THE FALLEN

5

ALSO BY
THOMAS E. SNIEGOSKI

THE FALLEN 1
THE FALLEN AND *LEVIATHAN*

THE FALLEN 2
AERIE AND *RECKONING*

THE FALLEN 3
END OF DAYS

THE FALLEN 4
FORSAKEN

THE FALLEN 5

ARMAGEDDON

Thomas E. Sniegoski

Simon Pulse

New York London Toronto Sydney New Delhi

This book is a work of fiction. Any references to historical events, real people, or real places are used fictitiously. Other names, characters, places, and events are products of the author's imagination, and any resemblance to actual events or places or persons, living or dead, is entirely coincidental.

SIMON PULSE
An imprint of Simon & Schuster Children's Publishing Division
1230 Avenue of the Americas, New York, NY 10020
First Simon Pulse paperback edition August 2013

For information about special discounts for bulk purchases, please contact Simon & Schuster Special Sales at 1-866-506-1949 or business@simonandschuster.com.
The Simon & Schuster Speakers Bureau can bring authors to your live event. For more information or to book an event contact the Simon & Schuster Speakers Bureau at 1-866-248-3049 or visit our website at www.simonspeakers.com.
Designed by Mike Rosamilia
The text of this book was set in Adobe Garamond.
Manufactured in the United States of America
2 4 6 8 10 9 7 5 3 1
The Library of Congress Cataloging-in-Publication Data
Sniegoski, Tom.
Armageddon / Thomas E. Sniegoski. — 1st Simon Pulse paperback edition.
p. cm. — (The fallen ; 5)
Summary: The war between Heaven and Hell rages to a dramatic conclusion as Aaron, half angel and half human, fights with the other Nephilim to protect humanity from Satan's wrath.
ISBN 978-1-4424-6005-8
[1. Angels—Fiction. 2. Good and evil—Fiction.
3. Love—Fiction. 4. Supernatural—Fiction.] I. Title.
PZ7.S68033Arm 2013
[Fic]—dc23
2013014870
ISBN 978-1-4424-6006-5 (eBook)

For David Kraus,

My friend, and brother.

Mondays are just not the same anymore.

August 10, 1963–January 12, 2013

For my wife, LeeAnne, who is much more than I deserve. And to Kirby for not killing me in my sleep.

Thanks also to Chris Golden, Annette Pollert, Liesa Abrams & James Mignogna, Erek Vaehne, Mom & Dad Sniegoski, Kate Schafer Testerman, Mom & Dad Fogg, Pete Donaldson, Pam Daly, Kathy Kraus, Paul Deane, Thomas Fitzgerald, Larry Johnson, Mark Snyder, Natalia Vargas, Pat & Bob, and Timothy Cole and the Inheritors of the Earth down at Cole's Comics in Lynn, Massachusetts.

And also a very special thanks to all the fans of The Fallen. I couldn't have done it without you.

—Tom

THE FALLEN

5

PROLOGUE

GENESIS:

IN THE BEGINNING, GOD CREATED THE HEAVENS AND THE EARTH.

THE EARTH WAS WITHOUT FORM, AND DARKNESS FILLED THE VOID.

THEN GOD SAID, "LET THERE BE LIGHT," AND THERE WAS LIGHT. . . .

So it began.

Seeing the enormity of the task before Him, the Lord God created the Architects, the first of those who would be known as angels. They would help Him shape the life of the fledgling world that meant so much to Him.

But when all was said and done, when the Architects had

completed the task for which they were created, their divine essence was to be absorbed back into the glory that was the power of God. The Almighty set about designing the next of His angels—the Seraphim, the Cherubim, the Principalities, the Powers—who would be His holy messengers.

But the Architects had survived, using the might bestowed upon them by their Creator to hide, and to continue to perform the function for which they had been designed. Unbeknownst to an already distracted God, they would make the earth what it was supposed to be, erasing all the errors in design until only perfection remained.

A task that they were now so very close to achieving.

But first there must be Armageddon.

CHAPTER ONE

NOW

Edna didn't know if it was night or day. It really didn't matter, since it was dark most of the time anyway.

She rolled slightly on the inflatable mattress to look at the windup travel clock that sat on the basement's cold concrete floor.

9:48.

Edna still didn't know if it was morning or night.

The world outside the house was growing more dangerous. There were . . . creatures in the nearly perpetual darkness. Creatures that would harm her family.

It was Edna's husband, Frank, who had thought it best for the family to move to the basement until things got better.

Until things got better. She let the words swim around in her brain as she listened to the steady, deep breathing of her sleeping husband and children. *Is it even possible to think of such a time?* she wondered.

The single basement window had been boarded up with heavy planks, and it was dark in the cellar, the only light coming from a battery-powered lantern atop an old plant stand in the far corner.

Is that light dimming?

She glanced at the faintly glowing clock again.

9:55.

For the first time that day—or was it night?—Edna allowed herself to think of her niece.

She allowed herself to think of Vilma.

An image took form in her mind. A dark-eyed little girl, scared and saddened by the death of her mother in Brazil.

Edna remembered this child, how she'd brought Vilma back to the States and raised the girl as her own. The child with the dark, soulful eyes growing into a beautiful young woman—

A beautiful young woman with a secret.

Another image took hold, also of Vilma. She was still beautiful, but with fearsome, feathered wings spreading from her back, a sword of holy fire burning in her hand.

Is it true? Can it be possible?

But Edna had only to remember what was outside, and she knew that it was.

Nephilim, Vilma had called herself, the offspring of one of

God's angels and a mortal woman, and, according to her niece, the saviors of the world.

Edna thought of the night Vilma had returned to their Lynn, Massachusetts, home and the stories the girl had told about the other young people like herself. She had brought her boyfriend with her.

Aaron. His name was Aaron, and something bad had happened to him. Vilma had said he'd been hurt while they were trying to save the world.

Edna's eyes focused on the lantern. Yes, the light was dimming.

Careful so as to not rouse her daughter, Nicole, or her son, Michael, Edna rolled from the air mattress onto the floor and crept toward the lantern.

The batteries are dying, she thought as she picked up the cheap plastic lantern they'd bought in case the power went out during a storm. She gave it a shake, knowing that it was likely to have little effect, but it didn't hurt to try.

The light grew dimmer.

Fear began to grip Edna as she considered what she would have to do if they were going to have light in the basement.

"Hey," her husband whispered in the darkness. "What are you doing?"

"The light's dimming. The batteries must be dying."

"Are there more down here?"

"No. They're upstairs."

"Why didn't you bring them down when—"

Edna could hear the annoyance in Frank's voice and interrupted him. "Because I didn't think of it till now."

"Where are they?"

"In the refrigerator," she told him. "Vegetable drawer."

"Seriously?"

"Yeah," she said. "My father always kept batteries in the fridge. He said they last longer that way."

"Your father was nuts."

"Don't start."

Silence fell between them, broken only by the sounds of the children's breathing. Edna was surprised that they hadn't woken up, but then again, since the business with Aaron and Vilma, since they'd left—were taken, she corrected herself—Nicole and Michael had been awfully quiet.

Edna still wasn't sure what had happened that night two weeks ago. She had awakened in the morning, somehow knowing that Vilma and Aaron were no longer in the house. She remembered it as if it was a dream, but she knew—as did her children and husband—that it hadn't been a dream. Somebody, or a group of somebodies, had come in while the family slept, and left with Vilma and Aaron.

"Edna?" Frank asked.

"Yeah?"

"You okay?"

"Yeah."

"Want me to go—"

"I'll go," Edna snapped, quickly setting the lantern back on the plant stand and starting toward the stairs.

"Edna, I—"

"It'll only take me a minute, I know right where the batteries are."

"The vegetable drawer," Frank said.

"Exactly."

"You're as crazy as your father."

Edna smiled at her husband in the darkness. "Be right back," she said, feeling for the railing that would lead her up to the kitchen.

Edna started to climb, the old, wooden steps creaking under her weight.

"Mama?" Nicole asked sleepily.

"Go back to sleep," Edna told her. "I've got to get something from the kitchen. I'll be right down."

"Get my Legos," Michael called from the darkness.

"Your mother is going upstairs to get batteries and that's all," Frank warned.

"I'll be right back," she said again as she reached for the hastily installed deadbolt. The bolt fought her for an instant, then slid back with a loud snap.

"Frank?" she called out.

"Yeah?" She could hear him moving toward the foot of the stairs.

"Come up here and lock this behind me."

"I don't think—"

"I don't want you to think," she said. "Close it, and lock it behind me."

Frank was silent.

"What if there's something up here?" she asked him. "What if there's something in the kitchen and—"

"All right, all right." He stomped up the steps behind her.

"I love you," she said so only he could hear.

"Yeah," he replied angrily, but then softened. "You're a pain in my ass, but I love you, too."

"Here I go," she said, taking a deep breath and pushing open the door.

She could feel him right behind her, ready to pull it shut as she stepped out into the kitchen.

Which was exactly what he did.

She stood still for a moment, allowing her eyes to adjust to the gloom.

The place was a shambles, which was not how it had been left. They'd had visitors since the family had taken to the cellar. An electric chill coursed down her spine.

"Everything okay?" she heard Frank ask softly from the other side of the door.

"Yeah," she whispered. She just needed to grab the batteries from the fridge and get back behind the locked door with her family. "Going for the batteries now."

Breathing deeply, she began to move through the kitchen, trying to avoid the debris strewn across her path. Whatever had been there had been searching for something, food perhaps, tearing open every door and cabinet. The refrigerator hung open before her. At least she was coming for batteries, not something to eat.

In her haste, Edna tripped over the legs of a broken chair and went sprawling across the kitchen floor. She lay there stunned, her heart hammering in her chest.

"Edna?"

She heard the click of the deadbolt snapping back.

"Don't," she called out. "Stay with the kids."

"What's going on? I heard—"

"I fell," she said, already getting to her feet—only to find herself face-to-face with a living nightmare.

Vilma had referred to the things by various names: goblins, trolls, and others that weren't fit to repeat in front of the children. But what they were called didn't matter; to Edna, they were all monsters.

As was what stood in her kitchen now, staring at her with eyes like big black buttons, eyes that looked right through her, turning her soul to ice.

Edna stifled a scream, knowing Frank would instantly appear at her side, leaving the children alone and exposed in the cellar below.

The creature remained perfectly still, its glistening eyes

fixed upon her. *Maybe it's as afraid of me as I am of it,* she thought.

Ever so slowly, she slid her foot behind her in an attempt to back away.

The thing's thick, leathery lips peeled back, revealing a mouth full of needle-sharp teeth, but it did not move. It began to growl, the sound growing in intensity and pitch.

Edna knew that she should have been more afraid, should have been screaming at the top of her lungs or passed out cold upon the kitchen floor, but she thought of her family—of her husband and children—and knew there was nothing more important than staying calm and focused to get back to them.

As she inched away from the creature, the growling became louder. Edna sensed that it was only a matter of seconds before she had a problem. She was about to turn and make a run for the basement when she heard the door open behind her.

"Are you all right?" Frank asked.

"Close the door!" Edna screamed, as the creature in her kitchen rushed toward her with an ear-piercing wail.

Edna tried to run, but her foot slid on the floor and she was falling again. She landed on her knees, the impact making her legs go numb. She could hear the labored breathing of the monster almost upon her. She struggled to stand, but her legs refused to help. It was as if they'd been shot full of Novocain. Instead, she began to frantically crawl across the floor.

Then suddenly something grabbed her. She cried out,

clawing at the body that was trying to pull her up from the floor.

"It's me!" yelled Frank, attempting to drag her to the cellar door.

The open cellar door.

"Frank, the door," she managed, her voice filled with panic. He didn't answer, his strong arms wrapped around her, practically carrying her.

"Daddy?" a voice called out from the cellar below.

"No," Edna said, twisting her head to locate the monster. She found it perched atop a nearby counter, its awful face pointed toward the open door, sniffing the air—smelling her children below.

And then it leaped.

The creature's body collided with them, and they fell against the wall beside the door to their sanctuary.

"What's going on up there?" Michael called up, and Edna thought she could hear the creak of stairs.

"Michael, stay where you are!" Edna screamed.

Her husband was on his hands and knees, his eyes locked on the creature that crouched mere inches from him.

"Get down the stairs," Frank ordered, refusing to look away from the beast. "Get down the stairs and lock the door behind you."

"Frank, you—"

"You heard me!" he shouted as the monster attacked.

The abomination wrapped its spindly arms around the man Edna had loved for well over twenty years. Frank fought back, using all his might to drive his attacker toward the center of the kitchen.

"Go!" Frank grunted with exertion as the monster growled with annoyance.

Edna couldn't leave her husband. She ran to the basement door, peering down the steps at her children, who stood there, their eyes shining white in the darkness below.

"Lock this door!" she commanded, slamming it closed.

Back pressed against the door, she heard the deadbolt slide into place and could not help but smile. *Good kids,* she thought, as she grabbed an overturned kitchen chair and swung it with all her might at the murderous beast that straddled her husband on the floor.

The creature cried out, falling from atop her husband to the floor. Edna went to Frank, reaching down to pull him to his feet. His face was wet, glistening in the faint light of the room, and she knew that it wasn't sweat.

"I thought I told you to—"

"When have I ever listened to you?" Edna asked, placing herself beneath his weight and helping him toward the cellar door.

The monster was suddenly before them, cutting them off, its mouth opening wider and wider as it hissed, raising its clawed hands, preparing to attack again.

But there came a rumble so loud and intense that it shook the house.

And then there was light—a searing white light that seemed to find its way into every corner of the room.

As the monster cowered, Frank and Edna froze in terror.

And Edna had to wonder, *Is this it? Have Vilma and Aaron—the Nephilim—failed?*

Is this the end of the world?

CHAPTER TWO

TWO WEEKS AGO

The rain continued to fall.

Gabriel sat in the shelter of the burned-out home, watching as his metal dish filled with the heavens' tears.

Though it appeared as if he was simply resting, the yellow Labrador retriever was on full alert, his black nose attuned to the scents of the unnatural. A pack of strange beasts, which the dog did not have a name for, had been prowling the neighborhood since he and his friend Dusty had arrived at the Stanleys' old, fire-ravaged home.

It made him sad to be there, but when Vilma had ordered him to take Dusty to a place where Gabriel felt safe, this was the first place to enter the dog's mind.

This was where he had been happiest—the most content. He and his boy.

He and his Aaron.

Gabriel looked away from his dish and out at the overgrown yard, remembering a simpler time with his master, before he was changed into what he was now.

The holy fire inside the retriever rolled, as if reminding him that it was there, not that Gabriel could ever forget it. It was Aaron's newly awakened power that had saved Gabriel after he'd been hit by a car.

Aaron's power had brought him back from the brink of death.

Aaron's power had changed him.

The dog spotted a muddy tennis ball nearly hidden in the tall grass at the far side of the yard. Rising to his feet, Gabriel trotted across the yard, lowering his nose to sniff at the ball.

It smelled of the past, before Aaron knew that he was Nephilim, before Aaron's foster parents were slain by the murderous angels called the Powers, before Gabriel's own transformation into . . .

Into what?

Was he even a dog anymore? Gabriel thought of the ferocious power that was now a part of him. It had been given to him by Aaron, and it had made him something else entirely.

And what that was concerned him.

Gabriel wished Aaron was there with him, that they could at least pretend things were the way they used to be.

A moan from inside the house caused the Labrador to

reluctantly leave the tennis ball and the scents of the past, and look in on Dusty.

Gabriel's water dish was practically full, and he lowered his head to carefully grip the edge of the bowl in his teeth, lifting it gingerly, barely spilling a drop. With equal care, he carried the bowl up the rickety back steps and through the torn screen in the porch door into the burned remains of the house.

It still smelled strongly of smoke.

Smoke and death.

The scents forced Gabriel to remember the horror of what he'd experienced here.

The horror of the angels that had come to kill his boy, but had taken the lives of Aaron's foster parents, Tom and Lori Stanley, instead. The horror that had set Aaron and Gabriel on their long journey to save the world.

He maneuvered through the rubble-strewn hallways, careful not to spill the water that he carried. Dusty moaned again, and Gabriel quickened his pace.

They'd found a dry place at the back of the house, in a room that had been the den. Using some old blankets that he'd found, Gabriel had made a makeshift bed for the injured Dusty.

Gabriel entered the room to find the young man lying atop the covers. Dusty's exposed flesh was damp with fever from the infected lacerations that covered his body. He appeared to be awake, his glassy eyes watching as the dog carried the water bowl closer.

"Good boy," Dusty managed, before his body was racked with convulsing chills.

Gabriel set the dish on the floor, only spilling a few drops, and approached his friend. He studied the angry wounds that covered just about every inch of the young man's body. Bits of darkened metal were imbedded deep beneath Dusty's skin. There was nothing Gabriel could do to remove the shrapnel from when the Abomination of Desolation's giant, mystical sword exploded. All he could do was try to keep the infection from growing worse.

He took a long drink of the fresh rainwater before he began what had become his ritual. He lowered his head and gently began to lick the wounds clean of infection.

Gabriel worried about the state of the world. The longer he and Dusty remained inactive, the worse it would become.

But mostly he worried about his boy, Aaron.

Worried that he might not see him again.

Worried that Aaron had succumbed to his own injuries sustained during the vicious attack upon the school where he and the other Nephilim had lived until a few days before.

Worried that he—and the world—might not be able to survive Aaron's demise.

Vilma lay on the cot in the tiny concrete room, staring up at the ceiling vent and listening to the hum of the artificially produced air, wondering what was happening in the world above.

It had been two weeks since she and Aaron had been taken from her family's home and brought to this underground installation. She'd heard nothing since about what was happening beyond these walls.

She sat up and pulled on her boots. She couldn't sleep, and lying there wasn't going to do her much good. She would go and sit with Aaron for a while.

She hesitated at the door, knowing what—who—she would find posted on the other side.

Vilma pushed down on the latch and pulled open the metal door.

Levi was at his post, sitting on the bench outside her quarters. His large, mechanical wings were unfurled, and he appeared to be sharpening the ends of his metal feathers.

The fallen angel stood upon seeing her. "Hello, miss," he said in a low, gravelly voice, and his mechanical wings disappeared back beneath the long, heavy coat his kind always wore.

"Hello, Levi," she responded.

Levi, and others like him, called themselves the Unforgiven. From what Vilma understood, these fallen angels had refused forgiveness for the crimes they had committed against Heaven during the Great War. Denied all divine abilities, the Unforgiven mastered magickally enhanced technology to carry out their mission against the Architects, as a way of penance for their crimes.

And to finally allow themselves to be forgiven.

"Couldn't sleep," she continued, letting the door close behind her.

The fallen angel nodded. "Not hard to believe during these turbulent times." He slid the file he'd been using to sharpen his wings into the pocket of his coat. "Is there anything I can do to assist you?"

Vilma shook her head. She could feel his stare from behind his goggles and hated that she could not see the fallen angel's eyes behind the dark lenses.

"A sleeping potion, perhaps?" Levi offered.

"No, that's all right," she said. "I'll just go and spend some time with Aaron."

"Very good," Levi said with a slight bow of his head.

"All right then," she said, starting down the harshly lit corridor. "If anybody is looking for me . . ." She'd just about reached the corner when the fallen angel called after her.

"Miss Corbet is with the lad, I believe."

Vilma turned to acknowledge that she'd heard him. He was honing the edges of his metal-feathered wings to razor sharpness again. She imagined the damage they could do in battle, and a shiver ran down her spine.

"Thanks," she said, trying not to sound irritated. *When isn't Miss Corbet with Aaron these days?*

Vilma rounded the bend and approached the elevator. The infirmary where Aaron was recovering was two levels below this one. She pressed the red button and waited for the car to arrive. Of all the places she could have ended up after fleeing the destruction at the Saint Athanasius School, she'd never thought it would be an abandoned, underground missile base.

But that's exactly where she and Aaron had been brought by the Unforgiven and Taylor Corbet—Aaron's mother.

Vilma leaned back against the cold cinder-block wall, listening to the metallic grinding of the gears and pulleys bringing the elevator down to her. Taylor had promised that the elevators, as well as the entire installation, were perfectly safe, but Vilma wasn't sure she believed that.

The elevator doors parted with a shrieking whine, and she stepped inside, pushing the number six. It took a moment, but the doors closed, and her descent began with a disturbing lurch.

Levi had explained that the Unforgiven claimed places that were abandoned. Deconsecrated churches, burned-out buildings, unfinished construction, and decommissioned military bases became their secret hideouts.

This particular base in Kansas had been abandoned since the late eighties.

The elevator stopped with a savage jolt, and Vilma found herself grabbing hold of the metal railing to steady herself. The lights flickered ominously, but the metal doors slid wide.

Vilma stepped out into the mint-green corridor. The paint

was chipping in many places, and there was a very specific smell to this floor. It smelled like a hospital.

She started toward the reception area, where another of the Unforgiven sat. She didn't know this one's name. He'd never offered it, even though she'd seen him just about every day since she and Aaron had arrived.

His head was bowed as if asleep, but Vilma knew better.

As she drew closer, he lifted his head, and she was again staring at her reflection in goggle-covered eyes.

"Here to see the boy again," the fallen angel stated.

"Yes," she answered, as she did every time she visited.

"He is still unconscious," the Unforgiven informed her, although she already knew that.

Vilma often thought of the day, or evening, when she would come and be greeted with news that he was awake. But for now, she had to be content with the fact that her boyfriend was still alive.

Images of the assault upon him flashed through her mind, no matter how hard she tried to keep them at bay. The armored figure of Lucifer Morningstar—his own father—plunging a blade of darkness, a blade of black fire into Aaron's stomach.

"Better than him being dead," she blurted out as she had since first speaking with this Unforgiven angel that watched over the infirmary.

"Yes, that is true," the Unforgiven replied.

"May I go and see him?" she asked.

The angel did not respond immediately. He never did.

"Miss Taylor Corbet is with him," the angel finally said flatly.

"She always is," Vilma responded, again attempting to keep the annoyance from her tone, but failing.

"I'm told it is a mother's concern for her child," the fallen angel explained.

A mother's concern, Vilma thought, feeling her ire rise. Where was her concern all those years he'd been without her? All the years he'd spent in foster care? Where was her concern then, when her son needed his mother?

Silence followed, and it looked as though the angel was meditating or whatever it was that he was doing behind the reception desk.

"I'd like to see him," Vilma stated.

"Of course," the angel said.

She took that as permission to proceed and started down the short hallway. Aaron's room was at the far end, on the left.

Her legs grew heavy the closer she got to his room. She hated to see him like this, clinging to life.

Barely.

Nobody could tell her what was wrong with him, other than that he'd sustained a serious injury and was trying to heal.

What more should she need, really?

How about that he was going to pull through? That the guy she loved with all her heart was going to live?

But nobody would tell her anything.

She stopped in the doorway of the darkened room, taking in the shadow of the bed where Aaron lay and the woman sitting at his bedside, holding his hand.

"Come in, dear," the woman said suddenly.

"Oh, hey," Vilma said, entering the room. "I thought you might be asleep."

"Not while I'm sitting with him," Taylor Corbet said. "Aaron gets my full attention as long as I'm here."

"That's nice," Vilma responded just to say something. "How's he doing?" She moved to the bed. Aaron was so incredibly still and pale. If she hadn't known better, she would have said that he was—

"Still unconscious, but I believe he's healing," Taylor said. "An engineer was by earlier to check on the healing ring we placed—"

"What?" Vilma interrupted. "Healing ring? What's that?"

Taylor stood and reached across her son to turn on a small light above the bed. "We felt that we could better improve his chances if we were to assist him with the healing process."

Vilma's anxiety grew. "And how does this healing ring work? What is it?"

Taylor pulled Aaron's sheet down to his waist, revealing a copper-colored ring with a glass center pulsing on his chest with an unearthly energy that seemed to mirror the beat of her boyfriend's heart.

"It's an Unforgiven design," Taylor explained. "It's a machine that uses stray life energies to boost the healing potential of the individual."

Vilma couldn't take her eyes from the circular machine. "And you couldn't tell me about this?" she asked.

"I just did, dear," Taylor said. "It's for his own good."

"But you could have come to me," Vilma insisted. "You could have told me that you were going to attach some . . . some magickal machine to my boyfriend's chest."

She could feel herself growing angrier by the second and reached down to take hold of Aaron's other hand. It was cold.

"It just would have been nice to know," she said, fighting to control herself.

"You're right," Taylor agreed. "We should have told you, but there is so much at stake that—"

Vilma glared at his mother. "I have just as much say in his care as you. I should have been told."

"I'm his mother," Taylor Corbet stated.

"Sure," Vilma said flatly. "I guess everybody has one, but I think there's a little bit more to it than just a title."

Vilma saw a flash of anger in the woman's eyes.

"You think I deserve that."

Vilma squeezed Aaron's hand tightly. "He thought you were dead."

"And you don't think that tears me up inside?" Taylor's voice began to rise. "Not a day went by that I didn't think of him, out there, needing me."

Vilma refused to look at the woman.

"I needed him as much as he needed me," Taylor continued. "But I loved him too much to go to him. I had to remind myself, day after endless day, that being with him would have been dangerous to Aaron, and the rest of the world."

Curious, Vilma found herself responding. "You stayed away to protect him?"

Taylor stared lovingly at her unconscious son. "That was the only thing that kept me away," she said. "The man that I had loved—Aaron's father—I had no idea who he truly was, or how powerful."

"Lucifer," Vilma said.

Taylor laughed, and then smiled. There were tears in her eyes. "I knew him as Sam."

"Sam?" Vilma asked. "Lucifer Morningstar called himself Sam?"

Taylor laughed again, and the tears tumbled from her eyes. "He did." She reached up to wipe her dampened face. "And to tell you the truth, he looked much more like a Sam to me than a Lucifer."

"So, you actually had no idea who he really was?" Vilma asked.

Taylor shook her head slowly. "Not until after Aaron was born."

Vilma's curiosity was getting the better of her.

"How did you find out?"

Aaron's mother's face grew very still. "It was after I'd given birth," she said, her voice sounding distant. "An angel told me . . . his name was Mallus, and he told me of my love's true identity, and how there were powerful forces out there in the world who would have used me, and my child, to acquire the power they wanted."

Vilma stared at the woman, as Taylor's gaze lifted to meet her own.

"But all that came after I'd already been declared dead, and Mallus was helping me to escape from the morgue."

THE HIMALAYAS

The storm raged around the two angels, and Mallus stopped for a moment to get his bearings. They'd already passed through the nearly deserted town of Lukla—the threat of the possible end of the world having dramatically cut into tourism and folks' desire to risk their lives climbing mountains.

A raging snowstorm wasn't helping matters much either.

Things had changed quite dramatically since Mallus and his companion were last here.

"Is it Thursday?" Tarshish, the last of the powerful angelic beings known as Malakim, suddenly asked.

Mallus looked in his direction as the snow swirled about his face. The Malakim had raised his body temperature so the snow could not collect upon him.

"I think so, why?" the fallen angel asked.

"Sloppy joe night," Tarshish said wistfully, referring to the old-age home where, until recently, he'd been hiding himself away. "I loved sloppy joe night."

Mallus sighed. It had been like this for their entire journey, the Malakim reminiscing about what he had left behind when they'd decided to help the Nephilim avert the decimation of the world. For their part, the two had embarked on a mission to retrieve the power of God that had been housed inside the Metatron—a heavenly being they had destroyed while working for the Architects in this very region countless millennia ago.

Mallus squinted through the white and shifting haze, sensing the presence of other preternaturals nearby. He'd heard rumors that there was a tavern in these mountains for those of an unearthly disposition. It would be just the place to gather their thoughts—and perhaps some information to help them on their mission.

"Perhaps it will be sloppy joe night wherever we're going," Mallus suggested, trudging effortlessly through the accumulating snow to where he sensed the tavern to be.

"Do you think?" Tarshish asked. "Wouldn't that be lovely."

"I wouldn't consider sloppy joes lovely," Mallus said, watching the mysterious tavern gradually take shape before him. If he were human, he would not have been able to see it.

"Obviously you've never had the real deal. I wonder if

they'd be made with hamburger," Tarshish pondered. "Maybe yak? Wonder how that would taste?"

Mallus ignored his companion's ramblings as he studied the magickal sigils, warding off evil forces, that had been carved into the wood of the tavern door. *A good sign,* he thought as he lifted the latch and pushed inside.

He recognized the smell almost immediately. It was the coppery tang of violence.

It was the smell of murder.

Blood was spattered everywhere, as were the remains of the supernatural beings who had been unlucky enough to have stopped in for a drink.

Nearly twenty large, apelike beasts stopped their feasting and glared at the intruders with glistening, yellow eyes. Their dingy white fur was matted with drying blood and other internal fluids.

These creatures had many different names—abominable snowmen, bigfoots, skunk apes—but Mallus had always called them yetis.

"Something tells me it's not sloppy joe night," Tarshish commented as the yetis roared their displeasure at the interruption of their meals and bounded across the tavern toward the two fallen angels.

"On your toes!" Mallus yelled to his companion, running to meet the first of the beastly attackers.

Though weakened by his fall from Heaven, the angel

still had enough divine strength to deal with the likes of these filthy creatures. He pulled back his arm and delivered a punch to a yeti's leathery face. The blow was solid, landing on the creature's snout with a loud, satisfying snap. The woolly monster stumbled backward, its own dark blood streaming from its nose.

"There's more where that came from," the former commander of the Morningstar's army informed the beast, as Mallus readied for the next wave.

The injured yeti emitted a terrible roar, leading the others in an all-out assault upon them. The monsters were on them in a wave of fur, fangs, and claws, each apparently starving for a feast of fallen angel flesh.

Mallus had no intention of being a yeti's meal. The angel soldier lashed out with his fists, shattering bone and rupturing internal workings with every blow. But there was confidence in the way the beasts fought, a self-assurance that showed in the savagery of their attack.

They seemed to fear nothing.

Mallus was yanked from the floor by the arm, and before he could react, his yeti captor sank its fangs into his shoulder, tugging at the flesh. The fallen angel screamed in pain, sinking his fingers into the tough, leathery flesh of the vile beast's face and ripping it from the yeti's skull. The snow creature released him with a gurgling grunt, while three others charged forward, driven mad by the scent of the angel's blood.

Despite his pain, Mallus continued to fight. But the more he lashed out, the more effort they put into trying to bring him down.

And he feared that it would not be long before they succeeded. Mallus's own blood streamed from his wounds to mix with that of the dead beings on the sticky floor.

"I've had just about enough of this," bellowed a voice.

Mallus looked toward the sound, as a mound of muscular, furred creatures suddenly exploded in a silent flash. Innards, blood, bone, and fur spattered the ceiling and walls like some twisted abstract work of art.

The yetis atop Mallus froze. Tarshish rose from the remains of the mound, his slacks, checked shirt, and light Windbreaker torn and covered in gore. His eyes glowed.

There was another flash, and the Malakim's clothing looked as though he'd just put it on fresh. "That's better," he said, admiring himself.

Survival instinct kicked in, and the yetis that still held Mallus began to back away.

"Do you want them to escape?" Tarshish asked his companion.

Mallus looked to the retreating snow beasts. Where was their confidence now? "No," he said.

The Malakim raised a hand, passing it through the air as if stirring bathwater. The remaining yetis evaporated into a cloud, raining a coppery mist onto the already gore-covered floor.

"That was unpleasant," Tarshish commented.

"Wasn't it," Mallus agreed, gingerly touching his shoulder. He could already feel himself beginning to heal.

"Why are we here again?" the Malakim asked, as he strode about the ravaged bar. He almost slipped in a puddle of blood and grabbed at a heavy wooden table to steady himself.

"I was hoping for a quiet moment to collect ourselves," Mallus answered. "And a chance to acquire some information."

"There won't be any of either, I'm afraid," Tarshish remarked. "Unless we're to extract that information from the dead."

Mallus was about to agree when he heard a faint wheezing. His gaze met the Malakim's. They'd both heard it.

The fallen angel moved carefully toward the bar. A bloodied figure was curled into a tight ball behind it.

"Over here," Mallus said, crouching beside the injured form. The man wore a barkeep's apron, and what little of his flesh wasn't covered in blood was a strange golden color. *Elf,* the Malakim thought, somewhat surprised. The elves were a quiet race, usually keeping to themselves in the hidden corners of the world.

The barkeep had a ghastly wound in his side, leaking what little remained of his life blood onto the cold, wooden floor.

"He won't be able to give us anything," Mallus told Tarshish as the Malakim came around the bar.

"He still looks alive to me," Tarshish commented.

"Not for much longer."

"What kind of attitude is that?" Tarshish said, kneeling down beside the elfin barkeep and placing a hand on his head. "If I'd known you were such a quitter, I'd have stayed at the home."

Before Mallus could respond, the Malakim's hand began to glow, and the elf appeared suddenly stronger.

"What have you done to him?"

"I've given him a little bit longer," Tarshish said. "Ask your questions. I can't keep this up all day."

The barkeep's eyes were wide, his mouth moving, trying to speak.

Mallus pulled him into his arms.

"They . . . they attacked without provocation . . . ," the barkeep whispered in his elvish language, but Mallus could understand, for he was an angel of Heaven—and even a fallen angel could understand all tongues.

"As creatures of a darker nature have a tendency to do," Mallus acknowledged.

"They broke through the wards of protection with ease," the barkeeper continued. "It is so, so much worse than we thought. . . ." The elf's voice trailed off as his body began to twitch and death attempted to claim its prize.

"Not much longer now," Tarshish announced.

"We're searching for what became of the Almighty's power after it was cut from the Metatron," Mallus quickly explained to the elf, feeling that ever-present twinge of guilt at his—their—past actions. "We believe that it created a kind of trinity, a dark trinity."

The elf's eyes went wide with understanding. "The Sisters," he whispered, fear in his weakening voice. "The Sisters of Umbra."

"Do you have any idea where we might find them?"

"He's almost done," Tarshish warned.

Mallus grabbed hold of the dying elf's chin, his gaze boring into the elf's eyes. "Do you have any idea where they are?" he repeated urgently.

"The body . . . ," the barkeep managed. "The . . . corpse . . . of the . . . fallen . . . god . . ."

"That's it for him," Tarshish said, rising to his feet. "Empty."

Mallus gently laid the corpse on the floor and stood, thinking about the elf's final words.

"I was hoping he could have been a little more specific," Tarshish said, perusing the dusty liquor bottles on the shelves behind the bar.

"He was helpful," Mallus replied.

The Malakim pulled a bottle from the back of a shelf and removed the cork with a loud pop. He sniffed the contents and made a face.

"He was?" he asked.

Mallus nodded grimly. "I think I know where he meant."

From the puzzled look on Tarshish's face, Mallus could tell that he did not understand at first, but then realization blossomed in the powerful being's ancient eyes.

"Right," Tarshish then answered him. "I should have known we would end up there."

"The scene of the crime."

CHAPTER THREE

The six demons crept past Mrs. Carmichael's sixth-grade classroom, hunting for prey in Brideview Elementary School. Seeing them in the building where she'd spent some of the happiest moments of her life filled Melissa with an anger that took nearly all her power to control.

But she waited, crouching behind the partially open door of the boys' bathroom, studying their movements. The filthy creatures carried an assortment of swords, knives, and spears, nothing that would stand up to the divine fire at her disposal. They wore armor, but what skin was exposed glistened wetly in the dusky light coming in from the corridor's large windows. She listened carefully as the demons spoke to one another, understanding their guttural language as she was able to understand all languages.

What Melissa heard did little to cool the anger that simmered in her breast. In fact, it burned all the hotter, desperate to be unleashed upon her enemies, as they talked about humans' delicious meat. One of the demons even pointed out that children were sweetest.

Melissa's angelic nature squirmed at the loathsomeness of it all, and sparks of holy fire began to leap from the tips of her fingers.

Bright enough to capture the demons' attention.

"Shit!" Melissa swore, bursting through the bathroom door, a massive sword made of the fires of Heaven appearing in her hands.

Her first swing cut through the leg of one demon, sending him to the floor with a shriek. She buried the crackling blade into his bald skull, and he burst into flames, casting an eerie glow in the corridor for her to see by.

Melissa was surprised that the others hadn't run. Instead, they simply stood, glaring at her with red, beady eyes.

She popped her wings, and the looks upon their monster faces were priceless. She could see that they were afraid of what she was. Even in the short time that her Nephilim band had existed, they had done a lot of damage to the Community of horrors, earning quite the reputation for their ferociousness.

"Boom," she said, and lunged at them.

Swinging her flaming sword into the neck of another demon, Melissa separated its head from its body and sent it tumbling down the hall. She could not help but wonder if the Nephilim had become the monsters' boogeymen: the punishment that monster mothers and fathers threatened their monster kids with if they didn't eat all their intestines for supper, or crawl into their coffins at bedtime.

The thought made her smile, but not for long.

There were four demons left. She methodically took two of them down, one after the other. She was much too fast for them, jumping up to fly over their heads, then dropping down to skewer them before they could figure out where she'd land.

The floor became sticky with their blood, which suddenly made Melissa think of the kindly Mr. Scartino, who was in charge of janitorial services at Brideview Elementary.

He wouldn't be happy with the mess she'd made.

A spear point narrowly missed her face. She had to pay attention. Aaron had always tried to instill the importance of keeping one's mind in the game.

Aaron.

She remembered how he'd looked after the injuries he had sustained, as they had all been forced to flee the school where they'd lived. He hadn't looked good, not at all.

She wondered if he was even still alive.

Melissa forced her thoughts back to the problem at hand, bringing her burning blade down upon a demon's spear, cutting it in two. As he tried to stab at her with the broken ends, she pushed off from the ground, her wings carrying her above the demon. Using both hands and all her might, she plunged the blade through his head, splitting the nightmarish beast in half.

She glared at the last remaining demonic soldier. The stink of death and evil hung heavy in the air, and Melissa was again reminded of how much she hated what the world had become.

It made her cranky, and when she was cranky, she could be so very cruel.

"I'll let you kill yourself," she told the last of the demons, in its nasty language. Surprise flashed upon its leathery face. "I'll stand right here and let you do it."

The demon held a knife that looked as though it had been carved from bone. He waved it around, attempting to intimidate her, but having very little success.

"That's about all the mercy I can muster for your kind," Melissa finished.

They faced off for a moment, neither of them moving.

"So what's it gonna be?" she finally asked the monster. "Are you gonna do it, or am I?"

The demon did pretty much what she expected. It threw its blade with deadly accuracy. Melissa caught the knife with ease, watching as the demon turned tail and fled. She willed flame into the demon blade, making it crackle and spark with the fires of Heaven.

"This would have been so much easier if you'd killed

yourself," she muttered as she took aim, and threw the burning blade with all her might.

The knife punched through the demon's skull, and it exploded in a flash of light and fire. The headless body slumped to the floor.

"She shoots, she scores," Melissa cried, pumping her fist in the air as she imitated a cheering crowd.

Then she turned to the corpses littering the floor and began to drag them into a pile in the center of the corridor. Taking the burning blade of her sword, she shoved it into the middle of the demon pile.

Demons were extremely flammable. They went up like oily rags.

Melissa watched, making sure that none of the holy fire jumped from the pyre to the walls of the school corridor. She didn't want to burn the building down. As soon as the bodies were nothing more than ash, she stuck her blade back into the smoldering pile, reclaiming the divine fire.

The school was silent. Melissa closed her eyes and extended her wings to be sure that no other beasts lurked nearby. The tips of her feathers were sensitive to the unnatural, but she could feel no vibrations alerting her to trouble. The school was now safe.

She took a final glance at the ashes, allowing one of her wings to sweep the pile across the corridor to mingle with the dust and dirt that had collected there since the world had fallen to pieces several weeks ago. Then she turned and headed for the concrete staircase that would take her into the basement, passing tattered posters on the walls promoting good hand hygiene during cold and flu season.

Colds and flu are the least of humanity's problems now, she thought as she pulled open the basement door and jogged down the steps. A second set of stairs took her farther underground to the bomb shelter.

From what she understood, these bomb shelters had been built in most public buildings during the 1950s, when the threat of nuclear attack was on everybody's mind. When Vilma ordered the Nephilim to flee to somewhere safe, it was the first place Melissa thought of. She had to wonder if the yellow-and-black poster depicting the symbol for radiation shouldn't be altered to show that the shelter could be used for monster attacks, too.

She rapped on the heavy metal door with her knuckle. "It's me."

She heard the sharp click of a metal bolt being slid back, and the door opened just enough for a set of old eyes to peer out from behind horn-rimmed glasses.

"You alone?" the old man, whose name was Charlie, asked cautiously.

"I certainly am," she answered. It was the same answer she gave him every time she returned to the shelter.

"Can't be too careful," he replied as he always did, stepping back and allowing her to enter.

Melissa entered the room, closing the door firmly behind her. The others watched with fearful eyes. There were six of them in all—Charlie, who had opened the door, and his wife, Loretta; a young mom, Doris, and her five-year-old daughter, Maggie; Tyrone, who was no older than her; and the school's middle-aged nighttime security guard, Scott.

They had all found their way here to the shelter, after the darkness fell permanently and the streets had become unsafe.

"So?" Scott asked, his hand creeping up to caress the can of Mace that he wore on his belt. "Did some of those things get in?"

"Yeah, they did," Melissa said, moving toward the elderly woman who was lying on a cot in the corner. "But I took care of it."

"Did you find anything to help Loretta?" the old man asked, following her to his wife.

Melissa dug in her pocket for the bottle of Advil she'd found in the teachers' lounge, before encountering the demons. "This might help," she said, opening the bottle and shaking out three of the pills.

Loretta looked sweaty, and Melissa was sure that she had a fever.

Her eyes went to the dirty bandage on the old woman's arm, and she reached out to take a peek at the wound beneath. It appeared to be getting worse. Something totally unnatural had bitten Loretta before she and Charlie had abandoned their home and come to the school looking for shelter.

"Hey, Loretta," Melissa said, as she took the woman's hand and gently squeezed. "Why don't you sit up for a minute and take these? They'll help with the pain."

Loretta's eyes opened to mere slits, and Melissa put her arm around the woman's shoulders, pulling her up.

Charlie stepped forward with a half-empty bottle of water. "I've been trying to get her to drink, but she won't."

"Thanks, Charlie." Melissa took the bottle, then put the pills on the old woman's tongue. "Here, swallow these," Melissa told her, carefully tilting the water to the woman's lips.

Loretta looked as though she was still asleep, but she managed to get the pills down. Melissa helped her to lie down again.

"Do you think those will help?" Charlie asked, fiddling with his glasses. He took them off, wiping the lenses on the front of his shirt.

"They won't hurt," Melissa replied. She turned away from the old woman to find the young man watching her. "Got something to add, Tyrone?"

The dark-skinned youth had given her nothing but attitude since they met. They all knew what she was. When she'd first arrived, the building had been overrun with giant, ratlike creatures. She'd quickly dispatched them, and everyone had appreciated it.

But Tyrone had continued to look at her like she was

as bad as the rat things. "You know we can't stay here much longer," he said.

The group had been there for close to a week before she had arrived. They were now wrapping up their second week there.

"I don't know that," she replied, walking past him to get her own bottle of water. There were five cases of bottled water stacked against the far wall. They had to be careful. It wouldn't last forever.

"We're gonna run out of water . . . out of food."

Several cases of ready-to-eat meals—MREs—were piled by the water. It was probably enough to last them a month, if they skipped some meals here and there.

"That's not a problem today," Melissa said, cracking the top on her first bottle of water for the day and taking a long swig.

"Yeah, so what are we gonna do when it is?" Tyrone asked.

Melissa knew he was right. They would have to do something before the food and water ran out, but she wasn't sure what yet.

"I'll know when the time comes," she replied. They were all watching her now.

They must have thought they were saved when they first saw her.

Sword of fire in hand, wings flapping powerfully upon her back.

Their prayers had been answered.

As she drank her water and glanced back at each of them, she had to wonder if they were still feeling that way.

Or if they were thinking that not even Heaven could save them now.

Verchiel haunted the remains of the Saint Athanasius School and Orphanage, wandering the grounds in search of answers to what had happened, and where the Nephilim had gone.

It was obvious that they had been driven from this place, although they had not gone quietly.

The bodies of trolls, goblins, and other nightmarish beasts still littered the grounds—there was even a dragon corpse.

No, the Nephilim had not left their home without a fight.

But the question still remained—where had they gone?

Something wriggled at the former Powers' leader's core, a feeling entirely unfamiliar to him. He paused where the science building and secret library had once stood, and where now not a trace of either remained, considering the odd sensation. He decided that it must be guilt. Guilt that he had not been here to help those who had once been his mortal enemies, but were now unlikely comrades. Guilt that he had been approached by servants of the Architects and had been invited to swear his allegiance to their cause.

His eyes ticked down to the pale skin of his forearm and the strange, snakelike mark that had appeared there. The three hooded sisters who spoke for their masters, the Architects, had given him the mark. They'd told him that once he had made his decision, they would know, and would call for him.

But Verchiel also had another choice to make. A choice that an ancient prophet had foretold in a painting. A decision would have repercussions on his future, the future of the world . . .

And the future of Heaven.

Verchiel seethed, his anger leaking from his divine form and setting the very ground around him afire. He had never seen the world in shades of gray before. As leader of the heavenly host Powers, he'd had no doubts about who his enemies were and what had to be done to purge their blight from the world.

But the Lord God Almighty had seen things differently, and Verchiel had been struck down by one of the very creatures the Powers' leader had sought to render extinct.

Verchiel's existence then grew more complex, as he was returned to life to work in alliance with the very beings he had once sought to destroy.

The fires of Heaven swirled ferociously around him, growing in intensity, reflecting his tumultuous emotions.

Why have I been brought back? the angel questioned again. *Is it to aid the Nephilim in purging the world of a cancerous evil, or is it for something more?*

Something bigger?

Something that would rest entirely upon a decision that he had yet to make?

Verchiel roared, and the fires responded in kind, spraying from his body and consuming whatever they touched. The ground and everything lying on it began to burn—the dead bodies, then the school and orphanage.

The angel raged in the eye of the firestorm. Divine flames spread from him in pulsing waves, on the verge of obliterating everything, when he realized what he was doing.

This isn't the answer, Verchiel thought, forcing himself to take control of his angry spirit. He called back the holy fire, taking it within himself, where it continued to fight before finally submitting to its master.

He surveyed the damage caused by his lack of control. Shame added to his guilt. Even with the school grounds reduced to nothing more than a memory, the decision he needed to make still haunted him.

He caught movement from the corner of his eye. The shape darted around the corner of a building that had somehow managed to survive his tantrum. Without a thought, the angel sprouted his wings and took to the air, flying across the still-smoldering grounds with blinding speed.

Verchiel's anger flamed again at the sight of a loathsome goblin scampering across the property. It looked over its shoulder to check if it had been seen. Verchiel flew toward it, his eyes locked upon the filthy creature, its armor crusted with dirt and blood. The goblin ran around the skeletal remains of an old greenhouse, and Verchiel temporarily lost sight of it.

Flapping his wings all the harder, the former Powers' leader dropped closer to the ground, smashing through the remnants of the greenhouse.

At first he did not see the one he pursued, but then he saw the goblin trying to dig itself into a hole in the ground.

Touching down, Verchiel recalled that the Nephilim had used this place as a burial ground, interring their dead beneath the earth. It was the Nephilim Melissa who often visited these graves, leaving flowers and polished baubles as reminders of who lay rotting in the ground beneath.

But now they appeared . . . empty.

Verchiel grabbed hold of the goblin's ankle, yanking the struggling creature from the dirt.

The goblin roared its displeasure, thrashing its legs and waving its arms. Verchiel threw the disgruntled creature to the ground.

It lay there, flat on its back, gazing up into the darkened skies, and Verchiel began to think that perhaps he'd thrown the creature a bit too hard. He loomed above the goblin, nudging the monster with the toe of his metal boot.

The goblin's scream was bloodcurdling, and Verchiel jumped back, a weapon of fire manifesting itself. Leaping to its feet, the goblin attempted to flee once again, but Verchiel no longer had the patience to deal with such things and simply used his wing to slap the goblin back to the dirt.

Verchiel stood over the goblin, sword of fire ready to strike.

"What are you doing here?" the angel demanded.

He could practically hear the little monster's thought process, the gears turning inside its malformed head.

"The greatest of battles was fought here, and I but a lowly soldier was badly injured in the skirmish," the goblin explained. "I was abandoned—left to fend for myself upon this battlefield." The goblin paused, cowering in the shadow of the angel.

"Where are your injuries?" Verchiel asked, head tilted to the side as he studied the creature. "Other than damaged armor . . ."

The goblin appeared startled. "Did I say injured?" he asked. "I meant to say, rendered unconscious. Yes, I was rendered unconscious. My comrades left me here, believing that I was dead."

Verchiel sensed that the creature was lying. He brought his sword up beneath the loose skin of the goblin's throat. "I tire of your lies. Prepare to meet your maker—if one even exists."

"Please!" the goblin begged, dropping to its knees. "I'll speak the truth, just don't—"

"Then speak it," Verchiel interrupted. "I'll know if you are lying to me again, and this time there will be no mercy."

"There was a great battle here, yes there was. And I was but one of the soldiers summoned to fight against the foes of the great Satan."

"Great . . . Satan?" Verchiel questioned.

"The one who now rules us all," the goblin excitedly explained. "All the beasts of the Community have sworn their fealty to the new Dark Master—the Lord of Shadows."

A nervous shiver of anxiety ran up the angel's spine. Lucifer Morningstar had been missing from the group for quite some time. Was it possible that he had somehow fallen to darkness again?

"Why are you here when the battle is done?" Verchiel asked.

The goblin cowered. "The battle was so very frightening. . . . I knew that if I fought, I would be slain for certain."

"You didn't fight, did you?"

"I didn't want to die," the goblin said with a sad shake of its head. "So I hid . . . hid beneath the bodies of my fallen brethren, and prayed to the dark gods of my long-departed ancestors that I would be spared a grisly fate."

"Coward," Verchiel snarled.

"If we are assigning labels, yes."

Verchiel was repulsed by the monster. Ending its life with a flick of his wrist would be too merciful.

"So, this is the life you would lead now? Scavenging from the battlefield and the dead?"

The goblin looked about, but held its tongue.

"And what have you done here?" Verchiel asked as his eyes fell upon the empty graves that once held the bodies of the fallen Nephilim. He could feel the fires of anger rising within him.

"Here?" the goblin asked. "I have done nothing."

Verchiel allowed the burning edge of the sword blade to touch the side of the goblin's neck. The sound was like the hiss of an angry serpent.

The cowardly beast cried out in pain, dropping its head to the ground and covering it with its hands. "Mercy, I beg of you!" the goblin wailed. "I told you that I have done nothing with those who were buried here. It was the Satan who ordered them harvested."

"The Satan did what?" Verchiel asked, taken aback.

The goblin slowly lifted its head to face the angel.

"Yes, it was the Satan. He ordered his army to dig for the decaying prizes."

Verchiel experienced the chill of impending dread.

"And what was done with these bodies?"

"Taken," the goblin said.

"Taken?" Verchiel repeated. "Taken where . . . and for what purpose?"

The goblin continued to cower. "Who is to say? The Satan . . . he works in mysterious ways."

Verchiel moved his deadly blade of flame away from the goblin, lost in thought. What would the leader of all darkness want with the corpses of slain Nephilim? The answer eluded any rational thought, but it did not keep the question from echoing repeatedly within his troubled mind.

Whatever the purpose, it would most certainly not be good.

Verchiel's keen hearing picked up the sound of escape, and he whipped around as the goblin attempted to flee.

Powerful wings opening in full, Verchiel bore down on the disgusting beast and drove it back to the ground.

"Where are you off to?" he asked.

"I've told you everything I know!" the goblin wailed, certain that it was about to meet its end.

"Which is practically nothing." Verchiel flapped his powerful, feathered appendages to intimidate the frightened beast. "I want to know more about this Satan, and why he has taken the bodies of my comrades."

"I can tell you no more!" the goblin exclaimed.

"What is your name?" Verchiel asked.

The creature appeared surprised by the question.

"Your name!" Verchiel bellowed. "What is your name?"

"Ergo," the goblin cried. "My name is Ergo."

The angel reached down, grabbing hold of the front of the goblin's filthy tunic and yanking it to its feet.

"Are you going to kill me?" the goblin whimpered.

Verchiel smiled coldly.

"It is your lucky day, Ergo," the angel said calmly. "For I have some questions, and I think we shall find the answers together."

* * *

Cameron imagined an ax.

Not the kind for fighting an army of demons or beheading a troll, but the kind used for chopping wood.

Night was cold in the woods, and he was going to have to build a fire.

He'd spent most of the day gathering wood from the forest, dragging the fallen limbs of large trees to the cabin. A sword of fire was good enough to chop the larger limbs into manageable pieces, but now, for tradition's sake, he was going to use an ax.

Holding out his hands, he manipulated the fire, shaping the stuff of Heaven into the ax that he remembered from his childhood.

The one his father had used when teaching him to chop wood.

Cameron admired the tool that he now held in his hand, finding it awesome that it was exactly how he remembered it—but constructed entirely of fire.

He hefted the ax in his hands, marveling at the fact that the tool even had the same weight as the original, and finding it strangely funny that he could remember the weight of an ax when so much of his past remained enshrouded.

Placing the first piece of wood on end upon the flat stump of a mighty oak, Cameron readied to split his first log.

The ax of fire descended with a crackling hiss, like grease

sputtering in the frying pan, and split the wood with ease. At this pace he would have all the wood split before lunchtime. Cameron grabbed another log and continued.

As he chopped, his thoughts drifted to memories of the besieged school grounds where he and his fellow Nephilim had lived, and Vilma's orders to leave immediately.

To find someplace safe.

What had brought him here?

The fire ax penetrated and split the log with a resounding crack.

Cameron couldn't even remember the last time that he'd thought of the cabin, but there it was, suddenly in his mind, as if waiting for him to remember. To return.

Someplace safe.

He quickened the pace of his chore, one log after the next, halved pieces falling to either side.

He couldn't recall the last time he'd been here, but now, the longer he stayed, the more those memories slowly surfaced.

It was almost like remembering somebody else's memories.

Warmed with exertion, Cameron removed his sweat-dampened shirt, enjoying the touch of the cool northern air on his muscles.

Even that simple act stirred thoughts of something long buried.

In his mind's eye, Cameron saw the back of a powerful man, standing in this very place, doing this very same chore, muscles rippling beneath suntanned flesh, a puckered crimson scar above each shoulder blade.

Where powerful wings used to be.

Cameron reached for the next log and found that there weren't any more. He allowed the ax to dissipate and set about piling the wood near the entrance to the cabin. Then he carried an armful inside and set it before the stone fireplace.

He went back out to get his shirt, and as he passed through the doorway, he had another flash of memory.

The man chopping wood—his father—stopped, turned to him, and smiled.

Cameron had never remembered the man's face so clearly before.

To be fair, he'd likely been only seven years old when he was last at the cabin with his parents, but it was as if his mind had been waiting to allow these memories to manifest themselves.

It was an interesting theory, and not all that strange when he considered his current situation, and that of the world.

Quickly retrieving his shirt, he decided that lunch was in order. He walked to the rear of the cabin and pulled back an old blanket to reveal a well-stocked cupboard of canned goods. He selected peaches and Spam, then grabbed a rusty hand-crank can opener and a fork on his way to the tiny table. He pulled out a chair and prepared to have his feast.

After hours of hard work, Cameron found himself enjoying the simple meal, even as the memories of his past continued to bubble to the surface.

To say that his childhood had been tumultuous was an understatement. Mostly it had been spent moving from one place to the next with his mother. He'd been under the assumption that they were going to eventually meet up with his father, a man whom Cameron barely knew.

He'd never really questioned his mother about his father. She'd explained that he was doing important things to help the world, and that had satisfied Cameron. As a young boy, he'd figured his father was a fireman, or an astronaut.

He'd never thought a fallen angel.

Cameron felt himself relax, his mind going into a kind of fugue state as he sat at the table, fork in hand. The memories rose up again, but this time he didn't hold them back. He was fascinated by the experiences that had been hidden in the folds of his brain.

He remembered his father handing him the ax. It wasn't a new memory, but this time it was so much clearer. And this time, his father spoke to him.

And he could hear each and every word as if they were being said to him now.

"There may come a time when you will have to fight."

His father's arm was around his shoulders, as he led Cameron to the pile of uncut wood.

"A time when your mother and I will not be here to help you . . . to guide you."

Cameron was in awe at the memory of his father's strong voice.

"But in times of despair, I want you to remember: this is all much larger than you, larger than me, larger than your mother."

The vision flowed into Cameron chopping wood; his pathetic first attempts, followed by an eventual success.

But his father kept talking.

"They believe they have a plan—that they know better than He, but that is not the case. Somebody has to stop them."

Cameron remembered that he'd chopped wood into the dark, and his mother had waited for them in the doorway to the cabin.

That was his old memory, but now it was different. Now he heard his father's voice.

"Someday, someone must challenge them . . . challenge them for the sake of the world."

It was like rewatching a familiar movie, but one where he'd missed some parts. The young boy—little Cameron—finally dropped the ax and turned toward his father.

"Who?" he asked. "Who must be challenged?"

And the father—his father—gently placed powerful hands upon Cameron's shoulders and looked deeply into his eyes.

"The Architects. The Architects must be challenged."

Cameron dropped his fork on his plate, the clatter snapping

him from his dreamlike state. He was breathing heavily, and suddenly had the worst headache.

It was as if something sharp was being pressed through the bone of his skull into the meat of his brain.

His father was pushing a very thin knife into his head as his mother watched.

The pain was incredible, and he surged from the chair, hands gripping his throbbing skull. There were things inside his head—things that had not been there before—things that had been locked away until . . .

Until they were needed.

The angelic part of his nature could not stand it anymore. His wings flowed from his back, and divine fire coursed through his veins. Cameron swayed in agony, trying desperately not to throw up.

What was happening?

He was afraid . . . this place . . . the cabin . . . was doing something to him. Lurching toward the door, he saw the markings on the frame. One at a time they ignited around the doorway, strange wriggling shapes in the wood.

This was insane. What was happening to him? Cameron panicked. His body felt as though it was on fire with fever. It was still daylight, but as he attempted to focus his throbbing eyes, the environment changed from day to night.

And in the night his father was waiting.

Yet another vision—his father kneeling before a hole in the

ground at the edge of the forest. He was pointing at something that had been laid to rest there.

"When it's time . . . when it's your time . . . you'll come here for this."

Cameron's gaze fell to the leaf-covered ground.

It took a moment for him to realize that he was no longer remembering. Instead, he was standing over the spot that his father had pointed out.

He dropped to his knees, sinking his fingers into the dirt. The ground was firm, and riddled with rock, but that didn't hinder his efforts, so focused was he on finding what was buried there. Cameron didn't want to think anymore—to remember—all he wanted was to dig.

It became increasingly cooler as the sun slowly set, but Cameron didn't stop. He thought about going in search of a shovel, but he feared that he'd return and find the hole filled in, as if he hadn't touched it.

Finally, his fingers scraped across a smooth surface. Cameron's breath caught in his chest as he bent forward, sweeping away the last of the dirt, to reveal a large wooden box. He stared at the filthy prize, then gasped as symbols similar to those on the door frame ignited on the lid of the box.

Hesitating only a moment, Cameron reached into the hole. The box was heavy, and he could only imagine what might be inside.

"When it's time . . . when it's your time . . . you'll come here for this."

Cameron looked for a latch to open the lid, but there didn't appear to be one.

The shapes on the box grew brighter, and as if compelled, Cameron laid his hands upon the damp wood.

There came a sudden muffled whirring from inside the box. Cameron quickly pulled his hand away and watched as a glowing vertical seam slowly manifested, and the two sides of the box flipped open.

A strange smell wafted up from the box, one that reminded him of Lorelei's secret library back at Saint Athanasius. Cautiously, Cameron leaned forward to look inside.

To see what his father had left him.

CHAPTER FOUR

The mouse named Milton scurried through the total darkness.

It was not familiar with this place, but that did not stop the mouse from exploring its new world.

Barely remembering how it came to be here, Milton recalled the human woman, Lorelei, and the library they'd been in as it came under attack.

The woman had sent the mouse away, ordering it to protect itself. After that, Milton's memories became a jumble of violent images and deafening sounds. But the tiny mouse's survival instincts kicked in to preserve its life.

Scurrying amid the destruction, the mouse had sought a haven, a place to hide, but the entire library had become filled with monsters and magick.

Milton had smelled the magick in the air, and felt it

in the floor trembling beneath its tiny paws. The magick that had preserved the library was breaking down. And no matter where the little mouse went, no matter what bookcase it hid beneath, it had sensed that it wouldn't be safe for long.

Then it had caught sight of the jagged hole in the floor, from which creatures of nightmare were still climbing up into the library.

A hole in the floor.

The mouse had seen that as its only option for escape. So it had darted across the wide expanse of floor, up and over the bodies of dead beasts, weaving through the chaos of battle that still raged around it and the books cascading down in a storm of paper to fill the hole in the floor.

Milton had stopped at the edge, its tiny nose twitching above the black cavern. For a moment, it didn't know which was more dangerous—the library that was collapsing, or the unknown void that awaited inside the hole.

The library moaned in its throes of death.

Survival instincts kicked in again, and the little mouse found itself springing from the jagged edge of the hole, down into the pool of black.

Into a world of darkness.

A world that Milton explored now, searching for a place it would again feel safe.

It stopped in the all-encompassing dark and turned its

pointy nose upward. Traces of what it had come to recognize as the scent of magick lingered in the gentle air currents.

Milton had not rested since coming to this strange, shadowy place, but something alerted every one of its animal senses.

The mouse breathed in a faint scent of something familiar; then it caught sight of the briefest flash of light and heard the softest of sighs.

Its tiny heart raced as the mouse scampered forward.

Drawn toward the scent of its friend.

Drawn deeper into the darkness toward the Morningstar.

The toddler emerged from behind a grouping of rusty metal barrels. He pitched precariously forward as he ran full tilt across the weed-covered tarmac, but the look on his young face was one of unbridled determination.

Then, suddenly, he fell. His little hands slapped the ground, barely preventing his chin from hitting the concrete. His face twisted in shock and fear, but instead of crying . . .

"Damn these legs!" the little boy shouted in anger.

The child struggled to his feet. He swayed momentarily and was about to run again, when he noticed that he was no longer alone.

The strange creatures that had been relentlessly hunting him and Jeremy had arrived.

One by one, the Agents slunk from hiding, their skintight

bodysuits refracting what little light managed to permeate the thick clouds that obstructed the sun, making them seem to become invisible, and then appear again. There were three of the thin, black-garbed assassins, and one by one they withdrew their blades.

The toddler could feel their eyes upon him as they scrutinized their prey through the masks over their faces. He stood as still as he was able, struggling to maintain his balance, disgusted that it was taking him so long to get the hang of this standing business.

The Agents moved closer, drawn to him like hungry dogs to a bloody piece of meat.

"C'mon," the child whispered. "Closer . . . closer. Yes, that's a good bunch of filthy murderers. Come close so you can't get away."

He noticed that one was turning away. The child couldn't have that. He needed the killers' attention 100 percent.

"Hey!" the boy yelled. "Look out! I might just take off in a flash." He did a little dance, turning in an awkward circle and almost falling on his butt, but his maneuver achieved what he wanted. All murderous eyes were riveted to him once more.

And it wouldn't be long now. They were just about where they needed to be in order for . . .

A god-awful scream and the sound of pounding wings interrupted the quiet.

Jeremy Fox dropped from the sky amid the group of Agents, his ax of fire clutched firmly in hand.

If the assassins were surprised by the Nephilim's sudden appearance, they did not show it as they shifted their attention to the young man.

The three attacked as one. The Agents thrust and slashed with their blades, spinning, leaping, and jumping in a graceful, yet murderous ballet.

There was nothing graceful about Jeremy Fox. He went at them with a cold, determined efficiency, swinging his burning battle-ax as if it was an extension of his body.

The first Agent to fall lunged, aiming his blade at the Nephilim's heart, when Jeremy's ax liberated his head from his body. This did nothing to slow the other assassins. Instead, they doubled their efforts in an attempt to bring down the Nephilim.

The child watched, mesmerized by the conflict, as the pair attempted to drive Jeremy away from the little boy.

Curious, the toddler thought, before sensing movement behind him. He turned as quickly as he could to see a fourth Agent raising his blade.

"Jeremy!" the child screeched.

"Roger!" Jeremy responded, and the toddler hoped—prayed—that the Nephilim would not be too late.

The Agent reached down, cobra quick, snatching the child by his chubby arm. The toddler struggled, kicking his feeble legs and waving his other arm. Then the air was knocked from his lungs, as the assassin slammed him to the ground, pinning his little body with one hand as the other drew its blade ominously closer.

The toddler thrashed, managing to wiggle out from beneath the restraining hand. But the Agent was faster, grabbing him around the middle with both hands so their faces were just inches apart.

Close enough for the toddler to act.

Gathering all his strength, the boy flailed his arms, jamming his chubby fingers into the assassin's eye.

The Agent grunted in pain, dropping the child as he reared back, clutching at his damaged orb.

The toddler crawled toward where Jeremy was still fighting.

He watched as Jeremy dispatched the other two Agents, one managing to sink his knife into the young man's shoulder just before Jeremy cut him in two at the waist. The other fell away as Jeremy buried his ax blade deep within the Agent's chest.

The toddler's eyes met Jeremy's as he heard the sound of rushing feet behind him.

"If you would be so kind as to finish that up for me," the child said.

Jeremy spread his wings and leaped into the air, killing the fourth assassin with a newly created knife of fire plunged deeply into his skull. Jeremy lay atop the still-twitching body of the Agent for a moment, then rolled off, fixing his gaze on the toddler.

"Are you all right, Roger?" Jeremy asked, out of breath and practically wheezing.

"Enoch," he corrected, pushing himself up from the ground and standing erect.

"What?"

"Not Roger," the toddler corrected. "My name is Enoch."

"Roger, Enoch, whatever you're calling yourself, you're still a pain in the ass," Jeremy said as he, too, stood.

"I'm a pain in the ass?" Enoch asked indignantly, tiny hand poised upon his chest. "Who's the one who doubted that we were being followed? And who agreed to put a child—a mere toddler—at risk, only to be proven wrong? Who? Who did this? Could it be some other pain in the ass? Maybe one with wings and flaming cutlery?"

"Cutlery?" Jeremy asked. "They're swords and battle-axes, not some sort of kitchen knives." He slowly pulled out the blade the second Agent had lodged in his shoulder. "That bloody hurts," he grunted, tossing the weapon to the ground.

"Well, it might as well have been cutlery," the toddler said, crossing his arms and approaching the dead bodies to examine them. "Did you happen to notice that I was almost killed?"

"Yeah, I saw," Jeremy said. "There were four instead of three. My mistake."

"Your mistake?" Enoch repeated, spinning to look at the young man. "Isn't it your job to be aware of such things, and protect me?"

"Yeah," Jeremy admitted. "I guess."

"You guess? Perhaps I should be searching for another angel to safeguard my wellbeing until—"

"Until what?" Jeremy interrupted. "What am I protecting you from anyway?"

The toddler fell silent, looking at the carnage around them. It wasn't the first attack since Enoch had remembered who he was, and they'd gone on the run.

"You're protecting me so that I can fulfill my special purpose," he said finally, turning his wide-eyed gaze to the Nephilim.

Jeremy sighed. He heated the tip of his finger with angel fire and cauterized his still-bleeding wound with a hiss. The young man grimaced in pain.

"Do you even know what that special purpose is?" he asked the child.

"No," Enoch admitted. "Not completely, but—"

"We should get out of here," Jeremy interrupted again. "If these guys tracked us, then there are probably more right behind them." He reached down, grabbing Enoch by the back of his pants and placing him on his shoulders.

"And there always seems to be at least one you miss," Enoch added.

"I don't always miss one," Jeremy corrected.

"You most certainly do," Enoch explained. "There was that one at the mall in Denmark . . . and then this?"

"I knew about the one at the mall," Jeremy said defensively.

"So you're intentionally putting me at risk?" the toddler asked.

"Now why would I do something nasty like that?" Jeremy asked. The Nephilim opened his wings to their fullest. "You're such a pleasant little bugger."

"You're being sarcastic. I may be a child, but I know sarcasm when I hear it."

Enoch couldn't quite make out Jeremy's answer as the Nephilim's wings closed around them.

Although he was certain that it was anything but pleasant.

Satan hung weightless in the black, cold vacuum of space, gazing down at the earth, now under his sway—or at least under the sway of creatures who swore their fealty to him.

Squinting his eyes, he could just about see through the shifting cover of gloom that prevented the light of the sun from shining upon the earth's surface. It was a world of shadow now, perfect for the monstrous breeds that served him. Great cities were in flames; historic monuments were crumbling, swallowed by a shifting ground that quaked as giant serpents burrowed beneath the earth's crust. From space, Satan, the Darkstar, admired the world that had been given over to chaos.

A world on the brink of oblivion. His dream for so very, very long.

But now, he had to wonder . . .

Is it enough?

Satan could not help himself. He turned his gaze from the orb slowly spinning below, to the star-filled void above—and the endless expanse beyond.

And the kingdom of Heaven that lay beyond that.

The earth was nearly under his control, but he found himself yearning for more.

The Lord God Almighty had stolen his universe of all-encompassing darkness with the utterance of four simple words, "Let there be light," leaving the Darkstar and his family to flee to any pocket of darkness that could hide them.

For eons, Satan had hidden himself away, planning and plotting, waiting for the time when he would take everything that the Lord God held dear.

But first, he would take away His earth.

Satan drifted closer to hear the anguished cries of those who had survived thus far. He took extra pleasure from their prayers that asked the Lord of Lords why He had abandoned them during their time of need. These pleas were another victory for the Darkstar, for he had broken the connection between Heaven and earth. The prayers of the planet's sad inhabitants would never reach their intended ears.

Entering the atmosphere, Satan felt the heat of re-entry

upon his body, which was nothing in comparison to the fires of hate that burned inside him.

He dropped through the heavy layers of cloud that kept the sun's rays from caressing the world, denying it warmth, and emerged in the night sky above the monolithic citadel that served as the base of his growing kingdom. Satan circled the fortress that he had raised from the depths of the ocean, then landed near its great stone doors.

A multitude of monsters had gathered to greet him. Many held weapons of war, while others—their bodies covered with scales and quills, mouths filled with razor-sharp teeth and poison—were weapons unto themselves.

They watched as the Darkstar gently touched down, his solid black wings splayed out on either side of his armored form. He was an awesome sight to behold, of that he was certain.

Not long ago, tribes of these creatures had fought against him, refusing to accept him as their one true liege. Many had died fighting his claim of supremacy, but after Satan had slain the planet's divine protectors—the Nephilim—they had at last accepted him for what he was.

Their king . . . their lord and master . . .

Their god.

Satan advanced toward the great cathedral's entrance, the gathering of monstrosities parting to create a path for him. He remained alert for signs of danger, for while they all had sworn their loyalty to him, the honor of such creatures was not to be trusted.

"All hail the Darkstar!" a beast proclaimed, raising a blood-encrusted sword above its malformed head as Satan approached.

"Hail!" the crowd shrieked as one.

The closer Satan got to the massive doors, the louder the beasts roared their allegiance, stamping their feet, tentacles, and cloven hooves upon the hard ground. He should have felt energized by their veneration, but instead he felt empty. It was as if he barely heard their cries of adulation, distracted by what was still denied to him. He would not be satisfied until Heaven, and the loathsome God enthroned within it, fell to his legions.

The cathedral opened to grant him access; then the stone doors slammed closed behind him, cutting off the cheers of the beasts outside. Satan stood in the shadowy silence.

"Do I sense troubles?" asked a creeping voice from somewhere within the vast chamber.

"Troubles? Who is troubled?" asked another voice.

"Certainly not the one who is now called king. What trouble could there be for one who rules us all?" questioned a third.

The Sisters of Umbra gradually shambled from a patch of impenetrable darkness, their robed and hooded forms swaying before him.

Satan strode into the sanctuary.

"You read my mood as if it were your own," the Darkstar said.

"How can this be?" asked one of the Sisters.

"Has the jubilation of your achievements waned so quickly?" asked the second.

"Certainly, we are mistaken," said the third.

Satan walked past the crones, moving deeper into the citadel, toward the throne that had been constructed from the bones of those who had denied his supremacy.

Furling his great wings of ebony, the Satan plopped his armored form down onto the skin-upholstered seat.

"You are not," he said.

The Sisters moved as one, slowly turning and shuffling to stand before him.

"But what could be troubling you, great Lord of Shadows?"

"Could it be that some of your enemies—though routed—remain at large?"

"And perhaps still threaten your glory?"

Satan scowled at the thought. Yes, some who opposed him had managed to avoid his wrath, but he had demonstrated his omnipotence. Surely the Nephilim were holed up somewhere, terrified by what he had done to their world, and waiting for the inevitable.

Waiting to die.

But the Sister's comment would not leave him. What if

the Nephilim were not hiding, but planning another assault against his rule?

"They are still out there," he said. "And as long as they are alive . . ."

The middle Sister finished his thought. "How can you truly enjoy what you have achieved?"

"Knowing that they are out there, plotting against you," added another Sister.

"Threatening to disrupt all that you have worked so hard to attain," said the last of them. "It would be enough to drive one mad, we'd imagine."

Satan knew that the Sisters were right—how could he possibly focus on conquering Heaven, knowing that he had enemies on earth who might thwart his plans?

"Scox!" Satan roared, his voice echoing through the vast stone structure. "Damn your eyes, where are you, servant?"

The red-fleshed creature, the last of an imp species wiped from existence by the angry Satan, ran breathlessly into the chamber.

"Forgive me, my Darkstar," the imp said, head bowed, hands before him. "I wasn't aware that you'd returned. I was watching the human military's latest attempt to attack us."

Satan cocked his head to the side. "And how did they fare?" he asked, mildly amused that humanity was still trying to fight back.

The imp slowly raised his head to gaze upon his lord and

master. "Quite poorly, my lord," he said with the hint of a smile. "A swarm of enthusiastic gargoyles tore the aircraft to pieces before they could pose a threat."

A threat. The word swirled around the Darkstar's thoughts. The humans, try as they might, would never be successful against him. But the others . . . the half-breeds . . . the Nephilim.

Even though their numbers had dwindled, and they were scattered to the far corners of the earth, hiding from his wrath . . . still . . .

A threat.

"Scox," Satan said.

"Yes, m'lord."

"The corpses."

"Corpses, m'lord?"

"The bodies of the dead Nephilim that I had exhumed from their graves."

"Ah, yes, the corpses," Scox affirmed.

"Bring them to me," Satan ordered. He glanced at the Sisters, who eagerly nodded their hooded heads.

"I hate to see perfectly good corpses going to waste."

CHAPTER FIVE

The Architects felt pity for the world of man.

Or at least it was the closest thing to emotion that such beings could feel. The twelve Architects saw imperfection and were called by duty to correct it.

In a place neither here nor there, the first of God's angels perched on ledges in the circular room they called Habitat, staring at a ghostly image of earth slowly spinning before them.

"Would it not have been easier to wipe it all away with fire or some cosmic event?" asked one of the pale-skinned creatures, his large, dark eyes fixed upon the globe.

"We've talked of this before," answered another dispassionately. "It was not our purpose to destroy or create anew. We were here—are here—to guide this world to its fulfillment. The raw materials that we require are present for us to utilize . . . clay to be shaped into something wonderful."

"It has proven to be nothing but a disappointment," another Architect added.

"We are in the process of fixing that," the one that they called the Overseer interjected.

The Overseer was the first to have been birthed by God, standing at the right side of the Almighty as his eleven Architect brothers were brought into existence.

The Overseer and the other Architects were the personification of the Lord's vision for a world in the throes of birth. They were to oversee its creation, helping to bring the Creator's vision for this wondrous place to fruition.

And when that job was done, they were to be no more.

But the Overseer looked upon the world and saw not perfection, but chaos, and knew that the Architects' job was far from complete.

And it wouldn't be until the earth was like unto Heaven.

A new Paradise.

The world had yet to attain that level of perfection . . . but with their assistance, it was closer now than it had ever been.

So very, very close.

The Overseer's mind could not help but wander, recalling soon after the earth was born when his Creator had deemed their services complete.

How can the Lord think that? the Overseer had thought. *This planet . . . this world . . . can He not see the pandemonium that will continue into perpetuity?*

But He was the Lord God Almighty, and to question Him—

The Overseer remembered the horror as he watched his fellow Architects fade from existence, one after the other, as he prepared to meet his own similar fate.

And was made nothing with just a thought.

Nothing.

The Overseer became slightly agitated with the recollection, as he often did when his thoughts returned to that moment. His brothers turned their watchful eyes from the facsimile of the world to him.

"You're thinking of our creation again," said one.

"Our second creation," the Overseer corrected, for he had willed himself and his brethren back into existence.

The Lord God had moved on to some other grand scheme pertaining to the creation of all things, carelessly leaving behind some minor spark of thought—some flame of inspiration—that took hold of the moment and shaped itself into an idea.

And then a purpose.

The Overseer was that idea, and thus lived again, and saw with even more clarity, what it must do to fulfill his beloved master's aspirations of perfection.

So it was the Overseer's time to influence, and his brothers were re-created from the same fires of inspiration that had brought him back.

It was important to stay focused. They were so close

to achieving the perfection their God had yearned for in the earliest of earth's days.

"And what of us then?" asked one of the twelve Architects. "What shall our purpose be when perfection is finally attained?"

The Overseer sensed tension in his brothers. It was thrilling to be on the verge of finally completing their task, but it was also a little frightening.

They had no desire to cease their existence.

"Perfection is so easily corrupted," the Overseer explained. "We will remain, ever vigilant, to ensure that it is maintained."

His brother Architects grew calmer, turning their gazes back to the ghostly representation of the world. They liked that answer.

And so did the Overseer.

The Morningstar was falling.

Lucifer, who had once been the most blessed of God's angels, plummeted into darkness, his body stolen by an ancient evil that possessed his physical form, driving his essence deep into hiding within his own damaged psyche.

Lucifer struggled to regain control, but the creature that called itself Satan was far stronger than he could ever have imagined. And the farther he fell, the harder it would be for him to return—to be forgiven for his sins.

To finally achieve redemption in the eyes of God.

Lucifer carried the burden of his many sins, and this misery lived within him. It became his strength. It had fueled his desire for redemption, but now Satan drew power from the Morningstar's pain.

Hiding in the recesses of his psyche, Lucifer's conscience was not spared accountability for the acts performed by the ancient evil inhabiting his skin. In fact, it pushed Lucifer even deeper within himself. From this darkness, he witnessed the murder of the Nephilim Lorelei, a magick user. Tricked by the trusted visage of her teammate, the sweet girl had been viciously struck down.

And as if that was not enough, Lucifer was forced to endure the agony of seeing Aaron, his only son, lured into an ambush by the guise of his father. As the evil entity plunged a sword of darkness through the boy's body, Lucifer Morningstar had felt Satan's supreme joy.

It had been more than he could bear.

But as the nothingness rose up to greet him, the Morningstar recollected a long-suppressed memory.

The memory of his creation.

He had sprung from nothing to kneel in the Lord's hand.

"And I shall call you the son of the morning," God had said, and the Morningstar had become filled with the light and love of his Creator.

The first of Lucifer's memories would now be his last.

And it would have been Lucifer's end—if it wasn't for the sound.

The Morningstar listened. There was something familiar about the noise.

The squeak came again.

Yes, Lucifer knew that sound, and he found himself smiling. It was the voice of the one creature who had befriended him when all others had turned away, who believed that he was good, and kind, and worthy of forgiveness.

It was the squeak of a mouse named Milton.

The pain was indescribable.

Dusty lay atop a moldy comforter and wished that he would just hurry up and die.

Fever racked his body, as if he were burning from the inside out. But that was just a minor discomfort in comparison to the pieces of the Abomination of Desolation's sword that were lodged in his flesh. Each sliver was vibrating at a different speed. As the shrapnel quivered, Dusty's head was filled with a cacophony of sound. Each piece of the sword screamed of futures to come.

A cold, wet nose, followed by the gentle lick of a warm tongue, was enough to send him into spasms. Dusty knew the dog meant well, but it was all too much.

He managed to turn his head to stare at the Labrador that sat patiently beside him. He could sense the worry radiating from the animal's deep, dark eyes. He wanted to tell the dog to leave him to his fate, but no sound would come from his lips.

The pain was incredible, and he couldn't stop himself from writhing in agony, which only drove the vibrating pieces of metal deeper into his body.

The dog, Gabriel, got to his feet. His hackles of golden yellow rose along his neck, and sparks of fire leaped from the ends of his fur.

The dog looked back at Dusty, a message passing between them. Dusty knew that he should try to remain silent, so as not to draw the attention of whatever was in the house.

Through pain-blurred eyes, he watched as the Labrador, their sole protector, turned gracefully and trotted from the room.

Again, Dusty was overcome by visions. It was as if each piece of the giant sword once wielded by the Abomination of Desolation was attempting to tell him something. The images were so fleeting that he could barely make out one before the next came crashing into view.

But Dusty saw a dog—Gabriel—being attacked.

It took almost every bit of strength that Dusty still had to process these flashes of prescience, to organize them in such a way that they made the slightest bit of sense. But he concentrated with all his might, and they started to vibrate—to speak—at the same frequency. Slowly, the images became more linear, and the pain began to subside.

From what he could understand, Gabriel was going to be overcome if . . .

But again the pieces of shrapnel were all communicating at once. Dusty was just about to slip into unconsciousness, when he managed to regain control, visualizing each piece of metal within him vibrating at the same speed.

Vibrating as one.

Suddenly it all became clear.

And Dusty saw what he could—what he would—do to save his friend.

Gabriel knew that trespassers were in the house. He could smell their pee-like scent hanging heavily in the air.

Cautiously he stalked down the rubble-strewn corridor toward the burned-out remains of the kitchen. The smell was stronger there.

Gabriel stood in the entryway, his enhanced canine vision searching the gloom for intruders. Gazing about the once-cheery place, the dog could not help but remember his family, and the happy times they had spent together there. Tom, Lori, and little Stevie; they were gone now. Only he and Aaron survived.

Aaron.

The dog felt a wave of panic, realizing that he didn't even know if his master was still alive.

Distracted by this disturbing thought, he did not notice the creatures in the shadows. They were small, about the size of cats, but walked erect like small children, and were covered in thick, shaggy fur.

They lunged. Mouths ringed with sawlike teeth, they screamed their excitement as they rushed him. Tiny, clawed hands grabbed at Gabriel's fur, and the dog released the most ferocious of barks, unleashing the power of the Nephilim.

Divine fire trailed from Gabriel's body as he sprang about the kitchen, attempting to elude the swarm of hungry creatures. They came at him from all sides, pouring in through broken windows and up from the basement. Gabriel fought as best he could, snatching the furry varmints in his mouth and shaking them as his holy fire ignited their fur. Then he tossed their flaming bodies into the expanding horde and grabbed for the next.

Suddenly, the creatures nearest the hallway began screaming, then fell dead. The others started swarming out the kitchen door.

Gabriel darted around the broken cabinets. There, in the hallway, stood a nearly naked Dusty, arms and legs spread wide. He wiggled his finger wildly, as if urging the creatures to come at him.

Has Dusty gone crazy? Gabriel wondered.

Then Dusty let out a horrible shriek, and his wounds began spurting blood. The advancing creatures fell with the dead on the floor, their furry bodies bleeding.

Gabriel couldn't understand what it was he was seeing.

More of the beasts swarmed Dusty, and again, he let out a yell.

More of them went down, while others tried to escape Dusty's reach.

Gabriel poked a dying creature with his paw. A jagged piece of dark metal stuck out from its fur, just above the creature's tooth-filled mouth.

A jagged piece of metal.

Suddenly, that piece of metal began to move, to vibrate, and it shot from the creature's body, boomeranging back into Dusty's flesh.

Is this even possible? the dog questioned, but realized that such a thought was completely foolish given this new, horrible world.

Gabriel picked his way to Dusty amid hundreds of dead and bleeding creatures, trying not to step on the furry bodies. Dusty had dropped to his knees, breathing heavily.

"Woof," Gabriel said to Dusty, who did not have the ability to speak any language as the Nephilim did.

Dusty lifted his head slowly. The cuts on his face and body were already beginning to heal. "It's all right now, boy," he said, a strange smile forming on his bloodstained face. "I've figured it all out."

Dusty reached out to pet Gabriel's head, but the Labrador stepped away, avoiding his touch. Moments ago, the young man had been so sick that he could barely move. What happened?

Dusty laughed again, looking toward his hand as he flexed his fingers.

"I know what I am now," he said with a firm nod to Gabriel. "I am the sword, and the sword is me."

CHAPTER SIX

Vilma brought Aaron's limp hand to her mouth and kissed it.

She watched him, imagining how she would react if his eyes suddenly opened.

"I miss you so much," she said, as much to him as to herself.

She was alone with Aaron. Taylor had been called away by one of the Unforgiven for a reason they chose not to share.

Which was perfectly all right with Vilma. A lot of Taylor's stories were disturbing, like when she'd explained where she'd been for the last twenty years.

Vilma couldn't imagine what it would have been like to go to the hospital to have a baby, then wake up inside a morgue drawer. She recalled Taylor's explanation of how Mallus, using angel magick, had made the doctors, and hospital staff, believe that she was dead. And the idea of never seeing one's newborn child, even if it meant saving said child, was just something that she could barely comprehend. It must have been beyond terrible.

"I know you don't know she's here yet, but when I found out who she was, I was pretty pissed," Vilma told her unconscious boyfriend. "I didn't think there was any excuse good enough, but now, after hearing why she stayed away . . .

"I wonder how I would have reacted," Vilma said, recalling the haunted look in Taylor's eyes as she told her story. "What must it have been like to learn that the man you've loved, the father of your child, was actually Lucifer?"

She thought about all the challenges she'd faced since meeting Aaron and learning that she, too, was Nephilim. It made it that much easier to accept Aaron's mother.

"I really think you'll like her," Vilma said to him. "She comes across as a little cold and distant, but I think that probably has something to do with living with the Unforgiven." She made a face. "Those guys give me the creeps."

Mallus had turned Taylor over to the Unforgiven to save her from the dangers of evil forces willing to use her against the angel whose heart she had captured. For her own safety, the safety of her son, and the safety of the world, Taylor Corbet had remained hidden. With the Unforgiven, she worked to keep the world from falling to the mysterious Architects.

It was an uphill battle.

Vilma stared at the mechanical healing ring attached to her boyfriend's chest. She watched the flashes of energy that coincided with the beating of his heart. The device made her nervous, but if it was going to help him . . .

The healing ring suddenly brightened, pulsing rapidly as Aaron's body began to twitch.

Is he waking up? Vilma jumped to her feet to summon help, but there was no call button. It wasn't really a hospital anymore. She hated to leave his side, but she had no choice.

Vilma bolted from the room. "Hey!" she cried.

The Unforgiven sentry who usually sat at the old reception desk was gone. The entire floor appeared to be empty.

"Is anybody here?" she shouted, but there was no response.

Vilma turned back to the room, watching Aaron's body twitch and shudder. He needed help. She ran back down the hallway and into a darkened stairway. She had no idea whether she should go up or down. Her panic escalated. She leaned against the wall for a moment, trying to calm herself.

There were scrapes, digs in the paint and stone, as if something—or someone—had rubbed up against it repeatedly. The image of the Unforgiven, their mechanical wings furled upon their backs, immediately came to mind.

They must use these stairs, she thought.

It was as good a theory as any.

And without a moment's hesitation, Vilma headed down the stairs, hoping that help awaited her somewhere below.

* * *

Aaron suddenly realized he'd been staring at the pulsing, geometric shapes on his computer screen.

Well, that's time well spent, he thought, rubbing his burning eyes.

He tapped his keyboard, and the screen saver vanished. He hadn't quite finished the Saint Athanasius School's income tax preparations, but better to finish it in the morning, rather than risk a mistake.

He saved his file, then noticed the time at the bottom of his screen.

8:36 p.m.

"Shit." He had no idea it had gotten so late. He thought of calling Vilma, but decided it would be better to just head home. He didn't want to waste any more time when he could be on the road.

He pushed back his chair, reached beneath his desk for his satchel, and stood. No one else was burning the proverbial midnight oil at Mallus, CPA, except for a cleaning crew. The sound of a vacuum cleaner could be heard coming from an office down the hall.

Aaron headed for the elevator, wondering if Jeremy would still be awake when he got home. Their four-year-old son had been having some difficulties sleeping: recurrent dreams about goblins, trolls, and an armored, winged giant with a huge, vibrating sword.

Aaron smirked. Jeremy was his kid, all right—what an imagination.

The elevator doors parted and he stepped into the empty cab, beginning his descent to the garage.

Aaron was exhausted. He had started working for Mallus, CPA, five years ago, after getting his business and accounting degree from Northeastern University. It was pretty much the job he'd hoped for: decent pay, providing an adequate life for his wife and child, even allowing for a small savings toward the house they wanted to purchase.

He was lucky.

No, he corrected himself. Not lucky. He'd busted his ass for the life he had—the only luck he'd had was in meeting Vilma.

Aaron's heart fluttered and flipped whenever he thought about his wife. He still had no clue as to why she'd ever agreed to go out with him, let alone marry him. That was luck.

The elevator reached the basement and shuddered. The doors began to part, then stopped. *What the hell?* Aaron thought. He tried to push them apart.

Peering out to what should have been the well-lighted parking garage, all he saw was darkness.

Total darkness.

Aaron stepped back, unnerved.

He wondered if there had been a power outage, but the elevator's lights were still on. And there should have been emergency lights above the rows of cars.

He grasped the doors once more and, grunting with exertion, shoved them apart. Standing in the doorway, he couldn't make out anything, not even the shapes of the cars that should have been parked there, no matter how hard he strained his eyes. He pulled his car keys from his satchel and hit the button to start his car, watching for the flash of lights and listening for the sound of the motor.

Nothing.

Aaron hit the button again. Nothing. There was nothing out there.

How is that possible?

He double-checked the panel inside the elevator. PG was lit. He should have been in the parking garage.

But he wasn't.

Part of him was tempted to go stumbling off into the darkness, but there was another part that warned him to be careful.

Something wasn't right.

Aaron hit the button to close the doors. He'd exit through the lobby and let security know there was an issue on the lower level.

The elevator reached the first floor with a *ping*. The cab shuddered. The doors parted.

Total darkness.

Impossible!

Aaron poked his foot out of the elevator. The ground was

solid. He reached out in front of him, hands searching for the wall, but finding empty space.

"What the hell is going on?" he asked aloud. "Hello?" he called out. "Anybody here? What's going on?"

His questions were met with an eerie silence. There was absolutely no sound. No buses, no cars, no noise filtering through the lobby from the busy Boston street outside.

Aaron suddenly experienced an excruciating pain in his stomach. He doubled over at its intensity.

Great, he thought, breathing rapidly through his nose in hopes of lessoning the agony. *I'm having a medical emergency in the middle of a blackout.*

As the pain began to subside, he reviewed what he'd eaten that day. Vilma's salad was super healthy; surely it wouldn't make him feel so terrible.

He turned back toward the elevator, and the doors closed. The darkness wrapped around him.

"Shit," he muttered, the all-encompassing black starting to make him feel a little bit dizzy and unsteady on his feet.

Again he took a deep, calming breath, trying to get a handle on the increasingly bizarre situation. He fished through his bag for his cell phone. He stared at its illuminated face, finding some comfort in its glow; then he hit the speed dial for home.

The call didn't go through.

He tried three more times without success and was tempted to throw the phone away, but managed to keep himself together.

Aaron used the light from his phone to try and see around the building lobby. The light only went so far before it was eaten up by the inky blackness. A chill ran up and down his spine.

Where there should have been marble tile, there was only shadow.

"I'm close to freaking out here," Aaron said aloud just to break the silence.

And then he saw a light, so faint that it must have been very far in the distance, but who could tell in this dark void?

"Hello?" he called, walking toward the pulsating beam. It almost looked like a flame, but what would be burning inside a Boston office building, and wouldn't there be smoke?

Aaron stopped. The lobby wasn't that big. Surely he should have hit a wall or a doorway by now.

"Hey!" he called out again, remaining perfectly still, eyes riveted to the light, which now seemed to be slowly—oh so slowly—moving toward him.

But the closer it got, the more it seemed that his eyes were playing tricks on him.

Two human shapes were making their way toward him.

But why does it look as though they're on fire?

Aaron suddenly had the urge to run. But his legs wouldn't move.

The figures walking toward him were burning.

Their clothes were charred, their exposed flesh melting like candle wax.

This is a nightmare. I need to wake up.

The figures were close enough now that Aaron could smell the awful aroma of their burning clothes and hair—

And he recognized their faces.

"Dad? Mom?" He started toward his foster parents but recoiled at the heat from their bodies.

"Tom . . . Lori, what's happening?" Aaron began to panic.

A sharp pain shot through his stomach once more. He cried out, dropping heavily to his knees. Was the pain somehow causing him to hallucinate?

His parents edged closer. The heat thrown from them was incredible.

"Please," he begged, looking up at their horrible, burning faces. "What's happening?"

"Take my hand," his father said. His voice sounded hoarse, choked with smoke.

The pain in Aaron's stomach intensified.

"Is this . . . is this a dream?" he struggled to ask.

His mother and father exchanged a glance, then looked back to him.

"It is a dream," his mother confirmed, her voice even more frightening than his father's. "This perfect life you've built here is a dream."

"Perfect life?" he asked, not understanding at all. "What do you . . . ?"

Aaron was ready to cry, the agony in his belly so bad that he could barely stand it.

"We've come to guide you," his father said, smoke billowing from his mouth.

"Guide me? Guide me where?" Aaron wanted to know.

"Either back to life, or . . ." His mother bent down to take him into her fiery embrace.

"Death."

Vilma felt as though she'd been descending the stairs for days. She'd encountered many locked doors, and floors that hadn't likely seen any activity since the installation had been abandoned.

On what appeared to be the lowest level, she found evidence of life; lights shone brightly through a thick glass window in a heavy metal door. Vilma peered through the glass at the shadows on the other side.

She pounded on the locked door. She needed to get somebody's attention so she could get back to Aaron.

What if he was taking a turn for the worse?

Pushing that disturbing thought aside, she pounded on the door some more.

"Hey! It's me, Vilma. Please—it's Aaron, he needs help!"

She waited for somebody to answer the door, but nobody came. Her frustration grew.

"Is Taylor in there? Hey! It's Aaron! Something's wrong!"

Shadows moved on the other side of the thick glass, but still there was no response.

"Hey!" she screamed, giving another powerful bang.

Nothing.

Anger flowed through her body as if liquid fire was being pumped into her veins. Vilma could hold back no longer. Stepping away from the door, she dropped her right hand to her side and imagined the weapon she'd need to break inside.

The sword was huge—a scimitar.

Vilma raised the flaming weapon with both hands and, with a scream of frustration, brought it down against the metal in an explosion of sound and fire.

The door melted, exposing a long hallway.

As Vilma withdrew her sword, multiple Unforgiven angels appeared, wings unfurled and weapons in hand.

"I don't care to be ignored," Vilma said, stepping through the opening, careful not to burn herself on the molten metal. "Especially not when the health of Aaron is concerned."

The Unforgiven looked as though they didn't know how to react.

Then Taylor Corbet appeared. "What the hell is going on?" she snapped at the Unforgiven. Her gaze traveled the hallway to the remains of the door. "Vilma?"

"Something's wrong with Aaron," Vilma said with irritation. "I was knocking, and nobody paid any attention, so I . . ."

Taylor looked to one of the Unforgiven. "Is he all right?"

The angel reached inside his coat and removed a square electronic device. "He's in an unusually heavy REM state, but otherwise appears to be fine."

"There's nothing wrong with Aaron," Taylor said, turning to leave. "Now if you'll excuse me—"

Vilma felt it in the air. Something unnatural caused the muscles in her back to tingle. Her wings were poised to emerge.

"What's happening?" she asked.

"Nothing of your concern," Taylor replied. "Return to Aaron."

"I can feel it," Vilma said. "There's some kind of disturbance here."

Taylor looked at the Unforgiven, and then back to Vilma.

"You can feel something?"

Vilma nodded.

Taylor stared at her for a moment, then motioned her down the hall.

Vilma followed, willing her sword away so she wouldn't accidentally burn anything. Around the corner, Taylor pushed open a set of double doors that led into a large room filled with complicated-looking pieces of machinery and multiple viewing screens.

Taylor stopped behind an Unforgiven who was seated in front of one of the screens.

"How's he doing?"

"All his vitals are being taxed at the maximum levels," the Unforgiven said.

From what Vilma could make out, they were watching an extremely thin man, who knelt inside another, rounded room. Wires trailed from his body into instrument panels hung upon the concave walls.

"Who's that?" Vilma asked. She couldn't take her eyes from the man on the screen.

As if at the sound of her voice, the man turned his gaze upward and raised his long, skinny arms to beckon to someone, or something.

"The angel's name is A'Dorial," Taylor said. "It was once his purpose to maintain the world's connection to Heaven."

"But that connection was broken," Vilma said, looking away from the angel, who slowly stood. "The Abomination of Desolation cut the earth's connection—didn't it?"

"The connection was severed," Aaron's mother confirmed. "But somehow . . ."

Vilma stared as A'Dorial's body exuded an unearthly light.

"He's . . . he's still maintaining a connection, isn't he?"

"Yes," Taylor answered. "As small as it is, he's somehow managed to keep the most fragile of links open."

A'Dorial's body suddenly dimmed, and he collapsed on the floor.

"Get in there," Taylor commanded the Unforgiven who

had gathered behind them. "Take care of him before his body temperature gets any higher."

The Unforgiven swarmed from the room, some carrying strange mechanical devices. Vilma could only imagine their purpose.

"What's wrong with him?" Vilma asked.

"He is straining to keep that link open. It's killing him."

"And if he should die?" Vilma asked, fearing the answer.

"Then our final connection to Heaven will be severed," Taylor said, appearing to grow quite nervous. "And I guess we would truly be on our own."

CHAPTER SEVEN

Lorelei died looking into the face of evil.

At first she had believed it was her friend and mentor Lucifer Morningstar, but just as his blade plunged into her body, she knew that it wasn't him at all. It was someone—something—else. Pure evil had somehow stolen his form.

And that just pissed her off.

She wished that she'd had the ability to react, but as her life slipped away, she had been too damn weak to do anything but die.

Lorelei felt bad leaving behind her Nephilim friends to deal with the darkness that had befallen the world, but what could she do? She was dead, and that was that.

As she understood it, once one died, the energy that comprised the life force—the soul—was released back into the universe, where it would live on in the perpetual cycle of creation, in one form or another.

So why am I still around? she wondered. *Why am I still able to think as me . . . as Lorelei?*

For a moment, she panicked.

Oh crap, am I a ghost?

The idea scared her. Unless she was the kind of ghost that could actually help her friends. That would be all right, she imagined.

Lorelei was aware of herself, and what had happened to her, but her current reality was a question.

Maybe this was all part of the process.

Or not.

Where was she anyway?

She didn't seem to have a body anymore, but . . .

It was as if she'd had her eyes closed, and suddenly they were open.

She could see blurry shapes standing before her. They—whoever they were—seemed to be watching her.

She tried to speak. If she could see, perhaps she had a voice, too.

Hello? Who's there? What's happening to me?

The sound wasn't sound at all, but a kind of mental projection. She was speaking with her mind.

The silhouettes stood clumped together behind a large gate of some kind, the shape of what looked to be a great city barely visible in the distance.

Lorelei suddenly felt fear. Whatever was happening to

her was unlike anything she'd ever experienced or read about.

The figures gradually began to fade.

What's happening? she asked, not really expecting an answer.

But there was an answer nonetheless. One of the silhouettes broke away from the group to approach her. It moved as if in slow motion. And then it spoke to her in a voice that she knew, and loved.

We don't have much time.

Dad? Dad, is that you?

Her father, the fallen angel Lehash, had been forgiven his sins through Aaron's redeeming powers, allowing him to return to the paradise of Heaven.

Lorelei had missed him more than life itself, but now that she was dead . . .

It is, darlin', Lehash said.

A wave of intense emotion flooded her at the sound of his Southern drawl.

But we ain't got much time.

What is it, Dad? What's going on? Where am I and what—

Listen to me. You've got to help them.

Who? I'm dead . . . aren't I?

Yes, you're dead. But that doesn't mean you're out of the runnin'.

She felt herself suddenly begin to shake, the silhouette of her father becoming more blurred.

Dad?

Listen to me good, Lorelei; you've got to help 'em in any way you can.

Who, Dad? Who am I supposed to help?

Your friends. The Nephilim. You gotta help 'em.

What? Lorelei was frantic to understand. *How can I help them if . . .*

It's too late. Her father's voice dropped in and out. *The link ain't strong enough.*

Dad! she cried out. *Please tell me what you can!*

Guide them to the place, Lorelei, Lehash said, his voice becoming fainter by the second. *They're the last chance we have. Lead them . . .*

Dad! Her sight faded to black.

Lead them to the Ladder, were the last words she heard her father say.

The next thing she knew, Lorelei was standing, completely naked, in a pile of ash and what looked to be bones.

She looked around her. She appeared to be on the grounds of the Saint Athanasius School. The sky was gray and dismal, but she felt no cold—even though she wasn't wearing clothing. Raising a hand, she scrutinized it. The skin appeared pale, and slightly translucent.

She could see the school through her hand.

What's happening? Take it easy, Lorelei, she told herself. *Deep breaths.*

And then she began to laugh. "Ghosts don't breathe," she said, fighting the urge to cry. "Ghosts can't do much of anything."

Her resolve started to crumble. She couldn't feel the ground beneath her feet, either. Panic crept over her as she focused on the pile of blackened ash and yellowed bone fragments that she was standing on.

Why am I here?

Slowly it dawned on her: She was standing on her remains. Her body had been burned after she had died.

Tearing her gaze from the ashes, Lorelei looked around. The seared corpse of the great dragon lay close by.

That must have been what burned her.

With her new understanding, Lorelei discovered that she could move.

And move she did.

She floated through the air like an untethered balloon. At first, it was sort of difficult to control her movement, but with some concentration, she was able to maneuver.

Is this what I have to look forward to? she wondered. *Flying around . . . naked?*

Glancing down at her body, Lorelei imagined herself fully clothed. Her flesh began to steam, and an ethereal mist flowed over her body to create a robelike covering.

"Would you look at that?" she uttered in awe.

Maybe there was more to this ghost business than she suspected.

There has to be. How else could Dad expect me to lead them? she thought as the mist coalesced around her head like a hood.

But there was still much that she didn't understand.

Lorelei drifted by the felled dragon. It was huge, but had been taken down by beings less than half its size.

The Nephilim.

Lorelei could not help but smile at the thought of her friends, but her smile quickly passed. Had they survived?

Her thoughts were suddenly, rudely, interrupted as a monster exploded out through the side of the dragon's corpse, ripping through the thick, scaled flesh with its huge pincers.

Lorelei screamed, recoiling from the loathsome creature that had been feeding on the dragon's insides. Its insectlike head was covered in gore. It shook violently, releasing a disturbing cry of its own.

Somehow Lorelei sensed that the beast could not perceive her ghostly shape, but it did not stop her from acting out in revulsion. She found herself reaching out to the creature's chitinous head, watching as her ghostly fingers passed into one of its bulging compound eyes. Her hand inside its head, she willed the monster to die.

The insect screeched one final time, before its head exploded.

Lorelei stared at her ghostly hand, stunned.

There was definitely more to being a ghost than she'd imagined.

* * *

Satan breathed in the thick aroma of the grave and imagined a time in the not-so-distant future when the entire atmosphere would smell like decay.

Glorious.

The Darkstar turned to the row of corpses laid out before him. The five bodies of the fallen Nephilim had been exhumed from the burial ground at the Saint Athanasius School.

The bodies had been interred in what looked to be bedsheets. The makeshift shrouds had started to rot.

One at a time, he studied the corpses, forming a unique bond with each. Satan, the Darkstar, saw great potential in these rotting forms.

"You shall be my children," he said to them, his eyes lovingly caressing the still corpses. "And in being so, you shall serve me loyally—unquestioningly."

Legions of beasts had sworn their allegiance to him over the last few weeks. But the Darkstar knew that their fealty was fleeting. It was the nature of such creatures to serve only their best interests. He knew if the opportunity ever presented itself, the foul beasts would hungrily knock him from his perch of command.

They served him only because they feared him. But now he would create his own army.

The armored Lord of Shadows tenderly lifted the decaying cloth to expose the corpses' faces. He studied each and every one in their various stages of decomposition, so he knew them as only a father knows his children.

The misery that came to be known as Hell, imprisoned within the form he had stolen, churned eagerly in anticipation of what it was going to be allowed to do.

It was a power so great, so awesome in its magnitude, that it scared even one such as him.

This had been God's punishment to Lucifer: all the sorrow of Heaven, all the sadness and pain caused by the Morningstar's revolt against the Heavenly Father and His Kingdom, stored away inside him, in order that he learn the folly of what he had done.

To the Son of the Morning, this was the ultimate punishment, but to one born in darkness, this was a power that bordered on unimaginable.

Satan admired his new children. A power such as this must be used sparingly—effectively—for even he was unsure that he could control it if unleashed completely.

Standing above his soon-to-be-reborn family, the Darkstar removed the black metal gauntlet that covered Lucifer's hand, exposing his pale flesh to the elements. He flexed his fingers.

If he was required to give any accolades to the Creator, it would be for the wonderful design of His divine beings. The angels truly were an achievement to behold.

And Satan found it fitting that the gift of new life, a

life born of darkness and misery, would come from a vessel originally forged in the fires of God's love.

A vessel strong enough to contain that which came to be known as Hell.

Satan conjured a knife of petrified shadow and brought it to his palm. Without hesitation, he pressed the edge of the blade against his fragile flesh, cutting a gash, unleashing the blood within.

Blood rich with the power of torment and sorrow.

"This is my blood," Satan recited, slowly tipping the wound in his palm over the mouths of the dead Nephilim. "It contains the power of my life, which I give unto you."

The Darkstar admired his work, the wound upon his hand already healing. Wishing his blade of night away, Satan searched for any sign that he had succeeded. His blood had been completely absorbed, and he visualized it working its way through the bodies, restoring a semblance of life to the cadavers' cells and organs.

Satan waited, then began to pace. To call the Lord of Shadows impatient was an understatement.

"Live!" he ordered them, believing his words contained the catalyst to bring forth the results he so desired. "I command you to live!"

The corpses showed no sign of life.

Suddenly there came a knock on the chamber's door. Satan turned in fury as the imp demon Scox intruded on his solitude.

"Master?" the red-skinned creature asked. "I heard you cry out, and I was uncertain if it was me that you called for or . . ."

"Did I not ask to be left alone?" the Darkstar demanded, feeling the urge to peel the flesh from the imp's musculature and use it to cover a cushion for one of his thrones.

"Yes, but I wasn't sure if . . ."

The imp trespassed farther into the chamber, and his eyes went wide.

The Darkstar spread his wings and vaulted across the expanse of room to land before the terrified servant.

"You weren't sure?" Satan leaned in to the flummoxed imp. "Weren't you listening to my explicit commands?"

Scox backed toward the door, but it had already closed behind him, trapping him with his angry master.

"Yes, yes, I was," he stammered. "But there have been times when I obeyed your requests for isolation, then incurred your wrath for not heeding your requests to—"

"Your insolence inspires me," Satan said, grabbing the imp by the throat and imagining the glorious screams that would act as a balm for his frustrations. He was just about to begin ripping the red flesh from the imp's face when—

"Master!"

"Scox, your pathetic begging will only spur me to work all the slower," Satan said, sinking his claws into his servant's leathery flesh.

"No, look!" the imp screeched.

Satan turned. The cadavers were moving.

He tossed Scox away, the promise of torture forgotten.

"Leave," the Darkstar commanded, wanting to be alone with his children as they were reborn.

Satan sensed the stone door open and the imp slip away, as he watched the corpses.

But as soon as the imp left, the bodies ceased any signs of life.

"What is this?" Satan growled. Why had they shown signs of life just seconds ago, but now . . .

Satan could think of only one difference, insane as it was.

"Scox!" he roared. "Come here, now!"

He was about to scream for the imp again, when the door opened.

"This time—this time, I am sure that you called for me."

The corpses were moving again, writhing as if the imp's presence somehow facilitated their return to life.

A strange realization came upon the Darkstar.

"An audience!" he exclaimed.

"Excuse me, my lord?"

"An audience," Satan repeated. "They wish their births to be witnessed."

Scox looked at the corpses, then back to his master. "If you say so, my liege."

Satan nodded. If an audience of one was enough to spur a few twitches, what would more spectators bring?

"Bring them in," Satan announced, his eyes still fixed upon his children.

"What?" Scox asked. "I don't know what you're—"

"The rabble outside," Satan explained. "The beasts that claim to serve me—bring them here."

Scox hesitated, but knew better than to question any further. The imp left the chamber, and the bodies stilled.

"Quickly, Scox!" Satan bellowed.

Squeaks, squeals, hisses, growls, and roars announced the arrival of the Darkstar's minions.

"Come in, come in," he waved.

He could tell that the monsters were confused, perhaps expecting some sort of trap, but they continued to lope, slither, undulate, and glide into the chamber.

Satan could barely contain his pleasure as his monstrous Community stared and the corpses writhed to life.

The beasts were asking questions, but it was not time for answers. Satan raised his hand for their attention.

"Silence!"

The chamber grew eerily quiet even though filled almost to capacity.

"You are all about to witness something . . . fantastic." Satan pointed to the shapes that squirmed across the stone floor like maggots atop a piece of rotting meat.

At his command, the movement of the five corpses became

more frantic, clawed fingers ripping through the remaining shrouds that covered their bodies.

Those that had been dead had returned to life, shucking off their burial garments like snakes leaving their old skin.

And what a spectacular sight they were.

Their bodies were now oily black as the Darkstar's blood, the surface of their skin reflecting the chamber's light with an unearthly shine. Their eyes glowed a sickly yellow, and their mouths, which were twisted in a rictus grin of pain, were filled with jagged, razor-sharp teeth.

Satan's new army crawled on all fours, their muscular backs bucking wildly with their transformation. One after the other, they tossed their heads back, crying out in a strange combination of agony and relief, as huge, batlike wings tore through the fabric of their flesh.

"Look at them," Satan commanded proudly. "My blessed angels of darkness, my angels of the void."

The Darkstar broke his gaze from his creations to take in his audience. His chest swelled with pride as he saw fear in their watchful eyes.

He smiled, for now he finally understood.

He knew what it was like to be God.

CHAPTER EIGHT

The fallen angel and the Malakim flitted about the storm-racked Himalayan mountains, as Tarshish's angel magick transported them here and there on their search.

"Does any of this look familiar to you?" Mallus asked, raising his voice above the howl of the frigid winds.

Tarshish shook his head. "Things have changed a lot since the early days," he said. "Who knows if the Metatron's body is even in the same place."

The Malakim paled. "I think I need to sit." He trudged through the snow to an outcropping of ice-covered rock and leaned against it.

"Are you all right?" Mallus asked.

"Fine," Tarshish answered. "Just not used to using my magick so freely. It's draining."

The two knew that the power they sought was not going to go with them willingly. They were likely in for a fight.

A fight that they might not survive.

"Do you think this'll do it?" Tarshish asked.

Mallus looked out at the swirling snow and the seemingly endless mountains beyond. "Depends on what you're talking about."

"If we can find the Metatron's remains, and locate God's power that we unleashed . . ."

"Yes, go on," Mallus urged.

"Do you think it would be enough to forgive us our sins?"

"That's a good question."

"And what do you think the answer would be?" Tarshish prodded. The Malakim must have realized that he was slowly being covered by the drifting snow, because in a sudden flash, the snow on his clothes turned to steam. "Go ahead and tell me whatever you're thinking. I can take it—I am the last of the Malakim, master of powerful angel magick and all that jazz."

"Let's just say I think we've done some serious bad throughout the ages," Mallus said. "But this could go a good distance in getting the Lord God Almighty to look upon us favorably again."

"So, no full pardon?"

"What do you seriously think?" Mallus asked him.

"Yeah," Tarshish agreed. "We were pretty nasty. Maybe we don't deserve to be forgiven."

"Perhaps," Mallus said.

"So why bother then?" Tarshish asked. "Why risk what little life we have left if for no reward?"

"Isn't that the kind of attitude that got us into this situation?" Mallus asked.

Tarshish shrugged. "Yeah, probably."

"We did a lot of damage to this world when we sided with the Architects," Mallus said. "I think we owe it to ourselves, as well as to all the others trying to make things right."

"But will it matter?"

"Won't know unless we try."

Tarshish stared at Mallus, the Malakim's ancient eyes seemingly dissecting him and then putting him back together.

"How did somebody so smart fall for all the crap the Morningstar was shoveling during the war?" the Malakim asked.

"I don't know, why don't you tell me."

They both had a good laugh.

"You rested now? Can we go?" Mallus asked finally.

"Yeah, I'm good." The Malakim pushed off from his rock, his body emitting waves of crackling energy.

Mallus stepped closer, feeling the Malakim magick take hold of him, as they prepared to teleport about the mountains again on their search.

"How close do you think we are to actually locating the Metatron's shell?" Mallus asked.

"I don't know, but there's something that I'd like to try."

And the pair was gone, the falling snow covering up any evidence that they had ever been there at all.

Jeremy opened the can of stew with his burning knife, while heating the contents with his hand.

"This should be hot enough," he said, his breath fogging.

It was cold in this abandoned cabin by the Baltic Sea, but the larder was relatively well stocked, if one enjoyed canned foods, that is.

Jeremy carried the food to the cot where Enoch lay beneath multiple blankets.

"Here," he prodded, bringing the steaming can and spoon to the toddler's mouth. "Sit up and have a bite. You need to keep up your strength."

"I'm not hungry," the child said from beneath the covers.

"Yeah, but you will be," Jeremy answered. "And once I'm done, you'll be telling me that you fancy a snack. Have a bite to eat now and avoid pissing me off later."

"I told you—"

"And I told you," Jeremy snapped, reaching over and pulling at the pile of blankets.

The child was curled into a tight little ball. His body, unnaturally large for one who had been born so recently, still appeared small and helpless.

"Please eat something," Jeremy said. He'd continued to will heat into the palm of his hand so that the contents of the can would not grow cold.

Enoch looked at him intensely; there was much anger in those eyes, as if Jeremy were somehow responsible for the troubles they'd been having.

"I'll eat," Enoch stated angrily. "But I won't like it."

"That's fine with me." Jeremy dragged a stool beside the cot and sat down. "Why don't you pull those covers over your shoulders?"

Enoch scowled but did it anyway, draping the blankets across him like a shawl.

Jeremy dipped the plastic spoon into the stew and brought it to the child's mouth.

"I shouldn't even be eating this," the baby said. "I'm less than two months old. This will probably wreak havoc with my digestive system."

"You've been doing fine," Jeremy said. "Baby food is only for real babies."

"I'm a real baby," Enoch protested.

"No, you're not," Jeremy retorted.

"Close enough."

"Not sure if I'd even go that far," Jeremy said, taking more stew onto the spoon and bringing it to Enoch's mouth.

"Bastard."

"Shut up and eat your stew."

Enoch took another mouthful, this time more eagerly. The baby was obviously hungry. Big surprise.

A roar sounded from somewhere outside. It was distant, but close enough.

A sword of fire immediately came to life in Jeremy's hand. He set down the can of stew and darted toward the window. The thin glass was covered in frost, distorting the view outside.

He could see something moving in the frozen water outside, its serpentine neck jutting up from the ice with another roar.

"What is it?" Enoch asked.

"I don't bloody know," Jeremy said. He held the sword down by his side so as not to alert the monster to their presence inside the hovel. "Sea serpent, I'd gather."

Enoch helped himself to the can of stew, having some difficulty using the spoon.

"It's hard to believe that there was a time when a creature like that would have been unheard of," Jeremy said.

"I never knew such a time," Enoch said, chewing noisily.

"Which is just my point," Jeremy stated. "You're only two months old, and a bloody sea serpent sighting is commonplace."

Enoch scooped more stew from the can, dribbling some of it down the front of his tiny blue jacket before shoving the rest into his yawning mouth.

"I'll try to fix that," the boy said. "Once I've had the chance to—"

"To what?" Jeremy asked. "What are you going to do?"

"I'm going to fix—this." Enoch waved the plastic spoon around. "I'm going to fix the world."

"That's what you keep telling me, but all we're doing is running around from one place to the next, with no rhyme or reason."

The toddler was frustrated. "You know how hard it is for me."

"Yeah, I know." Jeremy was tired of the whole thing. He returned to the stool and took the can from the child.

"My memory is incomplete," Enoch said. "I know what I was, but not what I'm supposed to be now."

Jeremy didn't answer. He'd heard it all before.

"I'm hoping that it will eventually come to me," Enoch explained. "I sense it out there . . . like a beacon trying to reach me. It's what brought me here, and to your mother's attention."

Jeremy flinched at the memory of his mum. He couldn't get the image of her dead body out of his mind.

"I'm here for a very special purpose, Jeremy," the child said, his tiny voice cracking from the strain.

And then he was crying, tears streaming down his cold, chubby face, his cheeks turning an even brighter red.

Finishing the rest of the stew, Jeremy remembered his mother's face as she died, her last word before her final breath:

Protect.

She wanted him to protect the little bugger, so here he was.

"Shush," Jeremy said, setting the empty can and plastic

spoon down on the floor. Enoch continued to wail, so worked up that calming him seemed impossible.

Jeremy sat next to him. Enoch tried to crawl away, but he was too overcome with emotion.

Jeremy could relate. He was frustrated too. He could only imagine what it was like for the toddler. Yes, Enoch spoke like an adult, but the truth was the little bugger was only eight weeks old. It was amazing that he was capable of holding it together as well as he did.

"C'mere," Jeremy said, grabbing for the squirming Enoch. The child fought him, but Jeremy was larger, and quite a bit stronger. He pulled the fussy babe into his arms and hugged him close. "Calm down now," he said, and started to rock.

Enoch continued to fight and screech.

"Wouldn't want that sea serpent to hear you now, would you?" Jeremy asked. "I'd have to toss you to him to make my escape."

"Damn . . . you . . . ," the baby wailed, between gulps of air.

Jeremy squeezed the child tighter. "That's it," he said, his voice soft and calming. "Let it all out, and then we'll be done."

"Don't . . . you . . . understand? I . . . have a job . . . to do . . ."

"I get it," Jeremy said. "I really do."

He knew that the child was here for a purpose, but it was nothing short of maddening, for Enoch as well as himself, not knowing exactly what that reason was. They simply had to keep fumbling along in the dark, until some light was shed on what Enoch's mission might be.

An earsplitting roar rattled the window.

Bloody hell, if his bit of fun with the baby hadn't come true.

"Wait here," Jeremy said, prying the child from his grasp.

"Where are you going?" Enoch demanded petulantly. "I haven't finished venting yet."

Jeremy walked toward the door, a sword of fire igniting in his grasp. "You have if you don't want to be eaten by a sea serpent," the Nephilim said.

That shut up the wailing child.

Jeremy placed his hand on the freezing door latch and looked back to Enoch. The child sat, arms crossed, sulking.

"Thought you were going to feed me to the beast," Enoch said in his sternest voice.

"Now would I do something mean and nasty like that?" Jeremy asked. "This shouldn't take but a minute." Then he stepped outside into the cold, slamming the door of the cabin closed behind him.

The serpent loomed above the cabin, its skin glistening like a rainbow in the dim light of day. Jeremy hated to admit it, but it was a beautiful sight to see.

But then the beast opened its mouth in a roar as it saw him standing there, showing off rows of milky-white, hooked teeth. He could just imagine the damage they could do when biting into tender flesh.

So much for beauty, Jeremy thought, sprouting his wings and flying at the beast, preparing his weapon of crackling flame to strike.

He could be pretty damaging when he wanted to be as well.

"It's all about choices," Tom Stanley said, his face having burned away to reveal a yellowed and charring skull.

Aaron wanted to scream and run, but he knew it would be pointless. Where was he going to go in all this darkness?

He couldn't stand to look at his foster dad, choosing instead to focus on Lori, his foster mom. She didn't look quite so horrible, even though her skin was burning too.

"What kind of choices?" Aaron asked. "I don't understand."

He wanted to believe that this was all some sort of nightmare, but no matter how hard he tried to wake himself, how hard he pinched the flesh of his arms and legs, he wasn't waking up.

Which meant that this was somehow real.

"You're in a bad way, Aaron," Lori said, puffs of smoke leaking from her mouth.

"What do you mean by a 'bad way'? I'm fine—or at least I was until I got in the elevator tonight and . . ."

"And it all disappeared," Tom finished with a knowing nod. "That's what we're trying to tell you, son. None of it was real."

Aaron just stared, dumbfounded, having no clue how to respond.

Lori stepped closer, and Aaron pulled away. He could see

that his actions were hurting her feelings, but he couldn't really help that right now. He needed to know what the hell was happening to him.

"None of this is real," Lori said, and then sighed. "Your job, your office, your life outside this place . . ."

It was as if somebody had taken a sledgehammer to his stomach.

"My life outside . . ." He couldn't even bring himself to finish. "This is crazy. Insane. You're not real. You're the figments of my imagination. . . ."

"We are," Tom agreed. "But we're your subconscious, here to try and help you."

Aaron's legs had become like rubber, and he was having a difficult time standing. "Help me? How are you helping me by telling me that everything I know and love . . ." Aaron stopped as more horror crept up on him.

"Wait," he said. "Vilma and Jeremy . . ."

His foster parents remained silent.

"Arrrrrrrrrrrrgh!" Aaron cried out, bending over in agony. "So this pain . . . isn't real either," he gasped.

"No," Tom said. "The pain is very real."

Lori reached out a flaming hand and laid it on his shoulder. "We just want to help you, Aaron."

The pain was getting stronger. It was like he was being stabbed with a large knife—or sword.

"What—what's happening to me . . ."

The pain was incredible, and getting stronger.

"Your body is forcing you to make up your mind," Tom said. Most of his lower face had been reduced to bone.

Aaron fell to his knees, shivering in a cold sweat.

His foster mom knelt beside him. "We're here to help you make the right choice."

"What choice?" Aaron demanded through gritted teeth. "Why is this pain real but nothing else is?"

"You brought the pain with you," Tom explained. "From your true reality."

"In fact, you built all of this to try and escape it," Lori said, her sparking hand caressing his arm supportively.

"What—what does it mean?" Aaron feared the answer, but he needed to know.

Lori glanced up at her husband.

"Do you want me to tell him, or . . . ," Tom began.

"No, I'll tell him," Lori said. "It means that you're either going to live, or . . . ," she said to Aaron.

"Die?" Aaron asked. "I'm going to die?"

"It's up to you," Tom explained.

"Of course I want to live," Aaron insisted.

Once again Lori and Tom shared a look.

"Do you really know what that means, Aaron?" Lori asked.

Aaron didn't.

"All this," Tom said, waving a blackened, skeletal hand around his head. "All this goes away."

Aaron's eyes darted around. "Looks to me like it already has."

"It all goes away," Lori repeated. "In here"—she pointed at his forehead—"as well as in here." She pointed to his chest.

"What do you mean it goes away?"

"Your wife, your child, the life you share with them," Lori said. "It all ceases to be if you choose to live."

Aaron could not wrap his brain around the meaning of Lori's words.

"Because they never really existed," Tom said with a shrug. "You've created it all to escape the reality of your current situation."

"You were mortally wounded in battle with the Darkstar, who took the form of your father," Lori added.

"My father," Aaron repeated.

The pain intensified, and with it came a barrage of images.

Aaron didn't know which hurt worse.

He remembered. He remembered his wedding day. The birth of his son. But those memories had been a dream. Creations of a perfect existence; what he wished to be true.

"Oh God," he said, voice cracking and eyes welling up with tears. "None of it . . . they're not real."

Aaron's reality rushed in to fill the void left by his shredded dreams.

"You could have stayed with them," Lori said sadly. "But that would have meant that you chose to die."

In a way he felt that he had.

Aaron pictured his son asleep, eyes suddenly opening and smiling a smile warmer than a thousand sunrises.

Then it faded.

"Oh God, I can't forget him—please . . ." He looked to his foster parents. They had always been there for him while growing up, but now he remembered how they had died.

And he knew why they were burning.

"I killed you," he said.

"No." Tom shook his head. "The Powers killed us. Verchiel killed us."

"But it was because of me."

"Shit happens."

Aaron gasped, desperate to hold on to the memory of something very important—something to do with a thousand sunrises—but it was gone. He couldn't remember.

He started to cry again, feeling a monumental loss, but not knowing what it was.

He thought of Vilma, and for a crazy moment, he remembered her as his wife.

Maybe someday, but not now.

"Are you all right, Aaron?" Lori asked. The flames flicked over her gentle features.

"Yeah," he answered. The pain in his stomach was still pretty intense, but he pushed himself to his feet. As he did, he was startled to see that a bloodstain had formed on his shirt. "This doesn't look good."

"It's not," Tom said. "We should probably move on, if you've made your decision."

Aaron looked around at the darkness and tried to imagine what had once occupied the void. If he had known, that knowledge was gone.

"We should probably do something about this," Aaron said, holding his arms up to draw attention to the expanding stain of blood.

"That's exactly what we intend to do," Lori said.

His foster parents turned, retreating farther into the darkness.

And Aaron followed close behind, pulled along by the light thrown from their burning bodies.

CHAPTER NINE

Those progeny of the divine and human, who had been called Nephilim before they'd died, had been transformed into some other entity entirely.

Their master—their father—called them his dark messengers . . . his Angels of the Void.

The five dark angels stood in their birth chamber, acclimating to their new environment. Slowly they flapped their leathery wings, allowing their slick ebony flesh to dry and their muscles to strengthen.

They vaguely recalled that they had once lived, flashes of memory from a time and place when they had served another God.

The memories filled the Angels of the Void with intense hatred, but also with purpose: to destroy those that had once been family to them.

The black messengers could sense their former brothers and sisters, somewhere else, and it caused them great pain.

A pain that they knew would not stop until—

"Do you feel them?"

The Angels of the Void turned toward the sound of their father's voice. He stared at them proudly. Others gathered around him, but they were not the ones of whom their father spoke.

"Out in the world," Satan said, pointing beyond their birthing chamber. "Hiding from me . . ."

Jagged memories of their former selves assaulted their senses, making the desire to destroy—to kill—all the more urgent.

"Hiding from you."

The angels knew that the Nephilim must suffer as they had suffered before surrendering to the darkness of death.

Before they had been reborn.

"You need to find them and you need to steal their lives . . . so that they, too, may receive the gift you were given."

The angels watched their father, understanding what was being asked of them.

What was expected.

"Find them," Satan instructed.

The Angels of the Void did as they were told, attempting to reestablish the connection they'd once had with their Nephilim siblings.

"Find them. And take away their lives."

Anticipating the coming hunt, the angels spread their black wings.

"Go," Satan, the Darkstar, commanded, and the dark messengers surged into the air, exploding through the domed ceiling of the citadel.

Out into the endless night.

The last thing Lorelei remembered was thinking about her friends.

She wasn't precisely sure what had happened then, only that the grounds of the school where she'd been had blurred all around her as if she were suddenly moving at an incredible speed, and she found herself in another place entirely.

Lorelei felt the urge to panic, but then remembered that she was dead, and that there really wasn't much to worry about anymore.

It wasn't like she could get hurt.

If she could have taken a few deep breaths to calm herself, she would have. Looking around at her new surroundings, she saw that she was in some sort of basement, her feet floating a few inches above a concrete floor.

It would have been cool, if she wasn't dead. That kind of threw cold water over anything that might have been exciting.

People were sleeping in the darkened room: a young woman and a little girl, a teenager, a middle-aged cop—or was he a security guard?—an old man, and an elderly woman. Lorelei was drawn to the old lady. She could feel the tethers that held the woman to life gradually loosening.

Lorelei had no idea why she was here, until she saw a familiar form asleep in the corner, away from the others.

"Melissa!" Lorelei squealed, but only she could hear. She floated across the room toward her sleeping friend, and that was when images—terrible images of creatures with black, armored skin, rising up from the earth—flashed through her mind.

Lorelei had no idea what these demons were, but she somehow knew that they were extremely dangerous.

Dangerous to the Nephilim.

Some sort of strange, inexplicable link seemed to exist between Lorelei and these awful beasts. She saw them as they crawled up from the dirt, spreading leathery, batlike wings.

"What are you?" Lorelei asked, oh so curious, but also afraid.

It was if the creatures were compelled to answer—to show her—the masks of black upon their faces melting away to reveal human faces beneath.

Lorelei reacted with a scream that only she could hear.

They were the dead, her friends, the Nephilim fallen in combat. But how? How could they be alive again?

And then it hit her, and for an instant she refused to believe, but then thought better. Maybe they weren't alive at all.

Lorelei tentatively reached out with her mind once again, connecting with the other armored creatures as they pulled themselves up from what had been their graves, and was shaken to the core.

The dead Nephilim had somehow been returned to life, brought back from death to serve as agents of a terrible force.

The Darkstar.

And those who had once been her beloved friends had a terrible purpose that they willingly shared with her. These things, these twisted mockeries of sacred life, were now hunters of the surviving Nephilim.

Stalkers of their still-living friends.

Lorelei could not allow this. She had to do something—but what?

Managing to sever the strange connection she'd made with her resurrected friends, Lorelei experienced a whole new level of frustration.

How could she help if she could not be heard? How could she reach out to her still-living friends and warn them about what was coming?

And then she remembered what she had done to the insect creature that had crawled from the body of the dragon, and stared at her translucent hand, not wanting to hurt in this instant, but to help.

Was there a way?

Lorelei drifted closer to the sleeping Melissa, still entwined within the grip of nightmare, and reached out to her with her ghostly hand. She didn't know exactly what she was doing, but instinct guided her.

The tips of Lorelei's fingers disappeared inside Melissa's head, establishing a tentative connection with the girl. It required a great deal of energy, and Lorelei knew that she could not hold the connection for long. She injected the fear of what she had seen into Melissa's subconscious, hoping that her friend would take it as some sort of sign.

A warning to be heeded.

Melissa had been happy to see her friends alive: Janice, Kirk, William, Russell, and even Samantha.

It was one of those moments when everything seemed right with the world. The sun was warm, and a gentle, cooling breeze only added to the perfection.

No one said a word, so as not to lose the flawless moment.

Melissa felt an intense connection to her Nephilim friends. She'd always wondered what it would be like to have brothers and sisters, and now, looking around her, she knew. She could burst from the joy.

"We're a family!" she blurted out, then panicked. Had she spoiled the moment?

Everyone simply stared.

"I love you all," she tried to explain.

The words seemed perfect as they left her mouth, but Melissa realized that she had only made things worse.

As her friends glowered at her, she wanted to defend her statement, to explain that this was what being a family was all about.

But she didn't get the opportunity, for the skies grew unusually dark, and the refreshing breeze turned cold and damp.

Melissa shuddered.

And it was then that she remembered that they had all died, and had been buried on that very spot.

That she had left trinkets and keepsakes on their graves from the places she had been while defending the world from encroaching evils.

She started to cry. It was as though nothing would ever be right again.

Then the muddy ground beneath her feet started to move, as something forced its way up from below. And it wasn't just one grave—it was all of them.

Dirt and rock exploded into the air. Melissa recoiled, peering out from between splayed fingers at the nightmarish figures that surrounded her.

Everything about them was black, from the glistening armor that covered their bodies to their batlike wings to the aura of foreboding they exuded in waves.

But the most disturbing aspect of all was that Melissa felt

that she knew them, that there was something overwhelmingly familiar about the nightmarish visages that now surrounded her.

"Who are you?" she frantically asked the black, armored wraiths that had emerged from the hold of the grave.

And suddenly she knew.

"We are your family," they announced as one.

"And we love you."

Melissa came awake in the darkness of the fallout shelter, stifling a scream, the stink of overturned dirt heavy in her nostrils.

She looked around, making sure that the black, armored things weren't there with her.

What the hell was that all about? she wondered.

"You okay, Melissa?" Charlie asked from the shadows. He always seemed to be awake.

"I'm good," she said, trying her best not to show the old man how absolutely terrified she was. There were some grunts and sighs as the others stirred in their sleep.

"Bad dreams," she said.

"Tell me about it," Charlie said. "Not sure I'd know a good dream if it bit me on the ass."

As her eyes adjusted to the darkness, she saw him sitting at the edge of the cot, by his wife's side, as he always was.

Melissa pushed herself up and approached him. She was

hoping that the longer she was actually awake, the faster this nearly overpowering sense of anxiety would pass.

But it wouldn't go away.

"What was it?" Charlie asked her.

"Excuse me?"

"The dream, would you tell me what it was?"

Goose bumps broke out on her flesh, and she rubbed her hands over her arms. "Old friends." Her eyes darted around the chamber, searching every shadow for . . .

For what? she wondered. Did she actually expect to see the creatures from her nightmare there in the bomb shelter? That was crazy.

But if it was so crazy, why did she have the overpowering urge to get the hell out of there?

She couldn't help but feel that this was some new Nephilim instinct that was trying to warn her.

"I keep having a nightmare about Retta getting bit," Charlie was saying. He looked to his wife, breathing shallowly on the cot.

"How's she doing?" Melissa asked, desperate for a distraction. "Did the Advil help?"

"Yeah," Charlie said, taking his wife's limp hand in his. "I think it did. She seems to be resting more peacefully."

"Good." Melissa studied the older woman, looking for a positive sign that her health was improving, but she saw no change.

"Your friends," Charlie began. "Were they . . . were they like you?"

Melissa nodded.

"And they died?" Charlie asked incredulously.

"And they died," Melissa repeated. "It's pretty rough out there."

"Tell me about it," Charlie said. "If I hadn't remembered this shelter was here from when our kids were in school, we wouldn't have made it."

Melissa thought of her nightmare again, and the awful things that had crawled up from her friends' graves. She couldn't shake the feeling that there might be some reality to the dream.

The panic became overwhelming, and her hands began to shake. Every instinct that she had told her to flee, to run, if she wanted to survive.

"Maybe you should take a few of those pills yourself," Charlie then said. "You're not looking too good."

"I'll be fine," she reassured the old man. "But I need to leave."

A preternatural intuition was telling her that this was exactly what she had to do.

"You're leaving?" Charlie asked, raising his voice. "But where are you going? What will we do if more of those things come back?"

"You'll be fine. You can't get more secure than this place."

She went to the backpack she'd put together while out exploring around the school, making sure that she had everything she would need.

"What's going on?" the security guard, Scott, asked.

"It's Melissa," Charlie answered. "She's leaving."

"What do you mean she's leaving?"

Melissa quickly rifled through the contents of her bag. There was a half-drunk bottle of water on the floor nearby and she snatched it up, stowing it in her backpack.

"Is this true, Melissa?" Scott asked, approaching her.

She hated her answer, but every fiber of her being told her that this was the way it had to be.

For their sakes, as well as her own.

"Yes," she said firmly, pulling the zipper closed.

"You can't leave us," Doris said, sitting up against the wall, her daughter coming awake in her lap. She had turned up the camping lantern, so the shelter was no longer in shadows.

"I have to," Melissa said, not sure how she could explain that if she didn't get out of there, something would come, and it would kill them all.

She started toward the door.

"Please," the mother pleaded, and Melissa could see that she was crying.

"Is that how it's gonna be?" Tyrone asked. She was waiting for him to get involved. "Get us all stoked that we're gonna make it—that God, or Heaven, or whatever, was looking out for us by sending you—and then drop us cold when things look tight?"

Melissa didn't respond. Conversations with Tyrone always ended up in an argument.

"Thought so," he said with a sneer. "Always told my mama that all that time in church, prayin' to God and Heaven and stuff, was all for nothin'."

"Listen," she said, her anger flaring. "I have to go or you'll all be in danger."

"What do you mean?" Doris asked, pulling her child closer.

"It's hard for me to explain. The Nephilim—they're supposed to stop things like what is going on out there."

"Good job so far." Tyrone's voice dripped with sarcasm.

It took everything that Melissa had not to summon a sword of fire and separate his obnoxious head from his shoulders.

"But things have gotten out of control," she went on. "Powerful, evil forces are keeping the world in darkness. No, we didn't do too well. But that doesn't mean we're finished. There are others like me out there, and we're going to set things right."

Melissa gritted her teeth. *Is that even true? Did the others even survive?* She had to believe they had, that they were still out there—ready to fight, as she was.

"I need to find them," she said. "Together we will save our home—our world—from this terrible fate."

"You said that if you stayed, we would all be in danger," Charlie said.

"I did."

"From what?"

She envisioned the dark, armored creatures that proclaimed their love for her. "The creatures destroying the world? They know that I'm going to try and stop them with everything I have. And they'll be looking for me."

Melissa slung the backpack over her shoulder. "I can't put you in danger any more than I already have."

She started for the door, but Tyrone blocked her.

"So you're really going," he said, wearing a look of disgust.

"I really am," she confirmed. "It's for our own good."

"Says you," he said, moving out of her path before she could push him out of the way. The look on his face was like a physical blow, but there was nothing more she could do, or say.

At the door she paused to listen and make sure that some creature wasn't on the other side, eager to get in.

She slid back the bolt, then turned toward the others, her hand on the thick metal knob.

"We're going to try and make this right again," she said, before turning her attention only to Tyrone.

"And I want you to put that bad attitude you're carrying to good use and keep these people safe," she told him.

She could see that Tyrone was going to give her more lip, but then his expression changed as he looked into her eyes.

He must've seen something there, maybe the fires of

Heaven that burned at the core of her being. Something that told him he'd be better off doing what she asked.

For the first time since she'd met him, Tyrone was speechless, and remained that way as she walked out the door, closing it firmly behind her.

Gabriel frowned. He could sense something different—unpredictable—about Dusty now.

It was raining again, and he and Dusty had sought shelter in the Stanleys' old playroom.

Dusty was up and about now, no longer affected by fever. In fact, he appeared healthier than Gabriel had ever seen him.

As he paced about the room, the expressions on his face changed, reacting to something that Gabriel—even though he truly tried—could not see.

"Are you sure you're all right?" Gabriel asked the young man.

Dusty had stopped, facing an area of mold-covered paneling, tilting his head from one side to the other. "I'm . . . I'm fine," he replied.

And it dawned on Gabriel that Dusty could understand him.

"You can understand me," Gabriel spoke in his canine tongue of growls and whines.

Momentarily distracted from his study of the wall, Dusty turned his attention to the dog. "Why yes," he answered, a large smile spreading across his face. "I guess I can."

Then he stared off into space again.

"What do you see?" Gabriel asked, slowly approaching his friend.

"I don't know how to explain it," Dusty said. "Before, with the Instrument, I was perpetually bombarded with sounds and visions of the horrible things that were happening, or would happen in the future. It was more than I could process. My brain couldn't handle all that information at once."

"And now?" Gabriel asked.

"Now, I can still see it all, but it's not so overwhelming. . . ."

Dusty looked down at Gabriel. A thick, milky film covered the young man's eyes, and the Labrador wondered how he could see anything.

"I understand that there are many potential outcomes."

Gabriel listened patiently, not really following.

"I see all the possibilities." He paused. "There are so many choices . . . so many futures."

Gabriel sat down, as if obeying a command for a very special treat. "You can see the future? Do we win?" he yipped excitedly.

Dusty spun to face another part of the room.

"It's not clear," he said. "Some decisions lead to victory, while others . . ."

Gabriel watched Dusty's expression turn to one of supreme grimness.

"What can we do?" the dog asked.

"As I am now the sword, we have an advantage," Dusty

said, almost dreamily. "Many decisions can lead us to victory, but there are no guarantees of success."

"We have to try," Gabriel said.

"Absolutely," Dusty agreed.

Gabriel leaped to his feet, ready for action. "What do we do first?" he barked excitedly.

"Influence," Dusty said. "We must look at the situation like a game of strategy, and move the pieces accordingly." He looked down at the eager Labrador. "You are going to take us to where we need to be."

"Okay," Gabriel answered, tail wagging. "Where is that?"

"I'll show you." Dusty brought his finger down toward Gabriel's face. "This might hurt."

Gabriel tensed, his eyes riveted on the young man's pointing finger. A dark piece of metal, a sliver of the sword, broke through the skin at the tip of Dusty's finger.

Before the Labrador could ask what was happening, the splinter shot into the flesh of his nose. Gabriel yelped, recoiling. It did hurt, quite a lot actually. The dog pawed at his nose, his dark-brown eyes watering. The pain began to rapidly diminish.

"What did you do?" Gabriel whined, in between violent sneezes.

Dusty stared at him with large, glazed-over eyes.

"I know where we need to go," he said. "And now you do too."

At first, Gabriel didn't understand, but then suddenly it was like he was seeing flashes of memories. Only these memories had yet to occur. At first he was afraid, the new responsibility looming large before him, but he quickly convinced himself that this was what he—they—were supposed to do.

"I see!" the dog barked.

"Now we can begin," Dusty said, reaching down to place his hand atop Gabriel's blocky head.

And Gabriel saw as clearly as if he were gazing out a window.

Without wasting another moment, in a rush of air and the crackle of divine fire, they were off on a path to shape the future.

CHAPTER TEN

It was getting dark inside the log cabin, and Cameron lit one of the lanterns so that he might see better what his father had left for him.

Most of the box's contents appeared to be old parchment paper. Cameron carefully removed the stacks of documents. They had an odd, waxy feel and gave off an earthy aroma. He scanned the ancient writing, somehow knowing that it was an angelic language and that he would be able to translate. The ink had a reddish tint, a result of the passing years, he imagined. But Cameron was focused on the books at the bottom of the box. He was almost afraid to touch them—certain that they were full of secrets, but not sure if he was ready to know them.

There were no titles on the covers, and finally, he picked up a volume and started to flip through it. They appeared to be journals.

Then came another painful flash of memory. He glimpsed an image of his father, bent over at the table, writing feverishly in a book.

One of these books.

Cameron stared at it for a long time before opening to a particular section and starting to read. Passage after passage, he read of his father's experiences, his voice in Cameron's head as if he were reading to his son.

His father wrote of his time on earth, cut off from Heaven and his Almighty God, but he also wrote of other things.

He wrote of the Architects.

WHO COULD EVEN DREAM OF STOPPING THE ARCHITECTS? I'VE CONSIDERED SEEKING OUT MY OTHER WAYWARD BROTHERS OF HEAVEN, BUT I KNOW THAT THEY WOULD NOT CARE—MANY FEELING DISDAIN FOR EARTH'S NATIVE LIFE THAT THE ALMIGHTY DEEMED SO SPECIAL.

THE ARCHITECTS' PLANS, FROM WHAT I'VE SURMISED, GO AGAINST EVERYTHING THE LORD GOD WANTS FOR THIS WORLD. IF ONLY I MIGHT REACH HIM, LET HIM KNOW OF THEIR TREACHERY.

BUT THE LORD OF LORDS WON'T LISTEN TO ONE SUCH AS ME, ONE WHO FEARED THE OUTCOME OF the Great War in Heaven and fled in cowardice to live among humanity.

Cameron flipped the pages of the journal until another passage caught his attention.

The Nephilim—the spawn of human and angel—who would have thought they'd be the cornerstone of the Architects' plans?

Yet it does make sense. They meld two of God's most favored creations, creatures of both Heaven and earth. If the Architects' plans carry through, these beings will inherit the earth.

"The Nephilim will inherit the earth," Cameron repeated aloud, his mind racing. Here was potentially the opportunity that they'd been waiting for. He needed to get this information to Aaron and the others, especially if there was a chance that the secrets found inside this box might help them in stopping—

Cameron caught movement outside his window. There had been deer, and the occasional raccoon in the yard, but this seemed bigger.

Always cautious, Cameron called forth a sword as he got up from the table and moved toward the door.

It was freezing outside, his warm breath clouding as he stood on the porch, eyes scanning the woods.

He did not expect to see a naked child.

Over by the pile of unchopped wood, a child no older than five or six cowered, his pale, naked flesh nearly glowing in the night.

"Hello?" Cameron called out as he approached the trembling youth. Not wanting to scare the little boy, Cameron sent his weapon away. "Hey there," he said, coming to stand no farther than six feet from the shivering child.

The child lifted his gaze, his face covered in dirt and what appeared to be dried blood.

"Are you all right?" Cameron asked, concern in his tone.

"Hungry," the child said. "We're all so very, very hungry."

The hair along the back of Cameron's neck stood on end. He stepped back, reconsidering his sword, and it sparked to life in his grasp. The light thrown by the weapon reflected strangely in the little boy's dark eyes. They glowed like an animal's.

The little boy tossed back his head and roared. It was a strange sound, unlike anything that might come from a human throat.

Cameron knew he was in trouble. From the corners of his eyes, he saw other naked children creeping from the forest.

Backing away slowly, he tried to keep his eyes on their moving shapes. More unearthly howls came from the woods. Cameron flexed the muscles in his shoulders, calling forth his wings.

The little boy with the dirty face let out a gleeful squeal.

"We've been smelling you for days," the child said. "We knew there was meat close by, but we didn't know how delicious and rare."

Cameron tensed.

"I'm the kind of meat that will seriously mess with your stomach," he said in a threatening voice, waving his blazing sword. *Maybe I can scare them away,* he thought. He didn't want to hurt a child, no matter how screwed up the kid was.

"No worries, special meat," the filthy boy said. "So hungry we be willing to take the risk."

The other children giggled, their laughter eerily transforming into growls. And then the little boy began to claw at his skin, ripping it away to reveal thick black fur beneath.

Even after all the crazy stuff he'd seen in his short Nephilim life, Cameron doubted he would ever get used to this.

The boy transformed into a muscular, bearlike creature. The thing roared, showing off thick yellow teeth designed especially for ripping flesh from bone. There then came a succession of similar growls and thrashing from behind Cameron, and the Nephilim saw that the other children were also shedding their skin.

"Okay then," Cameron said. "Demon bears? Why not."

They rushed at him all at once, wild eyes glistening and

fangs slavering. Cameron felt his angelic nature practically squeal with delight as it rushed forward to battle.

Cameron leaped into the air, hovering above the beasts' slashing claws. He lashed out with his sword of fire, hacking away limbs and singeing fur. The creatures' howls and cries mingled together in a nearly deafening cacophony of violence.

The demon bears retreated, and Cameron dropped to the ground, bracing for the next wave of attack. He had whittled down their numbers, some of the beasts holding back to nurse their wounds, but there were still quite a few with hunger in their gazes.

"Not used to your meat biting back, are you?" he said, crouching and switching his sword to the other hand.

The demon bears continued to growl fiercely, pacing back and forth as they decided what course they must take next to achieve their special meal.

"I'm feeling generous today," Cameron then said. "Leave me now, and we'll call it even. You won't get to eat me, and I won't cover my floor in new rugs."

The bears looked at one another.

"Special meat feels he is merciful," growled one.

The bear that Cameron believed to be the little boy by the woodpile came forward. "Save your mercy, special meat," he proclaimed. "You will fill our bellies before—"

Cameron wasn't quite sure what happened exactly.

One second, the bear was telling him how he would soon be inside their bellies, but the next he was gone—disappeared—into thin air.

The other demon bears sniffed the air, just as surprised by their comrade's sudden, inexplicable disappearance.

Suddenly, the demon's body dropped from the sky, landing in a twisted, bloody heap.

Cameron stared with the other beasts at the damaged body. Then he searched the night sky, the starlight obliterated by thick clouds.

Is that the flapping of wings? he wondered, straining his ears and scanning the velvety darkness.

"What did this?" one of the bears roared.

Another strode forward to sniff at the bloody corpse; then he, too, disappeared.

But this time Cameron saw a black shape with enormous wings, moving incredibly fast, drop from the sky to snatch another of the beasts.

"Holy crap," he whispered. A nearly overpowering sense of foreboding fell upon him, and he had the urge to escape—to run—to get away from this place before . . .

A life-form that seemed to be made from the darkness itself swooped down from the sky once more, attacking the bear demons with abandon. All Cameron could do was watch as the winged creature landed amongst the shifters and, with elongated, razor-sharp claws, eviscerated all who attacked. It was a scene out of nightmare.

Eyes locked upon the carnage, Cameron watched as the creature, armored in the stuff of shadow, bloodily dispatched the last of its attackers.

The killer slowly turned, its masked, featureless face, also as black as pitch, directed at Cameron.

Sword still blazing in hand, the Nephilim prepared for the worst.

Then the figure's shadow helmet faded, revealing a pale, female face.

A face that Cameron recognized, and had called a friend, before she had died.

"Hey, Cam," Janice said, her bloodless lips stretching into a smile. "It's been awhile."

Verchiel flew across the blighted lands ravaged by monsters and nearly endless night.

It both surprised and appalled him how quickly the world had fallen to darkness.

His eyes trailed upward, to the churning clouds that masked the sun, preventing light and warmth from touching the earth. Verchiel then turned his gaze down to the loathsome goblin that dangled from his hand.

"How did this happen?" Verchiel bellowed over the howl of the wind and the beating of his wings.

The goblin Ergo squirmed uneasily as he dangled precariously in the angel's grasp. Verchiel held on firmly to the collar of the goblin's armored chest plate.

"What?" the goblin asked, his voice even higher than usual from fear. "What are you talking—"

Verchiel gave the goblin a violent shake, and Ergo shrieked again.

"Please . . . please be careful . . . even in my armor, a fall from this height would—"

"Answer me!" Verchiel's voice boomed over the sounds of their flight.

"It is as I said before," Ergo cried, turning his gaze upward toward his captor. "Satan Darkstar controls powerful magicks, powerful enough to blot the sun from the sky."

The goblin had shared stories of how this mysterious leader—this Satan—had called together all the nightmares of the world, forcing them under one flag.

The banner of the Darkstar.

Any who fought back against the Darkstar's edict were destroyed.

Verchiel noticed that the goblin had stopped thrashing. He followed the creature's gaze to the encampment of tents in a mall parking area.

"Friends of yours?" he asked the goblin.

Ergo didn't answer, which made Verchiel guess that this was the battalion from which the goblin had defected.

The angel angled his body earthward, much to Ergo's chagrin.

"What are you doing?" he screeched. "Take me back up!"

Verchiel sneered. "I thought you would want to be reunited with your friends."

"They're no friends of mine," Ergo spat. "And besides, they think I'm dead."

Verchiel gave a powerful flap of his wings to slow his descent. "Then let's give them a surprise, shall we?" he said. "What joy the sight of you will bring when they realize that you are still among the living."

Verchiel released the goblin as his feet touched the ground. Ergo fell to all fours with the impact.

"You don't understand," the goblin said, his beady eyes riveted on the sprawling encampment.

"What is it that I don't understand, foul thing?" Verchiel asked.

Ergo turned to look at him pathetically. "They'll torture me for abandoning my position."

"Then we'll go together," Verchiel said. "Perhaps some of my courage will rub off on you as we walk." He yanked the goblin to his feet.

"Perhaps you would grant me a merciful death," Ergo suggested as they walked side by side, Verchiel's hand on the goblin's shoulder.

"Do you honestly believe that you deserve such a thing?" Verchiel asked as they reached the perimeter to the army encampment.

"Have I not been the perfect captive?" Ergo pleaded. "Sharing all that I know about our glorious leader? Surely this must count for something."

Nearby, a goblin soldier relieved itself on one of the parking lot's tall light posts. The goblin turned to look at them dully, as its liquid waste splashed on the concrete base. Its eyes grew saucer wide as the angel and his captive approached.

Barely finished, the goblin fumbled with a yellowed horn hanging over its shoulder, bringing it to its mouth and blowing an alert.

The horn brought the goblin army streaming from the tents.

"Kill me," Ergo begged, as the army came at them, weapons of war in hand.

"Why would I want to do that?" Verchiel asked, picking up the goblin and tossing him into the crowd. "Especially after we've become so close."

The army recoiled in caution as Ergo landed at their feet. They looked from Ergo, to Verchiel, and back again.

"A trade," Verchiel announced. "I give you this deserter, in exchange for an audience with your commander."

Ergo scrambled to his feet, but the goblin legion was

faster, grabbing him roughly and placing a sword beneath his chin.

"Traitor," Verchiel overheard one of the soldiers growl, as they dragged Ergo off into the mob, where he became lost amongst the hundreds of other loathsome goblins.

"So," Verchiel said, as pleasantly as he could. Aaron and the others had always scolded Verchiel for his lack of social skills, so he would see if the benefits they touted were indeed true. "Do we have a deal?"

The goblins looked to one another and began to laugh.

Verchiel wasn't amused.

Still laughing, the goblins charged, blood-encrusted weapons at the ready.

"I guess that would mean no," Verchiel said, shaping a weapon of fire in his hand.

The goblins fell upon him in a noxious wave of blood, sweat, and filthy flesh. They hacked and slashed at Verchiel, their weapons barely scratching the divine armor that adorned him, as he allowed their thirst for violence to arouse him. Then Verchiel struck back.

The air became suddenly filled with the screams of the dying. The goblins fought valiantly, but they were no match for a soldier of Heaven—even one who had fallen from the grace of God.

For a moment, Verchiel thought of the three hags and the offer they'd bestowed on him from their masters, the Architects.

Serve them.

The memory just enraged him, the rushing of the blood through his veins deafening him to the goblins' cries for mercy. If they had wanted mercy, then they should have done as he'd asked in the first place, and allowed him to speak with their commander.

The blacktop was awash in goblin blood, as Verchiel hovered upon his mighty wings, finishing off the stragglers still brave enough—insane enough—to come at him.

Then he flew through the encampment, setting the leathery tents ablaze with gouts of holy fire dispensed from the tip of his blade. Verchiel's fire was ravenous, devouring not only the tents, but all those still within them. Burning goblins ran about until they dropped to the ground, flaming pyres that lit Verchiel's way as he flew over the carnage he had wrought.

Ergo emerged through the flap of a burning tent, fleeing his captor, who was engulfed in angel fire.

"The commander," Verchiel demanded of him. "Where will I find him?"

Ergo turned his attention to the tents that remained untouched. There, across the lot, was a larger, more elaborate tent.

The frightened goblin pointed.

Verchiel stared at him for a moment, enjoying the sheer terror that rolled off the foul creature in waves. Then he flew toward the tent.

Touching down just outside, Verchiel was met with the shrieks and whoops of more armored goblins. They had as much effect on Verchiel as the previous goblin soldiers, dying just as quickly despite their fancy armor and weaponry.

Verchiel stood before the tent, the dead at his feet, watching the flaps blow invitingly in the breeze.

"Come out and face me," he proclaimed.

His request was met with silence.

From the corner of his eye, he watched as Ergo came to join him. "Perhaps you'd care to go inside to bring him out," Verchiel suggested.

"Perhaps you'd care to kiss my puffy rump," the goblin replied with a snarl, his anger at being turned over to his former comrades obviously outweighing his fear of the angel.

Having no desire to drag the commander out, Verchiel touched the edge of his burning sword to the entrance flap, setting it ablaze. It didn't take long for the commander to emerge.

"Ah, there you are," Verchiel said as the goblin leader dropped to his knees before him. "I wasn't sure if you'd heard me."

The goblin sprang up, a dagger in hand, poised to strike. Verchiel was having none of it, swatting his attacker back to the ground with a swipe from one of his huge wings.

"I called you before me to ask you a question," Verchiel said, watching as the commander recovered from the blow, groggily sitting up. "Are you listening?"

The commander spotted Ergo standing nearby. "You there," he bellowed, ignoring Verchiel's words. "Protect your superior!"

Ergo didn't move.

The commander appeared stunned as he rose to stand upon shaky legs.

"Are you listening?" Verchiel asked again, raising his voice.

The commander cowered, but slowly nodded his head.

"You have seen what I have done, and what I am capable of." Verchiel raised his arm, presenting what remained of the encampment. "After seeing all this," the angel continued, "who do you serve?"

The commander stared at Verchiel with hate-filled eyes, as the survivors of the goblin army drew closer, awaiting their leader's response.

"I don't . . . ," the commander started, then stopped.

"I will ask you again," Verchiel said. "Who do you serve?"

The commander again looked at the damage and those who had fallen under his command. Then he turned his gaze back to Verchiel.

"Who do you serve?" Verchiel repeated, stressing each word.

The commander spit something thick and black onto the ground, a sign of disrespect.

"I serve the one true lord," he declared. "I serve Satan, the Darkstar, with all my—"

Verchiel sliced the commander's head from his body before he could finish.

"Wrong answer."

Turning, Verchiel addressed the remaining survivors, with a slow, menacing flap of his wings. "You serve me now. Any questions?"

CHAPTER ELEVEN

The longer Aaron followed his parents, the more it all sank in: His life was an elaborate creation of his subconscious.

It was more than Aaron could take. He sat down on the solid shadow, unable to go on.

His parents stopped.

"Aaron?" his foster mother asked. "What are you doing?"

"I can't," he said, refusing to look at her. He stared at the brown dress shoes on his feet, shoes that he'd bought specifically for his job.

A job that didn't really exist.

"I can't go any farther," Aaron said, his strength beginning to ebb. "I can't do this."

"Aaron, please," his foster father said. "You have to go with us if—"

"I'm forgetting," Aaron interrupted. Even as he spoke, the memories that had once been rock solid inside his mind were already fading.

"Those experiences were never real to begin with," Lori told him. "They have to vanish to allow your real memories to come back."

"Real memories," Aaron said, then laughed sadly. "Up until a little while ago, they were my real memories."

"Aaron," Tom Stanley began. "We understand how hard this must be for you, but—"

"You understand?" Aaron asked. "You're not real either. You're some sort of screwed-up mechanism to help me get back to whatever screwed-up reality I left behind."

His parents shared a look.

"We're not going to say that you're wrong," Lori acknowledged.

Her face was now almost obliterated by flames. Tom's wasn't much better. All that remained of his human visage were a few tufts of hair.

"If I tried hard enough, I could probably wish you both away," Aaron said, returning his gaze to his shoes.

"Probably," Tom agreed.

"But would you really want to do that?" Lori asked.

Aaron shrugged.

"Maybe if you did, you'd hold on to your memories?" Lori prompted him.

Aaron was silent for a moment.

"We were going to get a dog," he said finally, playing with his shoelaces.

"You already have a dog," his mother reminded him.

"Aaron," Tom said. There was agitation in his tone. "It isn't safe here."

"What do you mean? It's my subconscious. Why wouldn't it be safe?"

Lori took her husband's burned skeletal hand in hers.

"You ended up in this place for a reason," his foster mother explained. "You escaped here to heal from . . ."

"From what?" Aaron urged.

"You were struck down. Some of what hurt you was left behind," Lori said.

"Kind of like a poison in your system," Tom added.

"Is it still inside me?"

His parents nodded their burning heads.

"Where?"

"Somewhere here, in the darkness," Lori said.

"Is that where you're taking me?"

Lori again nodded.

"You have to go there if . . . ," Tom began.

"If I want to live," Aaron finished. He stood.

"Are you coming with us then?" Lori asked hopefully.

"Sure," Aaron answered. He looked around; something was nagging at the back of his memory. No matter how hard he tried, he couldn't retrieve it. "I'm really not sure why we stopped to begin with."

His mother urged him to follow with a burning hand. "I guess we just got tired is all."

Aaron was still in a coma, no better, no worse.

Vilma had returned to her boyfriend's side with his mother. The two had not spoken since Vilma had learned of A'Dorial and his deteriorating connection to Heaven. She was certain that piece of information was important to their survival, as well as the survival of the world.

Staring down at the young man she loved, she wished him awake. She was sure if he were conscious, he would know what to do.

He'd figure out what all this meant in the greater scheme of things.

"You've been awfully quiet," Taylor commented, as she took a seat near the foot of Aaron's bed.

"Just thinking," Vilma answered. She reached down to Aaron's hand and touched his fingers. They were colder than usual. Time was running out.

"I think you need to talk to Levi," Taylor said.

"Levi?" Vilma questioned. "Why?"

"Levi is the leader of the Unforgiven," Aaron's mother said. "It would be good for you to learn how he sees the big picture."

Vilma didn't reply. She didn't want to leave Aaron.

"I'll let you know if anything changes," Taylor told her. "Go on, I think it will help you."

Vilma knew that if she were going to help save the Nephilim and the world, she would need to be part of the Unforgiven's plans.

"Where is Levi?"

"He's got a workshop on Level Five," Taylor said. "He's waiting for you there."

"He knows I'm coming?"

Taylor nodded. "We've been talking. We both feel it's time for you to learn more about the operation."

Vilma nodded, then hesitated. "How did you know I'd go?"

Taylor laughed quietly. "You're not a stupid girl, Vilma Santiago," she said, taking Aaron's hand in hers. "My son would never become involved with a stupid girl."

Vilma took the statement as a compliment, leaving the infirmary and walking to the elevator. It was waiting, doors open, and she got inside and pushed the button for Level 5. The doors slid shut, and the elevator lurched upward.

To say that she wasn't nervous would be a lie. Although she'd been living with the Unforgiven for several weeks, she was still unsettled by the odd, part-angelic, part-machine creatures.

There was something creepy about them.

The doors opened, and Vilma was greeted by total darkness. She hesitated, but when the elevator doors started to close again, she quickly stepped into the darkened hall.

"Abandon hope, all ye who enter here." She thought of the quote from *Paradise Lost*, which she'd read in Mr. Wormstead's high school literature class. She longed to be a student again, almost laughing as she remembered how complex she'd thought life to be then. Not.

"Hello?" she called out tentatively. "Levi? It's Vilma."

Proceeding down the hallway, she conjured a divine flame in the palm of her hand for illumination. At the end of the hall, she raised her fiery hand, looking left, then right, trying to decide which way to go, when she heard it.

Music.

Craning her neck, she determined that it was coming from the left, and followed the sound until she reached an office. She stopped outside for a moment to listen. The music was definitely coming from inside.

She knocked. "Hello? Levi?"

Silence greeted her. According to Taylor, she was expected, so Vilma let herself in, and was immediately immersed in a nearly deafening wave of classical music.

No wonder Levi hadn't heard her.

The room was larger than it looked, and filled with all manner of technology. There were pieces of computers, stacks of hard drives, and monitors just about everyplace she looked.

Strains of Beethoven's Ninth played as Vilma carefully picked her way around a barrier of flat-screen monitors. She started to call out Levi's name again, but quickly fell silent.

Levi, the leader of the Unforgiven, was shirtless and hunched over a worktable. Vilma was struck by how pale his flesh was—and how scarred. His back was covered with thick scars of various sizes and shapes. But her eyes were drawn to the two vertical metal pieces that protruded from just above his shoulder blades.

His wings. The fallen angel was working on his artificial wings.

Levi paused, raised what looked to be a screwdriver, then waved it in the air as if he were conducting a symphony.

Vilma was mesmerized. She'd thought of the Unforgiven as cold, emotionless beings—more like machines than anything else. But now, witnessing this . . .

The side of her foot bumped a pile of computer parts, which fell, knocking over a stack of plastic CD cases.

Levi immediately plucked one of the razor-sharp feathers from the wing on his worktable, raising it above his head defensively.

Vilma froze, fear and embarrassment etched on her face.

"Whoops," she said.

Levi lowered the feather blade, sliding it back into the configuration of others on the mechanical wing. He reached for something on the wheeled tool cart beside him and pointed a remote at the stereo.

The classical music ceased, plunging the room into deafening silence.

"I didn't know you were here," Levi said, without looking at her.

He hefted one of the wings from the table, his powerful muscles flexing as he draped it over his shoulder. The metal wing connected to the protrusion on his back with a loud snap. He attached the second.

"I'm sorry," Vilma said. "I called out, but when nobody answered . . ."

"That's perfectly fine," Levi said, still avoiding her gaze.

He wasn't wearing his goggles!

"I was lost in my work," he said as he recovered his shirt and quickly slipped into it. Then he snatched his goggles from the corner of the table and slid them over his eyes. "That's better," he said, adjusting the fit.

He reached for the remote again and used it to brighten the lights. "Now we can talk."

Vilma had squatted and was trying to clean up the mess she'd made. "I'm really sorry for disturbing you—and for making a mess."

"Your addition to the mess is barely noticeable," Levi answered. "May I get you a refreshment? Coffee, tea, water?"

"No, thank you," Vilma said, restacking the CDs. "There, as good as new." She stood, slipping her hands into the back pockets of her jeans.

"So," she said, cutting to the chase. "Taylor said you wanted to talk to me."

"Yes." Levi nodded. He gestured toward a desk chair in the corner. "Please."

Vilma took the offered chair, and Levi sat awkwardly beside her. The Unforgiven leader seemed as uncomfortable in her presence as she was in his.

But her curiosity about the angelic beings only intensified.

"Your wings," she said. "What were you doing to them?"

Levi seemed surprised by the question. "Routine maintenance."

"Cool," she said, nodding slightly. "Is it hard? Y'know, is it like tuning up a car or something?"

She could feel Levi's stare through the dark lenses of his goggles.

"Nothing like a car," he said flatly. "We get much better mileage."

It took her a moment to realize that he'd cracked a joke. She smiled, surprised.

"Good one."

"Was it? The Unforgiven aren't too adept at humor, I'm afraid. The world is very close to its end," he continued, without pause.

"Whoa," Vilma responded. "So much for humor."

"I told you we weren't very good at that—we've spent too long trying to keep the Architects from achieving their goals. It stifles the sense of humor."

"I guess so," Vilma said. "So what's the story with the Unforgiven and these Architects? What's the connection?"

"The Architects have been here since the beginning of time as we know it. They were the first of God's angels and have been manipulating world events to reflect what they perceive to be perfection."

"So a monster around every corner is perfection?"

"They believe that this is the road to perfection."

"Crazy," Vilma said.

"Yes, it is," Levi agreed. "We've been battling this crazy for quite some time. We, the Unforgiven, see it as our purpose, our penance for the transgressions we committed against our Holy Father during the Great War in Heaven."

"So you're among the fallen," Vilma said.

"We are fallen, yes," Levi confirmed. "But we finally understood the love that our Lord God Almighty had for this world, and swore to keep it safe from harm."

"Safe from the Architects."

Levi nodded. "They feel that God is mistaken. They believe this world has not yet reached its full potential—its zenith—and intend to guide it there."

Vilma wasn't quite sure how to respond. "We're not doing too well, are we?"

Levi shook his head. "We were holding our own—until the Abomination of Desolation severed the earth's connection to the divine."

Vilma made a face. "Yeah, we kinda dropped the ball on that."

"Heaven's ties to the world of man were severed, except . . ."

"A'Dorial," Vilma said.

"Though small, and diminishing, the angel A'Dorial managed to maintain a connection, sending out a cry for help to the power of Heaven when the Abomination threatened."

"It doesn't seem as though anybody was listening," Vilma commented.

"And that is where you'd be wrong," Levi said. "Responding to the severity of the situation, Heaven did send us a means for restoring the earth's connection to the divine."

"What was it?"

"A missing piece . . ."

Vilma waited patiently for Levi to continue.

"We're not one hundred percent sure, but we believe it was sent as a child. It was to be born into the world as—"

"A baby? You're talking about a baby," Vilma said, not believing her ears. Her strict Catholic upbringing was aroused at once, making her think of God's son, the savior, and how he, too, had been sent to help the world. She had to wonder what kind of child savior would be sent to save the world from threats of a monstrous kind.

"Yes. The baby was born in the presence of some of our human agents, but . . ."

"What happened?"

"The hospital facility was destroyed."

"And the baby?"

"Missing, although we have evidence that the child still lives."

"Somebody has the baby?" Vilma asked.

"And is protecting it."

"But you have no idea who?"

The Unforgiven leader shook his head. "It must be someone who understands the child's importance."

"You said this baby is a missing piece—what does that mean?"

"The child is a component of a powerful angelic being known as the Metatron."

"Sounds like a Japanese robot that turns into a bus," Vilma said, trying to inject a little humor, and immediately wishing she hadn't. "Sorry. What is the Metatron?"

"It is the ultimate divine entity. It is God, angel, and human; the culmination of all the Creator's greatest achievements. The Metatron was to be an extension of God on earth, but the Architects destroyed it. They slaughtered its humanity and dispersed the essence of God and the powers of angels."

"So the baby is the human part," Vilma said. "But what about the rest of the Metatron?"

"They continue to exist in the world," Levi said. "The Unforgiven have been tracking these powers for centuries, waiting for this very opportunity, when all three aspects of the Metatron are in the same place."

"So the Metatron gets rebuilt," Vilma said. "What then? Does it provide a way to defeat the Architects?"

"If only it were that easy," Levi said. "With the Metatron whole, we finally have a way of restoring the Ladder."

"The Ladder?" Vilma questioned. "What . . . ?"

"The Ladder is a means by which earth can again interact with Heaven."

"It could undo what the Abomination of Desolation destroyed?" she asked him hopefully.

"It could," the Unforgiven leader said, but his expression was grave. "But without its reactivation, I fear that the world will be unable to hold on for very much longer."

The skin of a hundred children had been stitched together and stretched along a moss-covered wall in one of the chambers inside Satan Darkstar's unholy cathedral.

Satan reclined upon a throne of human bones, likely supplied by the same children who'd provided the disturbing screen of flesh.

"I tire of waiting," Satan announced to the generals who stood before him.

Scox rushed to intervene. "What seems to be the problem? The Lord Satan does not have all day."

General Skeksis, a powerfully built creature of a reptilian

nature, stepped forward. "I beg the Dark Master's pardon," he said, bowing his scaly head. "It will only be a moment more."

The general reached out to the insectoid sorcerer who would be responsible for conjuring the visuals, and grabbed one of its many spindly limbs.

"What are we waiting for?" the general growled, nearly ripping the flimsy appendage from its socket.

"Spellz takez timez," the insectoid buzzed. "Patiencez, generalz."

Satan squirmed in his seat. "I'm very quickly running out of patience," he said petulantly.

Sensing the potential for danger, the insectoid pulled his arm from the general's clutches and continued to weave his spell. The magick user's voice buzzed like flies upon a rotting corpse as it danced about on its spindly legs. Then it darted forward to scrawl symbols of power on the bottom half of the tautly stretched skin of innocents.

Dark magicks were at work here.

"Enough," Satan Darkstar proclaimed, rising up from his chair. "I am finished here."

He was about to leave the room when the screen of skin began to undulate.

Almost as if it were alive.

It was enough to capture Satan's interest, but only for a moment.

"Here, my master!" General Skeksis pointed a stubby, clawed

finger at the screen as images began to gradually appear. "This is what has been done in your name."

Satan watched scenes of battle: armies of demons, trolls, goblins, and a myriad of other beasts of damnation, battling the human populace.

From the looks of it, the humans never had a chance.

Satan watched with moderate interest as cities across the globe fell into ruin, their armies crushed by legions of beasts.

He was then shown scenes of fearful, desperate humans being rounded up like cattle to be slaughtered.

"Does He see this?" Satan asked.

"Does who see, sir?" Scox asked. "The general? I'm sure the general sees just fine."

"The Lord God," Satan roared. "The Lightbringer—does He see what I am doing to those who believe, worship, and pray to Him?"

The images of slaughter continued to play upon the skin of innocence.

At one time, this was all that the Darkstar had hoped for. All those millennia, when he had hidden himself away in the shadows, waiting for a time when he might strike—at last, that time had come.

But with it came the realization that it was not enough. That he was unsatisfied.

All the darkness, all the innocent blood, did little to quench the Darkstar's thirst for revenge.

He did not want only the earth, but Heaven as well, and all that it contained. He would not be satisfied until he had it.

"Bring me the Sisters," Satan Darkstar announced, eyes still focused upon humanity's demise. They would know how to guide him to make his dreams a reality.

"Bring me the Sisters of Umbra."

CHAPTER TWELVE

Cameron remembered Janice as having been a nice kid; quiet, usually dressed all in black, and hair dyed bright colors. Some of the others had said that they believed she had a bit of a crush on him, but he'd never seen it.

And then she'd died.

He really hadn't thought much about her since she'd been speared by a troll in Russia while attempting to rescue some miners trapped in a tunnel collapse.

He certainly never expected to see her again. And certainly not like this.

Janice spread her arms and opened her batlike wings wide. "What do you think?" she asked. "Pretty bitchin', right?"

Cameron tensed. His every instinct screamed that he was in danger. But this was Janice—one of his own kind.

At least she used to be.

"I thought . . . ," he started, not liking the fear in his voice.

"You thought what?" Janice urged. She started toward him, stepping over the bodies of the shape-shifters she had murdered. "That I was dead?"

Cameron gripped his blade of divine flame as she came closer.

"You're right, I was," she continued. "But now I'm back, good as new."

She stopped and lifted her arms again to show him. "See? No holes."

Janice laughed. It was a cold sound, lacking any humor.

"How?" Cameron was intrigued, even though he knew that her being here with him, talking to him, was wrong.

"He came for me. The Darkstar pulled me from the darkness."

"The Darkstar," Cameron repeated.

His former comrade nodded vigorously. "He isn't our enemy, Cam. I was so afraid while I was dead," she explained. "I was all alone. Heaven never came. There was nothing, Cam—just a sad, cold oblivion."

She started toward him again.

"Stop," he warned, directing the point of his blade at her.

Janice smiled, continuing her advance.

"The Darkstar pulled me from the void and gave me a purpose. He showed me how wrong we'd been to serve the light, to serve an Almighty who would cast us aside once we'd completed our service."

Cameron slashed his blade of flame across the ground in front of his one-time friend, creating a line of divine fire between them.

Janice was repelled by the flames, rearing back with an animal-like hiss. The armored collar about her neck turned liquid and flowed up over her face as if to protect it.

"I'd hoped to convince you," Janice said, her voice strangely muffled by the helmet of shadow. "I wanted you to join me—to join the others."

Her words chilled him to the bone. Others?

He thought of the other Nephilim who had died, and imagined them clad in black armor, sporting wings of shadow.

"You've done this to the others?" Cameron asked, feeling a spike of nausea, as well as anger.

"I've done nothing but accept the gift offered to me," Janice said simply. "As have the other Nephilim who fell in battle."

Cameron seethed. "Out of respect for you—for what you once were—I'm asking you to leave."

"Or what?" Janice challenged.

"Or one of us will be dying again."

Janice extended her arms to either side of her body, as claws of darkness grew from the tips of her gauntleted hands. "I'd hoped you would understand," she said, flexing her fingers.

Cameron didn't even see her move, the attack was so swift. One second she was standing a foot away, the next . . .

Barely evading her grasp, Cameron threw himself to one side, watching as Janice's claws sliced through the bark on a nearby tree. She lunged, slashing at him again. He leaped into the air, but she anticipated his action, using her own batlike wings to leap as he did.

Cameron spun, landing in a crouch.

Then he felt it, an icy, tingling sensation in his midsection.

"First blood," Janice purred, bringing one of her hands to her face, as she squatted before him. The darkness of her helmet melted away to reveal her pale mouth, and she licked his blood from her claws. "What's that I taste?" she asked, smacking her lips loudly. "Is that fear?"

A chill raced up and down Cameron's spine as he tried to focus. The pain from his stomach was intensifying, and he could feel the warmth spreading down the front of his body.

It was his turn to bring her fear.

Cameron launched himself with a roar, flapping his powerful wings with such force that he was upon her in an instant. The force of their collision sent them hurtling backward, the two of them digging a small trench in the forest floor before hitting the base of an ancient pine tree.

Temporarily stunned, Cameron shook it off, bringing the pommel of his divine weapon down upon the armored face of his foe.

Janice cried out, struggling beneath his weight. But Cameron ignored her cries, relentlessly bringing down the end of his weapon again and again.

The Nephilim aspect of his nature knew his foe should be slain quickly, efficiently, for that was what was done with one's enemies.

But this was different, he rationalized. This was someone who had once been a friend. And no matter how hard he tried, he couldn't bring himself to deliver that final, decisive strike.

"Please," Janice begged, her wide, scared eyes looking up at him as he readied another blow.

Cameron hesitated.

It was all the time she needed.

A twisted smile appeared on Janice's pale, dead features. Before Cameron could react, she squirmed out from beneath him, slithered around his body, and crushed his mighty wings to his back, rendering him flightless.

Cameron tried to shake her off, spinning around and slamming her against a nearby tree.

Janice grunted with the impact, then began to laugh.

"You know, there was still a part of me that sorta died when you didn't surrender," she whispered in his ear. "That same part would have given just about anything to be this close to you."

Cameron felt something cold and wet tickle his ear.

Janice's tongue. A numbness crept into his legs, and he found it difficult to remain standing.

And still her grip intensified. She was crushing him.

Gathering up what strength he had left, Cameron attempted to ram himself against the tree, but one of his feet became entangled in a root, and he crashed to the forest floor.

Cameron lay on his back, looking up into the face of one he had once called friend, and instantly thought of the others, and how he was going to let them down.

Janice studied him with eyes as black as pitch.

"I want to remember you like this," she said as she raised her claws to strike. "Helpless before me. Helpless before the blessed power of the Darkstar."

Tarshish pulled the front of his jacket tighter about him, cowering in the frigid winds of the Himalayas.

"Can you feel that?" the last of the Malakim asked.

Mallus tilted his head back and closed his eyes, reaching out with his senses. "I feel something. Is it the shell?"

Tarshish looked older now, frailer. The more he used his power, the more it damaged his body.

"Not necessarily the shell," Tarshish said. "But the residual horror of what we did." He looked at Mallus, shame in his gaze. "Our actions were so contemptible that it left a permanent impression. A kind of stain."

Mallus tried to pick up more of what Tarshish was feeling. "I'm sensing something, but I'd never have guessed . . ."

"Maybe I just feel worse about it than you," the Malakim said. "Maybe I'm more sensitive to the fact that we murdered an extension of the Lord God."

"I feel pretty bad about that too," Mallus insisted.

Tarshish stepped away and spread out his arms. "The shell is somewhere around here. Just imagine what a few millennia of seismic activity does—all that shifting rock and accumulating ice."

"If it's here, it's buried deep," Mallus agreed.

The Malakim dropped to his knees in the snow. "Taken within the embrace of the mountain range, that which was divine hidden from lowly eyes."

"What are you doing?" Mallus asked him.

"Gonna make us a passage."

"How are you going to—"

There was a searing flash, followed by an intense explosion. Mallus hurtled through the air, carried by a shock wave.

His fall was cushioned by several feet of snow, but his body smoldered, burned by the intensity of the heat thrown by the blast. He lay there for a moment, dazed, then carefully sat up to see that the ice- and snow-covered landscape they'd just been standing on had been cleared. The ground steamed, and a yawning hole gaped before him.

"Tarshish!" Mallus called out.

"Here," answered a voice from inside the hole.

Mallus trudged toward the pit, stopped at its edge, and cautiously peered down. "Where are you?" he asked, waving away clouds of steam rising up from below.

"I think I might need some help," a weakened voice announced.

Mallus zeroed in on the voice and found Tarshish. He appeared even older, and more frail, than he had moments before. His clothes had burned away to reveal a nearly skeletal physique.

"What have you done?" Mallus asked, carefully descending to help.

"What was necessary," Tarshish replied, allowing Mallus to assist him to stand.

"So I'm guessing we're supposed to follow this path you've made."

"It would be a waste not to," Tarshish answered.

Mallus felt a shiver pass through Tarshish's body as he helped him along the circular stone passage that receded into the ground.

"Are you cold?"

"Quite," Tarshish said, his sunken eyes locked on the curving passage before them. "Can you feel it now?"

It took a moment, but Mallus did. "Yeah," he acknowledged, nearly overwhelmed by the waves of despair that wafted over him.

"It feels pretty awful, doesn't it?" Tarshish noted.

"It does."

"Think it's time to lay these ghosts to rest," Tarshish the Malakim said.

"I think you're right," Mallus agreed, firming his grip on his companion's frail body and continuing down the passage, deeper and deeper into the womb of the earth.

Gabriel and Dusty appeared on the darkened street in a flash of divine fire and a rush of air.

Tilting his head back to sniff, Gabriel made sure there were no imminent threats in the area.

Confident that they were safe, he turned to Dusty, only to find that his companion was gone.

"Dusty?" the Labrador barked.

He caught movement in a nearby storefront and padded toward it just in time to meet Dusty emerging, wearing a baggy pair of sweatpants and pulling an equally large, hooded sweatshirt over his head. Gabriel hadn't realized until then, because dogs seldom thought of such things, that Dusty had been practically naked, his clothes shredded when the Abomination's sword had exploded.

"I was starting to get a little cold," Dusty said.

"Sometimes it pays to have a double coat of fur," Gabriel said. "Why did we come here?"

Dusty wandered off a bit, then paused, as if to get his

bearings. "We need to go down here," he said, heading down the sidewalk.

Gabriel followed at his heels. "Is this how it's going to be?" the dog asked. "I follow you around, without knowing why?"

"It's complicated," Dusty said, his voice trailing off.

"I think I can handle complicated," Gabriel said, as his friend came to a stop. "What's wrong?"

"Hurry up or she won't be on time," Dusty ordered, ignoring the Labrador's question and walking faster.

"Who won't be on time?" the dog whined.

Dusty came to an awkward stop in front of what looked to be an old bookstore, its window shattered. "In here." He climbed through the broken window, careful to avoid the shards of glass that protruded like sharks' teeth from its frame.

"Who won't be on time?" Gabriel repeated, grumbling. He leaped through the window without waiting for an answer, knowing that one was not likely to come.

He found Dusty at the back of the store, standing, head tilted to the side.

"We're good," Dusty said. "She should be along in just a minute."

"I'm going to give you a good bite if you don't tell me who—"

Gabriel heard movement at the front of the store and immediately went on full alert. Someone, or something, had followed them in and was making its way to where they stood.

"Get behind me," Gabriel commanded, his voice dropping to a threatening growl.

"There's no need for that," Dusty said. "And even if there were . . ."

Gabriel couldn't believe his eyes as a familiar shape stepped into view.

"Right on time," Dusty said with a chuckle.

Melissa thought she saw the things from her nightmare around every corner, and found herself jumping at shadows.

She'd left the relative safety of Brideview Elementary's bomb shelter, driven by an overwhelming sense that if she stayed, something horrible was going to happen to her and anybody who happened to be near her.

Melissa couldn't bear to think of innocents being hurt because of her.

She stuck close to the shadows as she walked, the image of a sword poised on the periphery of her mind in case she needed to defend herself.

But for now, the activity on the street was unusually calm, which was perfectly fine with her. As good as she was at killing monsters, she didn't want to take any unnecessary chances.

The thought caused an odd sensation in the depths of her chest, a burning, churning feeling that she'd grown to relate with her angelic nature. As a Nephilim, she thrived on killing monsters.

As she passed the burned facade of her favorite used bookstore, Melissa stopped. She stepped up into the store through its broken window. Memories of the time she'd spent here, before she'd realized what she was and what she had to do, danced about her mind. She couldn't help but smile.

This was where she'd bought her favorite book of all time: Madeleine L'Engle's *A Wrinkle in Time*. She so wanted to be Meg Murry. Melissa remembered being swept up into the fantasy of the novel, wishing that it was all real, never realizing what her own future held.

She wandered into the area that had been reserved for story time and froze.

Something was wrong.

Something was there. . . .

Without a moment's hesitation, a sword of fire appeared in her hand. She was ready.

"Melissa!" Gabriel barked, but she didn't even look in his direction. Instead, Melissa turned to an open area at the back of the store. He was about to follow when he felt Dusty's hand touch his head, and a warm tingle spread through his back.

"She doesn't see us, does she?" Gabriel asked.

"No."

"Why?"

"It complicates things," Dusty said.

He left Gabriel, moving toward the girl. Dusty was no more than a foot away when Gabriel saw Melissa tense, spinning toward him, burning sword at the ready.

"Whoa!" Dusty said, stepping back a few steps. "She really is a sensitive one."

Melissa eyed every corner for a threat.

"What are you going to do?" Gabriel asked.

"I need to send her on her way or it's going to be too late."

"Should I even bother asking?"

Gabriel watched as Dusty carefully moved closer to the girl and rubbed his hands together vigorously. The Labrador was even more confused than ever. Then Dusty held his hand out toward the girl and gently blew on his palm into Melissa's face.

"Tiny particles of the sword," Dusty explained, stepping back to where Gabriel waited. "They should take effect right about—"

Melissa felt as though she'd been shocked. Staccato images exploded inside her head.

Feeling dizzy, she dropped down to one knee, her weapon still at the ready, just in case.

It took her a moment, but then she was able to process the vision. She saw Cameron in the woods. He was fighting one of those things from her nightmare.

And he didn't look as though he was winning.

Melissa reacted before she could even consider what she was doing. Her wings erupted from her back and wrapped her in their feathery embrace, to transport her to Cameron's side.

Dusty smiled. "That should do it," he said, turning to leave the store.

"Where did she go?" the Labrador asked, following at his heels.

"Where she was needed most," Dusty replied.

"Which was?" Gabriel prompted, the annoyance in his canine voice reaching new levels.

Dusty stopped, blinked his cataract-covered eyes, and then started through the broken window out onto the street. He viewed so many possibilities in his mind, but now, one path seemed more defined than the others.

"Melissa is helping Cameron with the dark angel," he said. He stopped, pointing at the dog just as he was about to leap.

"Be careful," Dusty warned. "There's a piece of glass beneath your left hind paw. If it slices the pad, you could get a nasty infection. We wouldn't want that."

Gabriel considered the floor beneath his paws and changed his position before springing to join Dusty on the sidewalk.

"Excellent!" Dusty smiled, the possibility of infection fading from his mind. Fading from the future.

"So Melissa has gone to help Cameron?" the dog said.

"She has," Dusty said patiently. He hoped that Gabriel

would eventually understand the enormity of Dusty's gift—curse—and trust what he had to say.

"How does she help him?" Gabriel asked as they began to walk down the center of the deserted street.

Dusty concentrated on the possible futures spread out before his mind's eye and focused on the one with the best outcome. "With Melissa's help, Cameron will find the army."

"The army?"

Dusty nodded. "The army that will fight in the final battle of Armageddon."

CHAPTER THIRTEEN

The mouse.

So tiny and frail in the grand scheme of things, but yet, so mighty.

Lucifer felt himself begin to rise up from the darkness, drawn toward the simple language of the rodent and its message.

It said that he was needed—that Lucifer Morningstar, even though he had been responsible for much horror in Heaven and in the world of man—was needed.

Oblivion pulled upon Lucifer, attempting to drag him down into the darkest void, where he would cease to be, replaced entirely by the imposter who had stolen his physical form.

But the mouse repeated his message, and Lucifer found the strength to claw his way back from the brink.

He was needed.

The Son of the Morning sank his fingers deep into the

environment of shadow that had tried so hard to claim him, using strength he didn't know he had to haul himself up from the sucking miasma of extinction toward existence.

He was needed.

In the simplest of terms, the mouse regaled him with stories of the world since his disappearance. Things had not been going well. The earth had been cut off from the influence of Heaven, the school attacked, its charges, still alive, scattered to the world.

The Morningstar again faced the agony of what he had done—what his body, controlled by another, had done.

He remembered the look on Aaron's face as a sword of darkness, wielded by his own hands, was plunged into his son's body.

Lucifer felt himself grow weaker, the tendrils of oblivion starting to pull him back.

You are needed.

The mouse squealed again, and though the Morningstar's sadness was nearly incomprehensible, he listened to the mouse. For a part of Lucifer that saw beyond his sorrow and guilt knew that if he were to succumb to the sucking despair, the world would end.

And the darkness would have won.

Despite the temptation to give in to his pain, Lucifer could not stand the idea of the nightmare that possessed his body inflicting more anguish upon the earth. Lucifer would take back all that belonged to him.

With a newfound vigor, the Son of the Morning pulled himself up from the pit of despair.

You. Are. Needed.

If he had been told that he had climbed from the mire of nonexistence for hundreds of years, Lucifer would have believed it. Never had he experienced such fatigue. But the Morningstar would not have it. He pushed through, for there was a purpose awaiting him on the other side.

He would see the darkness of evil burned away by the light of the Morningstar.

The Darkstar paused as the odd sensation reverberated through his body. He'd never experienced its like before, but then again, he'd never had a body such as this.

It was as if there was an irritation, just beyond his mental reach. He swayed slightly; then, as quickly as it came, the feeling was gone.

"Are you well, good master?" one of the Sisters asked.

"Perhaps you tire and are in need of rest," said another, vigorously nodding her hooded head.

"We will disturb you no longer," said the last of the three Sisters, shuffling for the door, the others following.

"You will stay where you are," Satan Morningstar proclaimed.

The Sisters stopped, staring intently at him, their eyes glowing eerily from the darkness of their hoods.

"I'm fine," Satan announced, standing tall and smiling at his servants. "Better than fine, actually."

The Sisters remained silent.

"This world is mine," he announced, spreading his arms and his black wings for effect. "There may be some out there in the desolation who would disagree, but I am in control."

Just saying the words brought a twisted grin to his face. Satan liked the feeling of the muscles in his face, his true form not able to perform such a function.

His true form really didn't have a face.

"I know that there are pockets of resistance, but they consist of poor, deluded souls who don't understand that their world has been stolen right out from underneath them."

Satan Morningstar paused, just in case the Sisters of Umbra had something to add to his assessment.

They did not.

"It's only a matter of time before all forms of defiance are quelled and my dark reign falls over the world." He paused, again waiting for a response that didn't appear to be coming.

"Don't you agree?" he finally asked his audience.

"Of course, Star of Darkness," replied one Sister. "Of course."

"It is inevitable they will fall," answered another.

The third considered her words before speaking. "Your enemies will most assuredly fall," she said. "But isn't it admirable that they have lasted this long against forces so great?"

Satan rankled at the words, rearing back.

"Admirable, but pointless," he said with a sneer. He liked sneering just as much as grinning—maybe more. "The poor souls don't even realize that they're already dead."

"Such an annoyance," one Sister said, shaking her hooded head and rubbing her clawed hands together.

"Even the tiniest of annoyances can ruin a day."

"Especially when these annoyances do not know they're dead."

These were not the words of encouragement the Darkstar had wanted to hear. As far as he was concerned, the world was his, and it was time to move on to grander pursuits.

Divine pursuits.

Beyond the veils of earth.

"Those annoyances are no longer my concern," Satan Darkstar said, a certain finality in his voice. "It is time to consider what is to come," he continued, not allowing an argument.

He pulled the gauntlet of black metal from his hand. Darkness leaked from the tips of his fingers. It floated in the air like oil injected into water, then gradually coalesced into a rendering of the globe.

"This is mine," Satan said, admiring his prize. "I always wanted this world, desired it more than anything else, but now that I have it . . ." He let his facsimile explode, returning his dark power to its squirming, liquid state.

"I can't keep my mind from wondering: What's next?"

The Darkstar looked to the Sisters. He could practically feel them bursting to respond, but they held their tongues, perhaps realizing that his question was purely rhetorical. He knew exactly what he wanted.

He guided the liquid shadow with his bare, outstretched hand.

"I always wanted to see Heaven," the Darkstar proclaimed wistfully. "The Golden City in which He resides."

The darkness attempted to re-create the great megalopolis, sprawling and elegant, awe-inspiring in its design. It tried, but it failed every time.

"But why would something as loathsome as me ever be allowed to look upon something so magnificent?" Satan Darkstar closed his hand into a fist, and the shadow ceased its attempts to re-create the great city of Heaven. "It is that question that now drives me."

He opened his fingers again, and more pitch flowed forth. It formed new patterns, until the air before them was filled with beings of every conceivable shape and size.

The darkness had made an army.

"When I first hid upon the earth, I watched the comings and goings of divine beings between earth and Heaven."

With Satan's words, the darkness started to create a ladder, and the shadowy army began to climb up toward Heaven.

"I wanted to go where these beings of gold, fire, and

feathers went. I wanted to look upon this place where I was forbidden to venture, then tear it down to nothing and drag it from the sky, sending it burning to the earth below."

The army of darkness still climbed the ladder before them.

"That was my dream then," Satan said to the Sisters. "But now . . ."

The darkness dispersed, as if carried away by a powerful gust of wind.

Satan stared at the Sisters. "I want to go to Heaven. I want to go to Heaven, leading an army of every nightmare conceivable. I want to march through the great gates into the Golden City, and into the halls of Heaven, where I shall rip the Lord God Almighty from his seat of power, claiming Heaven as my own."

One of the Sisters interrupted his rant, clearing her throat, which sounded as dry as the desert.

Satan contemplated wiping her from existence for daring such an interruption, but decided to listen to what the ancient seer had to say.

"The connection between the earthly realm and Heaven has been severed," she reminded.

"The surviving angels of the heavenly host Powers and the Abomination of Desolation saw to that," said a second Sister.

And the third, "But it would have been glorious to see."

The Darkstar spread his wings. "It will be glorious," he announced.

"But—," one Sister began.

"There will be no buts," Satan roared. "This is what I ask of you. This is how you will prove your fealty to me. You will find a way to restore the passage, to create a ladder that will allow me to ascend with my army to the gates of Heaven."

His purpose was right at the tip of his memory.

Jeremy sat Enoch inside the metal shopping cart and wheeled him up and down the department store aisles.

Enoch wasn't really sure why they had come here. It had something to do with Jeremy's jacket getting ripped while fighting a sea serpent or some such nonsense. Or maybe it was about food. Enoch couldn't remember, because he hadn't really been listening. He was too busy trying to recall his ultimate purpose.

Why had he been sent from Heaven back to the world?

His mind was filled with fragmented memories of the past, images that told of a previous time on the planet, before something truly awful had occurred.

"I'm heading down here for a second," Jeremy said, snapping his fingers in front of Enoch's face. "Hey!"

"Leave me alone!" the toddler screeched, waving his arms and trying to slap Jeremy's hand away. He probably would already have remembered his purpose if it wasn't for Jeremy's damnable interruptions.

"Chill out, lad," Jeremy said.

Enoch turned away in an attempt to recapture his train of thought. But that train had left the station without him.

"Damn him," Enoch grumbled, gazing around the dark, empty department store. Something caught his eye off in the distance. A purple dinosaur! His heart began to flutter.

He loved purple dinosaurs.

Enoch quickly maneuvered himself out of the cart's child seat.

That'll teach Jeremy for not buckling the safety belt.

The toddler climbed over the side of the metal cart to the floor, far more gracefully than he had anticipated.

Perhaps he was finally getting a handle on the coordination thing.

Enoch set off down an aisle. He felt a twinge of sadness connected with his love of colorful dinosaurs, for it had been Jeremy's mum who had first introduced him to them.

"Enoch!" Jeremy called from the front of the store. "Bloody hell! I thought I told you to stay with the cart."

A nasty smiled crept across Enoch's baby features, as he toddled all the faster down the aisle and turned the corner. This would serve Jeremy right for bothering him when he was so deep in thought.

Enoch ran along the wall at the far back of the store, past rows of seasonal supplies—grills, garden hoses, lawn furniture, outdoor paint. He searched for that elusive purple dinosaur.

And then he saw them ahead of him, against the back wall.

They were of varying sizes, some leaning against the racks, some hanging from large hooks.

He froze at the sight of them, as if each of his small, boot-covered feet weighed two hundred pounds.

He stood and stared . . . and remembered.

Enoch was the amalgamation of all that the Lord God was proud of: a mixture of supreme divinity, the angelic, and the human.

He was the Metatron, the physical manifestation of the power and the glory of Heaven on earth.

And Enoch remembered that there was a special place where the Metatron could communicate with his Holy Father.

A place where Heaven and earth touched—connected by the image of a ladder.

Enoch was staring at ladders: wooden ladders, metal ladders, ladders stacked on the floor and hanging from shelves.

He remembered.

And he began to scream.

CHAPTER FOURTEEN

Things became a little foggy when Vilma left Levi to return to Aaron's bedside.

She'd been trying to piece together everything she had learned from Levi, along with what she already knew. It was just too overwhelming.

She barely recalled getting into the elevator, never mind what button she'd pushed. But when the elevator came to a jarring stop and the doors slid open on the lowest level, she was certain she had pressed the wrong number.

Vilma.

At first the voice was so soft, she thought she'd imagined it—until she felt the tickle of a whisper in her ear.

Vilma.

The voice drew her into the deserted corridor.

Vilma.

She tried to follow the sound. It seemed to originate from one of the grilled vents in the upper part of the wall.

Vilma.

The voice called to her as it moved to another ventilation grill farther down the corridor. She was compelled to follow, expecting an Unforgiven sentry to stop her at any moment. But they were nowhere to be found.

Vilma.

The voice led her close to where she'd been mere hours before. Only this time, she passed the observation booth and headed directly toward an old missile silo.

To the place where A'Dorial was kept.

She easily opened the security doors, entering the huge concrete launching tube that had once held a nuclear missile but now held a sickly angel of Heaven. The walls had been singed black from the heat radiated from his body as he strove to maintain a connection with Heaven.

Vilma.

She found him, not as she'd seen him last—unconscious—but sitting up, his eyes strangely alive.

A'Dorial had been waiting for her.

"Vilma," he said again, his mouth barely moving.

Slowly, she approached the angel. "You called me here?"

He continued to stare, his gaze unblinking. "Yes."

"Where is everyone?" she asked him.

"Elsewhere," the angel whispered.

"Did you have something to do with that?"

A'Dorial just stared.

"I'll take that as a yes," she nervously answered her own question. "Why do you need me?"

The angel still did not blink, as his black eyes bored into hers.

Cautiously, she moved a little closer. "Well, what is it? Why have you summoned me here?"

The air around the angel's body started to shimmer, and Vilma felt the temperature in the room begin to rise. The heat from A'Dorial's body was intense, and she was beginning to wonder if she should leave, when—

"You have always been His hope," A'Dorial said, his voice barely a whisper.

"His?" she asked. "Do you mean . . ."

Her eyes darted upward, heavenward, and the ancient angel nodded ever so slightly.

"I'm not sure how hopeful He can be now," Vilma said sadly, her skin prickling with sweat. Standing near A'Dorial was like standing near an open oven. "We haven't done the best job protecting His world."

"Birth throes . . . ," A'Dorial said. "Birth throes of a new world."

Vilma tried to understand. "This world?" she asked him. "Birth throes connected to this world?"

"Perhaps it will live, but perhaps it will not. . . ."

Despite the intensifying heat, a chill ran down Vilma's spine.

"Are you saying—is God saying—that these changes, these birth throes might kill the world?"

A'Dorial was silent.

"What does this have to do with me?" Vilma asked, on the verge of panic, wishing yet again that Aaron was awake to deal with this. "What are you trying to tell me? Is there something that I—"

The angel sprang up from where he sat; the wires attached to his body broke loose, and shrill alarms began to sound.

A'Dorial threw his thin arms around her and pulled her tight to his blazing body. She struggled to keep her mind clear as her flesh began to blister.

She had no choice. Calling forth her Nephilim visage, Vilma unfurled her wings and released her inner fire. The heat of her body merged with A'Dorial's, and within moments, the two were surrounded by a divine fire that threatened to engulf the space.

"He wants you to fight for Him," the angel whispered in her ear. "For the sake of the world . . . for the kingdom of Heaven . . ."

The words left Vilma's mouth purely on instinct. "We will," she promised, though she had no idea how she would accomplish that task.

She could hear shouting from close by and looked up to see Taylor Corbet in the observation window. Then there came a whine and buzz from a nearby speaker, and Taylor spoke to her, anger in her tone.

"Vilma, what's going on?"

As Vilma began to reply, she felt A'Dorial's body go limp. His arms fell away from her, and he slid to the floor. Flames swirled around them.

"We have to get in there," she heard Taylor yell through the speaker.

But Vilma knew it was too late.

The heat from his form cooled immediately, and she drew back her own fire as she knelt beside the silent angel.

Unforgiven angels spilled in through the door.

"I think he's dead," Vilma cried as they pulled her away from him. She didn't want to leave him, but she knew there was nothing more she could do as the Unforgiven began to minister to him.

She watched for a moment, then turned to join Taylor and Levi, who stood in the corridor outside.

"He called me here," Vilma said, wanting to explain.

"It's all right, Vilma," Taylor said. She looked back to Levi. "When are they leaving?"

"As soon as we check the coordinates against the maps," Levi responded.

"What is going on?" Vilma asked.

The Unforgiven leader turned and strode away without a word, as Taylor focused her attention on Vilma.

"I don't know what was going on in there between you and A'Dorial, but he transmitted some important data to us before . . ." Her voice trailed off as her gaze moved to something behind Vilma.

She turned to see that the Unforgiven angels had ceased their ministrations and were now staring helplessly at the still form of A'Dorial.

"What kind of data?" Vilma finally asked, looking away from the sad sight.

"A location," Taylor replied. "We think we've found the child."

Cameron figured that there must have been something coating Janice's claws to numb his body, as if he'd been dipped in near-freezing water.

She sat astride him, her claws ready to slash open his throat.

But all he could do was watch.

He tried to thrash his body in a last-ditch effort to avoid the swipe of her claws, but he couldn't move.

She laughed at his pathetic struggle.

Cameron braced himself. Maybe if the pain was severe enough, his adrenaline would surge and he could shrug off the numbness and fight back a little. . . .

Before she finished him for good.

Cameron watched her claws begin their descent. They reminded him of black metal knives. He wondered if they were like the weapons the Nephilim made of divine fire.

The stupid crap you think of when you're about to die.

Then something struck Janice, something moving incredibly fast that knocked her off him before she could do the deed. It was just the break he needed. He struggled to his feet, the effort taking far more than he could even imagine.

And couldn't believe his eyes.

Standing between him and Janice was the most amazing sight that he could have ever wished for—Melissa, her wings full and flecked with fire, her burning sword pointed at their former teammate.

"Janice?" Melissa asked.

"Hey, girlfriend," Janice answered, climbing up from the dirt and spreading her own batlike wings.

"Watch out for her claws," Cameron managed. The numbness was passing, but slowly.

"What's happened to you?" There was genuine emotion in Melissa's voice, but she didn't let her guard down.

"Well, there was that dying business," Janice replied, her wings of solid black fanning the air ever so slowly. "And then I got better."

She leaped.

"Watch out!" Cameron screamed, attempting to maneuver between Melissa and her attacker, but stumbling.

"Get back!" Melissa commanded, lunging to meet Janice's attack.

There came an explosion of holy fire, tinged with spots

of darkness, as claws of shadow met sword of divine flame. The former friends were thrown apart, repelled by the force of their clash.

Cameron lurched toward Melissa, practically falling at her side. "Hey." He reached down and placed his arm around her. An unnatural black smoke snaked around her body as she tried to shake off the effects of the explosion. "You okay?"

Melissa blinked repeatedly and looked up at him, focusing on his face.

"Yeah," she said. "You?"

"Good now," he said, attempting to help her to stand. "Probably wouldn't have been so good if it wasn't for you."

"Glad I could help," she said, as they stood side by side.

Janice began to scream, and they turned their attention to their foe. Tongues of divine flame clung to her armor. She trembled violently, and sparks of golden fire fell like beads of water, to burn upon the ground.

Still screaming, the dark angel unfurled her wings and leaped into the sky, her cries slowly fading until she was gone.

Melissa suddenly leaned into Cameron. He grabbed her by the arm to steady her.

"You all right?" he asked, and she nodded. "What just happened?"

"I—I don't know," Melissa said. "I think it had something to do with the explosion. When my sword hit her claws, something happened. Some kind of connection was made. I saw what was going on in her mind, and I think she saw inside mine."

Cameron gazed up into the night sky, Janice's mournful scream fading in the night making the hair on the back of his neck prickle.

"If that's the kind of response a look around inside your skull gets," Cameron said, "in the future, remind me never to do that."

The power of God stirred within the shriveled breasts of the Sisters of Umbra.

Satan Darkstar had demanded that they re-establish a link between earth and Heaven, using ancient magicks at their disposal.

He did not know it by name, this connection—the Ladder—but he wanted it to exist again, so he could lead an attack on the gates of Heaven.

With just the thought of the Ladder, the power that had been theirs for countless millennia had become agitated.

And it was all that they could do to keep it under control.

The Sisters told the Darkstar that they needed time to research ancient texts to see if what he was seeking was within their powers to create, and they fled through a passage of shadow.

Back in the safety of their lair, the three experienced the full effects of the divine power as it struggled excitedly to take control.

As it attempted to free itself from the constraints of ancient flesh, blood, and bone.

The Sisters remembered how it had been—how the power came to be theirs.

They had been the high priestesses of the Mirthra tribe, an ancient people long forgotten to the mists of time. The Mirthra had been some of the first peoples of the planet, descendants of the world's first murderer, Cain, who killed his brother Abel and was sentenced by God to wander the world in punishment for his heinous act.

They were the descendants of Cain, and as if somehow marked by his murderous lineage, they were hated by the other tribes of the ancient world and forced to hide themselves or suffer the wrath of the superstitious rabble.

But the other tribes still knew of the Mirthra and blamed them for any ill fate that befell them. One of these tribes, having had a particularly dismal hunting season, and unfertile women, decided that the reason for their misfortune was all due to the existence of the Mirthra. And the Mirthra, already hiding themselves away, became the hunted of these angry ancient people, and met their fates at this tribe's hands.

The Sisters had prayed to their ancient deities, and even to the ancient father Cain himself, but the gods were not listening.

But something was.

As the high priestesses lay in a cave, dying from wounds

sustained in the genocidal attack on their tribesmen, the Architects came to them.

Beings of equal parts light and shadow, the Architects hung above them in observation, like the stars in the night sky. The priestesses had never seen their likes, and believed that these beings—these new gods—would be the last sights they saw.

The Architects stopped them from dying, freezing the moment of their passing from this world to the next, with a question.

"If allowed to live, will you serve us?"

Fearing the nothingness that clawed at them, threatening to drag them down into its hungry embrace, each of the Sisters accepted the offer of these new gods.

"Yes," croaked the first.

"Serve," managed another, beckoning to the gods above her with a blood-covered hand.

And the last, who had been injured the worst, just stared with her large eyes, her gaze providing the Architects the answer that they sought.

"So be it," the Architect's leader spoke, his words filling the cave.

And then the new god withdrew a pulsing sphere of light from within him. The Sisters remembered how bright it was, and the feeling that radiated from it as the orb gently floated from the Architect leader's hand, to hover in the air above their mortally wounded bodies.

They were terrified by the orb's presence, and though they had never admitted it to one another, each of them, at that very moment, believed that it might be best to die.

And to escape what was to follow.

The orb of light floated closer, tendrils of crackling light reaching out to caress the Sisters' withered flesh.

The orb wished to know them better, before . . .

Deep within their lair, the Sisters gasped with the sharpness of the memory, their clawed hands clutching at the front of their heavy robes as they again experienced the moments of their death.

And rebirth.

They recalled that the power had divided into three separate spheres of light—three miniature suns—that took position over their prone forms, waiting for the precise moment.

And the power that had once lived inside the godlike being, the Metatron, before being seized by the Architects, entered the Sisters' bodies just as the last spark of their existence was to flicker out, and reignited their dwindling life force to burning.

And the God power had burned inside the Sisters for thousands of years, providing them with the magickal means to serve their masters, the Architects, and to assist them in their plans to create a perfect world.

A Heaven here on earth.

But the wishes of Satan Darkstar had somehow stimulated the power that had once belonged to the Metatron, which had been theirs to control for so very long, rousing it to seek autonomy from its ancient hosts.

After oh so very long, the power remembered that it was of Heaven, and wanted at last to go home.

But the Sisters would not hear of it, for without the power that had returned them to life and sustained them for all these many millennia, they would cease to be.

And the Sisters could not imagine a world without them.

On the wall there was a vertical gash that glowed with an unnatural light. An opening into a reality inhabited by their masters, the Architects.

"We beseech you, masters," the first of the Sisters called out.

"Come to us," said the second.

"The Sisters of Umbra are in need of your counsel," said the third.

The split began to tremble ever so slightly, as the room filled with an intense humming that grew louder by the second.

The Sisters waited, as the light opened a window to another reality.

A reality that existed only for the Architects.

The Overseer floated weightless in an environment composed of multiple windows of ever-changing images, which looked over the world. An environment that the Architects used to steer the planet toward perfection.

The Sisters were quiet, waiting for the master of their masters to address them, but the Overseer did not acknowledge them.

When they could wait no more, the bravest of the three shambled toward their own window.

"We are in need of your counsel," she said.

The Overseer remained as silent as the grave.

"What is the subject?" the Overseer finally asked.

"It is the Darkstar," another of the three said, stepping forward.

"His aspirations, they threaten to undermine the plan."

"Satan seeks something from us that we fear to give," said another.

The Sisters felt it again: With the mere thought of what the Darkstar wanted from them, the power of the Metatron grew wild, struggling within them to escape its confines.

But they could not let the Overseer see.

They feared their master's reaction, feared that they would be stripped of the gift that had sustained them and had given them vast amounts of magickal strength for countless years.

No, their masters could not know. They would deal with the unruly power; they would wrest it back under control.

"What does the Darkstar ask of you?" the Overseer asked.

"He wishes us to reopen the original passage. . . ."

"To re-create the Ladder."

"The Ladder to Heaven, so that he may lead an invasion."

The Overseer of the Architects turned his golden eyes to them. They felt so very small under his gaze.

"You will not do this," he ordained. "We have worked too

hard to sever the connection between the earth and Heaven. We cannot risk the Lord seeing what we are doing before the world is ready."

The Architects had such grand plans for the world of man, and were desperate for the chance to show their Creator how wrong He'd been. The Architects were determined to save a world that would have obliterated itself if allowed to proceed without intervention.

They were so very excited to show Him what they would achieve, but first . . .

"You will tell him that it cannot be done," the Overseer said.

"Of course, but the Darkstar is not one to be denied his wants," said one of the Sisters.

"He will demand that we find a solution," responded another.

"And if he cannot get what he desires from us, he will seek out another source. He is most industrious."

The Overseer contemplated their argument. "Distract him."

The Sisters did not understand, but the Overseer clarified. "I'm sure that there are diversions that could take his attention away from you."

The Sisters considered this option. But how?

Before they could inquire further, they noticed that the glowing window began to close. Their audience was at an end.

The Sisters stepped back into the chamber as the ground began to violently shake, sending fragments of the ceiling raining down upon them.

Stumbling awkwardly to one side, they looked at one another in amazement.

"What was that?" one of the Sisters asked fearfully.

They shambled across their lair to investigate, when the entire room shook again with the sound of thunderous explosions in the distance.

"The unthinkable," answered a Sister brave enough to utter the words.

"There is no other option to consider. We are under attack," growled another angrily.

The Sisters of Umbra then joined hands, using their combined might to take control of the divine power once again.

And to ready themselves to deal with any who would dare attack their dwelling.

"May whatever gods they worship have mercy upon them," they spoke as one.

Leaving to confront their offenders.

CHAPTER FIFTEEN

"Why is that baby screaming at the ladders?" Gabriel asked, as he and Dusty arrived in the shadows of the gardening aisle in a department store.

"He is remembering what he is here for," Dusty responded as he watched the child shriek and cry.

"And it has something to do with ladders?" the dog asked.

"In a way, it does."

"If you say so."

It was getting easier for Gabriel to accept Dusty's vagueness. He knew that Dusty saw multiple possibilities and multiple futures, but the meaning of that was too much for the Labrador to grasp. He simply understood that his companion functioned on another level entirely and just did as he was told—shown. That had included transporting them both here, to a department store in Amsterdam.

There was a commotion from close by, and Gabriel tensed.

"Enoch!" a familiar voice yelled.

Gabriel was surprised to see Jeremy Fox run to scoop the screaming child into his arms.

"It's Jeremy!" Gabriel looked up at Dusty, his tail wagging.

"Yes, it is." Dusty was gazing off at what, Gabriel did not know.

"I was wondering what happened to him," the Labrador continued, observing how the British boy cared for the crying child. "I think he's changed."

Dusty suddenly moved, as if startled.

"What's wrong?" Gabriel asked, turning toward his companion.

"We have to leave. Now," Dusty answered, placing his hand on the top of Gabriel's head.

"I'm not even going to ask what you see," Gabriel commented. Sparks of divine fire began to leap from his thick yellow coat, as thoughts of their next destination filled his head.

"Good," Dusty said as they were swiftly transported away. "That means you're learning."

The Architects searched.

They were aware that those who opposed their efforts—

the Unforgiven—had reached out to Heaven in desperation when they realized what the Architects had set in motion.

The world was to be isolated from the divine.

The Unforgiven prayed for help, and Heaven answered the best it could in the time before their communication was cut off. Heaven's response was so quick—so desperate—that the mysterious answer to their prayers did not fall into the proper hands.

It was out in the world, needing to be found.

And so the Architects searched.

But the object sent from Heaven continued to elude them. The only balm to this disappointment was that the Unforgiven had not located the object either.

The world was in transition. Evil was overflowing the land. What it would do to God's chosen! Most would not survive, but that meant they were not fit to live.

It was the survivors who most interested the Architects: those who confronted the darkness and rose up from the wreckage of a once-great civilization.

It was the survivors who would claim this new world.

A world that God intended, but He did not know.

A world shaped by the Architects.

A world glorious to behold.

The Overseer experienced the first of the flashes while he gazed at the ghostly facsimile of the world as it slowly turned beneath him and his Architect brothers.

One of his brethren released a sound of alert, rousing all of them from their scrutiny of the world.

Another of his family made a similar sound, and that was when the Overseer began to feel it as well.

He took control of the representation of the world beneath him, moving it in such a way that all its dark, secret places would be more visible to his eyes, and the eyes of his brothers.

It was only a flash of light, a brief pulsation of red that could have been any number of strange anomalies that had dappled the globe since the Darkstar and his legions had overrun the planet.

But this was different.

"Alert the Agents to this location," the Overseer proclaimed.

The area on the ghostly globe had gone quiet once more, but the Overseer still saw it, flaring brightly in his mind's eye.

A beacon to exactly what the Architects had been yearning to find.

The cooling rock was slippery, and it took every ounce of coordination that Mallus had to keep himself and Tarshish on their feet.

"Are you sure the shell is here?" Mallus asked once again.

They had descended deeper and deeper into the earth through a tunnel formed by the Malakim's power.

"Patience, Mallus," Tarshish said, his voice sounding older—weaker. "You got a big date tonight or something?"

"Big date," Mallus repeated, reaching out a hand to steady

himself against the smooth walls. "If only it was something so trivial."

"It's here," Tarshish confirmed. "We haven't gone far enough yet. Looks like geological upheaval buried it good."

The farther they went, the warmer it got. Tarshish's nearly naked body had finally stopped shivering. Mallus had offered his shirt, but the Malakim had refused, muttering something about the discomfort being part of his penance.

The tunnel suddenly dipped precariously in the darkness, and Mallus lost his footing. The two of them fell, sliding a short distance to land in a heap on the floor of a much larger chamber.

"Are you all right?" Mallus asked as he climbed to his feet, then tried to help his companion.

Tarshish leaned back against the wall. "I'm fine," he answered, nodding toward the other side of the chamber.

Mallus followed his gaze and gasped.

What remained of the Metatron lay curled in the fetal position. The body's shell was huge, far larger than Mallus even remembered.

"How could we ever have brought down such a being?" Mallus asked, awe tinged with shame in his voice.

"Isn't the power of anger and jealousy amazing?" Tarshish asked. "That is what it was all about," he reminded Mallus. "We were mad at our God, so we lashed out, siding with those who coddled us. Told us what we wanted to hear. We were a couple of fools."

Mallus couldn't argue. "So the power of God is in there?"

"It is," Tarshish said. "Even though it has been tainted a bit over the millennia, I can still feel it."

"Are you up for this still?" Mallus asked, as he leaned down to pull the Malakim to his feet.

"I think I can manage." Tarshish shrugged off Mallus's hand and walked toward the giant armored body.

Mallus followed, and together, they entered the shell of the Metatron through an opening near where the stomach would be. The interior of the armor was illuminated by an eerily glowing moss that covered its surface.

"It appears that the remains' divinity has somehow affected some of the plant life," Tarshish commented, pointing out the luminescent patches that spread across the ceilings and walls. "I wonder—"

His words were cut off by a distant sound from inside the remains.

The sound intensified, and the glow brightened as whatever was approaching drew nearer.

Mallus tensed, not believing what he saw.

"I don't—," he began, but never finished.

The creatures resembled the apelike yetis from back at the tavern, only smaller in size and with luminescent fur. They surged at the angels in a shrieking wave, obviously annoyed by the invasion of their dwelling.

"I wondered if any other life-forms had been affected by

the divine radiation of the Metatron's remains," Tarshish said.

"I would guess so," Mallus answered, backing up. "What do you suggest we do now?"

"Fight them," Tarshish said simply.

"That is what I figured you'd say."

The first of the yetis sprang at them, glowing fangs bared and long, muscular arms swinging.

Mallus hauled back and then, using his superior strength, punched the creature in the face. Its skull exploded as if filled with dynamite, and its corpse crumpled to the cave floor.

"Good one," Tarshish acknowledged. It was his turn now. He unleashed a powerful flash of angelic magick that made the next four yetis explode in flames.

"Not bad yourself," Mallus said. More yetis came at him, and he shattered the bones of their limbs, leaving them screeching at his feet. "But we can't keep this up forever."

"We want them to take us," Tarshish announced, barely able to stand, but still unleashing gouts of destructive magick. "If my suspicions are correct, I believe they'll bring us to their master."

Mallus was horrified. "What if you're wrong?"

"Then we'll die, burdened by our own tremendous sin." Tarshish unleashed one more wave of magick that shook the hollowed-out body of the Metatron.

"I hope you're right," Mallus grumbled, as the two fallen angels allowed the yetis to overwhelm them.

A wave of filthy fur and claws dragged them down.

* * *

Even though she had gotten Melissa to leave the fallout shelter, Lorelei had stayed behind.

But for what? The whole ghost thing was really starting to get on her nerves.

She watched tough guy Tyrone and security guard Scott arguing about scavenging for more food, while Doris and her daughter, Maggie, attempted to play referee.

It was as if a hand gripped Lorelei by the shoulder, pulling her over to where Loretta lay, her husband sitting on the cot beside her, holding her hand.

Is this it? Lorelei wondered. *Is this why I'm still here?*

Lorelei floated before the woman, reaching out to lay a ghostly hand on her arm in comfort.

Loretta seemed to shiver at her touch, turning her head slowly to look at the Nephilim.

"Can you see me?" Lorelei asked. The woman's mouth quivered and then went slack, as the life left her.

Her husband brought her hand to his lips, kissing it lovingly. Then he laid his head on her chest, wrapped his arms around her, and began to sob.

"I wonder if he knows how much I love him?"

The voice startled Lorelei, and she turned to see Loretta now floating beside her.

"You're like me!" Lorelei exclaimed.

"No," Loretta said. "Not really."

Lorelei looked at her strangely.

"You're here for a reason," Loretta said simply. "I'm just waiting for you."

"Waiting for me?" Lorelei was even more confused.

"We're all waiting for you."

Before Lorelei could question her, the room was suddenly pulled away from them and replaced with another environment entirely.

The two women now stood in an open area of nothingness, but they weren't alone. As far as the eye could see, there were people: men, women, and children of all sizes, colors, and shapes.

"Who are they?" Lorelei asked in amazement.

"They are the souls who have passed since the world was cut off from Heaven," Loretta explained. "Their—our—energies have nowhere to go. We can't return to the source of all existence."

"So, let me guess, they're waiting for me to do something."

Loretta nodded.

"How am I supposed to help them pass on when even I couldn't pass on?" Lorelei panicked. Sure, she had connected with Melissa to warn her of approaching trouble, but this? She was clueless. "I don't know what to do!"

Loretta leaned forward and placed a hand on Lorelei's arm. "No worries, dear," the ghostly old woman said. "That's why he had me bring you here."

As if things weren't already confusing enough.

"Who? Who asked you to bring me here?"

Loretta only smiled, joining the countless others.

"Loretta?" Lorelei called. "Loretta, who had you bring me here?"

She searched the crowd for the older woman, but she was gone. Instead, the crowd moved aside, and Lorelei watched as someone approached from the distance.

She did not know who he was, but as he drew closer, she knew what he was.

The angel had a gentle smile upon his face. "Hello, Lorelei," he said, his ghostly, feathered wings gently fluttering behind him.

"My name is A'Dorial. Your father has sent me with a message from Heaven. He wants me to tell you about the Ladder."

CHAPTER SIXTEEN

Aaron had forgotten much as he traversed a seemingly endless region of shadow, but he also remembered. Fiction dissolved away, leaving behind only truth.

"Where are we going?" he called to his foster parents, whose bodies were completely engulfed in flames, their skeletal remains moving within an aura of fire.

"This is where the poison has gone," his mother said, her words making sparks dance from the yellow bone of her teeth.

"Where?" Aaron asked, joining them atop a hill. "Here?"

The shadows formed a large valley below them, and in the distance, he could see a wall of stone.

"Or behind that wall?"

His deep subconscious had become an annoying place, and he just wanted to be through with it. "Let's get this over with," he said, heading down the hill. Tom and Lori didn't follow. "What's the matter?" he called over his shoulder. "Aren't you coming?"

They continued to watch him, and for a moment he was reminded of how gruesome this particular aspect of his subconscious was. It seemed so morbid to be hanging around with two very important people in his life who had died horribly.

Because of him.

And with that thought, his foster parents disappeared, as if they'd never been there. Balls of color danced before his eyes as the darkness rushed in to claim the illuminated spot where they had stood.

Aaron sighed, reminding himself that they were only a manifestation of his memory. But it was still sad that they were gone again. He was painfully aware of how much he missed not having them in his life, and how dramatically everything had changed when his Nephilim birthright came into being.

He took a deep breath and focused on the wall in the distance, wondering how long it would take him to reach the other side of the valley. There was no way to really know, so Aaron just walked, curious as to what he would find once he got there.

He hadn't made it all that far when he noticed the shapes ahead. One after another they appeared. He could see that they were people, but he couldn't make out any more.

Aaron trudged on, eager to spend as little time as possible in this depressing place. As he drew closer, he could see that the figures were lining up a few hundred feet in front of the wall.

His curiosity outweighed his fear, and Aaron actually started to run, only to come to a sudden stop yards away from the long line of people.

They didn't have any faces. They were wearing normal clothes: jeans, dresses, suits, but their faces were blank—smooth, featureless flesh.

Aaron studied them, wishing that his parents had stayed long enough to maybe explain who they were.

One of the figures, tall and wearing a deliveryman's uniform, strode toward him. Aaron felt a tingling, then burning sensation in the palm of his hand as a sword of fire took shape there.

The faceless messenger continued, unhindered by the appearance of Aaron's weapon.

"You might want to stop there," Aaron warned, extending a hand, suddenly wondering if the person could even see or hear him, for he saw no visible eyes or ears.

The man walked a little faster.

Aaron started to back up, and the featureless figure began to run. Before Aaron could even think of evading him, the deliveryman leaped. He managed to raise his blade, but it wasn't a deterrent. The messenger ran right into the flaming sword, impaling himself.

Aaron watched in shock as the blade pierced the faceless man's chest. He started to pull back on the weapon, when his mind was filled with visions of the deliveryman, his truck, and the beasts of nightmare that besieged him as he drove down a lonely country road.

Aaron yanked the blade from the messenger's chest with a gasp. The faceless figure continued to stand before him, swaying.

There was a sudden flurry of movement close by, and Aaron saw that others were running toward them now. Still numbed by what he'd just experienced, he glanced around for a place to hide, but the people closed in too quickly.

The faceless wave grabbed at his clothes and clawed his skin. Desperately, Aaron swung his sword, but as each foe was cut by the flaming blade, powerful visions exploded in his mind. Aaron cried out, afraid that his skull might split with the sudden deluge of imagery.

Housewives snatched from their yards as they hung laundry, pulled into the sky by flying nightmares; children taken from school yards by things that burrowed up from their sandboxes; people aboard a packed airplane, swatted down by what could only be a dragon.

The realization of who these people were hit Aaron with twice the savagery of the visions themselves.

These were the people that he—and the Nephilim—were supposed to be protecting. These were the people they hadn't saved.

That he hadn't saved.

The sorrow was almost too much for him to bear, so Aaron wished his sword away, hoping that dissolving his fiery blade would perhaps cease the onslaught.

But it didn't.

Every touch was enough to cause multiple images to detonate inside his head.

And for his guilt to grow.

Aaron and the Nephilim had been put on earth to protect the human race, but they—he—had not done a very good job.

The faceless figures punched and kicked him, and he allowed it. He deserved everything that was being dealt him. He tried to say that he was sorry, but he was overwhelmed by their experiences.

A man was pulled beneath the sea, drowned by something covered in tentacles . . . an old woman had been dragged into the shadows of her basement by horrible, fur-covered things . . . joggers screamed in terror as they attempted to outrun a pack of slavering werewolves. . . .

It was all too much.

The images were as suffocating as the crowd. Aaron went down, the weight of the faceless assailants pushing him into darkness.

Drowning him beneath an ocean of guilt.

The Unforgiven installation was abuzz with activity.

Trench-coated, goggle-wearing angels rushed about as they

prepared to embark on their most important mission yet—to find the child.

Vilma caught up with Taylor as the woman was coming out of the control room. "I want to go with them," she said, rushing to keep up with Aaron's mother as she strode toward the elevator.

"I'm not sure that's wise," Taylor said.

"A'Dorial called to me," Vilma insisted, as they got into the elevator. "He said I was part of a plan, that I'm supposed to fight for God—for the sake of the world."

The elevator brought them to the infirmary.

"I understand that," Taylor said. "But I think you may want to stay here."

"Why? What's wrong?" Vilma asked, immediately concerned. "Is it Aaron?"

"I'm not sure," Taylor said, increasing her pace. "I received a call that I should come down."

There was a commotion by Aaron's room, and Vilma took off, racing down the hall and charging into the room. "Aaron?" she cried, as she entered.

Two Unforgiven angels stood over her boyfriend with odd-looking medical instruments. Aaron was thrashing about, his fists clenched as if to defend himself.

"What's wrong with him?" Vilma practically shouted. She pushed past the angels to Aaron's side and put her hand in his. His grip was incredible, almost hurting her.

The Unforgiven didn't answer, continuing to coldly observe Aaron through the lenses of their goggles.

"Did you hear me?" Vilma asked angrily. "I asked you a question."

"Answer her," Taylor commanded, entering the room.

"We don't know," one of the Unforgiven said, as he looked at the boxy instrument he was holding. "His entire metabolic system has gone into overdrive, as if he were performing some great physical act."

Vilma looked at Aaron's mother and saw concern on her face.

"Can we give him something to calm him down?" Taylor asked.

"We did," the other Unforgiven answered. "But his system burned it off in a matter of seconds."

Vilma gripped her boyfriend's hand all the tighter. Something was most definitely wrong. He was fighting with all his might.

The mechanical ring on his chest suddenly sparked and exploded, throwing off smoldering shards of glass and metal. Vilma reached out to grab the broken pieces of the device, throwing them off Aaron's exposed flesh. His skin was blazing hot.

"He's burning up," she said, fearing some sort of fever, the sign of something worse.

Fire appeared around where the ring had been attached, and

then started to spread down Aaron's body. His wings emerged as he lay, and they, too, were alight with fire. The bed's mattress was burning, and flames jumped hungrily to the floor and the walls. The Unforgiven angels were still attempting to discern data from their machines, but Vilma knew they were way beyond that stage.

She reacted on pure instinct. Her Nephilim visage surged to the surface, wings bursting from her back. She gathered Aaron up in her arms, the divine fire from his body attempting to burn her, but soon realizing that they were of the same species.

"Get him to the silo," Taylor shouted, thinking as she did.

Aaron thrashed in her arms, but Vilma held him tightly as she soared from the room and down the corridor, passing several Unforgiven carrying fire extinguishers on their way to the room. She burst through the stairway door at the end of the hall and headed for the lowest level. The heat from their bodies scorched the concrete walls black as they passed.

Just as they reached the bottom of the staircase, the door flew open to reveal four Unforgiven angels in protective suits.

"This way," one said, motioning for her to follow.

Vilma could feel the muscles in her arms straining, but she endured it, not wanting to set Aaron down until he was safe. She raced behind the Unforgiven as they led her through the concrete corridor and down another stairway to the old missile silo that had once housed A'Dorial.

She entered the chamber and gently laid Aaron's body on the floor. Stepping back, she wished that there was something she could have placed beneath his head to make him more comfortable, but she knew it would just burn.

"Let's go. Time to get out of there," one of the Unforgiven urged from the doorway. Eyes still fixed on her boyfriend, Vilma did what was asked of her, stepping out into the hallway as the two angels closed the heavy metal door, closing Aaron inside.

Through a small portal window, she watched him.

"What's happening to you?" she whispered, wanting more than anything to be with him, to comfort him, but unsure if she would have been able to withstand the intensity of his heat.

Tears flowed freely down her cheeks as she helplessly watched the man she loved, writhing on the cold concrete floor of the missile silo.

His body burning with holy fire.

Verchiel was amused by the stupidity of the dumb beasts, so stubborn they could not even see what was in their best interests. They could not fathom that pledging their allegiance to him would allow them to live another day.

The latest encampment of monsters came at him in an explosive rush of violence, choosing to fight with tooth, claw, sword, spear, knife, and ax—or whatever other instrument of murder they had at their disposal.

The angel met the onslaught with equal vigor, calling forth two swords of fire.

Wading in amongst them, he swung his weapons and watched the monsters fall, like chaff to the farmer's scythe. He considered giving them another chance to forget their dark overlord, and to bow their heads to him, but by then, he had slain them all.

Or at least those brave—stupid—enough to face him.

Verchiel was covered in the foul, stinking blood of his foes. He let the fire of the divine that coursed through his veins rise to the surface, heating his body and armor, baking the blood so it would flake to the ground.

He then turned, swords still in hand, to see if any more would challenge him. He hoped some would, but saw a small contingent of monsters huddled together. They immediately dropped their weapons and bowed in subservience.

Verchiel looked to the goblin, Ergo, standing with the other beasts that had decided they did not want to die—an army of foul creatures that now followed him.

What am I doing?

He thought of the three hags, and how they'd sought to entice him with an offer to serve the mysterious Architects.

Beings who supposedly had foreseen these dark times . . . who had helped make them happen.

Verchiel looked up at the cloud-filled sky, and then down at the corpses at his feet. The earth had become a Godless place, and he would do everything in his power to see it returned to its former glory.

What was he doing? He was forming an army.

Fighting fire with fire.

CHAPTER SEVENTEEN

She made him take his shirt off.

Cameron's body was bruised and scratched, but he had no major injuries.

"Hold still," Melissa ordered. She found a relatively clean rag and some bottled water. "Let me clean these up, just in case."

She got in close to him, dabbing at his wounds.

"How did you find me?" Cameron asked her.

Melissa stopped what she was doing to seriously consider the question. "I really don't know," she said. "It was like I suddenly knew you were in trouble, and where you were."

"Well, however you got here, I'm glad you did." He smiled at her, and she could not help but smile back.

"Yeah, me too," Melissa replied, returning to cleaning his cuts. She could see that he was already starting to heal. "That should do it," she said, setting the rag and bottle of water on the counter. "So, this was your safe place?" she asked, eyes darting around the log cabin.

"It was until . . . ," Cameron began. He'd grabbed a cleaner shirt from a pile in the corner, smelled it, and proceeded to put it on.

He looked as though he had more to say, so Melissa waited.

"That was Janice we were fighting," he finally said.

Melissa shook her head.

"No," she said emphatically. "Janice is dead. That thing just looked like her."

"You said that you were inside her . . . its head. If it wasn't Janice, what was it?"

Melissa was suddenly very cold. She wasn't sure if it was the temperature in the drafty cabin, or a connection to the memory of what she had seen.

"It's something wearing Janice's body," Melissa tried to explain. "Everything that made Janice a caring, loving person was gone—and something horrible, dark, and twisted has been put inside her body."

"But it knew me . . . us," Cameron said.

"Yeah," Melissa answered. "I think it's using Janice's memories."

"I think the same thing may have happened to the others," Cameron said haltingly. "The others who died."

"Yeah," Melissa confirmed, remembering her strange dream, suddenly feeling much colder.

Neither of them said anything more, really not sure how to respond to the idea that their departed friends had been resurrected as monsters. Silence seemed the most appropriate response.

Leaning up against the counter, Melissa noticed an old box sitting on the table. Just the sight of it made the flesh on the back of her neck tingle. "What's that?"

"Something that my father left for me to find. I didn't remember any of it until I came here," Cameron said, pulling the box closer. "It was like this place was the trigger to release the memory."

Melissa moved to the table and peered inside the box at his father's journal.

"Have you read that yet?" she asked.

"Some," Cameron answered. "He talks about a place where something very important is hidden . . . something that the Architects hid."

Melissa couldn't help herself; she reached into the box. There was something at the very bottom, a liner of some sort.

But one of the corners had peeled up, and on the other side, she saw some writing. As if compelled, she emptied the contents of the box.

"Hey, what are you doing?" Cam asked, annoyed.

She was so engrossed, she didn't answer. Melissa slowly peeled back the edges of the lining, careful so as not to tear it.

"What is it?" Cameron asked, reaching for it.

Melissa pulled away, claiming the discovery as her own. "I'm not sure, but there's writing on it."

She moved the wooden box and laid the paper on the table, gently smoothing the ancient parchment. Her eyes widened. There was writing on it, and so much more.

"It's a map."

"To what?" Cameron leaned in closer.

The writing was not a human language; it was angelic script, but Melissa could still read it.

"You said that your father wrote about something important," she said, growing excited. "Something that the Architects had hidden."

As Melissa looked at Cameron, she could see a similar spark in his eyes.

"What if it's something that can help us, something that could restore the world to the way it was?"

"I think this"—she laid her fingertips on the surface of the map—"can take us to it."

The glowing green yetis dragged Mallus and Tarshish by their feet through the seemingly endless passages within the shell of the fallen Metatron.

"You awake?" Tarshish asked.

"Yeah, I'm awake," Mallus replied to the beaten and bloody Malakim. "You don't look so good."

"Don't you worry about me," Tarshish said, the back of his

head bumping along the uneven ground. "I just need to hang on for a little while longer."

"Just a little while?"

"We're almost there." A sad smile appeared on Tarshish's bloody face. "A chance to make things right. Well, as right as they can be now. The rest will be up to you."

"What do you mean by that?" Mallus asked, suspicion in his tone.

"Just don't screw it up."

And that was when Mallus felt it: The angelic sigils tattooed on his body, which had served him well throughout the centuries, warning him of danger, began to tingle.

Warning him of the presence of an incredible, supernatural power.

Mallus felt his legs drop unceremoniously to the floor, and then the yetis' clawed hands were hauling him roughly to his feet. Tarshish was receiving the same treatment.

Mallus winced at the sight of the Malakim, his body so emaciated, and covered with cuts and bruises. He hoped that the angelic magick user could hold on long enough for them to finish their task.

Three heavily robed and hooded shapes emerged from the darkness.

"Are these the ones?" came a screeching voice from behind one of the hoods.

"How is this possible?" asked another. "Only a being of

great power could have . . ." Her voice trailed off as if sensing something.

"A being of great power," repeated the third, leaving her Sisters to draw closer to Mallus and Tarshish.

The hooded figure stopped before the two angels, studying them, then turned her focus to Tarshish. Mallus squirmed, but the yetis held him fast.

"Careful, Sister!" warned one of the two who hung back.

"Something isn't right with that one," said the other.

The Sister reached a spindly-fingered hand out from the sleeve of her robe, touching the center of Tarshish's bare chest, then quickly pulled it away.

"There is something about you," she said, curiosity evident in her horrible voice. "Something . . . familiar."

Tarshish laughed weakly. "Didn't think you'd recognize me in this condition," he said.

The other two Sisters moved a little closer.

"She is right, there is something strangely familiar," verified one.

"But I do not know why," added the other.

They huddled around the Malakim, his mystery drawing them nearer.

Mallus watched, not sure what Tarshish had planned.

"Looked a lot different way back when," the Malakim began to explain. "But then again, so did the power inside the three of you."

The Sisters recoiled with a gasp.

"It was pure then," Tarshish continued. "Radiant with the splendor of the Creator."

The Sisters of Umbra backed away from the mysterious stranger.

"You want to know why I seem familiar to you ladies?" Tarshish asked them. "I helped to place that power inside you."

"Blasphemy!" screeched one of the three.

"Lies!" cried another.

"He speaks the truth," admitted the third.

Tarshish nodded. "You see it now. Although I am nothing compared to what I was."

His frail body started to smolder, and then to glow.

"All right, Tarshish," Mallus said, struggling with his captors. "Time to let me in on the plan."

Tarshish ignored him, as his human flesh burned away to reveal something composed of pure energy, which leaked into the air, forming a humming cloud that swirled above the Malakim's head.

The Sisters had joined hands, their own magick emerging from their hooded forms.

"I was truly something back then, but so filled with arrogance that I couldn't see the big picture."

The Sisters extended their arms as one, casting a spell that screamed as it flew toward the Malakim.

"Do you get it now, Sisters?" Tarshish asked as he tossed

off his yeti captors. His energy flowed to engulf their spell and consume it. "I—we killed the Metatron. We set God's power, which ended up in your possession, free."

There was an explosion of force, light, and sound from Tarshish's body, and Mallus and his yeti captors were thrown back violently.

The Sisters of Umbra attempted to escape, but Tarshish would not have any of that.

The Malakim's human form was gone now. Tendrils of humming, divine energy reached out, ensnaring the three. The Sisters struggled in the Malakim's grasp, defenses of their own erupting from their ancient bodies.

Mallus managed to crawl over the wounded bodies of his primitive captors to make his way toward the struggle. There had to be something he could do to help Tarshish.

An awesome sight was suddenly before him, and Mallus threw his hands up to protect his vision. Through squinting eyes and splayed fingers, the fallen angel watched as the two conflicting powers battled, the light consuming the darkness, only to have the darkness expand outward to destroy the light from within.

For an instant, Mallus saw the Sisters emerge from within their shroud of protection. He saw the opportunity and took it. Removing from his pocket a knife that he had acquired from one of the Architects' Agents, who had tried unsuccessfully to kill him, Mallus stared into the miasma, imagining where his foes were, and threw the knife with every ounce of strength available to him.

At first Mallus believed that he had failed to hit his target, but then there came the most horrible cry. The maelstrom of light and darkness parted with a rush of air to reveal their opponents. Tarshish's barely recognizable form floated back and away, as two of the Sisters hovered over the fallen form of the third—the hilt of the Agent's knife protruding from the front of her robe.

"Sister!" one screamed, as she dropped to kneel beside her.

The other did the same, reaching out to scoop the limp body into her arms. "You will be well," she said.

"That's what I was waiting for," came a familiar voice from somewhere within the writhing mass of divine energy that was Tarshish. "Now don't screw it up," the voice told him.

Before Mallus could question the statement, a wall of energy propelled itself at the Sisters, engulfing them within its embrace. Above their plaintive shrieks, a rumble began that shook the enormity of the Metatron's shell.

The surviving yetis howled in fear, many of them fleeing the chamber, as pieces of the ceiling rained down upon them. The floor beneath his feet bucked wildly, and Mallus dropped to all fours. There then came a searing flash of the whitest light, its purity marred with branching capillaries of darkness, before it collapsed in upon itself with an earsplitting report.

Suddenly, it was silent within the confines of the shell.

Mallus rose, his eyes fixed on a sphere containing the power of God floating above the ground, where what remained of the Sisters writhed, their bodies having somehow been fused together in a writhing mass of flesh and limbs.

Mallus darted toward the sphere as a limb reached for it from the heap that used to be the Sisters.

"Give it back!" the twisted thing cried, multiple voices emanating from a cavernous maw in the lump of flesh that had once been three separate heads.

Mallus held the sphere in both hands, feeling the lingering presence of his friend. Tarshish had sacrificed himself to form a shell of supernatural energy that could contain the power of God for transport in order to re-create the Metatron.

"Please," the voice of the three Sisters begged. Six eyes in a sea of melted skin stared pleadingly at him.

Mallus turned from the misbegotten thing and headed down a passage he believed would lead him to the surface. The Sisters wailed behind him, and Tarshish's final words echoed in his mind.

Don't screw it up.

Mallus hoped that he wouldn't—but couldn't offer any guarantees.

Jeremy felt helpless.

He stood in the hardware aisle, watching as Enoch trembled and shook.

"What's the bloody problem?" he asked, irritation born of frustration in his tone.

All Enoch could do was cry and scream, then cry some more.

Jeremy knew that he had to do something for the child, but what?

He remembered one of the first times he'd tried to comfort the little monster during one of his tantrums. Jeremy had wound up with a tiny foot stuck in his bollocks. It wasn't the least bit pleasant. He considered leaving the child to work out his problem on his own, but he sensed that he shouldn't leave the boy alone.

"Enoch," he said again. The toddler had curled his body into a tight ball, and for a moment, Jeremy thought that he might've fallen asleep.

Squatting down, he reached out to touch him. Enoch let out an ear-piercing shriek, his entire body going rigid as a plank. The child continued carrying on, and Jeremy began to panic.

"Tell me what's wrong," he urged. "Are you hurt? What happened?"

Enoch writhed on the department store floor, his face scarlet from his continued outburst.

And that was when Jeremy noticed that the baby looked bigger.

At first he just believed it to be a trick of the light and

shadows, but as he looked more carefully, he saw that he was right. Enoch's clothes had become too small, the sleeves of his heavy sweater hiked halfway up his arm, his bare legs exposed below the cuffs of his heavy pants.

"Bloody hell, you're growing!" Jeremy exclaimed.

A noise from somewhere in the store captured his attention over Enoch's commotion.

"We have to go," Jeremy said, reaching out to touch the child.

Enoch yelled as if he was being murdered, and Jeremy quickly withdrew his hand. The child continued to moan and grow larger before Jeremy's eyes. He wished he had more of a chance to marvel at the transformation, but he heard more noise and knew they were no longer alone in the store.

Jeremy grabbed the child and started to run toward the shopping cart and their things. Enoch wailed.

"Quiet," Jeremy hissed. *It's like trying to hold on to a greased pig,* he thought as he reached the cart at the end of the aisle where he'd left it.

He unceremoniously dropped the toddler into the cart and began to stuff the supplies he'd collected into his backpack.

Jeremy realized that the boy had gone silent.

"Better?" he asked, arranging the items in the pack so that he could fit more.

Enoch was staring behind him, and Jeremy turned to see four shapes emerging from the darkness. Four masked killers like the others who'd been hunting them . . . like the one who'd killed his mother.

Enoch looked at Jeremy with fear in his tear-filled eyes.

"I've got this," Jeremy said, calling upon a sword of fire as he faced his enemies. More masked figures poured from the shadows behind the first, and Jeremy had a change of heart.

"On second thought," he said, shrugging his shoulder to release his wings.

Jeremy reached into the cart to haul Enoch out and transport them both away, when he felt a sudden sting. A puff of feathers suddenly filled the air, and an excruciating pain raced down the Nephilim's back.

Something had injured his wing. He dropped Enoch back into the cart.

The killers stalked carefully closer, the glint of knives in their hands.

Jeremy had no choice. "Hold on," he told Enoch, grabbing the handle of the shopping cart and spinning it away from their would-be attackers. The pain in his wing was incredible, but he tried to focus. Legs pumping with all his might, Jeremy propelled them to the front of the store.

More hunters emerged from the concealment of nooks and crannies around them.

"I did this," Enoch said. "I allowed them to find us."

"Shut it," Jeremy ordered, evading an attacker who sprang from the toy department, his knife slashing.

With one hand, Jeremy tossed a ball of divine fire into the face of his foe.

The killer sank to his knees, clawing at his face, which had become a raging inferno.

Jeremy was running with the cart again, taking a sharp left corner and smashing into two more attackers. They fell back in a tumble but quickly recovered, springing to their feet, brandishing their knives.

Jeremy reluctantly left Enoch alone in the cart, attacking swiftly with two swords of fire, killing both of the Agents before they could do any harm.

He heard a cry from behind him and gasped as he saw one of the masked assassins attempting to remove Enoch from the cart. The child had grabbed hold of its side, pulling the cart awkwardly along as the figure attempted to extract the little boy.

It gave Jeremy just enough time.

He used his wings to launch himself, though the pain was blinding. Landing just in front of the attacker, Jeremy summoned twin knives of fire, jabbing them into one of the eyeholes of the assailant's black mask, ending his life.

The killer slumped dead to the floor, the knives of fire protruding from his skull disappearing in a flash.

"I've got you," Jeremy said, taking the child protectively into his arms.

"You always have, haven't you," the little boy said, holding him tightly about the neck.

Jeremy experienced a strange pang of emotion for the child but pushed it aside to deal with more of the assassins.

He held Enoch tightly in his arms, swinging a sword of fire as he used his wings to leap across the aisles of the store, making his way toward freedom.

Jeremy charged toward the automatic door, calling forth a blazing battle-ax and cleaving the door in two.

He raced across the parking lot, flapping his wings, attempting to take flight, but the pain was still too much. Jeremy tripped, falling to his knees, and Enoch tumbled from his arms.

"Sorry," Jeremy said, gritting his teeth against the pain as he rested on all fours. Enoch grabbed his arm and tugged.

"We have to go," the child said frantically.

The black-suited assassins were coming from everywhere, converging on them.

This is it, Jeremy thought, centering himself for death.

"Listen to me," he said firmly so that the child would listen. "I want you to run." Jeremy was briefly taken aback that the child was no longer a toddler.

They grow up so fast, he thought, and wanted to laugh, but it really wasn't the time.

"No," Enoch said, pulling on his arm. "We can make it to the woods across the lot and—"

"Run!" Jeremy screamed at the boy, yanking his arm away, as he started to stand, creating two impressive swords of fire.

He watched to be sure that Enoch was getting away, before turning to confront his advancing foes.

"So," he said to them, a twinkle of danger in his eye. "Who wants to be first?"

CHAPTER EIGHTEEN

The Angel of the Void that had once been the Nephilim Janice, dropped from the turbulent sky, unable to keep aloft.

She landed on the hood of a car, the glass of the side windows exploding outward as the roof buckled beneath her weight. For a moment the stimulation of the fall helped to clear her thoughts of the unwanted memories since her mind had touched the Nephilim female's.

Melissa.

The dark angel moaned, rolling from the car roof to the glass-strewn street.

What had the Nephilim done to her?

She furled her large leathern wings and awkwardly climbed to her feet, swaying ever so slightly.

The images came fast and furiously, reinvigorating sections of her brain that had previously been shrouded in shadow.

"What did you do to me?" Janice wailed, reaching out to her fellow dark angels in a cry for help.

She attempted to focus, but it was so very hard. Janice saw images of what life had been like as burning flashes. She saw her end. She'd been wrapped in a net and pulled from the air, clubbed, then stabbed by two trolls, one wielding a three-pronged spear.

She gasped at the memory of the trident's points piercing her flesh.

Janice glanced at her midsection. Her shiny black armor became as if liquid, flowing away to reveal the pale flesh of her stomach.

And the puncture wounds where she'd been stabbed.

Remembering the fear and horror of her death, she gently touched the puckered scars.

That horror had brought her back from the cold oblivion. Her Dark Father had used it to give her life once more. But now, something else existed within her. Something from when her mind had touched the Nephilim's.

Janice saw a life before death, an existence that only truly began when the Nephilim came alive inside her, transforming her into an angelic being of Heaven and earth.

Crying as her mind became painfully crowded, the dark angel lashed out at her surroundings, razor-sharp claws extending from the ends of her fingers, allowing her to rip huge furrows in the door of the car before her. A part of her wished that it had been a thing of flesh and blood, something that would have cried out as its skin was torn.

But that desire was overwhelmed by the memories of valiant actions, the camaraderie that she'd shared with the others of her kind.

Nephilim.

They were her family, and she remembered how much she had grown to love them.

It felt as though burning-hot knives had been jammed into her skull, and the Angel of the Void savagely attacked another of the vehicles close to her. The rage was like a thing alive, and she took hold of the car, lifting it up from the street in a show of preternatural strength and hurling it through a nearby storefront.

Janice studied her handiwork, feeling a small satisfaction from her violent act—which quickly turned to surprise as a small group of people streamed out from the store in a panic, their hiding place revealed.

She was tempted to follow them, when she realized that they were already being hunted. A giant serpent slithered out from beneath the wreckage of a collapsed tenement, winding across the ground with incredible speed as it pursued its prey.

Most of the humans had found shelter, but two remained exposed. A younger man stopped to help an older woman who had fallen, despite the danger.

The thing that had been Janice eagerly watched the horror that was about to transpire, when she was stricken.

The memories that filled her head with what she'd been—what she'd done—surfaced again, like a viral infection.

Janice leaped. Her wings sprang open to capture the air, and she glided down the street to where the great serpent was about to feast upon the two human stragglers. She landed atop the snake's speckled back, sinking her claws into its thick, muscular flesh.

The snake hissed, sending a stream of yellow venom from its fanged mouth out into the air.

Janice caught the eyes of the man and woman. "Run!" she ordered them. "You've cheated death this day."

The serpent spun around, attempting to throw her from its back, but she held firm. Digging her claws deeper into the monster's flesh, she tore away bloody chunks of meat until its bony spine was revealed.

The snake's movements became so violent that Janice was finally sent sprawling, rolling across the street, to rise in a crouch, as the snake came at her.

Janice was ready. She sprang toward the giant reptile and delivered a killing blow, plunging her claws into the serpent's lidless eyes.

She wriggled her knifelike appendages in its skull, feeling for the demonic animal's tiny brain, as the monster twitched violently, and then went still.

Pulling her razored fingers from the reptile's skull with a wet, sucking sound, Janice took a step backward, in awe of what she had done.

But panic quickly set in again. This was not what she had been reborn to do. Janice tilted her head back to call her brothers and sisters to her side. They would know what to do. They would help her.

"No need to cry out, sister," came a soothing voice from behind her.

Janice spun away from the serpent's corpse to see the most welcome of sights.

Her dark family was already there, striding toward her.

"Something has happened," she began to explain, holding her blood-covered hands out for them to see.

The Void Angel that had once been the Nephilim William observed her with his head cocked oddly to one side. "It appears so."

"I found two of the Nephilim. One of them . . . she did something to me . . ."

"What did she do?" Samantha asked from her place beside William.

"Did you kill them?" Kirk wanted to know. He stood by William's other side.

Russell had wandered over to the serpent, bending down to look into its ruptured eye. "I don't think she killed anyone," he said.

Janice tried to figure out how to explain. "It was like she put things inside my head . . . memories of what I used to be before . . ."

"Before the Dark Father brought us back from oblivion," William finished.

"Yes," Janice agreed. "We were fighting, and my claws connected with her blade of fire and . . ." It was as if she experienced it all again.

William and the others circled her as she collapsed to her knees.

"Yes," William said. "I can sense it in you now—a light where none should exist."

Janice looked up at them. "Melissa did this to me. She . . . she infected me."

"A disease," Samantha confirmed.

"Yes," Janice agreed. "She gave me a disease." Her entire body trembled, but she was glad that her family had come. They would help her to overcome this affliction of light. "Do you think there is a cure for such an illness?"

"We do," William said.

And before she could ask, to beg him to tell her what it was, he lunged at her, claws extended, and swiped them across her middle, tearing away her armor and the pale skin beneath.

Janice's hands immediately went to the gaping wounds to keep her insides from spilling out.

"Is that the cure?" Russell asked him.

"It is," William answered, without emotion.

And then they all attacked, claws ripping her flesh and spilling the darkness that gave her life upon the ground.

But their attack also released a light, the memories of her past as a force for good, as death came for her a second time.

A cure?

Yes, perhaps it was.

"We should have waited until she showed us where the Nephilim are," Samantha said, licking blood as black as pitch from her fingers.

William considered that as he stared down upon Janice's mutilated remains. "She said that she fought them."

"Yes," Kirk agreed. "She did at that."

William knelt to retrieve one of Janice's hands, which had been severed from its wrist. He examined the limb as the others watched him, fascinated.

"She fought them, tooth—and claw," he said, raising the hand, and more specifically the fingers, to his nose. He sniffed beneath the claws, then brought one of the fingers close to his mouth, where his tongue darted out to lick the still slightly elongated nail.

William smacked his lips, tasting what had been left

behind from Janice's struggles. Then he tilted his head back, sniffing the air, searching for, and finding, the scent.

"There you are," he said, leathery wings unfurling from his back. He gave a powerful leap and took to the sky.

The other Angels of the Void followed in his wake.

Vilma found herself slipping into a kind of fugue, as she stared through the tiny window into the missile silo, at the man she loved.

She was worried for Aaron but found her mind wandering, her eyes slowly closing.

An image was suddenly, inexplicably in her head.

It was Jeremy Fox, swords of fire in each hand, mouth open in a scream of war as he charged.

Vilma's eyes snapped open. Aaron no longer lay in the silo.

It was Jeremy.

Recoiling from the door, Vilma rubbed at her eyes, cautiously returning to see that it was still indeed Aaron Corbet inside the protective chamber, his body radiating with an unnatural light.

What was that all about? she wondered. She was furious with her mind. Maybe it was a lack of sleep or her concern for Aaron. She would have been lying if she said that her thoughts had never wandered to the volatile British youth, and what might have happened to him since fleeing the school.

But to think of him at this time . . .

An uncomfortable sensation formed in the pit of her stomach the more she thought of Jeremy. Vilma felt ashamed. Aaron was her boyfriend. How could she even think of anyone else?

Vilma steeled herself, erecting a mental barrier inside her mind with Jeremy on the other side. Then she brought her Nephilim power forward. Her wings emerged, and divine fire coursed through her veins.

"Is everything all right?" asked one of the Unforgiven.

She nodded. "I'm going in."

"Are you sure that's wise?" the angel protested. "With the levels of heat he's throwing off, you might not be able to withstand—"

"I'll be fine," Vilma interrupted, pulling back on the metal latch and opening the door.

The heat drove the Unforgiven angel back, but Vilma slipped inside the silo. She let the blistering heat envelop her, closing her eyes and surrendering to it.

She lowered herself beside Aaron. Reaching over, she took his limp body and pulled him into her embrace.

Holding him tightly, their heat became as one, and Vilma's prayers for Aaron's recovery were all that she would think about.

Jeremy had heard it spoken of as the red of battle, a mental state one reaches when fighting to survive. It was said that a scarlet haze would color one's vision in this state of combat.

Jeremy indeed saw red as he swung his swords, a relentless killing machine cutting down one attacker after the next. Except that the red staining his vision was the blood of his enemies that splashed his face.

He wanted to be sure that Enoch had escaped, just a quick look to satisfy his curiosity, but his attackers would have none of it. They came at him in droves, climbing atop the bodies of their fallen comrades to get at the Nephilim, cutting and stabbing him with their glinting daggers.

Jeremy did not stay in one place for long, constantly zigging and zagging across the parking lot. He used the abandoned cars in the lot for protection when he could, and jumped atop them to force his foes to climb to reach him. Their numbers were so great that they swarmed the vehicles like ants, so it gave him little advantage.

He couldn't fly very far with his damaged wing. Short bursts allowed him to leap about, but he could feel himself growing tired. And the more tired he became, the more he found himself suddenly thinking of her.

Vilma.

If he needed an incentive other than Enoch to keep on fighting, to survive and live another day, he couldn't think of anybody better.

Things couldn't possibly be so bad in a world with her in it.

Jeremy jammed one of his swords into the belly of another assassin, while using a shorter blade of fire to sever his head.

Thoughts of Vilma spurred him on, the prize waiting for him at the end of the contest.

Yeah, he wished, knowing full well that her heart belonged to Aaron.

The muscles in his arms and chest strained with every swing of his swords. He couldn't keep up his defense much longer. Their knives cut into him and drew blood. He healed quickly, but with all his wounds . . .

Jeremy called upon his inner divinity, creating a roiling ball of holy fire that he threw toward the attacking wave. The explosion tossed the aggressors away but propelled him back with its force.

He scrambled to his feet as he crafted his weapon of choice, an enormous battle-ax of hissing orange flame. He'd hoped that the explosion would buy him a little time to catch his breath, but he saw as the smoke cleared that an even larger contingent of foes swarmed toward the jagged crater he'd created.

His enemies came at him with vicious abandon. Unafraid to die.

As Jeremy fought, a strange, mechanical, whirring sound rose above the clamor of battle. Were his foes readying some new weapon? he wondered as he fought.

Jeremy turned and saw that he was no longer the only one fighting the black-garbed foes; others had joined the fray. They all wore long trench coats and circular goggles over their eyes.

From their backs large mechanical wings sprouted, which they used with deadly efficiency against their common foe. He had no idea who they were, or where they'd come from, but at that moment he couldn't care less, for they were fighting with him, rather than against.

His guard was lowered for a moment, and Jeremy paid the price. Multiple knives were driven into his body, and he dropped to the ground, his vision already beginning to blur.

This was not the way he wanted to die. Jeremy surrendered his battle-ax and crafted a shield of crackling fire. His opponents sensed his weakness, and their attack on him intensified.

Jeremy wished he had the strength to call out to his mysterious benefactors, but it was all he could do to remain conscious.

All he could do now to stay alive.

The faceless throng flowed over Aaron, all demanding to know—

Why didn't you save me?

Aaron tried to push them off, but there were too many, and he crumbled beneath the weight of them, their pleas making it impossible to think.

He wanted to tell them that he was sorry, that there was only so much that he—and the others—could do.

The Nephilim had done their best.

But it wasn't enough for the crowd—or for him, really.

Aaron caved beneath the weight of his guilt. Perhaps it was the punishment he deserved.

With that thought, the weight disappeared. Aaron slowly—ever so cautiously—opened his eyes and unwrapped his body from its tight ball.

He wasn't out in the darkness anymore, and knew that he was now behind the wall. Cautiously he climbed to his feet, soaking in his new environment. Aaron knew this place: Ravenchild Estates, a high-end housing development that had been abandoned after it was discovered that the homes had been built atop an illegal dumping site for hazardous chemicals.

Not too long after that, the fallen angels had moved in, using powerful magicks to keep themselves hidden from the angels known as the Powers, who were hell-bent on destroying them and their Nephilim offspring.

The fallen angels and Nephilim had made Ravenchild their home—their Aerie.

Aaron looked around at the abandoned houses and the empty streets. But he wasn't alone. In the distance, he could see the figure of a child sitting quietly in the middle of the road.

He was drawn toward the figure, his mind racing. The child rocked from side to side, as if to the beat of some inaudible tune.

The realization hit like a shot from a gun. He knew this child . . . this little boy.

"Stevie," Aaron said in a choked whisper, overwhelmed with emotion at seeing his autistic foster brother again.

Stevie had died on this street.

And Aaron had been his killer.

He stopped just before the child, something keeping him from getting any closer. Stevie paid him no mind, soft moans escaping his mouth as he moved to and fro, lost in a world all his own.

Aaron squatted down on his haunches. They hadn't been real brothers, not of flesh and blood, but Aaron had always felt that they'd had a deep connection, almost on a psychic level.

"Stevie," Aaron said, his voice trembling as he struggled to hold back the tears.

Remembering what he had done.

It hadn't been this defenseless child whom Aaron had struck down, but something far deadlier.

Stevie had been kidnapped by Verchiel and the Powers, when the angel warrior still believed that the Nephilim were an abomination to God. The Powers were determined to wipe them from the earth at any cost, and had transformed his foster brother into an armored killing machine called Malak.

"I am so sorry," Aaron said, watching the rocking child.

Then Stevie stopped his movement, slowly raising his head to look directly at Aaron with clear, focused eyes.

"Sad," Stevie said in his soft, unemotional voice.

"Yeah," Aaron agreed, feeling a tear roll down the length of his face. "Yeah, I am."

Stevie smiled, but there was nothing joyous in his expression; in fact, Aaron found it completely chilling.

"Good," the child said, beginning to rock again, and clapping his hands wildly. "Good. Good!"

Aaron rose and backed away, as all his self-preservation instincts came alive.

Stevie peeled away the skin of his seven-year-old self and shucked it away like an old blanket, revealing a red-armored monster hiding beneath.

"Good!" Malak screeched, leaping at Aaron, a spear appearing in his hands, the point aimed at his chest.

Aaron tripped on his own feet, falling to his side. He watched as the spear point plunged into the pavement, only narrowly missing him.

"Stevie," Aaron pleaded, pushing himself up from the ground as the armored warrior yanked his weapon from the street's grip. "I'm not going to allow this to happen again."

Malak charged.

This time Aaron was ready, lunging forward to grab hold of the spear. The power of the Nephilim came alive, filling Aaron's hands with divine fire, superheating the metal spear until it glowed and began to melt.

Malak savagely kneed Aaron's side. Aaron cried out, leaping back in pain. It felt like he'd broken a few ribs.

Malak tossed the melted spear aside and drew a sword from the air. It, too, was forged of a dark metal that glinted in the faint sunlight of the abandoned housing development.

"Please," Aaron begged.

Malak moved like a dangerous thought, sudden and swift. Aaron shrugged the powerful muscles in his shoulders, allowing his wings to emerge. He leaped from the path of Malak's sword, flying over his foster brother's head to land behind him.

"I don't want to do this," Aaron said desperately. He was painfully aware that this was all happening just like it had that day.

The day he'd killed his brother.

Malak spun around, his movements a blur despite the weight of the armor he wore. He charged at Aaron, the impact sending them both crashing to the ground.

Their struggles were ferocious. Malak no longer wielded a sword, but now had a black-bladed dagger that descended inexorably toward Aaron's face. The Nephilim twisted to one side, and the point of the blade stabbed into the ground. Aaron flexed his powerful wings, bucking his body and flipping Malak from atop him.

There wasn't a moment's hesitation from his foe as he recovered immediately, coming back at him. Aaron had no choice but to defend himself, calling on a weapon of his own. He pictured something large and majestic and watched as it grew to life in his hand, just in time to drive Malak back with a halfhearted swipe.

"I don't want to do this again," Aaron said with finality.

The blade burned brightly, and Malak stood back from the crackling yellow-and-orange fire.

Then he began to laugh.

It was an insane sound.

"You were supposed to protect us," Malak said from behind his mask. "Keep us from harm."

Aaron was about to protest when he saw the street filling with faceless figures.

"That was your purpose," Malak continued. "At first God thought you were a mistake, but then He saw your potential."

Malak's voice changed, becoming high and squeaky. "Hey, maybe the Nephilim aren't monsters at all. Maybe they'll be a force for good in the trying times to come."

The faceless throng gathered behind Malak.

"He was wrong, Aaron," Malak told him. For once, the voice behind the mask sounded incredibly rational. The armored figure reached up to remove his scarlet helmet, revealing the face of his preternaturally matured sibling.

This is who Stevie would have become if . . .

If I hadn't been forced to . . .

Aaron's sword of fire suddenly became so very, very heavy. It was all he could do to hold it aloft.

His brother was silent, as were the countless others, their accusations an enormous weight on his weapon.

"I never wanted to . . ."

Aaron didn't know what to do or say. He hadn't been born a hero, and as far as he knew, neither had the other Nephilim. It had been thrust upon them, whether or not they wanted the responsibility.

"I just wanted a good life," Aaron said. He gasped at a vision of another life, of his job, his wife . . . his son.

We were going to get a dog.

Aaron looked at his weapon with utter contempt.

"I don't want this."

The sword vanished, as did the wings upon his back. He could feel the sigils of power that adorned his flesh in times of battle gradually cooling and starting to fade.

"I never wanted any of this."

The faceless throng surged closer to Malak, their forms blending with the armored killer's, causing him to grow in stature.

Aaron stared, dumbfounded, at his brother, who now towered above him.

A monster consisting of Aaron's greatest failures.

"Admit it, the Lord God was wrong," the giant said in a chorus of booming voices.

"He was wrong," Aaron repeated dully.

"There is no place on this earth for the likes of you and your kind."

"There is no place." Aaron's voice was weak, filled with failure.

"Do you accept your fate?" the giant demanded to know.

Aaron was done, finished with it all. His despair overwhelmed his heart.

"Yes," he whispered.

Malak grabbed him with an enormous scarlet mitt, raising the Nephilim to his face.

Aaron did not struggle, his fate already sealed.

"Welcome to oblivion," the giant said, opening his mouth and tossing Aaron inside like a measly snack.

And everything was as it should have been.

Dusty sat at a small table inside the empty convenience store, eating a sandwich and contemplating the future.

"I wonder who Bob was," Gabriel said, nibbling at the dry dog food in front of him.

"Hmm?" Dusty questioned, momentarily distracted from his visions.

"I wonder who Bob was," Gabriel repeated, while munching his kibble.

"Bob?" Dusty asked.

"This store," Gabriel said. "Bob's Famous Foodmart."

"Oh." Dusty gazed out the filthy windows at the parking lot and the road sign for Bob's Famous Foodmart. "I don't know."

"Well, whoever he was, he had a nice store," Gabriel said. The dog moved his attention to his bowl of water, lapping loudly.

Dusty imagined the place before the Abomination of Desolation severed the earth's ties with Heaven and the world had become a nightmare. "Yeah," he said, picking up what was left of his cheese sandwich. "I'm sure it was a nice store."

"Do you think there will be a time when there are nice stores again?" the dog asked.

Dusty chewed a bite of sandwich, thinking of an appropriate answer. "Are you asking me if there will come a time when everything will return to the way it was?"

"I guess," Gabriel answered.

"Afraid not. The good old days are gone. But the future . . ." Dusty stared outside again, images of potential futures vying for position. "The future could be interesting." Dusty's heart started to race. "We have to leave," he said, standing and extending his hand.

Gabriel nuzzled his head against Dusty's waiting fingers. "Is the future calling?" the dog asked.

"It very well could be."

And then they were off.

CHAPTER NINETEEN

Satan had waited long enough.

He'd told the Sisters of Umbra his most special desires, and they had left to consider his requests.

He'd warned them that his impatience was a hungry thing, and it would serve them well to act swiftly, or they would be consumed by its voraciousness.

His anger at being kept waiting was further agitated by the fact that they'd put some sort of magickal lock on their door, in an attempt to prevent him from gaining entrance to their lair.

How dare they, he thought as he drew upon magicks far older and stronger than theirs to shred the barrier and allow him access.

His arrival was like the most destructive of storms. Satan emerged in all his fearsome glory, half expecting the Sisters to be cowering in fear at his coming. But what he found was far more disturbing and bothersome.

The bodies of dead yetis lay scattered about, their once-glowing forms dimming as they began to decay.

"What has happened here?" he asked, walking amongst the dead. He could sense a power here, one that was not part of the armored remains where the Sisters resided.

An ancient power. A divine power.

A power potentially dangerous to him.

Feeling unsettled, the Darkstar was about to retreat when he heard something alive amid the dead. He created a fearsome blade from the shadows of the chamber to vanquish any who hid in wait for him.

He heard the sound again. Carefully, he picked his way through the yeti corpses, toward the faint, gurgling sound. It was as if someone were trying to breathe through water—or blood.

Satan's keen, predatory eyes caught a hint of movement, and he took to the air, flying across the vast chamber.

He believed himself ready for anything, but nothing could have prepared him for what he saw—a large, fleshy mass with limbs sticking out haphazardly from its misshapen form.

"What manner of monstrosity . . . ," Satan began, as what might have been a head rose up from the body to fix him in a multi-eyed gaze.

"Dark . . . sssssssstar," it wheezed pathetically.

"What happened here?" Satan demanded, studying the horrendous form before him, knowing exactly what—who—it was.

The mass that had once been the Sisters of Umbra shuddered, its limbs flailing as it attempted to respond.

Satan knelt beside the horrible thing. "Tell me what did this to you." He leaned toward the twisted hole that he believed was a mouth.

There was no reply.

Satan became annoyed by the creature's pathetic efforts. "Is that the best you can do?"

Tears began to leak from the thing's eyes, and the Darkstar was repulsed. He could see that it did not have long to live.

"Did you do what I asked?" he pressed.

The fleshy monster quivered in an attempt to answer him, but Satan did not understand.

Which made him all the angrier.

"The passage . . . did you find me a way in which I and my armies can reach Heaven?"

Again it moaned, but it did not answer.

Satan looked deeply into its multiple eyes, searching for his answer.

"Yes," he hissed, allowing his weapon of shadow to dissipate, freeing both his hands to grasp the abomination's head. "I do believe I see what I'm looking for in there."

Satan tightly held the thrashing head with one hand,

while he pushed his fingers into the soft flesh around its eyes, penetrating its malformed skull. It took a moment of fishing, but his fingers caressed the wrinkled surface of the conjoined brains, and he smiled.

"I'll apologize in advance for the agony I'm likely to cause," Satan Darkstar said. "But know that I have truly appreciated your guidance, and for that I thank you."

Satan pushed his hand and most of his wrist into the brain's soft gray matter. The Sisters ceased their struggle, giving in to the Darkstar's unholy act. He allowed his power to flow, darkness leaking from his fingertips to spread throughout the gray matter.

The Darkstar absorbed all the Sisters' memories of the life they'd led before their transformation, and the countless years that followed after they'd been infused with the power of God.

So much accumulated experience . . . so much accumulated knowledge.

In an instant, Satan took from them all that they knew. All that made them what they were.

He pulled his hand free with a nauseating squelch and stared at his dripping fingers, clenching and unclenching them as if pumping the information through his own being. He saw how it all started for the Sisters of Umbra, right through to the very end.

And amidst all that, Satan found what he had been searching for—

As well as who had invaded the Sisters' dwelling.

Satan now knew where the attacker had gone with the power of God.

The power that Satan would require to rebuild the passage to Heaven.

Satan growled, spreading his wings and taking flight.

In pursuit of the power that was his destiny.

A power that would shake the very pillars of Heaven till it fell to ruin.

"What am I looking at?" Lorelei asked the ghostly, angelic being called A'Dorial.

"These are the plains of Megiddo," the angel said, gesturing to an aerial image of a desert that the angel spirit had conjured for them. "Humanity calls this region the Middle East."

"I'm guessing this place has something to do with the Ladder you've been talking about."

"It does," the angel said. "For this was where Beth-El was built."

"Beth-El?"

"The House of God."

"And this was where the Ladder was kept?" Lorelei asked.

A'Dorial considered the question. "Yes, in a way. You see, Beth-El is the Ladder."

Lorelei waited patiently for the angel to explain.

"Beth-El was erected in the early days of humankind, as the

place where Heaven and earth met. It was the prophet Jacob who gave it its other name, Jacob's Ladder. He was third in the line of patriarchs of Israel, on his way to the city of Haran to take a wife. At the end of his first day of travel, he laid his head down upon a stone in the valley and slept."

The aerial view shifted to what Jacob had seen in his visions.

"He dreamed that there was a ladder from earth, reaching to Heaven. He dreamed that the angels of God used it to ascend and descend."

"Was there really a ladder?" Lorelei asked.

"Not as you'd know it, but he processed his visions using references that were familiar to him."

The picture of divine beings flying to and from Heaven quickly morphed into another image. It looked to be a temple-like structure, shaped like a pyramid with its top cut off.

"What's that?"

"That is Beth-El after the fall of the Metatron," the angel explained. "Cold and lifeless. The direct path to Heaven cut off by God when the Metatron ceased to be. It is only with the Metatron's power that it can be restored."

"The Metatron," Lorelei said, remembering what she had learned of the powerful angelic being that was an extension of God upon the earth. "Where is its power now?"

A'Dorial grew thoughtful, his soft, ghostly wings drawing about his body as if to protect him from the cold. "It is an elusive thing, this power," he said finally. "And sought by many; the good, as well as the evil."

He paused. The scene again changed, and an image of the earth appeared. Lorelei was captivated by how tranquil it appeared from space, even though she was very aware of all that was happening on its surface.

"This power will determine the fate of the world," A'Dorial stated. "The fate of the living, as well as the dead."

Countless spectral shapes appeared before them.

So many had died with no place for their life energies to go.

"You will assist the forces of good," A'Dorial stated.

Lorelei agreed. "I will."

"You will help return things to the way they have always been. The energies of the dead must return to the source of all life . . . to the stuff of creation."

It was a huge responsibility, Lorelei knew, especially for somebody who was dead, but now she truly understood the importance of why she was still here.

Melissa and Cameron decided they would follow the map.

"Ready?" Melissa asked. She was still seated at the tiny table with the old box. She had read Cameron's father's journals, marveling at the history that was expressed there, but the most fascinating aspect had been the map, and what they would find if they followed it.

Cameron stood in the center of the room, looking around the cabin as if memorizing every inch.

"Yeah, I'm good," he said. "Any idea where we're going?"

Melissa stood, the map in her hand. She stared at the yellowed paper and pointed to an area near its center. "We're going right here."

"How are we going to get there?" Cam asked.

"Weren't you paying attention in those classes with Aaron and Vilma, when they were showing our Nephilim powers?"

"I paid attention," Cameron snapped at her defensively.

"Well, obviously not that closely when we were learning about traveling."

"What's to know? You picture where you want to go, or Lorelei would put an image in our heads."

"That's one way," Melissa said, still studying the lines and drawings on the map.

"There's another?"

"See, not paying attention."

"Screw you."

She laughed, and closed her eyes to see the surface of the map in her mind. "Aaron said that there were other ways to travel. Like reading maps and studying photographs."

Cameron made a disgusted face. "How do we do that?"

"Well, maps are made to show us where something is in the world, and photographs are moments frozen in place and time," she explained. "Look, the map shows a particular place in relation to the world. We know of it by looking at where it is."

"I'm not sure that I . . ."

Melissa sighed, striding toward her friend. "Well I'm willing to give it a try," she said firmly.

"Have you ever done this before?"

She could not help but smile. "I wanted to go to China," she said.

"And did you?"

"I ended up at a Chinese restaurant in San Francisco."

"What went wrong?" Cameron asked.

Melissa shrugged. "I didn't know what I was doing."

"And you do now?"

"No." She shook her head. "But I'm willing to try. There's too much at stake not to."

That seemed to sink in.

"You're right," Cameron agreed. "So, what do we do?"

Melissa moved closer to him, flexing the muscles in her back and calling upon her wings.

"Let me drive," she told him.

She wrapped her wings around them both, while staring at the map to make sure she remembered every detail. She'd always known that those rainy-day recesses, playing with the world globe, would someday pay off.

"This makes me incredibly nervous," Cameron said, avoiding Melissa's gaze.

"What, the traveling or being this close to me?"

Their eyes locked for a second, before he looked away again.

That was interesting, Melissa thought, before quickly taking control of the moment.

She closed her eyes, picturing the ancient map. Closing her wings tighter about Cameron, she felt that odd sensation that she experienced when traveling great distances.

When traveling from here—

—to there.

They appeared in a rush of warm, tropical air, the ground beneath their feet loose.

Melissa opened her wings and gasped at the beauty of it. They were on the side of a rocky mountain island, surrounded by nothing but white, billowing clouds and deep-blue sea.

Cameron tried to maneuver for a better view.

"Where are we?" he asked, just as a large section of the rock he was standing on crumbled, and he fell.

Melissa grabbed for him, but only brushed her fingertips against his before he disappeared from view, obscured by the clouds that drifted about the mountain.

"Cameron!" she cried out. She waited, listening past the rushing winds and water, searching for a sign of her friend.

Something moved below, exploding upward at a tremendous speed.

She couldn't help but smile as she watched Cameron bank around, his powerful wings beating the air.

"For a minute I thought you might've forgotten how to fly," she said, as she moved to give him space on the ledge beside her.

"I wasn't asleep during all our classes," he teased. "This place is beautiful. Any idea where it is?"

"Tristan da Cunha," Melissa said. "It's in an archipelago in the South Atlantic Ocean." She squinted her eyes, looking out over the water. "The nearest land is South Africa."

Cameron stared at her.

"What?"

"How do you know all that?" he asked, admiration in his tone.

Melissa considered the question, realizing that she had no idea. She just did. "Special Nephilim powers," she said with a wink. There was still so much to learn about what they were. She just hoped that between saving the world and keeping it from being consumed by darkness, they would get the chance.

She glanced at the map, then up the mountain. "I think we have to go up there," she said. "There should be an entrance."

"Meet you there." Cameron spread his wings and took flight.

Melissa followed. Together, they surveyed the rocky surface for an opening that would take them inside the mountain.

"Is that it?" Cameron asked, flapping his powerful wings as he hung in the air.

She didn't see it at first. The entrance was thin, like so many of the other cracks and crevices in the mountainside.

"I think it is," she said as the two flew in closer.

There was no place to perch this time. The entrance to the cave would have been accessible to only the most experienced mountain climbers, or those who could fly.

"After you." Cameron gestured for her to go in first.

"When did you become such a gentleman?" she asked, ducking her head.

"When I realized that there might be booby traps."

Melissa smacked him as she passed. "Jerk."

She pretended to be annoyed, but it was good to be with someone. She liked having another person to watch her back and share in the adventure. She'd missed that since the Nephilim had disbanded, and wondered if they would ever be close like that again.

There were no traps inside the cave, but there was a pretty substantial drop. Melissa peered down into the darkness. "Well, shall we?"

"We've come this far, might as well."

"Shall we go together?" she asked, hoping the closeness wouldn't scare him away.

"Sure," he said. "Ready?"

They leaped at the same time, their wings fanning out behind them to slow their descent, flames of divine fire in their hands to light the way. After a moment, a bridge of stone appeared below them, and they touched down upon it.

Cameron looked around. "Which way?"

Melissa listened. At first she thought she heard the sound of running water, but as she tuned in, she became convinced that it was something altogether different.

Something mechanical.

"Do you hear that? Like the hum of a machine or something," she said. "Sounds like it's coming from down here."

She started to walk along the bridge, Cameron right beside her.

It was dark up ahead, and she held out her hand to create a weapon of fire, primarily for illumination, but also just in case.

Cameron also created a weapon. "You okay?"

"Yeah. I'm good."

"I missed this," he said, almost shyly. "Y'know, getting into things with somebody else. Being alone surrounded by monsters was getting kinda boring."

She was going to tell him how glad she was that they had found each other again, and that maybe—

Cameron's arm shot across her middle, stopping her cold.

"Why did you do—," she began, lifting her sword to light the path before her—or lack there of. The stone bridge came to an abrupt stop.

"Sorry to hit you in the stomach," Cameron said.

"That's all right," she answered. "I would have looked pretty stupid falling."

"Yeah, you would have." Cameron held his sword up to

illuminate what was above them. "I think there's something up there."

Melissa used her divine fire to shape a bow and arrow. She shot a flame into the air above them. The arrow stuck in a section of the stone, and the flare shed light on a metal door in the wall at least fifty feet above them.

"Would you look at that," Cameron said.

"This has to be it," Melissa said excitedly, allowing the bow to disintegrate, though the divine arrow continued to burn.

"Just like the entrance," Cameron said, flexing his wings. "Only way to get there is to fly."

Melissa jumped, her wings carrying her up to flutter before the door.

"Doesn't seem to be any way to open it," she said.

Cameron joined her, darting around, inspecting every aspect of the heavy door, but realizing that she was right.

Melissa laid a hand on the metal. Cameron followed suit, placing his own hands against the cold metal surface.

They heard it first, the grinding of gears, and they flew back as the circular door swung open on its own.

"Did you do something?" Cameron asked, bewildered.

"I think maybe we both did," she said.

Melissa flew through the entryway, landing just inside. The mechanical humming became all the more prominent inside the stone cavern.

"Last chance to leave," Cameron said, watching as the door slammed closed behind them. "Too late."

"Wouldn't want you in here all alone anyway," Melissa said to him. "You might get into trouble."

"I was thinking the same about you."

It was dark, and Melissa again called upon a sword of fire to light their way. "Might as well have a look around."

They'd gotten maybe five feet inside, when the chamber was illuminated by rows of small circles of white light.

A scene of past carnage lay before them.

Melissa and Cameron stopped, their eyes locked on the skeletal remains. Desiccated bodies were strewn about the floor. There were at least six of them, their bones yellowed with age and covered with the dust of time and cobwebs.

"What . . . what happened here?" Melissa asked.

"A fight," Cameron said. He approached the corpses, walking slowly around them. "Some of the bones have been broken, like they've been cut with a sword."

Melissa drew closer to Cameron as he reached for something amidst the bones.

Cameron pulled a large feather from the remains. "I think they were angels."

Melissa looked around. There were many feathers amongst the bones. She shuddered, giving the pile of the dead a wide berth as she continued farther into the chamber.

Which revealed yet another startling sight.

A large chair, a throne really, dominated the space. Sitting in the chair were the remains of an armored angel, slumped forward, his armor filthy with the passing of time. His wings, furled tightly upon his back, looked as though they'd been draped with sheets, spiders having wrapped them in thick white webbing.

"Who do you think this is?" Melissa whispered.

"I don't have a clue," Cam answered. "But he is in one piece, and sitting in the big chair." He turned his gaze back to the pile of dead. "I'd say he was the winner of the fight."

The corpse shifted. Melissa thought it was a trick of the eye, the soft lighting playing upon the armor. But then the corpse sprang from the throne, its web-enshrouded wings opening with a powerful rush as his armored form flew at them.

A sword of fire came to life in the ancient angel's hand as he landed, slashing first at Melissa—who barely had the time to create her own sword to block the savage strike—before he launched himself at Cameron.

"Melissa!" Cameron cried out, already locked in battle with the armored angel.

"I'm all right," Melissa answered, rushing to his aid.

The armored angel was relentless. He slashed at them, putting them on the defensive. There was no doubt now that this being was responsible for the pile of corpses.

The skin of the angel's face was practically translucent, like parchment paper, with a gray mustache and beard, but it was his eyes that truly captivated her attention. They were like two LED lights floating in pools of oil.

Cameron sprang into the air, and as he did, wished his sword into an enormous battle mace. He brought the spiked mace down upon the attacking angel's weapon with a thunderous clamor, driving the angel back.

Melissa saw her opportunity and lunged. She drove the tip of her sword into the angel's armored side, causing an explosion of energy that hurled her and Cameron back.

Dots of multicolored Christmas lights danced before her eyes as she fought to regain her composure. She had landed atop the pile of skeletal remains, but she was determined not to meet the same fate. Jumping up, she called out to Cameron.

"We can't let him recover," Melissa said, already wielding another sword of fire and making her way toward their foe, who had been knocked onto his back beside his throne.

Cameron agreed, following her closely.

The armored angel got to his knees and examined the hole in the left-hand side of his armor. Their shadows fell across him, as they prepared to strike him down.

"It takes a great deal of power to do this extent of damage," the angel spoke in a voice as dry as dust, sticking his mail-covered finger into the hole and moving it around.

The angel then turned his eyes on them.

Cameron came at him, sword above his head, poised to

bring the burning blade down in a lethal blow, when Melissa stopped him.

"Wait!"

Cameron stopped, confused.

The angel smiled. "A great deal of power indeed," he reiterated, studying them both. "A mating pair. Of course . . ."

He grunted as he hauled his armored body to his feet, using the arm of the great throne for support.

"Now, which one of you would care to explain how you got out of your cages?"

The power of God in his hands, Mallus struggled to keep his footing as he made his way back to the surface.

The surviving mutated yetis were hot on his heels. As he fled, he'd slow to turn and point the sphere of divine energy at them, releasing destructive blasts to drive them back. But the side effects did not last long. They were practically breathing down his neck.

Mallus could feel the temperature in the tunnel growing colder and knew that he was getting close to the surface.

"I didn't think we'd get this far," Mallus said to the ball. It seemed to respond to his statement, its color shifting to a softer shade.

He believed that the Malakim was still present here. He'd reverted to pure energy in order to contain God's power, though he retained some level of sentience. That was what

Mallus liked to believe. After so many years of solitude, he'd enjoyed Tarshish's company and didn't care to be alone.

Especially when on the run from an army of yetis.

As the passage's incline became more dramatic, he knew that he was almost there. Careful with his footing, Mallus increased his speed, watching as the sky appeared through the melted, circular opening just ahead.

The yetis yowled with fury. They knew his escape was imminent. Mallus considered blasting them again but did not want to slow his pace.

No, he would push on, striving for the murky light just above him.

Mallus could smell the yetis' filthy stink as they bore down upon him. He pushed himself, wishing more than any other time that he still had his wings so he might fly from their desperate clutches.

But the fates, or perhaps it was the power of God, saw fit to aid him. The passage grew narrower as he climbed upward, and the throng of yetis—so desperate to claim their prey—were stuck in a logjam of seething fury.

Mallus sprang from the opening, falling to his knees, the sphere of radiance slipping from his grasp. The ball of divine energy rolled across the ground, then came to a sudden stop. Around it, the layers of ice and snow melted away.

"I should be thankful that thing isn't fragile," Mallus remarked, getting up to retrieve the sphere.

Now came the hard part, he thought. Tarshish had been their transportation. What now?

Mallus looked around at the frozen wasteland of the Himalayas.

The yetis exploded up from the earth, searching for their prey. Even though the sun barely shone, Mallus could see that they were not accustomed to the brightness of being aboveground. They slowed, shielding their eyes from the murky light.

Mallus began to run, hoping he'd find some kind of cover to hide him until he could devise a plan.

The yetis, catching sight of their prize on the run, immediately forgot their fear of the surface and swarmed in pursuit of him.

The snow slowed Mallus's progress. He held the sphere out before him, to melt a path. But if he melted a path for himself, he also melted a passage for his pursuers.

Mallus chanced a quick look behind him, and did not like what he saw. The yetis were gaining. It was only a matter of seconds before they would overtake him.

Deciding to use a blast of God's power to buy himself a little more time, Mallus turned and aimed the ball.

The ground around them began to shake, and something exploded upward in a shower of ice and rock to hang in the frigid air.

The yetis paused, fearfully looking about to see what could

have caused the earth to quake so violently. Mallus used the diversion to make his escape.

"Where is it?" boomed a powerful voice across the icy expanse. "Where is what has been stolen from me?"

Mallus's first instinct as a warrior of Heaven was to fight, to throw himself at the enemy, and to take him down by any means. But he knew that it couldn't be like that, especially if the world was to survive. He needed to protect his prize and escape by any means necessary.

The armored figure that had exploded up from the ground loomed above the white landscape. It swooped down upon the yetis, its wings of black decimating their ranks with a mere swipe.

"Where is it?" he bellowed as the few surviving creatures cowered.

Mallus had managed to find cover behind an outcropping of ice and snow, and considered his options—which were pretty much none.

The hairs on the back of his neck stood up. Mallus grasped the sphere in both hands and spun, ready to fire a blast of divine fury at his attacker, but was taken aback by the sight of a young man in a baggy sweat suit. And a yellow dog.

It took a moment for his brain to shake off the shock. He knew these two.

"Where did you come from?" Mallus asked.

"Long story," the dog named Gabriel barked.

"Will you come with us?" Dusty asked.

Mallus could feel evil approaching them, and he looked at them both with desperate eyes.

"You won't have to ask me twice," he said, the sphere of God power growing bright as the sun in his grasp.

CHAPTER TWENTY

There was nothing—and that was exactly what Aaron wanted.

He didn't want to feel the pain of failure anymore, the disappointment of all who had suffered because he wasn't good enough.

Nothing was exactly what he deserved.

But suddenly, he was disturbed by the strangest sensation.

Something cold touched his nose, pulling Aaron back from the void. He opened his eyes to find two beady eyes staring at him, and a pink nose twitching.

It was a mouse, and Aaron remembered that his name was Milton.

"What are you . . . ," Aaron began, as a hand reached into his field of vision and scooped the mouse away.

Aaron rolled onto his back and looked up into the face of his father.

"Hello, Aaron," Lucifer said, placing the rodent on his shoulder. "I'm sorry to see you here."

"Is that you?" Aaron asked, recalling the last time he had seen his father. He had plunged a sword of darkness into the Nephilim's chest. "Are you *you* now?"

"In this place, I am," Lucifer said. "But out there . . ." The Morningstar looked out into the perpetual shadow. "I'm afraid that I'm still not in control."

Aaron sat up with a grunt, his every muscle protesting the movement. It felt as though he'd been lying inert for weeks.

"What happened to you?" Aaron demanded.

"Let's just say I let my guard down," Lucifer explained. "I let my guard down and a very old, very powerful evil took root inside my body."

"The Darkstar," Aaron said, remembering the name he'd heard from a goblin warrior.

"Satan, the Darkstar," Lucifer corrected.

"But I thought that you were . . ."

"Satan? Never took the title, despite what others have said throughout the ages. But now he's taken over my body and turned me into the monster that legend made me out to be."

"We have to stop him," Aaron said, rising to his feet. "We have to get you back."

"Yes," Lucifer agreed. He reached up and gently petted the

mouse perched on his shoulder. "But I think we need to deal with you first."

"Me?" Aaron asked, surprised. "There's nothing wrong with—"

"He's inside you," Lucifer said, touching Aaron in the center of his chest.

Aaron winced, the pain suddenly excruciating.

"When you were stabbed, he planted a seed of darkness in your soul."

The skin on Aaron's chest burned, and he ripped open his shirt to reveal a large, jagged, black circle in the center of his chest.

"What is this?" he asked his father in surprise.

"The seed is growing."

"How do I—" Aaron dropped to the ground, bent over with agony.

"The darkness always leaves a piece of itself behind, to fester and grow. It's preventing you from healing. It's feeding on your courage, making you doubt who you are—what you are."

Aaron mustered a short laugh through his pain. "That's where you're mistaken," he choked. "I'm not at all who you think I am or what I'm supposed to be."

"You're wrong," Lucifer countered. "You're special, Aaron. Capable of so much more than you even realize."

"I've failed in just about everything that I've tried to do."

"And that's how the darkness wins," Lucifer scolded. "You

might've failed at some things, here and there, but they're only minor pieces of the whole plan."

Lucifer knelt down, placing a firm hand upon Aaron's shoulder. "The victor of the battle is yet to be determined."

Aaron looked down worriedly at his chest. The black mark was growing larger. "How can I stop this?"

Lucifer's grip on Aaron's shoulder intensified, and his eyes bored into his son's. "Deep inside you is the strength of many."

Aaron felt a new sensation within his chest. "My skin!" He tore off his shirt, which had started to smolder, to burn. His sigils were prominent, blazing red, superheated from within his body. "What's happening?"

"Those marks," Lucifer stated, pointing to the designs on Aaron's skin. "Each represents a warrior of Heaven who fell in service to me—to my misguided cause—during the war with Heaven."

Aaron gazed down upon his chest. The sigils surrounded the circle of black, seemingly stopping its advance.

"These marks give you a portion of the power that those soldiers gave to me when they swore their allegiance."

Aaron could feel the divine fires burning within him.

"My destiny," he said.

"You will save the fallen, and realign the world with Heaven."

"My destiny," Aaron repeated, rising to his feet as his body crackled with energy.

"The creature that possesses my flesh—Satan Darkstar—has certain plans for Heaven," Lucifer told him. "Plans that must be deterred. But before any of this can happen, you must leave this place."

Aaron's wings exploded from his back. Lucifer seemed to grow smaller, but then Aaron realized that he was growing larger.

"You have to defeat the darkness," Lucifer called up to Aaron. "Not only out there . . ." He gestured toward the outside world, then pointed to his own chest. "But in here."

Aaron towered above his father. "Are you real?" he asked. "Or are you just another manifestation of my subconscious?"

"Does it really matter?" Lucifer asked, turning with a wave before disappearing behind a curtain of black.

Aaron considered the question, turning his eyes up to the pinprick of light above him. He extended his arms toward the growing light. It had been so long since he had seen light.

The passage of shadow, up toward the light, grew smaller—more constricted—the harder he tried to reach it.

His wings flapped mightily, until there was no more room for them to move. He sank his fingers into the darkness of the tunnel walls and hauled himself upward, closer, and closer still.

And then the passage began to move, thrashing and undulating as if caught within some sort of powerful storm.

But Aaron held on, bracing himself with his legs and feet, while he continued to climb, inch by inch, until the opening was just above him. He was feeling weaker the closer he came, but the sigils upon his flesh blazed hotly, reminding him once more of what they represented. Their power helped to spur him on.

He climbed into a tiny chamber, a wall of white tile all that stood between Aaron and his freedom. He hauled back his fist, punching at the barrier. But it did not break. The confining space continued to shake, dislodging him from his perch and sending him tumbling back down into the constricting passage.

Aaron scrambled back up and punched at the tiles again, this time with a furious scream. The sigils flared upon his skin, illuminating the confined space. The surface beneath him was wet, soft, and pink, and quivered at his assault.

The chamber shook violently again, and he could feel something in the passage below him. It was as if something had come up from below him and was attempting to pull him back down into the darkness.

Aaron's anger flared, the sigils igniting. Actual flames of divine fire leaped from the names, and Aaron felt their warriors' fury and again pulled back his fist, and with a cry of utter determination delivered a blow shattering the tiles outward in a shower of ivory.

Aaron shot into the daylight and landed on the ground of Aerie.

Crouched on the ground, he watched the giant Malak stumble back, hands going to his shattered teeth.

The knowledge that he'd been inside Stevie hit him like a slap, and for a moment Aaron felt pangs of sympathy for the injured and moaning giant, before his Nephilim spirit again usurped his feelings with its unbridled fury.

Aaron crouched down, calling upon a sword of fire.

Lucifer's words whispered in his ear, as the armored giant roared through jagged and broken teeth, charging at Aaron.

You have to defeat the darkness.

Malak pulled his arm back as he ran, a sword of ebony black taking shape in his grasp.

Aaron sprang from the ground, flying directly at the distorted visage of his little brother. He swung his own blade of fire directly at Malak's face, striking the giant in the side of the head in a shower of sparks.

There was a sudden flash, and Aaron was thrown back to the ground, the impact of his body shattering the street beneath him. He rose, shaking off the rubble to resume his battle.

Not only out there . . . Aaron heard Lucifer's voice say.

He looked down to his bare chest, at the circular black mark, and found that it had grown smaller.

But in here.

In his thoughts Aaron saw Lucifer touch the center of his chest, showing him where the most corrosive darkness existed.

And with that Aaron understood exactly what needed to be done.

Through the wafting dust and smoke, he heard the sound

of a child in distress. Instinctively Aaron advanced to help, but stopped when he saw his foster brother sitting in the center of the street, crying pitifully.

"You killed us, Aaron," Stevie cried, tears streaming down his face. "You did nothing to protect us, and so we died."

Aaron felt a tightening in his chest as his black mark grew a little larger.

The faceless unsaved appeared again behind the crying child, and they, too, began to wail.

"God put you here for a purpose," Stevie said. "But you failed him, Aaron." Stevie's eyes fixed him with a glacial stare. "You failed us all."

The darkness inside Aaron started to churn. But he would have none of it.

The sigils burning on his skin, he reached for his chest, sinking his fingers into the skin around the dark mark, taking hold of the darkness and ripping the cancerous mass from his body.

"What have you done?" Stevie screamed. "What have you done?"

Aaron willed the divine fires into his hand and watched the darkness be consumed by the fires of light. Stevie ran at him, the seven-year-old transforming into an armored engine of hate.

Aaron understood now that victory was not to be judged by the tiny failures, but how the final battle was fought.

A battle that could only be fought without self-doubt.

Malak bellowed, his voice echoing from within the scarlet helmet he wore. His hands had become like knives, long and razor sharp, ready to cut flesh from bone.

Aaron fashioned a sword unlike any other he'd made, as if it had been forged in the fiery passions of God's heart.

He'd carried the guilt of what he had done to Stevie for so long, allowing it to fester deep inside him.

Allowing it to grow.

He'd given that guilt a certain strength, a power over him, and now he knew that it was time to let it go. To accept what he had done. It was a necessary loss. If he had to do it again, there would be no choice.

"What. Have. You. Done?" Malak's claws were ready to rip Aaron's still-beating heart from his chest.

But it wasn't to be.

Aaron pivoted at the waist, God's blade of heavenly fire held tightly in his grasp, cutting through his foe's armored neck, severing the helmeted head from its body. He watched the head spin in the air, as Malak's armored form crumpled like a marionette whose strings had been cut.

The head continued to spin in space. All around them grew dark and cold. The head burst into flame, and in that flame, Aaron saw a face.

A beautiful face that called his name.

"Aaron."

He grinned, for not only had he been delivered from darkness—

But he had been delivered into the arms of the one whom he loved with all his heart and soul.

"Vilma," he whispered.

Enoch ran across the mall's parking lot and into the woods as fast as his legs would carry him.

He was bigger now, stronger, and it was all because of the memories that had been restored to him.

Enoch knew exactly why he had been sent back to earth—and what God had told him to do. But in order to fulfill God's commandment, he needed to get away. No matter how much it pained him to leave Jeremy behind, he had to escape. Without him alive, the world, and all of God's creatures, would meet a terrible fate.

Enoch was amazed at how sure he was of his body. No longer being a toddler made it that much easier for him to run. He had outgrown his shoes and was running barefoot, cautious not to step on anything sharp and injure himself.

The black-suited assassin appeared out of nowhere.

Enoch screamed, struggling with his foe, but even though he had grown, he was no match for his preternatural opponent.

The attacker moved to pin him, but Enoch flailed his arms, grabbing at the figure's black mask and twisting it violently, before it came away in his hands. He was stunned by his attacker's apelike visage. Its yellow eyes glinted as it snarled, showing off a pronounced set of canine teeth.

Enoch had readied himself for a terrible fate, when his attacker bent down and sniffed at the child's face and body. Still pinning Enoch to the ground with its superior strength, the apelike creature reared back, eyes twinkling—as if it had learned something from Enoch's scent.

The creature emitted a terrible howling sound and hauled him up from the ground. Enoch struggled as he was dragged back toward the mall parking lot, but his efforts were fruitless. The creature simply picked him up and placed him under its arm as it barreled through the woods.

He was in a panic, thrashing his arms and legs wildly, when suddenly Enoch found himself falling. His attacker dropped beside him, lifeless, a knife—no, it was a metal feather—sticking out from its apelike face. The child scrambled away from the body, only to be stopped by a figure in a long coat, with huge wings.

Huge metal wings.

"Who?" the child asked, as the angelic figure loomed above him.

"Child of God," the man said, "I know of you and have sworn to help restore the Metatron."

Enoch could not believe his ears. "You know me?" he asked excitedly.

The strange angel stiffened, his head flying back in a silent scream. All Enoch could do was watch in terror as he collapsed, dead.

Three more of the masked assassins walked toward him, knives in hand, and Enoch spun around to escape.

Only to run directly into the arms of another killer, who had come up on him from behind.

Satan Darkstar had returned to space.

The Lord of Shadows floated above the earth's atmosphere, studying his prize.

He should have been happy—satisfied—taking it all away from God and from humanity itself.

But this was just one small victory. The battle that he foresaw gnawed at him like a wolf chewing on a bone.

It seems so small now, Satan thought of his prize.

The Sisters' memories were fresh in his mind. The ancient power that had been in their possession for so very, very long provided him with tantalizing glimpses of how to make his desires a reality.

A being of tremendous power, the Metatron, had been sent from Heaven to the world of man. The Metatron had been given a special path to come and go as he pleased, but this thoroughfare had been closed off when the being met with a horrible fate.

But though it was closed, the door remained.

All he needed was the key to open it.

Satan felt his ire rise. He had lost God's power in the Himalayas, but surely there were other keys. Keys that if used correctly could perform the function that he required.

What did the humans call them? These special keys? Skeleton keys.

He would use a skeleton key. He would replace the power of God that had been given to the Metatron with another power of similar strength.

Now where could something of equal divine power be found? Satan Darkstar thought as he floated in the vacuum of space. A cruel smile teased the corners of his angelic visage, for he already knew the answer.

This body he had stolen. There was power unlike any other deep inside it. A power that had been created by an act of supreme defiance—

When this creation challenged its Creator.

As a punishment for this act of insolence, the Creator took all the pain and misery that had been created from Lucifer's defiant act and placed it inside His rebellious creation.

Lucifer would endure the hell of what he had done to remind him of his sins against his Creator, his Holy Father.

Satan Darkstar felt the energy churn inside him, a reminder of what existed at this body's core.

Hell was inside him: a power to rival that of God and Heaven.

This would be his skeleton key.

Satan opened his wings of black and dropped back down into the atmosphere, through the thick shroud of clouds, to the world—

His world.

Waiting below.

There was much to do before the conquest of Heaven. He needed to call upon his troops.

He needed to gather his armies, for there was a war soon to be fought.

CHAPTER TWENTY-ONE

Vilma wasn't sure how much more her body could take. The room had become like the surface of the sun, or at least what she imagined the surface of the sun to feel like.

Aaron's body was white hot, his skin covered with the glowing angelic sigils that were his birthright.

"I love you so much," she whispered in his ear, as she held him tightly. Her own skin tingled painfully, on the verge of blistering. "Please, come back to me."

Aaron's body grew hotter still.

"Can you hear me? I need you. The world needs you."

Vilma could no longer bear the searing heat. She released her hold on him—the hardest thing she had ever done.

He burned so brightly now that she could barely look at

him, and had to raise a hand to shield her eyes. "Aaron!" she cried desperately.

She knew that the Unforgiven were waiting right outside the chamber door, ready to release her as soon as she was ready. But not yet; she wanted to be with him for as long as she could, in case it was the last time she would ever be by his side.

The concrete walls began to crack and disintegrate, falling away in huge, dry chunks.

The heat finally became more than she could stand. It was time. Her heart breaking, she turned away from the man she loved and gestured for the Unforgiven to open the door. It would do no one any good if she were dead. There was still a battle to fight, an enemy to be defeated.

And if Aaron could not be there to lead them, she would act in his place.

Vilma heard a noise behind her, and suddenly, the blinding radiance was gone. She spun around to see a naked Aaron kneeling on the broken floor, his majestic ebony wings spread wide. The sigils that had blazed red on his pale skin were once again black. He was conscious and looking at her, his mouth struggling to move.

"I . . . I hear you," he said through trembling lips. "And I need you, too."

Aaron pitched forward, and she darted across the chamber

to catch him as he fell. He grunted in her arms as she lowered him to the floor. His wings furled, disappearing beneath the flesh of his back, and the sigils began to fade.

"Hello!" Vilma cried toward the door. "Help us, please!"

Aaron tried to raise his hand, to touch her face. "I missed you so much," he whispered.

She couldn't contain herself. She leaned down and kissed him passionately on the lips. His soft flesh was still hot, but she didn't mind.

She heard the clanking of the door mechanism and the creak of the hinges as two of the Unforgiven technicians entered the room, clad in their heavy, heat-resistant outfits.

"He seems to be awake now," she told them. "We need to get him back to the infirmary as quickly as—"

"No," Aaron said, trying to push away from her.

"Aaron," Vilma said, trying to be stern. "You've been in a coma for the last three weeks. You can't—"

"Have to," he interrupted. He stumbled slightly but managed to stand. "I think I'm good," Aaron said, gently poking the puckered scar in the center of his chest. "The darkness inside . . . it's gone."

Taylor abruptly pushed past the two technicians. She stopped cold as her eyes fell on her naked son. "Oh God," she whispered, her body beginning to tremble.

Aaron's gaze quickly went to Vilma, and then back to the dark-haired woman who headed toward him.

But Vilma said nothing, watching as Taylor threw her arms around the young man.

"I've waited so very long for this day," Taylor cried, her voice muffled as she spoke into his neck. "The day I would finally get to hold you."

Aaron's face wore a look of shock, then slowly relaxed into one of understanding. Vilma had no doubt in her mind that he instinctively knew who this woman was, as he threw his arms around her.

Taylor was the first to pull away. She reached up and took his face in her hands, staring at him in wide-eyed wonder.

"You're my mother," Aaron said, his voice as soft as a feather.

Vilma felt her eyes begin to tear at their raw emotion.

"I am," Taylor said. "And you're my son."

An Unforgiven angel came into the chamber with blankets, handing one to Vilma, and then to Aaron.

Vilma nearly laughed out loud when she saw Aaron's realization that he was naked in front of her and his mother.

He quickly pulled the blanket around himself.

"I always believed I would have so much to say to you, but now . . . ," Aaron trailed off.

"We'll have plenty of time to catch up." Taylor reached out to stroke his arm lovingly.

But will they? Vilma suddenly wondered as a grim-faced Levi entered the silo.

Taylor turned her adoring gaze away from her son. "Levi," she acknowledged, the joy on her face draining as she saw his expression.

"We lost him," the Unforgiven leader said woefully. "We lost the child."

The ancient angel appeared distracted.

"That will never do, never do at all," he muttered to himself, seeming to forget that Melissa and Cameron were even there. He turned abruptly then, heading deeper into the darkened chamber.

Melissa looked to Cameron. He appeared just as confused as she was. He shrugged, and they began to follow the angel as he continued to mumble to himself.

The chamber grew larger the deeper they went; the inside of the mountain had been hollowed out to create this vast space.

Melissa stopped, taking it all in as the lighting grew brighter, and she attempted to understand.

"What is this place?" she wondered aloud.

The walls on either side of the room were honeycombed with what looked to be frosted, podlike chambers. There had to be at least a hundred of them, probably more.

The armored angel spread his wings, which got an immediate rise out of Cameron, who created a sword of fire—just in case.

But the angel didn't seem in the least bit concerned. He

flew his armored body up and around the frosted containers, examining one after the other.

"What are those things?" Cameron asked, still clutching his blade.

"I'm not sure," Melissa answered, attempting to see behind the frost. Her thoughts kept replaying what the angel had called them, a mating pair, and that he'd asked how they had escaped from their cages.

The angel dropped in front of them, and Cameron crouched, ready to fight.

The angel just looked confused. "They're all there," he said, bringing an armored finger to his pale, lined face and tapping at his chin. "All accounted for, but if they're all . . ." It was as if he suddenly remembered that Melissa and Cameron were there with him. "Who are you?" the angel asked, a sword of shifting golden colors in his hand.

"We could be asking the same of you," Melissa spoke up.

"Me?" he asked, uncertainty in his tone. "Why, I'm the Custodian."

"We're Cameron and Melissa," she said.

"Cameron and Melissa," the Custodian repeated. He said it again, as if attempting to jar something from his memory. "No," he said slowly. "I don't know you. You're not on the manifest."

"Manifest?" Melissa repeated, eyes again darting around the room.

"What is this place, Custodian?" Cameron asked, drawn to the frosty compartments on the lower levels.

"It is the repository," the angel said, as if they should have known. He focused his attention on Cameron. "The waiting place."

"For what?" Melissa asked.

"For what?" the angel repeated, a bemused smile creeping across his ancient features. "For the Inheritors, of course."

"Who are the Inheritors?"

"Hey! There are people in here!" Cameron exclaimed, before the Custodian could answer Melissa's question. Cameron stood beside one of the chambers, wiping away the frost.

"Is that who is stored here?" Melissa asked the ancient angel. "The Inheritors?"

Cameron spread his wings and flew about the chamber to examine more of the pods. "They're all filled with people."

"Not people," the Custodian corrected sharply. "They're like you. They're the Inheritors."

"What do you mean they're like us?" Melissa felt her excitement growing.

"They are what you are." The Custodian seemed bewildered by her ignorance.

Cameron continued to flit around the upper levels, peering into each of the icy chambers, as if attempting to convince himself that they were indeed full of people.

"Get down from there!" the Custodian bellowed. "The stasis pods are extremely delicate!"

Melissa felt her heart rate quicken. She reached out to grasp the Custodian's armored shoulder and recapture his attention. "How are we like these Inheritors?"

The Custodian looked at her, his eyes twinkling eerily. "They are all Nephilim. They who will inherit the earth."

"What are you talking about, inherit the earth how?"

"The Architects have blessed your kind with their favor," the Custodian explained. "They have seen great potential in your species, and they have deemed you worthy of this future Paradise."

Cameron returned to Melissa's side. "There's got to be over a hundred people frozen here!"

"They're Nephilim," Melissa told him.

"What do you mean they're Nephilim?" Cameron asked incredulously. "Most of them were killed when the Powers—"

"The Powers!" the Custodian exclaimed, his eyes blazing. "They were quite troublesome to the Architects' plans, but that's where my legion came into the picture." The angel beamed proudly, gesturing at the stasis pods. "When we realized what the Powers were doing, the Architects had us gather the Inheritors. These were the cream of the crop, the strongest of the breeding program."

"Breeding program?" Cameron asked. "The Architects were making Nephilim?"

The Custodian grinned. "How else were they to create the perfect beings to populate their new Heaven? But the Powers almost mucked it all up," he continued with a snarl. "They deemed the Nephilim abominations. Can you believe it? As if the perfect blend of the human and the divine could be such a thing." The old angel shook his head in disgust. "We had to work in secret. We snatched up the best of the children throughout the centuries."

"Centuries?" Cameron asked. "You and your boys have been doing this for centuries?"

The Custodian looked quite sad. "There were many we couldn't save. Many who died beneath the Powers' swords, and others who took up arms against our holy mission."

Melissa gestured back in the direction of the decayed bodies that they'd first encountered upon entering. "Were those the angels who tried to stop you?"

"Some," the Custodian admitted. "But some were also my brothers, who were helping to fulfill the dreams of the Architects. They fought bravely against our foes." His eyes became distant at his memory of the past. "Why would they want to stop us? Why would they want to deny the birth of a new Paradise? A new Heaven?"

"What was wrong with the old one?" Cameron asked.

"What was wrong with the old one?" the Custodian growled, suddenly angry. Melissa wanted to kick Cameron as hard as she could.

But the Custodian's anger seemed quickly forgotten as he explained. "The old Heaven had become tainted by war. Brother against brother. It was like poison coursed through the veins of a once-perfect life."

He paused. "The Lord God had failed us. It was time for the Architects to rebuild what had been lost."

For the first time, Melissa understood the threat that the Architects posed. "They're going to destroy our world, to rebuild their Heaven."

The Custodian nodded ever so slightly. "Humanity has had its day. It failed. But it won't be forgotten, for its essence lives on in the Nephilim."

"That's insane," Cameron stated matter-of-factly.

"Do you have any idea what's going on out there in the world?" Melissa asked.

"I've been watching over my charges for a very long time, waiting for the day when the Architects would tell me that the world was ready for the Inheritors."

"Well, if things keep up the way they have been, there won't be a world for them to claim," Melissa said.

The Custodian cocked his head in confusion.

"The world has been cut off from Heaven and become overrun—with monsters," she explained to him. "Beasts, creatures of nightmare—of darkness. They've completely taken over the planet. The entire human race has gone into hiding."

The Custodian stroked his grizzled chin. "Monsters, you

say. The Architects do indeed work in mysterious ways."

"So you're saying that this chaos is all part of some master plan?" Cameron asked incredulously.

"I am saying that there isn't much the Architects haven't accounted for."

"Well, they didn't account for us," Cameron growled. His sword was back, burning like his anger.

"Is that what you think, Nephilim?" the Custodian asked.

Melissa and Cameron glared defiantly.

"Look at where you are," the Custodian waved his armored arm about the chamber. "A mating pair of Nephilim, in the nest of other mating pairs." He smiled.

A strange hissing sound emanated from the far end of the chamber, and more lights turned on, illuminating two empty stasis pods. The angel's armor suddenly blazed.

"You're exactly where you need to be."

Before either Nephilim could react, the Custodian manifested a net of holy fire in his hands, tossing it over them. They tried to move out from beneath the covering, but it was infused with an unnatural power that sapped away their strength as they dropped to the floor beneath its weight.

Melissa watched as Cameron's sword sputtered and died.

"The two of you will be better off in stasis," the Custodian attempted to reassure them. "And once the Architects deem the world is ready . . ."

He grabbed the end of the netting, cinching it closed, and

began to drag them over to the waiting pods, when there came a severe pounding at the entrance doors.

"What is this?" the Custodian grumbled, annoyed that his work had been disturbed.

The beating upon the door persisted; pieces of rock surrounding the door cracked away and crashed to the floor of the inner chamber.

Melissa managed to turn herself within the net to get a better view. She didn't have a good feeling about this.

"Let us out," she hollered. "Let us out before—"

"Silence!" The Custodian advanced toward the door.

The pounding intensified, and the center of the metal door began to dent.

Melissa struggled to pull the netting off them, but she was too weak from its enchantments.

The pounding was relentless, and the door finally succumbed, smashing into the chamber along with a large portion of the mountain wall that had secured it.

Melissa caught movement in the shadows, and practically screamed when she saw what had flown inside the chamber and now crouched before the Custodian.

"What manner of beasts are you?" the Custodian demanded of the intruders.

But Melissa knew, and panic nearly overtook her. These were angels of a different, far darker nature.

Angels of the Void.

CHAPTER TWENTY-TWO

Lorelei had been thinking of her friends, and before she even realized what was happening, she'd been transported to another place completely unfamiliar to her.

The ghost angel A'Dorial had told her that she was supposed to assist the forces of good. Now he was nowhere to be seen, although the spirits of those who had passed since the earth had been cut off from Heaven were still around her.

But they had proven to be less than talkative.

Lorelei decided to concentrate on her location. She had to figure out why thinking of her Nephilim friends had brought her here. As she was starting to learn since dying, nothing happened by accident.

She had manifested at the edge of a large parking lot, with a few cars scattered throughout. There was a department store on the other end of the lot. *Might as well start there,* she thought, gliding weightlessly toward it.

That was when she noticed them.

Bodies.

Bodies littered the pavement. Many seemed to be the black-garbed Agents that had attacked Mallus at Saint Athanasius before everything went to hell. Several were still burning, leaving her in no doubt that their wounds were caused by divine weaponry.

The closer she floated to the store, the more bodies she found, although some of these were dressed in long trench coats with funky-looking goggles over their eyes. *Are those mechanical wings?* she wondered as she drifted toward them for a closer look.

Then something in a pile of smoldering bodies caught her eye. She propelled herself closer and gasped in recognition, guessing that she now knew why she had been transported there.

His face was bloody and bruised, but there was no mistaking Jeremy Fox.

"Lorelei?"

The voice had come from behind, and she turned, stunned to see a ghostly Jeremy standing there.

"Jeremy," she whispered, a broad smile spreading across her face. But that same smile began to fade as she realized what it meant to see Jeremy this way. She quickly glanced to his body lying on the ground of the parking lot, before looking back to his ghostly form.

"I never expected you to be here," he said, rushing toward her in an unusual display of affection. He threw his arms around her, but simply passed right through her.

"What the bloody hell . . . ," he exclaimed.

"First off, I'm dead," she began to explain, the smile returning to her face. She had felt something as he'd passed through her, and it meant that things weren't as bad as she'd believed.

"Dead?"

"I'm a ghost," she confirmed with a nod.

Jeremy brought a hand to his face. "Bollocks, now I'm seeing bloody ghosts!"

He then noticed where she'd been standing, and the pile of dead bodies there. "Wait a minute," he began.

"It's not as bad as you think," Lorelei said quickly.

Jeremy had come closer to the dead. "That's me!" he shouted, pointing at the body peeking out beneath the others, and then looking at her. "I'm lying there on the ground—which means that I'm bloody well dead too."

"No," Lorelei tried to calm him. "Well, not quite yet anyway."

Jeremy stared at her.

"You need to hold on," she said. "Can you hear me?"

He continued to stare at her, then at his body.

"Yeah, yeah, I can hear you."

"You're still alive, but barely," she told him. "When you passed through me, I could feel that you were on the cusp between life and death."

"The cusp?" he repeated.

Lorelei nodded. "You could go either way, but the longer your spirit is out of your body . . ."

He had drifted closer to his earthly form. "You mean I have to get back in there?" he asked, sounding oddly horrified.

"Yeah, something like that."

"How?"

Lorelei shrugged. "I really don't know. But I don't think we have much time."

"Well, I bloody well don't know what to do!" Jeremy screamed.

Lorelei thought for moment, then floated down toward Jeremy's body. "I'm going to try something," she said nervously.

Kneeling beside the dying Nephilim, she placed her hand over his chest. She sensed a shift in the energies around her, and turned to see the many who had died since the planet had been cut off from Heaven gathered around her.

She'd used their energy once to kill a monster.

Now she was going to attempt the opposite—she was going to attempt to rekindle life.

She drew their power into her ghostly hand. It was wild, untamed, with a potential for destruction, but also for life.

Jeremy began to ask a question, but she wasn't listening. She was attempting to focus the soul energies of thousands, and if she wasn't careful . . .

She plunged her hand into Jeremy's chest and heard the ghostly version of the Nephilim gasp. Then Lorelei released the energy she had gathered in one powerful burst, drawing back her hand just in time to see Jeremy's ghost fade away.

Lorelei could not help but smile as the body that lay partially buried returned to life with a scream and an explosion of divine fire, which tossed away the dead that had been strewn atop him.

"Wouldn't want to do that every day," Jeremy said, as he stood, flexing his wings. He scanned the parking lot, countless corpses of enemies and mysterious allies laid out before him.

"Are you still here, Lorelei?" he asked. "Can you still hear me?"

There was no response.

"Well, I'm going to talk to you anyway."

He pulled his wings back within himself and started to walk quickly across the lot toward the woods.

"Hopefully, you can keep up," he said.

Jeremy was amazed at how good he felt. Whatever Lorelei had done had recharged his spiritual and physical batteries. He felt well enough to take on the world, which could very well be what he needed to do.

"I know I left the school and all, but I was given a huge

responsibility—to watch over a very special child. I believe he was sent here to help the world with its current predicament."

"Enoch!" he cried, as he reached the line of trees. "You can come out now. You're safe."

There was no answer.

"Enoch!" Jeremy called again, in the direction where he'd seen the child run. "It's me. We're safe for now."

"The child's name is Enoch, if you haven't figured that out," Jeremy said to Lorelei. "And it's very important that I find him."

He made his way into the wooded area, stopping short as he came across more bodies. There was a dead Agent, as well as one of the metal-winged beings.

Jeremy circled them, searching for any sign of what had transpired. He knelt down and touched the ground with his fingers, then brought them up to his nose to sniff. The scent was there, sharp and pungent.

The smell of the unnatural. Jeremy had smelled it before.

"I have to find him," he said, in a panic. "If they have him, everyone is in danger."

The body of the dead Agent suddenly sat up, and Jeremy reacted, a sword of divine fire springing to life. He was ready to cleave the skull of his foe when it spoke.

"It's me!" came a rough, gravelly voice.

Jeremy held his swing. "Me who?"

"Lorelei," the figure said with great difficulty. The Agent

moved stiffly as it attempted to stand. "I've possessed this body so I can interact with you," she said. The body listed to one side. "This takes some getting used to."

Jeremy lowered his sword but remained on guard. Starting to pace, he said, "I need to find Enoch."

The possessed corpse went stiff, and Jeremy was starting to become concerned that something was the matter when it began to speak again.

"I think I might be able to help with that," Lorelei said, using the voice of the Agent. "I think I can find out what's happened to Enoch."

Lorelei hated the feeling of being inside the Agent's corpse.

It felt wrong, and she had the sense that if she stayed too long, she'd be trapped.

"How?" Jeremy was asking, desperation in his tone. "How can you find Enoch?"

She was still getting used to her connection with the corpse, and her motor functions were improving. "I think I might be able to access his thoughts," she managed.

"Can you find out who these guys are?" Jeremy asked.

Lorelei had forgotten that Jeremy wasn't around when the Agents had first revealed themselves at the school and Mallus had explained who they were.

"They're a form of enhanced primitive men, used by a group of mysterious angelic beings called the Architects."

"Guess that explains why they look like bloody monkeys," Jeremy said. "But these Architects, what's their story?"

"To put it simply, they are angels who think they can do a better job than God—and want to prove it here, on earth."

"What do you mean by that?" Jeremy asked.

"They want to turn earth into their idea of Heaven," Lorelei said.

"Bloody hell," Jeremy muttered. "So why are they so hell-bent on having Enoch?"

"Because Enoch was sent by God," Lorelei said, as she began to access the memories of the Agent assassin. It was a disgusting process, something akin to wading through an ocean of foul-smelling waste. "The Architects want to stop God from having any involvement in what they're doing."

"But the world is going to Hell."

Lorelei waded deeper into the memories of the Agent, taking what she could from the fragmented thoughts. The Agent's brain was beginning to decay, and its memories were deteriorating.

"Which seems to be part of the plan," she said, experiencing a sudden wave of overwhelming nausea, even though she was dead. "I have to get out of this body," she told Jeremy.

"Not yet," Jeremy ordered. "You need to find out where they've taken Enoch."

The Agent corpse collapsed to its knees. "Have to leave the body," it growled. "Before I'm trapped."

Jeremy knelt and grasped the corpse's shoulder. "I need to know where he is."

It was like being inside a house as it collapsed around her, but Lorelei knew how important the information was, not only to Jeremy, but to the world. She rooted through the decaying gray matter as it bubbled and frothed, sorting through centuries of seemingly senseless murders mandated by the Architects.

Grabbing hold of a memory near the Agent's moment of death, she followed it back down the line to where he'd first learned of his last mission.

"Lorelei?" Jeremy called, but he sounded so very far away.

She was out of time—she had to leave—and wriggled from the Agent's decaying body like a snake shedding its skin.

Jeremy stared helplessly at the Agent's corpse as it lay perfectly still on the ground where it had fallen.

"Lorelei," he said, nudging the body with the toe of his boot. It didn't move. "Lorelei," he called again, his voice cracking with desperation. Enoch needed him—the world needed him to find Enoch, but without Lorelei's help . . .

"Jeremy!" a rough-sounding voice interrupted his thoughts, and he watched another of the black-garbed assassins trudge toward him from the trees.

"Any luck?" Jeremy asked, striding toward the Agent possessed by Lorelei's spirit.

"I think so." The Agent's arm lifted, and Jeremy saw that

the tight-fitting stealth suit had been peeled away to reveal the pale, mottled flesh of its hand.

Jeremy drew closer, noticing the strange arrow tattoo on the back of the Agent's hand. His Nephilim senses told him that the mark was filled with preternatural power. "It's like a directional signal. I just need to figure out how to make it work," Lorelei explained in her distorted voice.

He hoped that it wouldn't take too long. The thought of baby Enoch out there, in the hands of the enemy . . . it was almost more than he could stand.

CHAPTER TWENTY-THREE

The Unforgiven tried to make Aaron rest—but that wasn't going to happen.

He'd pretended to sleep, waiting just long enough for the angel attendants to leave before getting up and searching out Vilma and his mother.

His mother.

He wondered how long it would take for him to get used to that concept.

Standing in the center of his room in the infirmary wing, Aaron closed his eyes and thought of Vilma. The connection he had with his girlfriend was a special one, and he didn't think there would ever come a time when they would be truly apart. With his mind locked upon her image, he spread his wings and wrapped them tightly about himself, imagining that he was at her side.

It took more out of him than he'd thought it would.

He appeared at the back of the conference room with a rush of air, stumbling to one side, crashing against a freestanding chalkboard that was covered in notes.

From the corner of his eye he saw his mother stand and Vilma hurry across to him.

"Sorry," he mumbled, righting himself and attempting to straighten the chalkboard.

He could feel the cold stares of the fallen angels in the room. What had Vilma called them? The Unforgiven.

"I thought you were resting," Vilma said, wrapping an arm around his waist.

"No time for that," Aaron said, regaining some of his composure. "There's too much to be done, and I've already been out of the picture for too long."

"Aaron, please," Taylor said. "We have the situation well in hand. Go back to the infirmary—rest, we'll keep you informed—"

"A dark force has taken possession of the Morningstar's body, and in turn, his power," Aaron interrupted. "I'll be fine, thank you."

The leader of the Unforgiven, Aaron believed that his name was Levi, stood up from his seat at the conference table to address him.

"The Morningstar is possessed?" he asked. "Where did you come by this information?"

"It was this Satan Darkstar, wearing the body of my father, who put me in a coma."

"How can you be so sure that he was possessed?" Levi asked, as the other Unforgiven around him nodded in agreement. "The Morningstar is not known for his trustworthiness."

Aaron grimaced at the implications but could understand where their doubts were coming from, especially since many of them had followed Lucifer during the Great War in Heaven.

"Let's just say that he's changed over the centuries. Anyway, he told me of the possession while I was in the coma."

Levi looked around the table at his brothers. "He 'told' you?"

"I know it sounds nuts, but somehow he visited my subconscious. He explained the situation and told me what Satan Darkstar is planning. We have to stop him."

"I suppose it is possible that they communicated on some psychic level," the Unforgiven leader postulated. "The Morningstar is one of the most powerful of us, and the two do share the same blood."

"If we were to believe all that you tell us," Levi said to Aaron, "what did your father say this Satan Darkstar had planned?"

"Besides overrunning the planet with monsters?" Aaron started. He found himself flexing the powerful muscles on his back, his black wings slowly unfurling, and then closing again. "The Darkstar is planning some kind of attack against Heaven."

The Unforgiven looked at one another. Their eyes remained hidden behind the goggles, but Aaron could tell that a message was passing among them.

"We will take your concerns under consideration, Aaron Corbet." Levi turned to Taylor, who had returned to her seat beside him. "If you would please escort your son back to the infirmary, we will continue our briefing."

Taylor opened her mouth to argue, but seemed to think better of it. Instead, she stood and moved around the table to join Aaron and Vilma.

"C'mon, Aaron," Vilma said. "We should go."

"So that's the way this is going to be?" Aaron asked, feeling his ire rise. "You're not going to listen to me?"

"We will take what you have said under consideration." The Unforgiven leader then turned away, dismissing him.

Aaron didn't care for that. Not in the least.

He stepped away from Vilma, his wings erupting in a rush, the sound like that of a sail being caught in a powerful wind. The angelic sigils of power, part of his father's birthright, rose to the surface of his skin.

"You're not taking me seriously." Aaron's voice boomed in the confines of the meeting room. "And that makes me angry."

Some of the Unforgiven had risen from their chairs, the sharp feathers of their mechanical wings flared.

Aaron did not want to fight them, but if that was what it took to get them to listen, then so be it.

"Aaron, please," his mother begged, but he did not back down.

"Why won't you listen to me?" he asked.

Levi stood calmly, and his followers closed their wings.

"The world is on the brink of ruin," he said. "And with the child missing, and believed to be in the hands of the Architects, we are closer to annihilation than ever before."

Levi paused.

"The child must be our focus now. Only with him can we stop this Satan Darkstar."

Aaron thought for a moment, reviewing the Unforgiven's words, and realized that he was right. The mysterious child that he had been told about seemed to be crucial to their continued survival. He willed his wings away, calming the angelic fire churning through his body so that the sigils receded.

"I can help you," he said. But a wave of light-headedness washed over him, and he pitched forward.

Luckily, Vilma was there to catch him.

"It is noted," Levi said. "But before you can be useful to anyone, you must heal."

That wasn't what Aaron wanted to hear, but he had to admit that Levi was right. He'd been close to death for nearly two months. It was going to take some time to recuperate.

But time was something he was afraid that they—and the world— had little of.

Even still, he was allowing Vilma and his mother to escort him out of the room, when the alarms began to sound.

The Unforgiven snapped to attention and quickly made their way toward the exits.

"What's going on?" Aaron asked.

"Intruders," Taylor Corbet said. "Our perimeter has been breached."

Gabriel eyed the guard booth near the yawning entrance to the tunnel into the mountain. The windows were broken, and he could see, as well as smell, the blood that stained the walls inside.

"Are we just going to stand here?" he asked.

"We're waiting to be noticed," Dusty said.

He and Mallus stood beside the Labrador, Dusty staring fixedly at the crackling ball of power that Mallus still held.

Gabriel looked around at the desolate mountain road. There didn't appear to be anyone, or anything for that matter, around to notice them.

"By who?" he asked, his eyes going back to the booth and the dark stains inside it. "Or should I ask, what?"

Dusty tore his gaze from the powerful object in Mallus's possession.

"Huh," he said. "Didn't see that coming."

"What?" Gabriel asked.

"Nothing that I can talk about right now," Dusty said, as

cryptically as usual. "But it appears that I'm not the only one helping to captain the boat."

"I'm afraid I don't know anything about boats," the dog said. He looked at Mallus. It was shocking how bad the angel was looking. He appeared older, smaller, his clothes hanging on a far ganglier frame than when they'd first set out.

"He doesn't look so good," Gabriel commented.

"It's a lot of work to be responsible for the power of God," Dusty explained. "But his sacrifice will be well worth it."

"His sacrifice?"

But Gabriel's question would remain unanswered, as the trio suddenly found themselves surrounded.

The trench-coat-wearing individuals seemed to appear out of nowhere, and Gabriel was startled to see that they had metal, not feathers, on their wings.

The dog sniffed the air as the strangers stalked closer to them. There was no doubt about it; they were angels, but they were unlike any angels he had ever encountered.

"What should we do?" Gabriel asked. He could feel the power of Heaven roused in his body.

"Nothing," Dusty replied. "This is who we've been waiting for."

The strange angels seemed to be transfixed by Mallus, who appeared to be having some difficulty keeping the power that he held in line.

Dusty stepped forward, distracting the angels, whose wings came to life in a defensive stance.

"We mean no harm," he said calmly, raising his hands in surrender. As his sweatshirt sleeves fell back toward his elbows, Gabriel noticed that his friend's skin had taken on an almost gray shade, as if the fragments of metal trapped below its surface had begun to expand.

"We've come to make a delivery," Dusty added, turning his gaze once more on Mallus and his powerful prize.

Aaron didn't want to go back to his room.

"You're practically falling down," Vilma argued.

"I'm fine," Aaron protested.

"Maybe he'll listen to you," Vilma said to Taylor.

"Aaron, you heard Levi," his mother began. "You won't be doing anybody any good until you're fully healed."

"Any way of knowing what set off the alarms?" he asked, ignoring her as well.

"Aaron, please," Taylor begged, as he pushed past her in the direction of the Unforgiven.

"I just want to see," he said.

Taylor sighed exasperatedly.

"I wonder where he gets it from?" Vilma asked. "You, or his father?"

"Definitely his father," Aaron heard his mother say as he rounded a corner, walking into Levi and five other Unforgiven angels, who clustered around a doorway that opened into a stairwell.

"I thought you were going back to the infirmary," Levi said.

"I got distracted."

"That seems to be a persistent problem of yours."

"Really? I hadn't noticed." Aaron tried to resist the urge to be a wiseass, but failed miserably.

Levi said nothing further, turning back to the metal stairs that led from the main entrance to the many-leveled base below.

Aaron could hear a commotion above, the sounds of multiple footfalls as the Unforgiven sentries returned with their findings.

But there was another sound as well. Aaron found himself moving closer to Levi and the other angels, drawn toward the stairs.

"Where do you think you're going?" Levi asked.

"Aaron, what are you . . . ?" Vilma began as she and Taylor caught up with him.

"Get him away from there," Levi commanded. His men rushed forward to grab Aaron's arms.

"Wait!" Aaron cried, shrugging off the Unforgiven by calling on his wings to push them away. "I know one of them."

And he was right.

"Gabriel!" he shouted, as the yellow Labrador retriever bounded down the stairs ahead of the others. Aaron could barely contain himself, dropping to his knees as Gabriel leaped on him.

"Aaron!" the dog yelped pathetically. "It's you! It's really, really you!"

Aaron did his best to hug his friend as the dog nearly danced with excitement, his rear claws clicking on the concrete floor. Gabriel frantically licked Aaron's face, his affection for his boy overwhelming, and Aaron let him, dispensing his own kisses upon the dog's blocky head.

"I've missed you so much," he told the dog.

"You're all right," Gabriel said with relief. "When I last saw you, you were hurt—bad—but you're all right."

"How could I be anything but?" Aaron asked him, ruffling his floppy, golden-yellow ears. "I would never leave my best friend."

"Vilma!" Gabriel suddenly barked, and raced down the hall to bestow the same affections upon her.

Aaron stood to join them, but noticed that Levi and his men remained focused on the figures that had just reached the bottom of the stairs.

Aaron couldn't help but smile when he saw Dusty, but that smile quickly disappeared when he caught sight of Mallus. The former general in the Morningstar's army looked as though he had aged a hundred years since Aaron had last seen him.

"What happened?" Aaron asked, looking to Dusty. "And what's that?" He gestured at the pulsing sphere in Mallus's hands.

"It couldn't be," Levi said, awe in his tone. He stepped toward Mallus and the glowing sphere.

"If you're thinking the power of God, then you're right," Dusty said.

"The power of . . . ," Aaron began, but didn't finish, as Mallus turned his weary eyes to him.

"Are you ready, Aaron Corbet, son of the Morningstar?" he asked. "Are you ready to become the next Metatron?"

Verchiel had never seen a beast like this before.

Its arm lashed out, striking him square in the chest plate and hurling him backward with such force that he smashed through the front of the office building, into the lobby.

Eager to do more damage, the beast lumbered in pursuit. Its body was huge and muscular, its flesh a sickly green. Its head was a mass of writhing tentacles and eyes, and it roared as it came at him.

Finally, Verchiel thought as he used his wings to push himself up from where he lay. *A foe that just might be worth my time.*

His objective was to cause chaos among the various monster armies. He wanted to let them know that he was as strong as, if not stronger than, their mysterious dark lord.

The beast hopped in through the broken window. From the corner of his eye, Verchiel could see the monsters that had become his ragtag army outside, waiting.

Watching.

The green-skinned beast screamed, and Verchiel created a sword of fire from the stuff of Heaven, hefting it above his shoulder as he prepared to swing.

But the beast proved faster. It ducked below his swipe, reaching out with a three-fingered hand to grasp Verchiel's arm and wrench it savagely to one side.

Verchiel dropped his flaming weapon as the monster yanked him into the air, then whipped him onto the floor. Tiles shattered, and even through his heavenly armor, Verchiel felt the ferocity of the impact.

Before he could get to his feet, the beast grabbed him by the armor and flung him across the lobby.

This time, Verchiel's fall was cushioned by a large, overstuffed sofa, which tipped over as he landed, spilling him to the floor. As he readied to stand, he could already hear the lumbering footfalls of his opponent, its eager breathing quickened with the potential of victory.

It would be a cold day in Heaven before the likes of something this foul prevailed against a soldier of the Almighty.

Verchiel shot up from the floor, screaming his own battle cry.

The two powerful forces collided and dropped to the ground, landing atop a heavy wooden table and smashing it to splinters under their combined weight.

Verchiel drove his armored fist into the monster's face, feeling its tentacles spasm as he struck. They wrapped around his hand and forearm, but Verchiel yanked his arm free, tearing away some of the offending tendrils. The beast cried out in pain.

The rabble outside entered the building, watching the battle eagerly. They had seen this scene repeated hundreds of times already, and always Verchiel had been victorious.

As he would most assuredly be again.

The green-skinned beast grabbled hold of a broken table leg and swung it at the side of Verchiel's face. The wood connected, nearly knocking his head from his shoulders.

But the angel quickly recovered.

This adversary actually puts up a good fight, he thought as the beast came at him once more.

It still held the table leg like a club, raising it high. Verchiel summoned another blade of flame and slashed across the beast's stomach, just above its thick belt of rotting children's heads, as the table leg came down, grazing his shoulder.

Stepping back, Verchiel watched the beast. It was preparing to attack again, when it stopped short. Its belly had parted like a mouth, vomiting coils of internal workings and stinking liquid on the lobby floor. It let go of the table leg and frantically tried to shove its innards back into the gaping slit.

"A valiant attempt," the angel said, as the creature withered.

Verchiel was going to be merciful and end the abomination's life, when he heard a low, tremulous moan.

He looked at his followers and saw that they heard it as

well. Panic started to grip them as the moan gradually became a sound more akin to the blare of a trumpet.

"What is that noise?" Verchiel asked aloud.

The sound frayed his nerves, affecting him in a way that he could not understand, or explain.

"It's him," the beast kneeling defeated before him said in a language as horrible-sounding as the creature looked. "He calls to us."

"Who?" Verchiel asked.

The sound crescendoed like a trumpet fanfare, sending Verchiel's army of monsters into a frenzy, hands clasped over their ears.

"Who calls to you?" Verchiel demanded.

The thing's multiple eyes looked toward the ceiling.

"The master of us all," the creature gurgled. "He summons us. He summons us to him."

The beast attempted to stand, but slipped on the coil of something that might have been intestine. It fell back, flailing pathetically as it again tried to rise.

Verchiel severed the creature's head from its muscular body with an offhanded slash of his sword. It would hear nothing anymore.

The sound continued to blare from outside the building. Verchiel strode across the lobby. The monsters that now called him leader no longer had the good sense to move from his path, and he swatted them aside as he passed.

Verchiel stepped out onto the street. The bodies of those that had chosen not to surrender to the angel lay broken and burning about him.

Ergo came to cower at his side.

"It's some sort of summons," Verchiel stated.

"Yes," the goblin confirmed, his ugly face twisted in pain. "A summons to him."

Verchiel proceeded down the street, stepping over the dead, drawn to the horrible sound. He could sense his army of faithful beasts behind him, following in his wake.

Rounding a corner, Verchiel stopped.

A huge portal of swirling darkness had appeared, and the sound was coming from within.

He watched as random monsters entered the vortex, answering the call of their master.

A strange sensation came over the lower portion of Verchiel's face. He was smiling.

Turing toward Ergo, he watched the goblin recoil.

"What's the matter with your face?" the loathsome creature asked.

Verchiel did not answer. Instead he started toward the tunnel of shadow, what remained of his army at his heels.

"Where are you going?" Ergo cried out from behind him.

"Isn't it obvious?" Verchiel asked. "I'm answering the call. "I don't want to keep the Darkstar waiting."

CHAPTER TWENTY-FOUR

The Angels of the Void were terrible and swift.

The four flew into the Nephilim chamber like streaks of black lightning, circling the Custodian, then attacking the ancient sentry in unison.

All Melissa and Cameron could do was watch, as the golden netting continued to drain their strength. Melissa tried to look away, but even the effort of moving her head proved to be too much.

The Void Angels were like feral cats, playing with their prey. Each took a turn attacking with razor-sharp claws.

"What manner of foul things are you?" the ancient warrior cried out, blocking a slash from one of the Void Angel's claws.

Melissa knew that the Custodian wore armor, but something roiling in the pit of her belly told her that it would be little defense against these angels.

"They're Nephilim," she managed to cry out. "Nephilim that were brought back from the dead."

"Shhhhh!" one of the angels hissed, and held a long, hooked claw up to its helmet where a mouth should have been. The face mask melted away to reveal a smiling Samantha. "You'll give all our secrets away."

And with that, she spun and leaped, her black wings carrying her up and over the Custodian, who was distracted by the other three.

"Watch out!" Cameron screamed, making a pathetic attempt to thrash against the netting.

Samantha proved Melissa's suspicions correct, as the Void Angel's claws tore through the Custodian's armor, shredding it like paper, and slicing into his shoulder.

The old angel yelled and shifted his attention from the three he fought to Samantha flying above him.

Not good. Not good at all.

The three terrible creatures moved as one. They darted in and out, cutting through the ancient angel's dull golden armor, even as he swung his mighty sword of fire.

The Void Angels evaded the crackling blade, laughing, and continuing their attack.

The others had dropped their face masks now, revealing their pasty white visages, as if wanting to show the old sentry what was about to end his life.

"Your blood is old," Kirk said, licking the tips of his claws with a gray, sluglike tongue. "But it is filled with the power of the divine. Delicious."

Melissa watched in horror, then suddenly realized that Janice was not with the others. It gave her a spark of hope that they had been responsible for her defeat.

A spark of hope.

But sometimes that was all it took to build a raging fire.

The Custodian was hurt, his armor torn and the angelic flesh beneath bleeding. The Void Angels were circling him again, and he slowly turned as they did, his sword at the ready.

Melissa willed him to look at her, hoping to share her spark with him, perhaps to reignite the smoldering core of his being. Their eyes locked, and although they did not speak, Melissa sensed that he understood.

The Custodian cried out. Tongues of flame jumped from his armored body as he lifted his burning sword and spread wide his white, speckled wings, leaping into the air.

The Void Angels recoiled, screeching in surprise, each taking off in pursuit of the Nephilim caretaker.

The Custodian quickly changed his course to attack the Void Angels with renewed vigor. But his rally was to be short-lived. He was outnumbered and the Void Angels fought viciously, raking and tearing away pieces of his armor.

Melissa heard Cameron gasp beside her, and shared his horror as they viewed the old angel plummeting to the ground, crashing violently upon the stone floor.

The Void Angels cackled, dropping down from the air to finish what they had started.

"Get up!" Cameron cried. Once again, he attempted to escape the netting, but did not have the strength.

The Custodian lay still as the Void Angels casually sauntered closer.

"First we kill the old angel," William stated. "And then we deal with our friends in the net." He gestured toward them with a clawed hand. Melissa was disgusted by the ribbons of bloody skin that hung from his razor-sharp fingertips.

"I think we should take our time with them," Kirk said, "seeing as they're pretty much helpless."

"Helpless is just how I like my prey," Russell added. "You can be really creative then."

Melissa noticed the Custodian move.

"Get up!" she screamed. "Get up or you're dead for sure—we're all dead for sure!"

The old angel's eyes flickered and his body tensed.

The Void Angels were almost upon him.

Suddenly, he bolted up from the ground with a grunt, his wings flapping pathetically as he charged haphazardly forward. One of his wings was badly broken, and Melissa was stunned by the amount of blood that had pooled beneath him.

"Get him!" William screeched.

The Custodian was almost at the net covering Melissa and Cameron, when Russell, Kirk, and Samantha jumped him, their claws mercilessly slashing at what was left of his armor and his flesh beneath.

He did not scream as they tore him apart. So lost were the dark angels in their vicious work that they did not notice the Custodian extending his arm toward the golden netting.

Melissa held her breath, watching as the angel's fingertips brushed against the woven strands of fire. The netting evaporated in a rush of air.

The Void Angels stopped their savage attack on the ancient sentry as Melissa jumped to her feet, feeling her strength return. She glanced to her left to see that Cameron had recovered as well and was ready for a fight.

"Oh poo," Russell said, disappointed. "I was looking forward to making Melissa scream while Cameron watched."

"Do you want to hear me scream?" Melissa asked Cameron, her eyes locked upon the Void Angels as William joined them.

"Not really," Cameron said. "Laughing would be good. Screaming I could live without."

"How about these guys, though?" she asked, gesturing toward the Void Angels with her chin. "Any interest in hearing them scream?" A sword of fire ignited in her hand.

Cameron paused for a second, and smiled cockily. "Now that you mention it."

The Nephilim attacked, remembering their extensive combat training from the likes of Aaron, Vilma, Verchiel, and the Morningstar. They were perfect together, one's attacks complementing the other's. It was like a force of many as they leaped and spun in the air, their swords of fire putting the hideous shadows of their deceased friends on the offensive.

Melissa and Cameron were a sight to behold, and would have made their teachers proud.

Back to back they paused, their breath coming in short gasps as they assessed their situation.

The Void Angels had been driven back toward the entrance, but they suddenly darted off, each in a separate direction, disappearing into the shadows.

"I don't like that much," Melissa said.

"Not crazy about it myself," Cameron agreed.

Darkness spread like a living cloud, swallowing up the light as it flowed toward them like water across the floor.

"Must be one of their nasty little tricks," Melissa said.

"Shadows don't like light," Cameron stated, and she noticed that his sword had brightened and his skin had taken on a luminescence as well.

She too focused her inner divinity on her weapon and her body.

The two of them together, glowing like a star.

Darkness oozed around them, trying to smother their divine light. Walls of shadow built around them, and Melissa felt Cameron tense at her back.

"I think something's about to—," he began, but stopped as the Void Angels exploded from their curtain of concealment.

Without another word, the two Nephilim lunged at the shadows, plunging into its cold embrace.

It's like being underwater, Melissa thought, the darkness attempting to force its way into her mouth. But she would not stand for it, willing herself to burn all the brighter, as she hacked and slashed with her weapon of flame.

She could sense the Void Angels swimming in the shadows like sharks. Holding her blade close to her face, she waited for the inevitable.

It was two-pronged—Samantha coming from the right, and Kirk from above and to the left. Their claws slashed at her, and she replied in kind, swinging her sword with all her might. The Void Angels screamed their rage at her, furious that she would not submit to their violent intentions.

Then their attacks suddenly ceased. The darkness continued to flow about her like the thickest of fogs, and she spun slowly, ready to strike at whatever came at her.

In the light of her sword she caught a glimpse of something that turned her blood to ice. The four Void Angels were preparing to converge on Cameron.

"Cameron!" she cried out. "You're surrounded!"

Melissa threw herself into the black, thrusting her sword out before her in an attempt to reach her friend before their enemies.

Screams rang out close by, but she could not find her friend. Panic gripped her. She willed her body to burn, brighter and brighter still, but it wasn't enough. Cameron was still hidden in the darkness.

Then Melissa stopped. She turned her sword in her hands so its point was toward the ground. She lifted it high and, with all her strength, plunged it down into the rock.

The chamber was filled with an explosion of absolute brilliance. Divine radiance overwhelmed the shadow with its holy purity.

The Void Angels wailed, recoiling from Cameron's limp form. Melissa was already diving across the expanse of space to get to her friend.

Kneeling down beside him, she quickly assessed his situation. His clothing was torn and he was bleeding, but none of his injuries appeared to be fatal.

But she knew that could change in an instant, for shadows were already beginning to swirl and coalesce in the chamber.

Cameron moaned as she helped him to his feet.

"We need to find someplace where we can hold them off," she said.

Laughter echoed from the stone walls, as the Void Angels reappeared.

Melissa tried to maneuver away from their advancing foes, Cameron leaning heavily on her.

"Leave me here," he grumbled, attempting to free himself from her support. "Get to the back. Gotta be a place there for you to fight them off."

"Not a chance," Melissa said. "We're in this together, or not at all."

He looked at her, his dark eyes attempting to focus on hers.

"Besides, we're a mated pair." She winked at him, then created a particularly nasty-looking sword of holy fire in her hand.

The Void Angels were closer now.

"Tell you what," William began, his voice dripping with malice. "We'll kill you quickly, and then I'll put a special request in to the master for you to join my team."

Cameron managed to hold on to his balance, calling upon his own weapon.

"You all right?" Melissa asked, not taking her eyes from their enemies.

"To take care of these punks?" he returned, trying to sound confident. "Absolutely."

The air crackled with electric anticipation; a powerful storm of chaos about to break.

Then the chamber shook violently, and a nearly deafening hissing sound came from behind them.

Melissa spun around to see what new threat was at her back.

A thick cloud of rolling white mist billowed toward them, and within the mist moved something—a great many somethings.

A ragged and bloody Custodian stumbled out from the mist.

"What did you do?" Melissa asked, suspecting the truth, and finding herself suddenly terrified.

"Thought we could use some help," the old angel wheezed.

Nephilim—more than Melissa had ever seen before in one place—emerged from the fog, each and every one clutching a weapon of fire.

And looking very, very angry.

Aaron never again wanted to see such a look in his lover's eyes.

"What does that mean?" she was asking him, a hint of hysteria in her tone.

"It means that I'd be the Metatron," he said flatly. "The personification of God's power on earth. I'd be able to set things right."

"You hope," Taylor interjected, also disapproving of Aaron's decision.

"And once things are set right?" Vilma probed.

Aaron was silent, not sure what would follow after he assumed the guise of the Metatron.

"You don't know," Vilma answered her own question. "You're planning to take this power into yourself, fix the world's problems, and you have no idea what it means for you—for us."

"Vilma, please," Aaron said. He reached out to her, but she pulled away.

She might as well have stabbed him.

"I don't have any choice."

"There's always a choice," Taylor countered.

"Look me in the eye and tell me there's a genuine alternative," Aaron said, fixing his mother with a steely gaze.

She met his eyes, but quickly looked away. "I haven't waited all these years to have you in my life, only to lose you," she said, folding her arms across her chest.

Vilma moved over and put her arm around the woman's shoulders.

At any other time, Aaron would have been thrilled to see his girlfriend and his mother getting along so well, but now he was just annoyed, for he knew he wouldn't get anywhere arguing with either.

Gabriel had been strangely silent, lying on the floor, watching the entire discussion, and Aaron turned to him, hoping for some support. "What do you think?"

Gabriel pondered the question before answering. "Maybe we should ask Dusty," he suggested.

From what Aaron could gather, something had happened to Dusty back at the school after his encounter with the Abomination of Desolation's exploding sword.

Something about being able to see multiple aspects of the future.

Dusty had gone off with Mallus and the Unforgiven to prepare a place for the transference. There was no doubt as to what they and Levi believed should be done.

"Maybe we should," Aaron agreed, looking over to his mother and Vilma to see if that might satisfy them.

They just stared back at him with disappointment in their eyes.

Gabriel stood and walked to the office door before turning back to Aaron. "Are we going?" he asked.

Aaron waited to see if Vilma and Taylor would join them, but they just stood there.

"Yeah," he said, opening the door so he and his dog could leave.

The two started down the cold concrete corridor, Aaron lost in his thoughts until the dog interrupted them.

"This means you're going away forever, doesn't it?" Gabriel asked.

"Yeah, probably," Aaron said. "And no matter what you, Vilma, and Taylor think, I'm not okay with it, but it's . . ."

"It's the only answer right now," Gabriel finished. "A long time ago I probably wouldn't have been able to understand that myself, but since my change, I get it."

"Thanks," Aaron said.

"You're welcome."

They were about to enter a garage area where the army had kept their vehicles, and where Mallus had been brought by the Unforgiven, when Gabriel paused.

"Aaron?"

"Yes, Gabriel?"

"You are the best friend a dog could have." Gabriel turned his dark-brown eyes to Aaron. "And I will never forget you."

"You are the best dog," Aaron told him, doing everything in his power to keep his voice from cracking. "And I will never forget you."

"Aaron!"

Vilma was coming down the corridor, Taylor close behind.

Taylor opened the door, allowing Gabriel to enter the garage first, then followed him in. "We'll be inside," she said, leaving Aaron and Vilma alone in the corridor.

Aaron knew how strong Vilma was, how powerful, but right then, before him, she looked like she might shatter.

He was afraid of what would happen if he moved closer, but he was inexorably drawn to her, and there was no way he could resist her pull.

"Vilma, I—," he began, desperate to make things right between them before—

She came at him full force, throwing her arms about his body and squeezing him so tightly that he feared she might break him.

"I know what you're doing, and I completely understand," she said, pressing her face to his chest. "It doesn't mean that I like it or I accept it, only that I understand it."

"If there was any other way," he said, holding her just as tightly.

"I know," she said. "And if I'm not careful, I get selfish and think, why him? Why does it have to be the one I love more than anything in this world?" She looked up at him, her eyes brimming with tears. "Haven't we already sacrificed enough?"

He had no answer for her, as he brought his lips down to kiss the top of her head.

"Maybe this will be it," he said. "Maybe after it's done, everything will return to normal."

"It won't ever be normal again," she told him.

He held her as she started to sob.

"You have to promise me that you'll be strong. The others are going to need you."

"We don't even know if they're still alive," she said pathetically.

"They're alive," he told her, not sure how he knew, but he did. "They're going to need you, and so are Gabriel and my mother."

"I like her," Vilma said. "At first I hated her for what she did to you as a baby, but now that I've gotten to know her, I see what a strong woman she is."

"I'm going to need you both to be strong, to carry on what we started," he said. "No matter what I do, the world is never going to be as it was, and humanity will need you and my mom, and the others, to help guide it."

Aaron reached down and took her beautiful face in his hands, tilting it up to him. "Will you do that for me?" he asked.

"I would move the world for you if I could," she said.

She reached out, placing a hand gently around the back of his neck, and pulled his face down to kiss him.

If there was anything he needed to inspire him to endure, it was in that kiss. If it had lasted a lifetime, it would still have been too short, and Aaron wished that he could kiss Vilma forever. But it was time.

They said nothing as they stepped apart. Aaron took her hand in his for one last bit of physical contact, as they approached the double doors and pushed through them into the large concrete room.

Gabriel was standing there to greet them, along with Dusty. Aaron was a bit taken aback by the young man's appearance; his skin was covered in dark gray patches that appeared almost metallic.

"Gabriel says you have a question," Dusty said before Aaron could ask how he was.

"Yeah," Aaron answered, knowing that it was only a formality for Vilma and his mother. He knew exactly what he had to do. "So, what I'm about to do . . ." Aaron trailed off.

Dusty considered his words for a moment. "It's so much worse if you don't," he finally said.

Aaron nodded. It was as he thought. He looked to Vilma, who squeezed his hand, acknowledging that she understood as well.

"If this is going to happen, we might want to make it

quick," Levi called out. "I'm not quite sure how much longer Mallus has."

Levi was standing near Mallus in the far corner of the garage. The angel's gaze was focused entirely on the sphere that he still held in his hands. He looked even skinnier than when he'd first arrived.

Aaron gave Vilma one last kiss, staring into her eyes for what very well might be the last time.

"Love you forever," he whispered.

"Love you forever," she echoed.

He squatted down in front of Gabriel and threw his arms around the Labrador's thick neck, squeezing tightly, breathing in the comforting smell of the animal.

Then he rose and headed toward Mallus.

Taylor Corbet intercepted him, taking him by the arm. "I wish we could have had more time."

"It would have been nice," Aaron agreed.

"You've made me very proud." She touched his cheek.

"And you're every bit as beautiful as I thought you would be," he said, wrapping his arms around her in a loving hug. "I'm so grateful that we got the chance to do this."

And with those words, they released each other. Taylor stepped back. There was so much more that they could have said, but they would have to be satisfied with what they had shared.

The fallen angel lifted his gaze at Aaron's approach. "It's about time," he said weakly.

"Had some things to get in order first," Aaron told him.

"Understood," Mallus said. "Are we ready to try this?"

"As I'll ever be," Aaron answered. "What do I need to do?"

Mallus's eyes had returned to the sphere. "Hope with all your heart that it accepts you."

Aaron braced himself for what was to come.

"Here goes." Mallus leaned his face in toward the crackling sphere. "You can let it out now, Tarshish. The kid's here, ready and willing."

The halo that had once been the Malakim, Tarshish, gradually began to break down, and the divine energy that once belonged to the Almighty began to pulse and grow all the more intense as it was released from its confinement.

"Let's see if he's able," Mallus said, thrusting the power of God at Aaron.

Vilma had no idea what to expect. She didn't know any more than any of the others did.

Mallus was going to give Aaron some kind of power that might—

Might.

Be able to help them save the world.

As she stood beside Aaron's mother, Vilma's mind raced. She thought of what was happening in the world outside, of her uncle, aunt, and cousins, of the other Nephilim, but mostly she thought of Aaron and how much she loved him, and how she was now going to have to share him with this new power.

Mallus looked as though he had aged fifty years, and Vilma had to wonder if the same would happen to Aaron. She feared for the fallen angel. He had only been part of their group for a short time, but during times like these, people bonded quickly. Could she bear to lose another friend?

She watched from across the vast garage as Mallus turned toward Aaron, that glowing sphere in his outstretched hands.

He offered the power to Aaron. It was the passing of the guard, so to speak.

Vilma had to fight the urge to tell him not to take it, to cry out that they would come up with another way.

To everyone else, the power of God represented a chance to right what had been done to the world. But Vilma saw it as an end to any happiness she might ever have had.

A warm hand slipped into hers, and she started. It was Taylor Corbet.

Aaron's mother stared ahead at the scene unfolding before them, sharing her strength. It couldn't be any easier for Taylor; meeting her son after so much sacrifice, only to lose him to this.

Vilma gave the woman's hand a gentle squeeze, acknowledging that she was there for her—that they were there for each other.

Aaron stepped closer to Mallus, and the fallen angel thrust his prize toward Aaron's chest.

She didn't know what to expect; none of them did.

Which made what happened then all the more scary.

Mallus felt his life slipping away.

He wondered if this had been God's plan all along.

He thought of his past, of how he'd followed Lucifer Morningstar into war, escaping God's wrath by coming to earth, and falling in with the Architects and their mad plans to make the earth superior to Heaven, no matter the cost. Those were interesting times, but what had been even more interesting was his change of heart. A change of heart brought on by the Morningstar's transformation, nonetheless. In watching Taylor and his former commander, Mallus had been able to see the beauty of this world, and all the good that God had intended for it.

Mallus's failing eyes searched the garage for a sign of her, the human woman who had transformed the Son of the Morning: Taylor Corbet. Across the room, she looked as beautiful as when he'd first seen her. There was something special about that one.

Mallus chuckled to himself. Of course there was; she had managed to tame the Morningstar. And, in the process, she had given birth to the savior Nephilim, the one who would restore the fallen to Heaven. And now he could very well be saving both earth and Heaven, if all went as hoped. If there was anything that Mallus had learned as he'd wandered this world, it was that God was always two steps ahead. One might think that He had turned His attention elsewhere, but He was there. Everywhere. In some form—He was there.

Mallus felt God's power leave him. He watched Aaron's face, not sure if this mad plan was even going to work.

But if what Mallus believed was true, then this, too, was all part of God's divine plan.

For a split second Aaron wanted to change his mind.

The little selfish part of him that made him human grew incredibly strong for an instant, almost swaying his decision. But the true Aaron was stronger than that selfish part, and he accepted the gift offered to him.

He reached out for it, to hold between his hands, but the power would have none of that, surging into his chest.

It was like nothing he had ever experienced before, it was like dying, and being born again, over and over. It was like having the sun placed inside you, so wonderful and warm, but deadly hot.

But you don't want to let it go, enduring the pain for as long as you possibly can, for to release it would be—

Awful.

The energy of God swirled around his soul, before settling in for its stay.

For now.

A soundless explosion of sheer force emanated from his

body, the way in which the force of Heaven let them all know that it was staying. Aaron watched as Mallus's body was carried away by the silent emission, his now ancient skin and bones dissolving in the force of the blast, leaving nothing behind to show that he had even been there at all.

And as quickly as it had started, the sounds of the world returned, and Aaron found himself quickly turning around to see what this sudden release had wrought.

The concrete garage was still intact, but the walls were cracked in some places, and in others huge chunks had fallen away to litter the floor.

But his main concern was for his family, for Vilma, his mother, Gabriel, and the others. He turned and saw them there, staring at him in awe.

"Are you well, Aaron Corbet?" the Unforgiven Levi asked, carefully approaching.

Aaron did not answer at first, holding his hands out before him and feeling the rush of power to his fingertips.

"Never felt better," he announced.

"Now, let's go to war."

CHAPTER TWENTY-FIVE

The Lord of Shadows saw the memory as the Sisters had.

The natives called it Beth-El.

The House of God.

But the memory was of another time; the passage of many years layered upon it.

Satan opened his eyes to the here and now. He sat on his ancient throne, in a vast and empty chamber. He needed to be alone, as alone as he had been when the Almighty had taken away his place of being with those four catastrophic words—

Let. There. Be. Light.

He cringed, remembering the pain of it, remembering how his world had been torn to ribbons by the razor-sharp light of the Almighty's creation.

Clinging to what shadows remained, he and his brothers

and sisters had managed to survive. And in doing so, Satan plotted his revenge. The question had always been, what can I do to make you suffer as I have?

The answer had always turned him toward Heaven.

Just the thought of the place was enough to fill him with an intense loathing.

A loathing that spurred him to action.

Satan rose, crossing the empty room, his armored footfalls echoing throughout the chamber.

He threw open the mammoth metal doors, nearly crushing Scox against the wall.

The imp scampered away from harm, while clutching his horn in his clawed hands.

"Did you make the call?" Satan Darkstar asked, turning his gaze to his ever-obedient servant.

"I did," Scox told him, stroking the musical instrument made from pounded brass and the thighbone from the last of a particularly cruel species.

"And?"

Scox smiled, showing small sharp teeth. "Oh yes," the imp said. "I blew the horn, and they answered."

If he was going to lead an invasion of Heaven, Satan was going to need an army. Heaven would not fall easily, of that the Lord of Shadows was sure. He needed every able-bodied beast to join his charge.

Satan strode through his cathedral, Scox following at a safe distance. He paused before the immense doors that would lead outside.

"How do I look?" he asked Scox, just to be certain that none of his armor was amiss.

"Like the master of the world that you are," the imp praised him.

The Darkstar could not help but agree.

He nodded to Scox, spurring the imp to action.

The scarlet-skinned demon ran around his master, snapping his bony fingers. From the shadows on either side of the room, great stone beasts lumbered. It was their job to guard the entrance and open the impressive doors when needed.

The golems' movements appeared synchronized. They reached out, with squared, four-fingered hands to grip the thick metal rings that hung from the center of each door. They pulled upon the rings, and the doors swung inward, the gray light of the world melting the shadow.

Satan breathed in the smell of the sea, tainted with the stink of decay, then strode out to address those who had answered his call.

He was quite pleased indeed. Portals of shadow yawned open, spilling their vile but lovely contents at his doorstep. The Darkstar could hear their many voices, buzzing like flies circling dead flesh.

A hush spread out through the gathering as they noticed their commander's arrival.

"So nice of you all to come," his voice boomed so that all could hear. "For it is time to raze the pillars of Heaven!"

A roar went up from the crowd.

He was their leader. They would fight and die for him.

And he wouldn't have it any other way.

Lucifer knew what waited behind the door in his subconscious. He had been the one to make it.

It was a large door, and normally it was covered with chains and the most intricate and sturdy of locks. But now, the broken chains and locks lay on the ground at his feet.

His greatest fear had been realized.

Milton the mouse squeaked warily upon his shoulder.

"Yes, it is as bad as I suspected—worse, actually. The monster has gained access." Lucifer recalled the last time that what lay behind this door was unleashed upon the world.

Milton's nose twitched, the whiskers on the sides of his snout tickling the flesh of Lucifer's neck.

"Would you like me to put you down? I'm sure you could run—"

The mouse replied before the Morningstar could finish.

"And there is no other that I would rather have by my side, or on my shoulder." Lucifer reached up to gently pat the rodent, who remained perched on his shoulder. "So, should we see about getting this nasty business out of the way?"

Milton made a small, guttural sound, and Lucifer understood.

The Morningstar then delivered a powerful kick to the door, shattering what he had created so very long ago to contain the punishment meted out to him by the Lord God Almighty.

The barrier disintegrated before his onslaught, and Lucifer stumbled back as a blast of heat, which stank of blood and despair, assaulted him.

In retaliation for his crimes against God and Heaven, the Almighty had collected all the pain, horror, sadness, and misery that Lucifer had caused. One could call it Hell.

And God had taken that Hell and put it inside the Morningstar, a perpetual reminder of the crimes he had committed.

Now Lucifer stood in Hell as it swirled and screamed about him, reliving every moment of his loathsome sin against his Creator and His creations. The turmoil pounced heavily upon him, driving him to his knees, wanting him to relive the Great War.

It no longer fazed him, though, for how could he ever possibly forget? He remembered what he had been responsible for every waking moment.

Lucifer slowly rose.

"Are you all right?" he asked the mouse, burying his face in the crook of Lucifer's neck.

Milton did not answer, but he could feel the animal trembling, its tiny heart beating rapidly in fear. Lucifer carefully removed him from his shoulder and placed the animal safely within his robes, up against his heart. "You'll be safer there," he told his friend, as the environment raged about him.

Hell descended upon him again, furious for all the time it had been held prisoner. Power such as this could be totally devastating, especially in the wrong hands. Lucifer knew the ramifications of it being unleashed by Satan Darkstar.

And he wondered if he was strong enough to prevent that from happening.

Verchiel emerged from the vortex with his ragtag army of monstrosities close at his heels.

He'd thought he was prepared for anything.

But he was wrong.

Verchiel found himself on an island of cooling volcanic rock, on top of which sat a great stone citadel, covered in moss. Molten rock seemed to have bubbled up from the ocean around the island, creating more tiny islands of steaming black. The surface of the sea was also littered with the twisted wreckage of mankind's folly—great warships and carriers, as well as aircraft, lost in one battle or another.

His body tensed, and the divine fire that resided at the core of his being began to stir. He was surrounded by a gathering of abominations, so large he could not hope to defeat them all.

But they paid him no mind. In fact, they barely noticed that he was even there.

Verchiel gazed down into a pool of seawater at his feet and

was shocked by what he saw. He appeared to himself as a visage of death, his hair and face caked with the dried blood of the vanquished. His armor had been forged in the fires of Heaven, but after trekking across the blighted land, it was hidden under the mud and spatter of combat.

He appeared to himself as a monster.

It was no wonder that he could walk amongst them.

The angel's thoughts were interrupted as a hush fell over the gathering. The monsters' attentions were all directed toward the citadel.

Someone had just stepped through the enormous stone doors to address the crowd of monsters. Squinting his eyes, Verchiel looked upon the black-armored figure as he heard the name whispered in multiple languages throughout the legions.

The Darkstar.

But Verchiel knew him by another.

And that name was Lucifer Morningstar.

CHAPTER TWENTY-SIX

Vilma wanted to see Aaron, to make sure that he was all right and tell him that she loved him with all her heart.

After he had absorbed the power of God, the Unforgiven had taken him to the old missile silo, concerned that he might not be able to control the intense heat that now radiated from his body.

"I'm here to see him," she told the two Unforgiven angels who stood guard outside the silo.

"No one is allowed inside," one of the pair stated.

"But I'm his girlfriend. I need to see him," she said angrily. "So if you would please—" She moved toward the door, but the Unforgiven blocked her way.

"Those are our orders."

"I don't care about your orders. Get out of my way or—"

The Unforgiven sentries spread their metallic wings wide. "We have our orders, Miss Santiago."

Vilma's true nature rose in her chest, the burning sensation slowly intensifying as the Nephilim readied to exert itself.

But it wasn't needed.

The door behind them unlatched, and an authoritative voice came from inside. "Let her in." It was Aaron's voice, but there was something strange about it. Something different.

The guards were about to protest, when Aaron interjected. "Let me remind you that I am not a prisoner."

"But Commander Levi—"

"Your commander should worry about what's to come, not who is or isn't allowed to see me. Let her in."

The sentries closed their wings and stepped aside. Vilma passed through the doorway and closed the door firmly behind her.

Aaron turned toward her.

He had changed.

It wasn't necessarily a bad change, but it was a change.

Where he had once been about five-eight, five-eight and a half, he was now more than six feet. And his skin . . .

He wasn't wearing a shirt, and his skin had taken on a kind of golden-brown coloring, his muscles larger and much more pronounced.

"Been working out?" she asked nervously.

Aaron looked down at himself and smiled.

"Pretty crazy, right?" he said. "Guess the power of God is doing a bit of remodeling."

"Are you . . . ?" she began, but didn't finish as she stared into his eyes.

"I'm fine," he said. "It really didn't hurt at all. In fact, I didn't realize how much I've changed until my mother pointed it out."

"Has she been in to see you?"

He nodded. "Yeah, Frick and Frack out there let her by without any problem. Fringe benefit of being best friends with Levi, I guess."

Vilma reached out to touch his muscular arm. It was very warm.

"Any problem with the heat?" she asked.

At first he looked at her quizzically, but then understood. "Oh, you mean the internal fire?"

"Yeah."

"Early on," Aaron said. "But I've figured out how to keep it under control. In fact . . ." Aaron stepped away from her. "Watch this."

Vilma was shocked when divine fire suddenly appeared upon his exposed flesh, as if ignited with a lighter.

He saw the concern on her face and smiled. "It's okay, really," he said, his calmness putting her more at ease.

The fire then wrapped itself around his biceps. The holy

flame began to solidify, becoming a golden metal that sparked as if reflecting light upon a mirrored surface.

"What do you think?" he asked, obviously proud of his achievement. "Pretty impressive, right?"

The fire had spread over his entire body, armoring him from the neck down. He extended his arm toward her, and she reached out tentatively to touch the armor. It was only slightly warm to the touch.

"It feels like metal," she said.

"And for all intents and purposes, it is. Metal made from divine fire."

There was a lag in conversation as they admired his armor, but Vilma could not hold back any longer.

"How does it feel?"

He smiled. "The armor? It feels like—"

She shook her head. "No, what you have inside you."

"It feels fine," Aaron told her, but she could always tell when he was lying.

"How does it feel, Aaron?" she repeated quietly.

His face became more serious. "You know when you're at the zoo, and you look into the tiger's cage and it's just lying there, chilling in the sun, but you know that it could jump up at any moment and kill anything it wanted?"

Vilma nodded.

"That's what it feels like," he said. "It's just chilling, waiting until . . ."

He seemed afraid, and she reached out, taking his armored hand in hers. As she did this the golden metal returned to fire, and then vanished, the flesh of her hand now touching his.

Vilma wanted to tell him that everything would be all right, but the look in his eyes told her differently.

"It's changing me," he said softly. "I can feel it working inside me. It's trying to make me a better fit, but I was never made for this."

She squeezed Aaron's hand, not at all liking what she was hearing, but knowing that she needed to be strong.

For him.

"I'm not sure how much longer I'll be me," he continued. "I want you to know how much I love you, just in case I . . ."

Vilma stood on her tiptoes and silenced his words with a kiss. She wanted him to know that she loved him. But she couldn't tell him they would be okay. She didn't want to make promises that she might not be able to keep.

Their lips parted and she gazed lovingly into his eyes, but something wasn't right.

Where there had been love a mere second ago, now there was a strange blankness.

"Aaron?" she asked.

"They're coming," he said flatly, unceremoniously releasing her hand, as his flesh caught fire, and divine armor again took shape upon his body.

Levi suddenly appeared in the doorway, the Unforgiven lined up behind him.

"Are you ready?" the leader of the fallen angels asked.

Without answering, Aaron strode from the chamber, leaving Vilma standing there alone.

The warmth of his kiss already cold upon her lips.

Dusty stood before the restroom mirror, seeing himself in the now, but at the same time glimpsing his future.

The Instrument was spreading.

The pieces of the shattered sword were joining together in his body.

Dusty removed his sweatshirt. In the flickering fluorescent light, it looked as though he was wearing a gray metal chest plate, only he hadn't put on any armor. Yet that was what his chest had become . . . what all of his flesh was slowly becoming.

"Dusty?" a gruff voice called to him from outside the restroom.

He quickly put his sweatshirt back on, just as Gabriel nudged open the door and padded in across the tile floor.

"Everything okay?" the dog asked, looking up at him.

"I'm good," Dusty said. "What's up?"

"Everyone is gathering in one of the classrooms for a strategy session," the dog explained. "Thought you'd like to come, maybe help guide the conversation."

"I'm leaving," Dusty said unemotionally.

"You're leaving?" Gabriel questioned. "Where are you going?"

Dusty again turned toward the mirror for a glimpse of the futures—his futures, and the world's.

"Can't really say," he said. "Sorry."

"Well, I'm going with you," Gabriel said bravely. "We're in this together. We started this journey together, and that's how we'll end it."

"What about Aaron?"

Gabriel had to think about that. "He'll be fine," he said after a moment. "He's got to do what he's got to do, and I have to do what I have to do."

"And you have to be with him," Dusty said. He turned back to the mirror, tapping the glass with the tips of his fingers. "I see so many reasons for you to be at his side."

"But what about you?" Gabriel asked.

Dusty could feel the Labrador's eyes upon him, as the metallic tinge crept up the exposed skin of his neck. He pulled the hood of the sweatshirt up over his head. "What about me?"

"I'm your ride, remember."

"I remember."

Dusty headed for the hallway, Gabriel walking behind him.

Dusty looked down the passage.

"The meeting is that way," he told the dog. "And I'm going this way." He hooked a thumb in the opposite direction.

"Are you sure about this?" Gabriel asked.

Dusty laughed. "No way," he said. "There are a ton of ways that this could go wrong."

"Then let me go with you," the dog begged. "Let me help to make it right."

Gabriel's words created a rush of visions, slightly different from the last set.

"You'll be helping by staying here," Dusty said. "Go with him."

He started to walk away.

"You're going to make me worry about you," Gabriel grumbled.

"Don't," Dusty said, without looking back. "We've all got a part to play, and I've got a date with the future.

"If everything goes as I expect, it's going to get pretty damn interesting."

Enoch dreamed of his past, and the glory that was his when chosen by God to become the first Metatron.

Yes, there was much glory, but there was also fear.

Lots and lots of fear.

To be a lowly man, taken up to Heaven, paraded before God and his holy messengers. Yes, lots and lots of fear.

But the Lord God had explained that Enoch was chosen. He was the perfect human form in which to create the ultimate being that would watch over the earth while God was away—

While God was away?

While God was elsewhere doing what God does.

Enoch had embraced this new identity, doing as the Creator had intended until—

Until I was murdered.

The memory of the experience returned to his consciousness. The power of God and His angels had been viciously cut away, and his human aspect had been left to die.

The trinity torn asunder.

Slowly, Enoch opened his young eyes, remembering how he had been taken by the black-garbed Agents of . . .

The Architects.

Enoch awoke with a start. He was encased in a transparent sphere of energy, a bubble of sorts that hung in the air above the great room where the Architects had gathered.

The child knelt in the bubble, placing his hands on the surface of the sphere to observe his captors.

Twelve Architects stood around a ghostly interpretation of the world. Visuals of what was happening across the world would suddenly pop up, showing some sort of event, but each quickly went away to be replaced by another.

The events depicted changed as quickly as the Architects themselves.

They transformed before Enoch's eyes; first appearing as rolling spheres of fire covered in all-seeing eyes, and then morphing to a more human shape, with multiple sets of gigantic wings growing from their backs, and then to enormously tall figures, covered head to toe in robes that seemed to be cut from the fabric of the night sky—stars and all.

It was almost as if they couldn't make up their minds as to what they wanted to look like, deciding that they would look like many things.

They had assumed the form of the roiling balls of fire covered in eyes again, when he cried out for their attention.

"Hello!" Enoch called out, his high child's voice echoing inside the bubble. He banged on the surface, causing his prison to emit a loud humming sound.

One of the Architects noticed, many eyes flowing into one single orb fixed upon him.

Enoch waved at the eye. "Hello," he said again. "I'm awake."

"You are," said the flaming orb in a nearly deafening voice that the boy heard inside his head.

"May I ask where you have brought me, and why?"

The flaming body of the orb continued to spin, but the large, unblinking eye remained in place and just stared.

"You have been brought to the Habitat," the voice inside Enoch's head spoke. "To prevent the pursuit of perfection from being interrupted."

"Perfection?" Enoch repeated. "You mean out there?" He gestured outside his bubble, at their hologram of the world, and laughed. "You're joking."

"Joking?"

"Have you been outside your Habitat?" Enoch asked. "It's chaos out there. There isn't a sign of perfection to be found anywhere."

"We are making perfection," said the Architect.

"From chaos? You think you're going to create something perfect from that mess?"

"It is our intention, yes."

"Let me see if I understand this," Enoch said. "My existence is somehow threatening your vision of perfection."

"It is."

"Even though I'm here because of the Creator—because of your Creator."

The Architect remained silent.

"So, you thought that you would prevent God from spoiling your plans by getting me out of the way."

The Architect still did not respond.

Enoch's voice grew louder. "That if you brought me here and held me captive, everything would work out as you planned."

The Architect rejoined his brothers, all ignoring Enoch as they continued to guide the world toward what they perceived to be perfection.

"But you don't understand," Enoch chuckled to himself. He sat down, legs splayed out before him. "You haven't removed me from the equation at all. . . .

"I'm exactly where I need to be."

CHAPTER TWENTY-SEVEN

Satan Darkstar flew over his armies, his wings of ebony pounding the air as he flew beyond the circle of islands and wasted crafts of war to where the ocean pulsed and churned.

"Follow me!" he cried, his voice booming with the intensity of the most powerful of storms.

His legions surged forward, marching into the churning ocean.

Satan smiled at their obedience. They were willing to die at his command, but he could not afford to be wasteful. Every able-bodied servant of the Community would be needed if they were to effectively march their way into Heaven.

Darting down toward the restless sea, the Darkstar produced a spear of shadow and reared back to throw it, piercing the ocean waters.

It did not take long for this action to bear fruit, the waters starting to glow with an eerie yellow light, and then to bubble and churn.

Satan flew higher as something of great size slowly rose up from beneath.

The gray-skinned behemoth broke the surface with an earsplitting roar, its tiny dark eyes, accustomed to the black of the lower depths, squinting even in the feeble daylight. The creature splashed wildly in the froth, its flat tail slapping the surface, creating enormous swells that crashed upon the island shores, dispersing those of his armies that collected there.

The gray-skinned beast was a cousin of sorts, the spawn between one of Satan's dead sisters and a primordial aquatic life-form. They had only been able to create one child, but to Satan it was a most magnificent child indeed.

Satan flew down past the beast's blunt head, to where he believed one of its ears would be, and whispered what he wished of it, before flying off to take care of the most important of tasks.

Above the wide expanse of ocean, Satan Darkstar summoned a sword of endless night. The blade was enormous, and bolts of darkness like tendrils of electric current leaped from the shaft of the blade.

Satan had created it not for battle, but for cutting through the fabric of reality.

For making passages from here, to there.

But this would not be just any passage, but an entrance large enough to march his legions through to where the war to end all wars would begin.

Armageddon.

Satan hovered in the air and closed his eyes. He remembered what the Sisters of Umbra had seen, what the power of God had recalled.

The Darkstar lifted the mighty sword and slashed at what appeared to be nothing, but in actuality was creating a perforation in the planes of existence. An enormous gash appeared before the Lord of Shadows, but he did not stop there, hacking and slashing away, making the slit larger, and larger still, until he believed that the hole that he'd cut was large enough.

Once satisfied, Satan turned to observe the great sea beast.

The behemoth swam close to the islands, allowing the legions who could not reach the passage on their own to climb upon its massive back for transport.

Hovering before his portal, Satan Darkstar raised the sword of endless night to the shifting skies.

"Onward to Beth-El," he bellowed, his voice carried like thunder on the wind across the ocean.

"Onward to the House of God."

A fully armored Aaron strode into the Unforgiven command center with Levi by his side.

The place was abuzz with activity. Unforgiven agents darted about the large, circular room in front of a curved wall, made up of multiple monitors showing events transpiring across the globe.

From what Aaron could see of the broadcasts, it was eerily silent around the world. There didn't seem to be a monster around.

And he was about to find out why.

"Status update," Levi ordered, descending from the chamber entrance to the floor where the agents worked.

"Portals of transference have manifested across the globe," one of the fallen angels reported. "And the monster hordes have been using them to leave their territories."

Aaron followed Levi to the thick of the command center.

"Portals of transference?" Aaron questioned as his eyes darted to the monitors, some of which showed scenes of empty cities, while others showed swirling portals of black energy, armies of nightmare beasts marching obediently inside. "But transference to where?"

It was the first that the Unforgiven workers noticed him, their attention drawn to him as he waited for an answer. They seemed almost mesmerized by the sight of him.

By the being that was gradually becoming the new Metatron.

Levi stepped forward, punching some keys on one of the control panels. Three smaller screens merged into a larger one.

"We have some difficulty seeing through the thick cloud cover, but it appears they started here," the fallen angel said.

Aaron felt an icy chill electrify his spine at the sight of the churchlike structure that rose up from the middle of the ocean like a victory flag. There were other, smaller islands surrounding the larger, as well as what appeared to be a graveyard of ruined warships and aircraft; attempts at aggression easily thwarted.

"What is this place?" he asked in awe.

"It has been hidden to our satellites up until now," Levi said, hitting buttons and twisting knobs, trying to get a better view of the nightmarish place.

And suddenly the answer came to Aaron in a flash of pain.

"The Darkstar," he said, eyes locked on the ominous-looking citadel. "This is his place."

The screens were intermittently marred with static, the satellites' signals being disturbed by outside forces, but they could still see through the disturbance.

"Possibly," Levi said as he continued to play with the controls. "Our sensors currently indicate that the transference portals all opened here."

"All right," Aaron said as he leaned forward for a closer look. "Then where are they?"

"I don't know," the fallen angel said gravely.

"Sir," one of the other Unforgiven technicians called. "I've managed to clarify a video transmission from a weather buoy close to that vicinity that you should look at," the tech said.

"Put it up," Levi commanded, pointing toward the great screen before them.

The Unforgiven tech's fingers danced over a computer keyboard.

The major monitor shifted to hissing static, before a moving image appeared. Attached to an ocean buoy, the picture rose and fell with the waves, the lens splashed periodically by the sea.

At first Aaron could make out nothing, but then . . .

"What is that?" he asked, leaning in closer to better discern the image.

There was something enormous in the water. The unknown creature was whale-like, but with short, muscular limbs that propelled its cumbersome body. The sea beast was swimming toward what looked to be another portal, only this one was easily ten times the size of the ones they'd seen across the world, and it hung just above the ocean.

"Look at its back," Levi stated, pointing to the screen.

Aaron focused on the great beast moving in the water, finally seeing what it was that the Unforgiven leader was calling attention to.

Riding upon the sea monster's back were what could have been hundreds—maybe thousands—of nightmarish beasts, heading toward the larger portal of transference.

"Looks like we found the missing legions," Aaron said as the behemoth rose up out of the water to begin to climb up into the swirling passage torn in the fabric of reality.

"We still don't know where they are going. See if we can recalibrate one of the satellites to give us even a glimpse into that portal," the Unforgiven leader commanded.

The techs immediately went to work. The camera on the buoy shared a final glimpse of the great beast, its finned tail swishing as the monster disappeared through the supernatural doorway, with all its riders, to the other side.

"We have something!" one of the techs announced. They all turned their attention to the latest signal.

"Freeze that image," Levi commanded.

The techs were cleaning up the image when Aaron felt it. Just as when he'd recognized the home of the Darkstar, he suddenly knew what was waiting on the other side of the transference portal. The power of God that now resided within him told him all he needed to know.

"I know this place," Aaron announced, his voice sounding out with divine intensity.

As the image improved, they saw a desert.

"This is where it is buried," Aaron proclaimed.

"Where what is buried?" Levi asked him.

"Beneath the sands of this Israeli desert lie the remains of the ancient city of Megiddo," Aaron proclaimed. "And beneath that, I fear, is the prize that the Darkstar seeks."

"Megiddo," Levi repeated. "Where it has been prophesied that the final battle between good and evil would occur." Onscreen the vast armies of monsters swarmed around the desert.

"He is searching for Beth-El," Aaron said. "The Darkstar is searching for the House of God."

It took a moment, but Aaron saw from the looks upon the Unforgiven's faces that they understood the enormity of the situation.

"The Ladder," Levi stated flatly.

"Yes," Aaron answered him. "This was where the Ladder once existed, and where Satan Darkstar plans for it to exist again."

"But that's impossible," Levi protested. "Without the power of God . . ."

"He has something just as powerful in his possession," Aaron explained. "He has the power of the Son of the Morning—the power of Lucifer . . .

The power of Hell itself."

Undeterred by the superior number of the newly awakened Nephilim Inheritors, the Angels of the Void attacked without hesitation.

Cameron recoiled from the scenes of wanton savagery.

William drew first blood, eviscerating two of the revived Nephilim who came at him. The expressions of shock and fear on their faces as they realized that they had been killed were truly chilling. The other Void Angels followed their leader, leaping into the fray with cries of excitement.

"We have to help them," Cameron said, still attempting to shrug off the effects of the Void Angel's poisoned claws.

Melissa went to the Custodian, who lay still on the floor.

"I think he's dying," she cried.

Cameron managed to stand, focusing on his divine fire to try and burn away the poison's effects.

"We'll all be dead if we don't do something," he told her. They both looked up at the maelstrom of wings, fiery weapons, and slashing claws. The blood and bodies of Nephilim rained down within the chamber.

"These Nephilim have been in cold storage for God knows how many years," Cameron said. "They haven't a clue what they're up against."

"We barely understand what they are," Melissa agreed.

"Yeah, but you beat one," he reminded her. "How?"

"I don't know," she answered. "We connected somehow and . . ."

"How did you connect?"

She shook her head. "We were fighting, my sword struck her claws, and . . . I really don't remember."

"Is that how you did it?" he asked.

Melissa watched the slaughter unfold above them. The Nephilim were dying, one after the other, the Void Angels cutting them down with ease.

"It was the connection," Melissa then said.

"We've already established that—but how did you connect?"

"No, it's the connection," Melissa said as she placed a hand upon her chest. "Us to them."

She looked at him. "These Nephilim have no connection to them," she attempted to explain. "They're just enemies to be cut down."

"We have the connection: our friendship," Cameron said, at last understanding what Melissa was getting at.

"Only we can stop them," she said.

"I knew you were going to say that," Cameron said.

"It's the only way to save those who are still alive."

"Then we better get going," Cameron said as he spread his wings and leaped into the air. "Wouldn't want to be responsible for the loss of any more lives."

Satan Darkstar remembered the desert landscape as it had once been.

He saw not the broad expanse of desert with its sparse vegetation that spread before him, but a thriving city.

Megiddo.

And nestled deep within the bosom of the earth, existing before the great city had even been built, was his prize.

The House of God.

It was not Satan's own memory, but that of the Sisters of

Umbra, who had acquired the recollection from God's power, which they had received from the Architects.

The Architects.

Satan realized that there would soon come a day when he would need to deal with these mysterious angelic beings, but today was for other concerns.

A horrible, mournful death cry rolled across the harsh desert region.

The great beast of the sea that had transported Satan's troops across the ocean was dying.

Cut off from the sea, the gray-skinned behemoth thrashed in the white desert sand in the throes of death. His legions fled from the monster, not wanting to be crushed.

The Darkstar reached out to the creature with his mind. The behemoth begged for mercy, begged to be returned to its blessed sea, but the Darkstar ignored its pleas.

It would be far more convenient to just let the beast die.

Which it did, slumping in the sand with a final, mournful groan.

And with the beast's death, Satan looked upon the passage he had created and wished it no more.

The pulsating tear crackled and hummed at the edges as reality attempted to repair itself, and he allowed it. The hole grew smaller, collapsing upon itself in a rush of air and the nearly deafening crack of a sonic boom.

His legions trained their gazes on him, every one of their monstrous eyes fixed upon his glory.

This was what the Darkstar had been missing; this was why he still existed.

This was what it must feel like to be God.

The thought spurred him on, and a sword of war grew in his hand.

Satan raised his weapon as he marched across the desert, urging his armies to follow, the movement of the vast gathering causing the very floor of the desert to tremble with their footfalls.

An archeological dig existed in the location where his prize was hidden, layers of the city of Megiddo exposed to the world after countless centuries.

The archeologists might have uncovered priceless historical artifacts, but they had yet to come across the true prize.

Satan took to the air, his black-feathered wings carrying him above the monstrous throng.

"Dragons!" he roared.

Four of the large reptilian beasts removed themselves from the gathering, taking flight to join him in the skies. They flew in languid circles about him, waiting for commands.

"Reveal to me my prize!"

Satan directed his sword at the timeworn city.

The great sky beasts screeched in compliance, arcing their

bodies toward the desert below. Positioning themselves around the dig, the great dragons reared back their heads, taking in enormous lungfuls of air to mix with the heavily combustible fluids produced from venom sacks in the backs of their cavernous mouths for an explosive and fiery effect.

The dragons spewed their fire at what was exposed of Megiddo, billowing clouds of fire and black smoke roiling up from below as the reptiles' venom ate away at the primordial sands to expose what lay hidden beneath.

Satan returned to earth, touching down upon the desert, which had been crystallized to glass from the intensity of the heat.

The dragons ceased their spew, rearing back to circle what they had exposed. Satan waited patiently as the steam cleared. As the location began to cool, Satan saw that what remained of Megiddo, as well as layers upon layers of the desert strata, had been burned away. Waiting for him below, he saw his prize.

Beth-El was an odd-shaped structure, like a pyramid with its point sliced away. Satan leaped into the hole, using his wings to slow his descent. Landing before the looming structure, he was amused by the stairs of gold that led up to an even larger set of doors.

With memories not belonging to him, he recalled climbing these mighty steps with ease in the form of the great armored Metatron.

Excitement the likes of which he'd never experienced

coursed through the Darkstar as he ascended the remaining steps to the House of God. There was no discernable way to open the mammoth doors except to pry them apart by force.

Sword still in hand, Satan Darkstar jammed his shadow blade in the seam between the doors, using all his might to try and pry the pair apart.

Wings pounding the air, Satan leaned and pushed upon the sword, crying out with exertion.

He was nearly exhausted when he felt movement.

Yes, yes it was moving.

A new strength born of the promise of triumph fueled him. The left-side door bulged outward with a serpentine hiss as the seal was broken.

Satan marveled at his feat, sending his sword back into the shadows as he approached the door, grabbing it in both hands and pulling it toward him.

As the door inexorably came open, he was struck by a gout of heavenly fire.

It burned both physically and mentally, and Satan Darkstar screamed as he threw himself away from the entrance, and the threat within.

His armored form, still engulfed in the caustic flames of the divine, tumbled down the steps of giants.

Calling upon the shadows, the Darkstar pulled the darkness around him like a cocoon, engulfing his entire body to extinguish the holy fire. Satan then cast the cloak away, his black armor still smoldering, as he prepared to deal with that which would keep him from his reward.

Turning his gaze to the top of the stairs, he saw them, as deadly-looking in the flesh as they were in memory.

Two of them glared down at him from the entrance to Beth-El. Their bodies were lion-like, large and powerful, with human heads that stared at him voraciously. From their furred, muscular backs sprang two sets of fiery wings that slowly fanned the air as they watched their prey from above.

These were the Cherubim.

The guardians of the House of God.

It was their job to keep him from gaining entrance to this holy place.

And it was the Darkstar's mission to see these bestial angels dead at his feet.

CHAPTER TWENTY-EIGHT

Through ghostly eyes, Lorelei stared at the dark arrow tattoo on the hand of the body she currently possessed.

"So you think it will take us to Enoch?" Jeremy asked.

She tried not to look at him as he removed his torn and bloodstained clothing and slipped into one of the tight, black leather outfits that the Agents of the Architects wore.

"It will take us to the Architects," Lorelei answered in the gruff voice of the corpse. "It seems pretty simple."

"Then that should do it." Jeremy moved to stand beside her, staring at her expectantly.

"And then what?" Lorelei asked.

He looked at her as though she had two heads. "Then we save Enoch and get out of there."

"That's your plan?" she asked. She could feel the corpse

decaying. She'd need to find another relatively soon if they kept this up.

"It's all I can think of," he said, showing an emotional side that she'd never seen at the school. "I made a promise to protect the little tinker and haven't done a job of it. Do you have any other ideas?"

She thought for a moment, attempting to access the corpse's memories. There wasn't much there to use. "Not really," she had to admit.

"That's it then. We go with my plan—get to the Architects, find Enoch, and get the hell out."

"You make it sound so simple," Lorelei said.

"That's what you have to keep telling yourself when you're in the thick of it." The hint of a smile appeared on Jeremy's blood-spattered face. "So, can you make it work?" he asked, gesturing with his chin at the tattoo on the corpse's arm.

"Yeah, I think I can," she answered. "It's pretty straightforward. I just press it to activate the spell."

"Then I should probably get close," Jeremy said, sidling up beside her. "Oh, wait a sec." He pulled the black mask that the Agents wore over his face. "Okay. I'm good."

"You better be, if we're going to get out of this alive."

"What do you care?" Jeremy asked. "You're already dead."

Same old Jeremy, Lorelei thought as she raised the corpse's bare arm and applied pressure to the tattoo.

It was as if the world had dropped out from beneath them.

One moment they were standing in the woods, the next—

Jeremy bent over, violently retching, pulling the mask from his face so as not to throw up in it.

"What the bloody hell was that?" he asked, wiping vomit from the side of his mouth.

"From what I could see, it wasn't much different from how the Nephilim travel," Lorelei said. "It's where we are that has me curious."

They were in a circular room, standing on a raised dais. Everything was smooth, rounded.

"It reminds me of a seashell," he said. "Like this place was grown, not built."

"We're between the moments," Lorelei blurted out.

Jeremy looked at her as though she was crazy. "And what, pray tell, does that mean?"

"This place, the Architects have created it between moments in time, between the then and the now."

"Now you're just giving me a headache," Jeremy said. "Any idea where they've taken Enoch?"

She tried to pull more information from the corpse's memories, but got nothing. She was going to need to find a new vehicle to possess very soon.

"Let's go out here," she suggested, heading toward the only door in the room.

Jeremy slipped the mask back over his face as he followed her into an equally rounded hallway. "Which way?"

As if on cue, an Agent came around the bend, stopping before them. "Uh," Jeremy began. "Where have they taken the child?"

Without a word, a knife appeared in the Agent's hand.

"They don't speak," Lorelei said.

"Whoops." Jeremy created a sword of fire to meet the Agent's attack.

"Don't damage the body too much," Lorelei cried out. "I'll need it if—"

Jeremy screamed like a madman, swinging the sword with such force and accuracy that the flaming blade sliced through the Agent's neck, its head flying through the air as its body collapsed to the floor.

The Agent's head rolled to Lorelei's feet, bulging eyes, shocked by death, staring up at her through the eyeholes in the mask.

"Sorry," Jeremy offered, but no amount of apology could keep her in the body she currently inhabited. She had to leave or risk being trapped forever.

"Not good," was all she could manage before she pulled herself free to float above the decaying corpse as it crumbled to the floor.

"Not good at all," Lorelei stressed, her voice no longer heard by anyone but herself.

Melissa and Cameron soared upward within the mountain's chamber into the aerial battle between the revived Nephilim and the Angels of the Void.

The Nephilim fought with all their heart, weapons of fire striking at their bat-winged enemies, but they were just not strong enough. Centuries of inactivity had made them far too slow.

The Void Angels moved at the speed of thought. It would be a slaughter, unless Melissa and Cameron intervened.

"I'm going in," Cameron yelled, thrusting with his wings to collide with Russell, as the dark angel was about to tear out the throat of a female Nephilim he had pinned to the rocky wall.

Melissa set her sights on Samantha.

"Feeling brave, are we?" the Void Angel asked as she ripped the wings from a struggling Nephilim, letting him plummet in a pathetic spiral to the ground below.

Melissa held her tongue, focusing everything on her attack. She lunged at Samantha, but the black angel was quick, evading her with incredible precision, slashing at her as she passed.

Melissa evaded the claws, but barely, crashing into the wall with enough force to daze her. Shaking her head to clear it, she saw that Samantha was almost upon her, the girl's mouth twisted in a malicious grin.

Folding her wings tight to her back, Melissa allowed herself to drop as Samantha's claws scraped across the stone wall, just missing her. Then she reached up, grabbing hold of the Void Angel's ankles, pulling her down. Samantha shrieked, struggling ferociously as they fell.

Her leathery wings flapped wildly, slowing their descent, and proving to be the distraction that Melissa needed.

Filling her mind with thoughts of when they'd first met at the school, scared of what they had become and what the future had in store for them, Melissa remembered how Aaron and Vilma had helped them, how they'd helped each other.

The pair bounced off rock protruding from the mountain wall, and Melissa was forced to release the dark angel. But before Samantha could recover, Melissa created a sword of fire, slashing at her foe. Samantha did exactly as Melissa had expected, blocking the sword strike with her elongated claws.

There was a strange explosion of light, tinged with darkness, and the two were forcibly repelled from one another, both plummeting to the ground below.

Even though Cameron had Russell pinned to the ground, the Void Angel was incredibly fast, jabbing the razor-sharp claw on his index finger into Cameron's side.

The Nephilim cried out, jumping away before the dark angel could do further damage. He pressed a hand to his side to stanch the flow of blood.

"Did you really think you'd have a chance?" Russell taunted. "Look around you, Cam. The ground is covered with dead Nephilim."

And he was right.

Cameron was beginning to feel woozy. He tried to focus on the divine fire coursing through his veins—

As well as the memories of his dead friends that would allow him to defeat the evil angels.

"You thought you were such a badass," Russell continued. "The quiet warrior." He smiled a wicked smile, and all Cameron wanted to do was punch his face in.

But that wasn't the solution. Cameron needed to remember their time together, when they were family.

When they were all Nephilim.

"Are you still burning yourself after every kill?" Russell asked.

Cameron must have looked shocked.

"What, you didn't know I knew? Oh yeah, I knew. Watched you do it, burning your flesh with the edge of your sword."

Cameron didn't know what to say.

"I used to think you were so cool," Russell spat with contempt. "But then I died. And when I was brought back, I could see you for what you truly are." He paused, and Cameron noticed the muscles in the Void Angel's legs tense.

"Doomed," Russell cried as he sprang.

There wasn't much of an opportunity to think, never mind act. Cameron relied entirely on instinct, reaching for what was the closest object to protect himself from the slashing, razor-sharp claws.

The Nephilim corpse took the brunt of the damage as

Cameron thrust it at his foe, buying himself a few precious seconds.

"Have you no respect for the dead, Cam?" Russell asked, tossing the corpse aside.

But Cameron was ready as Russell flapped his powerful wings, charging at him with incredible speed. Cameron met the attack, swinging his sword of fire and conjuring the memory of the bond the two had shared before Russell's untimely death.

"What—what have you done to me?" Samantha asked, her speech slurring.

Melissa felt incredibly cold, experiencing what her former teammate had endured when her life had been taken, and after some semblance of that life had been returned by the power of darkness. Melissa wanted nothing more than to curl up in a dark corner with her eyes tightly shut, but that most certainly would have meant her death.

She knew there was still some sort of connection between the Nephilim and the Angels of the Void. It was the answer to defeating them.

Samantha tried to get away, but Melissa couldn't allow that to happen.

"You're going nowhere," she managed, forcing herself across the expanse of floor and jumping on Samantha's back before the dark angel could take flight.

"Get off of me!" Samantha screeched groggily, still reeling from the effects of Melissa's heartfelt memories.

Samantha spun around, her claws growing in length, and Melissa reacted as a true warrior, swinging her arm with great force and connecting with Samantha's chin. The severity of the blow snapped the girl's head to one side, allowing Melissa the chance she had waited for.

"There's still some divine inside you," Melissa said, taking the black-armor-garbed girl in her embrace. "We're still connected."

Samantha screamed, her wings beating the air as she fought to escape.

But Melissa held fast, the fire of the Nephilim igniting within her body, even as the darkness welled up within Samantha.

"Don't touch me!" Samantha wailed. She almost slipped from Melissa's grasp, but the Nephilim would have none of that, head-butting her foe, stunning her yet again.

The darkness and light flowed from their bodies, forming a cocoon about them; fire and darkness swirling around their struggling bodies, as ancient forces, good and evil, vied for supremacy.

Melissa knew that these two forces could very easily destroy them both, but it was the only way to truly defeat her foe—

And grant her friend the final rest that she deserved.

And then Melissa saw it.

It was just a fleeting glance, but at the center of her foe, where she had always imagined the soul to be, Melissa saw what remained of her friend. It was like a jagged piece of flint lying at the center of the black miasma, gone cold and dark with the coming of death.

A piece of Samantha's soul that Melissa could reignite if she was strong enough.

The darkness was winning, driving her to the ground, forcing its way into her body to suffocate the light of her divine birthright.

But Melissa remembered what she had seen in the center of the Void Angel's being and held on to that image.

She dropped her guard, letting the darkness overwhelm her, letting it become overconfident.

And just when it thought it had won—

The fire of Heaven was in her hand. Melissa reached through the darkness for Samantha's hard, blackened soul.

And wrapped her burning hand around it.

Cameron wasn't sure how much longer he would last.

He swung with his sword, but Russell's claws were just as effective, blocking his swipes and putting him back on the defensive.

His wound was still bleeding, flowing down his side and into the waistline of his pants.

Cameron tried to do as Melissa instructed, putting the

memories of his deceased friends at the forefront of his thoughts.

He could see that it was having some effect, but not necessarily the one he had been hoping for.

The memories of the life they'd shared at Saint Athanasius just seemed to make the reanimated Nephilim all the more furious. Russell screamed, clouds of darkness rising from his body as they continued to battle one another.

Cameron's sword of flame shattered with Russell's latest attack, and suddenly Cameron realized that he was in trouble. His mind felt foggy as he tried to re-create the blade.

"What's the matter, Cam?" Russell taunted. "Not the badass you thought you were?"

Cameron pushed himself across the floor, struggling to pull his thoughts together, but the poison was wreaking havoc on his system.

"I see your memories," Russell said, reaching down and running his claws across Cameron's leg.

The Nephilim screamed as they cut through his jeans to the flesh beneath.

"It was all a lie—all of it," Russell spat.

A sword sparked to life, and Cameron slashed at Russell to drive him back. The Void Angel just swatted it away, reducing the blade to sparks.

"We weren't a family. We were just fodder for God. Poor, pathetic creatures who had no real understanding of our place, or what we were even supposed to do."

"You're wrong," Cameron said. He created a shield of fire as Russell's claws descended upon him again.

"I died afraid . . . praying for God to save me," Russell growled. "And what did I get?"

The claws came again and again, slashing at the shield of fire.

"I think you know the answer."

Cameron couldn't remember the good times anymore, that sense of family that all the Nephilim had shared.

All he felt was an awful cold.

"Will you pray to God, Cam?" Russell asked. "Will you beg for Him to save you, even though you know He isn't listening?"

Overwhelmed by fear and depression, Cameron felt himself succumbing to Russell. He knew he was going to die, and for the briefest of moments, he welcomed it.

But then he changed his mind.

Cameron's internal fire sparked, shining through the cloud of shadow that wished to take him down. And it was all he needed to rekindle his yearning for life.

The darkness still pressed upon him, and through that thick, liquid black, he sensed Russell's claws. They were descending on him, ready to rip his flesh from the bone, to open him wide and let the darkness in.

But Cameron had other plans.

He thought of a knife with a blade sharp enough to cut through the shadow, thicker than night.

With a point keen enough to reach the core.

Cameron surged up.

Plunging the blade into a heart of darkness.

Samantha screamed, but Melissa did not let go, continuing to will the fire of God into her hand, which clutched the blackened piece of the Void Angel's soul.

And as she cried and begged, and thrashed her arms, legs, and wings, Melissa held on until the soul began to glow.

Melissa released the soul fragment, repelled by the thrashing of the dark angel.

"What is this?" Samantha wailed, looking down at herself.

The armor that she wore began to disintegrate, rays of divine light breaking through cracks that had formed in metal forged of shadow. Pieces began to fall away, clattering to the floor.

Samantha tried to fly away, to join with her brethren, but as she unfurled her wings, they immediately started to disintegrate. She fell to the ground as the light in her body intensified. She was crying now, sobbing pitifully as the last fragments of shadow that had clung to her dissolved away.

"I'm so sorry," Samantha said, raising her head to look at Melissa. "I never wanted to do this. . . ."

Melissa took her friend in her arms. The girl's body glowed hotly, but she shivered as if freezing. "Don't be afraid. It's all right now."

"Yes," Samantha agreed as the light grew even more intense. "It is."

There came a searing flash, and then the girl was no longer in Melissa's arms, but she was far from gone.

Melissa felt Samantha inside her. The fallen Nephilim's inner fire joined with hers.

There was another flash of blinding brilliance, and Melissa saw Cameron kneeling amid wisps of fleeting shadow, as his own foe returned to the light.

From across the expanse they shared a look of understanding.

It had become so much more now than just defeating their enemies.

They owed their friends another chance for peace.

The warmth of Samantha's presence inside Melissa gave her a whole new level of confidence and strength. She could see the same in Cameron as he approached, and they both turned toward the battle that still raged between the Nephilim and the surviving Angels of the Void.

"Enough!" Melissa screamed, her voice echoing through the stone chamber.

The creatures that had once been Kirk and William looked to them, cruel smiles forming at the corners of their pale, twisted mouths. But those looks of perverse pleasure were short-lived, as they recognized traces of Samantha and Russell within Melissa and Cameron.

The darkness exploded from the surviving Void Angels

in waves, propelling both across the room, but Melissa and Cameron were ready. They allowed the glow from their bodies to expand—the light driving back the Void Angels.

"What have you done?" William cried out, his face twisted in rage.

"You're not leaving here either," Melissa told the two dark angels.

"At least not in the way you came in," Cameron finished.

Kirk laughed evilly. With a roar, the Void Angels sprang as one, their wings of darkness propelling them into the air, darkness masking their retreat like squids squirting clouds of ink.

It only took a moment for Melissa and Cameron to realize what was happening.

"They're going to escape," Melissa said.

The other Nephilim dropped from the air to pin the Void Angels to the floor. William raged, his claws finding flesh and bone, but the surviving Nephilim were not deterred.

Melissa drew closer to the struggle, Cameron at her side. William and Kirk continued their horrible taunts, as the darkness from their awful bodies created a heavy pall in the atmosphere of the chamber, which now reeked of despair.

One of the Nephilim turned to look at them, and a message was passed with a glance.

"They understand," Melissa said. "The Nephilim understand that it has to be us."

She took Cameron's hand, joining her inner light with his.

Each summoned a weapon of divine fire—a short sword for Melissa, the knife for Cameron.

At the sight of these burning weapons, the Void Angels began to fight all the harder, but the Nephilim redoubled their efforts, holding the murderous pair in place as Melissa and Cameron advanced.

"You can't do this!" William yelled. "We're his children. Do you know what he'll do to you if—"

Melissa drove the point of her sword into the center of William's armored chest.

The results were immediate. The dark angel twitched and sputtered as his armor began to break down, allowing the rekindled light from within to escape.

Kirk knew that it was his end as well, but still he begged for mercy. Ignoring the dark angel's pleas, Cameron leaned in, sliding his knife into his former friend just beneath his breast plate, reigniting what remained of Kirk's soul.

The Nephilim leaped back as the light intensified. There was a searing flash, and the light was gone, as were Kirk's and William's bodies.

We did it, Melissa thought, experiencing an overwhelming sense of satisfaction. They had not only vanquished their enemies, but they had also restored their fallen friends' peace.

Cameron still held her hand tightly. She was tempted to tell him that he could let go, but she thought better of it. She liked the way her hand felt in his.

Like it's supposed to be this way.

The Nephilim, no longer fighting for their lives, gazed about the vast mountain chamber.

"Where are we?" one of them asked. "What happened to us?"

Melissa was about to explain when she heard coughing.

"What happened?" the Custodian asked, struggling to sit. "You have been chosen." His dark eyes glistened.

"You are the Inheritors of the world."

CHAPTER TWENTY-NINE

Satan Darkstar felt the eyes of his legions upon him as they amassed above him along the lip of the crater.

The Cherubim waited, the muscles beneath their golden fur rippling as they paced, catlike, before the entrance to the House of God.

Satan watched the Lord God's guardians. *What unusual beasts they are,* he thought. So much more bestial in their design, as if He wanted them to be feared.

To keep away those who did not belong in His house.

There was a commotion above as Satan's armies attempted to come to his aid, but the Darkstar would have none of it.

"No!" he cried out. He pointed his blade of darkness toward them, and flames of shadow picked off those eager enough to brave the dangers of the crater. "This is my fight!" the Darkstar proclaimed. "And mine alone!"

He wanted them to bear witness to his might.

Satan spread his wings and launched himself toward the House of God. One of the great beasts leaped from its perch, its two sets of wings flapping powerfully as it charged at him with incredible speed.

It slashed at him, claws trailing fire. Satan narrowly evaded the attack by ducking below its forward momentum. Then he surged up toward the Cherubim's underside, willing his armor to change. Long spikes grew up from his back and shoulders.

Satan impaled the Cherubim's stomach with his spiked armor.

The cry of pain was unmistakable, and he could not help but smile.

Retracting the spikes, he moved away, evading the bestial angel's fury.

Satan Darkstar laughed aloud, flying above the Cherubim as it chased him. Then he shot down toward a ledge protruding from the crater wall and pretended he was going to hit it. At the last moment, Satan pulled his wings about himself, disappearing into shadow, only to reappear in another pool of darkness nearby. The pursuing Cherubim crashed into the wall of the crater, raining rock to the floor below.

The great animal fell, lying upon the ground, stunned.

Satan saw the great beasts' flaws. Their size and ferocity worked against them. They were creatures of power and emotion, and that would be their downfall.

For he did not fear them.

Touching down not far from the Cherubim, Satan Darkstar watched as the creature struggled to its feet. Its belly was bleeding, and one of its wings was twisted unnaturally to one side. Its human face eyed him suspiciously. Suddenly, the monstrous Cherubim reared its head back, spewing a gout of angel fire at the Darkstar.

Satan reacted with the speed of a thought, a shield forged of shadow appearing on his arm. The liquid fire pelted its shiny black surface, eating away at the darkness. He knew that the shield would not hold for much longer, and in his other hand, he created the most lethal of spears. As the Cherubim ceased its spew, the Lord of Shadows pounced. He lunged at the divine beast and thrust the spear up under its chin, pinning its mouth shut before it could vomit more heavenly fire.

The Cherubim struggled, but the Darkstar pressed the attack, until the spear of darkness emerged through one of its eyes.

The fire it was preparing to release backed up inside its skull, and the Cherubim's head detonated in a shower of bone and blood.

Satan tried to avoid the splash, but the corrosive gore covered his body. He dropped to his knees as the divine fluids ate away at the darkness that clothed his body.

He was so close now. He would not fail.

The Darkstar forced himself to his feet, his armor bubbling

and smoldering, as he turned his attention to the top of the temple steps—to the second Cherubim guard, who continued to watch from its post.

The Darkstar simply smiled.

Aaron and the Unforgiven stared at the static that filled the screen of the monitors.

They'd lost most of the visuals as soon as the dragons had taken to the sky.

Aaron stood perfectly still, concentrating on the various screens, hoping that the power within him would have some sort of effect on the signal.

But it wasn't to be.

He looked around and saw the looks on the Unforgiven's faces.

They were afraid.

Aaron turned to Vilma, his mother, and Gabriel. He wished he could spare them the fear of what they had seen.

"Can we get the signal back?" Levi asked. The leader of the Unforgiven stood close to the largest monitor, his back to them.

"We're trying, sir, but . . ." The technician's voice trailed off, overwhelmed by the sound of hissing static.

Aaron felt the power coursing through his changing body. He knew it was up to him now. Taking hold of the power, he made it his own and used it to fuel his courage.

"We all saw what's happening out there," he said, the change in his voice surprising him for a moment. "We don't need to see any more." The armor forged of fire crackled and sparked along his frame, and he felt their eyes upon him. "We know what has to be done."

Levi turned toward Aaron and his own men.

"Yes," the fallen angel agreed. "It's what we have been wanting to do since our fall."

The Unforgiven remained silent until one brave soul spoke up.

"But our numbers are so small," he stated, looking around the room at his brothers. "You saw what we will be facing."

Aaron knew that this was his moment, his opportunity to show that they could put their trust in him, that as the Metatron he could lead them to . . .

Power surged within him, writhing like some great beast at the end of a snare. Aaron doubled over in pain, wild fire leaping from his armor to burn on the floor.

He could feel the Unforgiven staring at him, knowing that they now saw him not as their leader—their savior—but as a risk.

He tried to control the power, as he had learned to control the Nephilim when it had first emerged within him.

But the power of God would have none of that.

Aaron screamed as the essence of God beat him down.

Gabriel was suddenly there, avoiding the small pyres of fire that burned around him. "Aaron."

"So sorry, Gabe," Aaron managed. He had never felt this level of failure before.

Vilma and his mother were beside him as well. Vilma braced herself under his heavy, armored arm and attempted to help him stand.

"What we saw on those screens is inconsequential," Levi picked up, trying to distract his brothers from Aaron. "We swore allegiance to a cause," he reminded them. "We said we would never allow ourselves a moment of peace, until we prevailed against the machinations of the Architects."

He fixed them all with his goggled stare.

"And we have yet to do that."

Aaron felt some of his strength returning and moved to stand on his own.

"You okay?" Vilma asked.

He nodded as he looked at the woman he loved. She looked so small next to his new height, but also so strong. "Yeah, I think I've got it."

"We will gather our number across the globe," Levi spoke. "And we will fight together." Mechanical wings sprang from his back like a knife from a switchblade. "We will fight until the last of us is gone if need be."

Levi's words stirred something inside Aaron.

It was the voice of the power that now filled him.

The Metatron had something to say.

And it spoke with the voice of God.

It surprised Jeremy how much he didn't like being alone.

He had always been a loner, but since discovering his birthright, and others with the same affliction, he'd realized that having people around wasn't all that bad.

Never mind the fact that he'd just spent the last four weeks or so with a nasty toddler whose vocabulary was better than his.

On second thought, maybe being alone isn't so horrible, he thought as he padded down the rounded white corridor. There was still no sign of the ghostly Lorelei, and he wondered if she had vanished forever after surrendering her last body.

Putting that thought out of his mind, Jeremy focused on finding Enoch. He knew that the child was special. He'd known that deep inside his bones when he'd first heard his mother speak of him. He also knew the child was not safe in the possession of these Architects.

The twisting corridors seemed to go on forever. He reached yet another junction that could take him either to the left or the right, and his frustration grew. His face had begun to sweat and itch beneath the leather mask.

"C'mon, you bloody little monkey," he muttered, as if Enoch could hear. "Where the hell are you?"

As if in answer to his question, two black-garbed Agents appeared at the far end of the hallway to his right. They did not see him, for he was using the function of the stealth suit he wore to blend with his surroundings. They passed him, and Jeremy began to follow at a safe distance.

One passage after the next, Jeremy saw no end in sight, but something told him not to give up. He wondered if it could have been Lorelei's influence, or maybe even Enoch's.

The two Agents came to an abrupt stop, cocking their heads as if hearing something that he could not. At once they changed their course, heading back toward him.

Jeremy pressed himself flat into the curve of the wall and waited for them to go by.

And pass they did. Jeremy was about to peel himself away from the wall and follow, when one of the Agents stopped suddenly, turning around to face in his direction.

The Agent tilted his head back, as if sniffing the air of the passage. Jeremy felt that twinge of panic; he and Enoch had been on the run for quite some time, and a hot shower wasn't something that they'd had an opportunity to enjoy.

He hoped he didn't smell bad enough to get caught.

The Agent then turned back to his partner, and the two started walking again.

Jeremy breathed out a quiet sigh of relief.

And that was when the Agents chose to attack.

They came at him, bounding down the hallway, their ultrathin blades at the ready.

Jeremy called upon a large sword of fire.

The assassins were fast and moved in tandem, so Jeremy had to be faster. Allowing his wings to emerge, he took the battle briefly to the air, striking at the two of them from above. The Agents were completely unfazed. One sprang off the side of the wall to grab him around the waist and drag him down, as the other's knife strikes came dangerously close, slicing through the thick, leathery fabric to his skin beneath. *With a bit more practice they'll skewer my internal organs for sure.* Jeremy knew that he needed to take at least one of them soon.

One Agent thrust his dagger toward Jeremy's heart. Jeremy avoided the strike, stepping in close and pinning the Agent's arm under his own. He conjured a short sword and brought it swiftly around, chopping off the top of the Agent's head.

Releasing his foe, Jeremy watched him stumble about for a moment, his head bubbling over with blood and gray matter, before he fell sideways to the floor.

The other Agent wasted no time, lunging at Jeremy. The two tumbled backward, grappling for the upper hand. Jeremy flapped his wings powerfully, attempting to throw the knife-wielding killer off of him, but the assassin held tight, slashing and jabbing.

Their fight carried them down the hallway, rebounding off walls from one side of the corridor to the other.

Suddenly they were in an open space, and in that space, there was a large door.

Jeremy sensed something deep in the pit of his stomach, something that was calling to him. He intensified his fight, managing to get one of his legs beneath the assassin and kick him away. The Agent flew backward, bouncing off the door. Thinking quickly, Jeremy created throwing stars—he'd always loved kung fu movies as a kid—and let the weapons fly. The killer tried to leap from the path of the flaming stars but was too late. They penetrated the Agent's leather suit and pinned him against the door, where his body burst into flames.

Jeremy cautiously approached the door but was interrupted by the sound of footfalls from the corridor behind him. He turned to meet a gaggle of at least ten masked Agents, running toward him with murder in their intent.

There's no peace for the wicked, his mother had always said.

He was beginning to understand what she'd meant.

Lucifer Morningstar sat in the eye of the maelstrom, calmly stroking the soft gray fur of the mouse.

Hell raged about him; a simple name really, to describe the magnitude of what he had done so very long ago.

It had taken him many millennia to understand and accept his curse. It had been God's will to saddle him with this burden, to make him carry it with him wherever he might go.

The Morningstar recognized the destructive capacity of the ultimate sadness and misery within him, and he guarded it well.

But now there was another in possession of his form, another who wished to unleash this power.

Lucifer would not stand for it.

Hell raged about the Morningstar's psyche, but he exuded a sense of calm. Eventually, he would wrangle control, but for now, the cumulative effect of his crimes against Heaven raged unabated.

If there was one thing that the Morningstar had—

It was patience.

CHAPTER THIRTY

The voice of God cried out to the world.

Aaron Corbet, wearing the guise of the Metatron, stood in the control center of the Unforgiven's base, armored head tilted back as the message flowed from his mouth in all the languages spoken on the planet.

"Hear me, citizens of the world. Let all who oppose the darkness come forth. Climb out from your hiding places and take back what has been stolen from you. Join the fight against the evil that has grown like a cancer across the land. Drive back the darkness from whence it came, and take light into your heart."

The words reverberated throughout the room.

And the Unforgiven dropped to their knees, the Metatron's message the first balm to their tortured beings since their fall from Heaven.

* * *

Vilma Santiago was mesmerized by the sight of the man she loved, and what he had become. The Metatron's words brought her great comfort. Finally, she felt as though they had not been forsaken.

But what of her love? What of Aaron Corbet?

Was he still in there somewhere, overcome by the power of God, or had his usefulness been proven, and his individual light extinguished?

Taylor Corbet dropped to one knee and bowed her head before the Metatron.

She knew that it was her son, but at the same time knew that it wasn't. Aaron's body was being used as an instrument of a higher power. She didn't know exactly how she felt about that, having waited for so very long to have her boy back in her life again. But this purpose that he now served . . .

Taylor could not help but be proud.

The message was nothing short of inspirational.

Levi had known that their chances of surviving against the forces of darkness and the plans of the Architects were rather slim, but he had accepted their fate. He and his brothers had chosen this as their penance. They had sworn to protect God's world from any and all otherworldly threats, without hesitation.

No matter the outcome.

If they were to die in their endeavors, then so be it.

But now . . .

The words of God, as spoken by the Metatron, gave him hope. Their seemingly never-ending battle against God's foes was not for naught.

They had a chance.

Gabriel was compelled to bark.

Yes, he cried out in his canine voice. *Yes, we will emerge from hiding and fight the things that have crawled from the darkness.*

We will make them fear us!

And we will triumph!

Still wearing the blood and viscera of his enemies, Verchiel pushed his way through the seemingly endless sea of monstrosities to the edge of the deep impression in the desert sand.

Having followed Satan's army from the citadel to the desert, he was now compelled to see what new, terrible act the Morningstar was responsible for. It shook him to his core that Lucifer was again up to mischief.

Verchiel scowled as he pushed aside ogres, trolls, and demons of all shapes and sizes. To think he'd actually started to believe that the Son of the Morning had seen the error of his ways and now served the will of God. The Nephilim had been so sure of Lucifer's reform that they'd been shocked when he went missing.

Missing. Verchiel would have chuckled if he wasn't so thoroughly repulsed.

The Morningstar had remained true to at least one of his other monikers.

The Prince of Lies.

The largest of the foul creatures were crowded around the rim, and Verchiel was tempted to lash out with his divine might and smite them all, when he heard it. He froze. The nightmares around him paid no attention. They could not hear it, for they were not of the divine.

The voice of God was inside his head, and Verchiel could barely contain his joy. How long it had been since he'd heard the dulcet tones of the Creator's voice.

The message was a call to arms against the forces of darkness.

"What's wrong with you?" an ogre grunted, its loathsome body armored with the bones of fallen enemies.

Verchiel realized that he had dropped to his knees in reverence, drawing unwanted attention to himself.

The ogre loomed above him menacingly, as others of similar size and ferocity drew near.

Let them come, Verchiel thought. He rose to his full and impressive height. Let them come, for the Lord God Almighty had spoken to him—to him—and asked that he fight.

And it had filled Verchiel with great joy.

"What's wrong with me, you vile beast?" Verchiel asked.

He let the fires of his divinity surge forth, their heat burning away the blood and whatever foul pieces of offal that clung to him after his endless skirmishes.

Revealing the angel beneath.

"There is nothing wrong with me," he proclaimed, calling upon his blade of fire.

The monsters around him barely had time to react before Verchiel killed them. He leaped into the air, carried by wings no longer weighed down by the dried fluids of death. And when the former leader of the heavenly host Powers finally touched down upon the desert sand, a wide circle of death surrounded him.

If the Lord God wished him to stand against evil, he would be more than happy to comply.

But a mournful wail interrupted Verchiel's thoughts and pulled him to the edge of the great desert hole, where the beasts still gathered there cowered in the shadow of his divine light.

Crouching at the lip, Verchiel's gaze fell on the body of the first Cherubim, its head nothing more than a stain upon the hard-packed sand.

Another wail of pain sounded from below, and Verchiel saw a sight that turned his fiery blood to ice. The Morningstar stood at the entrance to a temple of God, holding the throat of another Cherubim, lifting it to expose its belly and plunging a blade into the divine being.

The Cherubim wailed in rage and disappointment. It had not been able to stop the interloper from befouling this holy place.

Verchiel was compelled to action. He spread his wings and dove into the hole to do something that he wished he had done on the battlefields of Heaven: kill the Morningstar.

"Lucifer!" he bellowed, landing not far from the body of the other Cherubim.

"Are you talking to me?" the Morningstar asked, and released the flailing Cherubim, whose burning blood now covered his armored form. The angelic beast flopped pitifully on the top step to the temple, its every movement causing more of its life to spill out upon the ancient stone.

The more Verchiel saw, the more enraged he became. He stalked toward the bottom of the giant steps.

"Aren't you a pretty little thing," Lucifer Morningstar said.

And as Verchiel looked at him, he had the strangest of thoughts. *This isn't the Morningstar at all.*

This is something worse.

Verchiel flew into the air, landing before the Morningstar and looking into the eyes of his foe. Where there had once burned the fires of righteous indignation, Verchiel saw only darkness, so deep and black that it threatened to suck him in.

"See something you like?" Lucifer asked.

Even his voice sounded wrong.

"You're not him," Verchiel said with stark realization.

"I'm something more," the thing wearing the body of the Morningstar announced.

Verchiel braced himself as the being lunged at him, crackling black energy trailing from the assailant's blade.

And then he felt a sudden, intense burning upon his arm. The arrowlike tattoo placed there by the three Sisters pulsed and throbbed, as if it would leap from his flesh.

And before he could even consider what it might mean, he was gone.

Enoch heard the call.

He knew it was the voice of God—the voice that should have been his—the human aspect of what was to be the new Metatron.

He sat up in his bubble, which still hovered over the Architects' control center. Something was most definitely wrong.

He pressed the palms of his young hands and his forehead against the surface of the sphere.

Could the Architects have heard it also? he wondered. It was a possibility. After all, they were beings of God, even if they felt they could do better than He.

Multiple images showing great unrest on earth flashed across the large, concave walls. And they appeared to be making the Architects very uneasy.

"Is something wrong out there?" Enoch called from his bubble.

The Architects paid him no mind, murmuring amongst themselves, their attention directed on the Architect that Enoch imagined was their leader.

"Something not going according to plan, perhaps?"

The leader's shape began to change. Suddenly, Enoch was looking at an incredibly tall figure clad in robes of scarlet. From his back sprang multiple sets of wings that were colored like a rainbow, but unlike a rainbow, their surface was covered in eyes.

"Everything is progressing as planned," the head Architect, the Overseer, stated, the sound of his voice like the blast of a pipe organ within the confines of a church. "It is impossible for anything to go awry."

"That's good to know," Enoch said. "Because from where I'm sitting, it appears that you all are a little nervous."

"Nervous?" The Overseer removed himself from the others. "We are the Architects, the first of God's beings, made to supervise the creation of what would have been His greatest achievement. What could possibly make us nervous?"

The eyes upon his many wings, and the single orb from within the hood of his robe, held Enoch in a paralyzing stare.

"He wanted to give you a chance," Enoch said, finally pulling his attention back to the other, agitated Architects, and the myriad scenes that still flashed upon the wall. "But it seems you just don't want to listen."

"We heard nothing," the Overseer replied.

Enoch smiled sadly, looking down at the angelic being. "First you disobey Him, ignore all that He asked of you, and now you lie about hearing His voice."

The Overseer remained silent, drifting back toward the gathering of Architects.

"That's what you were trying to prevent, wasn't it?" Enoch continued. "Capturing me was going to prevent the voice of God from being heard again, the Metatron from being reborn. Doesn't appear to have worked. The Metatron has found its voice anyway."

"That will be corrected," the Overseer stated.

A single image repeated itself on the walls of the chamber, and Enoch gasped as memories long buried floated to the surface of his mind.

He saw a desert inhabited by armies of monsters, and at their center was an enormous crater. And in that crater was . . .

"Beth-El," Enoch whispered.

"The evil has reached the House of God," one of the Architects announced, its usual dispassionate voice raised ever so slightly.

This sent a flurry of excitement through the others.

Enoch could see that there was something—someone—at the doors of Heaven. "Is this part of the plan?" he asked. "How are you going to manipulate this so it benefits you?"

The Overseer turned to the child once more. "We are the plan," his voice boomed.

But as the Overseer spoke, each of the Architects turned their attention to their leader.

"I know that you believe that," Enoch said. "But do they?"

The Overseer followed the child's gaze and saw that he was being scrutinized by his brethren.

Enoch chanced a wry smile at the heavenly being, only to have it quickly disappear as the Architects began to advance on their leader. *Are they attacking?* the child wondered, but then it all became clear.

One by one, the Overseer absorbed the other Architects. They flowed toward him, effortlessly merging with his body.

"Who ever said that they had a choice?" the Overseer then asked.

Enoch was confused. "What have you done?"

"I have merely taken back what was mine to begin with," the Overseer explained. "They were all aspects of me, as I was an aspect of God."

"Was?" Enoch questioned.

The Overseer's many wings spread wide. "I am so much more than what I was when I was first created," he declared with great certainty. "And once I've achieved my goals . . ."

"After all that you've seen," Enoch said, gesturing toward the walls, which were now blank, "you still believe that your plans will carry through?"

There came a tremendous racket from somewhere outside the chamber.

"What was that?" Enoch asked, moving about in his bubble.

"A minor annoyance," the Overseer replied.

"Another aspect to be considered and absorbed?" the child taunted.

"Perhaps," the Overseer acknowledged with a shrug. "Or maybe the disturbance simply needs to be excised."

The commotion grew louder, and Enoch could see that it troubled the remaining Architect.

"A tool is needed," the Overseer then said.

He turned his attention to an empty part of the room and raised a bony arm from within the scarlet robe. He kneaded the air with long fingers, creating a disturbance that grew cloudy, and then coalesced.

Where there had been nothing, a figure appeared, clad in the armor of Heaven. His powerful wings unfurled from his back, a sword of fire ready for battle clutched in one hand.

Enoch could do nothing but stare, another memory bubbling up from within him, a memory placed there by a higher power.

And within that memory there was a name.

The angel looked about him, his eyes wild with fury and confusion.

"Verchiel," Enoch whispered as he looked upon the angel conjured by the Overseer. "His name is Verchiel."

CHAPTER THIRTY-ONE

The clouds above him were thick and dark, and Dusty had no idea if it was day or night as he walked the lonely stretch of road away from the Unforgiven's base.

The snatches of visions that he perceived were telling him that the world was reaching a critical moment in time. Many events were on the verge of coming together—to effect the outcome of the looming conflict.

To effect Armageddon.

Some of them he had set in motion himself, but others . . .

Dusty paused as a new, and particularly gruesome, vision invaded his thoughts. It did not show much hope for the planet's survival.

At that, his body became racked with extreme cramps.

He dropped to his knees, trying to muffle his cries of pain, so as not to attract the attention of any nightmarish creatures prowling in the area.

He could feel the metal—moving—encasing his body.

It had been spreading slowly, but now . . .

Dusty lifted his sweatshirt. His entire stomach was covered by the metal. With a trembling hand he touched where the warm flesh had once been, and felt only cold metal. There was a tingling in his fingertips, and he raised his hand before his face to see the metal spreading over the digits, across the back of his hand, and down his arm.

At first he was afraid.

Afraid of what was happening to him . . . afraid of what he was becoming, but a soft voice that he believed to be the spirit of the Instrument whispered inside his mind.

This will benefit the world.

Letting go of his fear, Dusty opened himself to the will of the Instrument, and it obliged him, spreading with greater speed over his remaining flesh.

His face was the last to change, metal traveling up his neck, over his chin, into his mouth, and beyond.

Kneeling on the pavement, Dusty felt one last twinge of pain as his inner workings were transformed, and he surrendered the final threads of his humanity.

The being that had once been Dustin "Dusty" Handy

slowly rose to its full height, tearing away the flimsy sweat suit that had adorned its human body, reading multiple futures with unemotional eyes.

It raised its arm and looked upon the changing shape of the once-human hand, watching with deep curiosity as the fingers that had once been composed of flesh, blood, and bone transformed into a more useful shape for the moment.

Its fingers had merged together to form a blade, a knife as sharp as it needed to be in order to cut through the fabric of time and space, providing the Instrument passage to where it knew it was needed.

For the voice of God had summoned.

And the Instrument would answer His call.

The Metatron finished its address and allowed its power to recede, giving Aaron back control of his body.

Aaron felt weaker than he had before. The power that now resided within him was too much, even for his Nephilim body, and he knew it would eventually destroy him.

But that was a worry for another time.

Aaron saw that while the Metatron had been in control, they had moved from the mission control center to a staging area deep within the mountain stronghold, where all the Unforgiven had gathered before him.

It took a moment to access those memories, but he now recalled that he had summoned them there.

Levi, weapon in hand, approached Aaron from the side. "We're ready."

And as the words left his mouth, Levi's metal wings—as did the metal wings of all the Unforgiven gathered there—sprang from his back.

Aaron felt the divine power stir inside him at the sight of the army that had been assembled to fight in His name.

"So you are," Aaron answered. His voice was still not entirely his.

His own wings suddenly asserted themselves, the black-feathered appendages exploding from his back with a rush of air. "Gather round me," he ordered, his voice booming with authority.

The Unforgiven did as they were told, forming a tight circle around him. Vilma, Taylor, and Gabriel were pressed among them.

Aaron wished there was something he could say to assure them all that they were going to be safe, but he knew there were no such assurances. He himself only felt an overwhelming desire to see his enemy vanquished and the earth reconnected to Heaven.

He raised his arms and spread his wings to their full span. Reaching out with the power of the Almighty, he pulled them all into his embrace.

Delivering them from the calm, to the battlefield.

From a whisper to a scream.

* * *

Melissa couldn't believe what she'd just experienced, and the look on Cameron's face told her that neither could he.

"I know this is going to sound stupid," Cameron said. "But did you just hear God in your head?"

All she could do was nod, overwhelmed by emotion.

The newly revived Nephilim had clearly heard it as well. Many of them stood perfectly still, eyes tightly closed, faces turned toward the cave's ceiling. Others had dropped to their knees, their feathered wings wrapped around their trembling bodies.

At the sound of heavy footfalls, Melissa turned.

The Custodian, who had been on the brink of death, made his way awkwardly toward them.

She summoned a sword of fire to be on the safe side, just in case he was some sort of screwed-up zombie or something.

"There's no need of that," the old angel said, his voice soft and weak. He gestured for her to put the fiery blade away.

"I thought you were . . ."

"Dying?" he asked, and then coughed. There was now blood on his lips. "Later," he said. Then, after thinking a bit, "But maybe sooner would be better.

"Did you hear it?" the Custodian asked, his pale face brightening. "Did you hear the call?"

"We did." From the corner of her eye, Melissa saw the other Nephilim responding with nods.

"And will you answer it?" the Custodian asked.

Melissa knew that she and Cameron would, but she couldn't speak for the other Nephilim.

One of them stepped forward. He was a large man with a head of curly black hair. His skin was dark and covered with scars. There was no doubt that he had been a fighter.

"We have been awakened for a purpose," he said. Melissa could tell that he was speaking in some ancient language, but she understood perfectly, as was the Nephilim gift.

"As you have," the Custodian agreed. He coughed again, bringing up more blood. He lost his balance and fell backward against the stone wall, his tarnished armor clattering.

"The longer that I am awake, the more I feel it," the Custodian continued. "There is a terrible darkness upon the world now."

Is his voice getting weaker? Melissa wondered.

They all drew closer to hear the ancient being.

"The voice of God has called to those who believe in the righteousness of His power." The old angel seemed to drift off then.

Melissa stepped forward and knelt beside him, placing a hand on his armored shoulder. He stirred, and turned his head to gaze up at her.

"Perhaps I have been wrong these endless years," he said wistfully. "Perhaps I gathered the Nephilim here not to inherit the world, but to save it."

She considered the angel's contrition, watching as his pale flesh became more ashen. She felt Cameron come to stand beside her.

"You will lead them, my mated pair," he said, his dark eyes brightening for an instant. "Take on the darkness, before it's too . . ."

His last words never came.

Melissa stood, bumping into Cameron behind her.

"So what are we doing?" he asked her.

Melissa felt anxious, confused. She knew that they should answer the call, but she had no idea what their responsibilities were to the others.

The Nephilim simply stared at her, waiting, and that just added to her frustration.

But then she saw the flares of light as the Nephilim brought to life their weapons of divine fire and raised them above their heads.

"You wanted to know what we're doing?" she asked Cameron, never taking her eyes from the inspiring sight before her.

"We're leading an army into battle."

Satan Darkstar wasn't sure what had happened to his angel adversary, but he wouldn't let that worry him now.

There were more important things to be done.

Flying back up to the temple entrance, the Darkstar

reached out and tore the two huge doors from their hinges, casting them aside.

This was what the Cherubim guard dogs were protecting.

Inside was the prize that he had been seeking.

Satan strode into the chamber and immediately felt His presence. Even though the world had been cut off from Heaven, it did not diminish the residual power of what had once been active here.

In the center of the empty chamber was what appeared to be a simple rectangle of stone, but Satan could feel the power that still radiated from it.

An intricate shape had been carved into the center of the stone's surface.

It resembled a keyhole.

The Darkstar knew that he did not possess the actual key—the power of God—that had been inside the murdered Metatron, but he had something equally as strong.

He placed his black-gauntleted hands upon either side of the stone and stared into the darkness of the keyhole, imagining the wonders that existed beyond the lock.

He was not the Metatron. He was a thing of darkness, clothed in the embodiment of what had once been the Almighty's most favored angel, and housed within that angelic body was a grim force to rival the power of creation.

The time for thinking was at an end. Now was the moment for action. Satan Darkstar leaned closer to the keyhole and attempted to stir the power locked deep inside the body that he wore.

The power of disappointment, sadness, anger, fear, and despair.

The power that was known as Hell.

Lucifer Morningstar had become the personification of calm.

With Milton nestled in the palm of one hand, he sat amongst the maelstrom that was his inner Hell and extended his control.

He could sense the intruder who wore his skin attempting to draw upon the powerful feelings, and they were more than happy to oblige the interloper. The Hell knew him as its captor, and it seethed about him. It wanted to destroy him with its fury. It wanted to be free, to feed upon the raw emotions it would create with its release into the world.

But Lucifer remained the quiet at the eye of the storm. The more Hell raged, the more intense became his resolve to keep its destructive force in check.

He continued to gently stroke the tiny animal. The mouse was far stronger than anyone could ever have imagined, and it selflessly lent its willpower to the Morningstar's cause.

And though the hellish force continued to howl and rage, Lucifer held it tight, slowly pulling it closer to him.

* * *

Satan felt the power begin to emerge; all that accumulated pain, misery, and rage beginning to seep from his skin beneath the ebony armor.

He continued to focus on the lock. He had no idea what would happen when this catastrophic force was released, but he didn't really care.

His prize was within his grasp. Let all else be damned.

The power was there in all its glorious fury; the screams and cries of divine beings who died during that most profound of conflicts creating a symphony of discordance that threatened to cause his very head to explode.

And just as it was about to be released—

Hell receded.

Satan nearly collapsed, stumbling away from the stone slab that held his prize. He could still feel it inside him, writhing and dangerous, but there was something else there as well.

Something that was holding it back.

The Darkstar screamed his rage, bringing an armored fist down upon the slab of stone, but it remained untouched, impervious to his anger.

A blast of heavenly fire suddenly burned him with the intensity of those very first rays of light at the dawn of creation, and Satan found himself draped over the stone that contained his prize. His back was aflame as the armor forged of darkness attempted to repair itself.

He forced himself up from the stone and spun to face his attacker.

"Who dares?" the Darkstar demanded, his voice seething with malice.

The armored giant looming in the doorway to the temple was a sight to behold, causing Satan Darkstar to experience an unwelcome sensation that took him a moment to identify.

It was fear.

"I dare," the angelic being bellowed. "I, the Metatron."

And suddenly things didn't quite seem so bad, for standing before the Darkstar was the true key to the box that held his prize.

All he had to do was take it.

CHAPTER THIRTY-TWO

Verchiel was confused.

Mere seconds ago he had been battling ultimate evil, and now—

The painful tingling from the tattoo on his forearm reminded him of how he came to be here, but where was here?

"It is time for you to make a choice, Verchiel," said an angelic being looming before him.

Verchiel focused on the striking figure. There was a strength that radiated from this one, a strength that he had not felt in a very long time.

A strength he'd last felt while in the presence of the Lord.

There came a terrible pounding that made the plain white room tremble, followed by the sound of a ruckus that seemed to come from somewhere outside the chamber.

"Listen to me," commanded the divine being, as he moved closer to regain Verchiel's attention.

"Once, you had a vision for this world," the being continued. "You saw its potential, and attempted to make it so."

Images flooded into Verchiel's mind: memories of how he had come to the world of God's man in pursuit of criminals from Heaven's war, and how that mission had been tainted when he discovered an even larger threat.

Nephilim.

That obsession caused him to fall farther from God than the criminals he originally hunted, and eventually became his end.

Verchiel remembered how it had been, how his body had literally started to decay from the hate he had for his enemies.

And he remembered the moment of his death.

But the chosen one of the Nephilim—Aaron Corbet—had consigned him back to God.

Consigned him to oblivion.

He recalled the cold numbness and dropped to his knees.

"You were diverted from your true mission," the angelic voice stated.

"Yes," Verchiel agreed.

"I can give you purpose again," the being offered. "I can set your mission back on course. Together, we can transform this horribly tainted place into a Paradise."

"Yes," Verchiel said, feeling his strength return, a new purpose coursing through his veins. *This is it,* he thought. *This is the reason why God sent me back.*

He rose to his feet, the past forgotten, the future so clear to him now. This was the being that would guide him in purging the sins of the past to create a new and glorious future.

"Have you made your choice, Verchiel?" the towering angelic figure asked.

Verchiel was about to answer, when someone else spoke to him.

"Choose wisely, Verchiel," said a soft, childlike voice.

He turned to see a young child floating in a transparent sphere above the room. The child watched him intently.

"You," Verchiel said in surprise.

The child nodded. "So nice to see you again."

Verchiel felt as though powerful, godly hands had reached inside his skull and scooped out his brain, carrying it from this strange, simple room, into the cold of space—

A backdrop of twinkling stars transformed itself into a work of art, and the former leader of the Powers found himself within the confines of a familiar underground chamber, standing before a thin, raggedy figure.

The prophet.

The old man furiously painted images from a future he had foreseen.

"A frozen moment," Verchiel said, watching as the ancient artist acknowledged him, his face spattered with the efforts of his art.

"A choice not yet made." The prophet stepped away from his work, and Verchiel drew closer.

He called upon the fires within him, making his hand burn like a torch so that he might see what the prophet already understood.

"A choice," Verchiel repeated, his eyes studying the images he remembered from his first encounter with the old seer—images foretelling the coming of the Nephilim and their place in the world, images that had once sent him on his obsessive mission to cleanse the world of these abominations.

His eyes locked upon one in particular, one he hadn't seen before. It was a tiny illustration, nearly overwhelmed by all the others.

But it said so very much.

The painting was of him, the likeness not all that flattering, but it was obvious who the crude interpretation was supposed to represent. In his arms—amid turmoil and fire—Verchiel held a child.

"A choice not yet made," the prophet repeated, as the paintings faded, replaced by the stark white walls of the chamber.

"No, a choice made," Verchiel said with certainty.

Enoch remembered his visit to the angel called Verchiel. The Lord God had been so disappointed in this one and was determined to discover what had caused him to so fail.

The Almighty had dissected His warrior angel, examining

each piece and particle, but He saw no obvious defect. Verchiel had simply made choices, and it was those choices that had led to his downfall.

Enoch remembered how God had told him that this angel, despite all his faults, was special.

This one's name is Verchiel, God had said, as He reassembled the angel. *Remember it, for he will be important.*

Enoch saw a flash of recognition in the angel's eyes.

"Quickly now," the child ordered. "There is still much to be done."

Verchiel nodded at the child, as a hand fell firmly upon his shoulder.

"A choice," the being that reeked of God's power reminded him.

There was a great explosion from outside the room, and a section of wall tumbled in. Verchiel's attention was drawn to the scene, as an angelic being—a Nephilim, of this he was sure—fought against black-garbed foes.

The grip on his shoulder suddenly intensified. "A choice," the being repeated all the more forcefully, the sound of his voice echoing painfully in Verchiel's head.

"Yes," Verchiel answered above the commotion.

For the first time in so very long, his mission was clear.

A sword of fire came to life with the power of his thought, and he wrenched his shoulder from the angel's powerful grip.

He raised the sword of fire above his head as his wings carried him up, and with all his might, he drove the sword into the sphere that contained the child.

There was a blinding, deafening release of force as the bubble exploded, but above the din, he heard the angelic being's voice, dripping with supreme disappointment.

"Verchiel! What have you done?"

One moment Lorelei was in the Architects' stronghold, and the next, she was standing before a large stone slab in what appeared to be a temple.

The ghost of the angel A'Dorial was beside her, with the countless number who had died since the world was cut off from Heaven, waiting ever so patiently for the opportunity to continue their journey.

"Where am I?"

"This is what your father wanted you to see," A'Dorial said.

"What is it?" Lorelei asked. She could feel something emanating from the stone in waves, and the best word she could think to describe it was . . .

Potential.

"Is this it?" she asked the angelic ghost. "Is this the Ladder?"

"It is," A'Dorial acknowledged. "Though it is dormant."

She drifted closer to the slab, letting her hand float over its smooth surface. Her fingers entered the stone, and a warm tingle reminded her of the sensations she'd felt when still alive.

"How do we turn it on?" she asked.

"That is why the child is needed," A'Dorial answered.

She looked at the ghost. "Then I have to go back. I have to help Jeremy save the child. . . ."

The scene around them abruptly changed, the quiet of the temple erupting with the violence of battle.

"What is this?" she cried out, as gouts of fire exploded around her. Even though she could not be hurt, she still found herself shying away from the destructive forces.

"The battle has begun," A'Dorial stated. "Armageddon is in full swing."

Signs of struggle were everywhere. Angels with metal wings, which she recognized from the department store parking lot where she'd found Jeremy, wrestled beasts of every conceivable size and nature. For a brief moment her attention was totally transfixed upon the chaos unfolding before her, but she then became distracted by the sight of something far more awesome.

An angel of great size, his body clothed in golden armor, was squaring off against a being of darkness.

If Lorelei had still been able to breathe, she would have gasped at what she saw next. The golden angel's opponent was clad in armor that seemed to be made from solidified night, and he wore the face of her friend and confidant, the Morningstar.

He had been the one to kill her.

The desert sands exploded about them as the two forces

waged their war, and suddenly, Lorelei felt her own abilities awaken.

"Is this how you wish to use their life energies?" A'Dorial asked.

"What do you mean?" Lorelei asked, her desire for vengeance against the one who had hurt her fully aroused.

"The power that you use belongs to them." A'Dorial gestured toward the dead who watched. "Their residual energies are there for your disposal," the angel continued. "But are you certain this is the right battle?"

She watched the giant angel of Heaven swing a sword of fire at his darkling foe. Light would perpetually struggle against dark, and Lorelei knew that she had her own part to play in that struggle.

"The child," she said. "We have to help the child."

A'Dorial smiled.

"Good choice."

Jeremy drove on, slashing at the Architects' Agents, never pausing, even as he fought his way inside their sanctum.

He knew that he could not slow his attacks. He had to bring the Agents down before they brought him down with their superior numbers and savagery.

Switching from sword to battle-ax, Jeremy swung the enormous blade, cutting a flaming swath through a charge of attackers, their bisected bodies spilling harmlessly to either side of him, as the next wave of Agents came at him without pause.

"Bloody hell!" the boy cried out, starting to feel the effects of exhaustion. "Don't you guys ever quit?"

And that was when he caught another movement from the corner of his eye. He glanced toward the back of the room, where a glass sphere hung.

Enoch.

The sight of the little boy made the Nephilim fight all the harder. He was determined to rescue him.

He took his eyes from the sphere to dispatch two knife-wielding Agents with a grunting swipe of his ax blade, and when he glanced back, an angel clad in armor hovered near the floating bubble, a sword of fire raised above his head.

Fear coursed through Jeremy. There was no doubt in his mind what the angel's intentions were. He lashed out in any way he could, frantically trying to cut through the endless wave of Agents.

But the angel's sword came down with great sound and fury, a shock wave flowing across the chamber, knocking the Nephilim off his feet.

Jeremy was already on the move to see if the child was safe, when he heard a booming voice cry out. "Verchiel! What have you done?"

At the mention of the name, Jeremy's blood turned to ice in his veins.

Verchiel, he thought with escalating terror. *That's the bloke who nearly wiped us out.*

Jeremy fought with renewed purpose now. His ax struck the Agents down with double the fury, as he charged toward the back of the chamber. He spread his wings as he leaped, battle-ax of fire crackling as he propelled himself toward the armored visage of Verchiel.

Heaven help the angel if he'd harmed the child.

The Overseer had expected Verchiel to accept his offer. Together, they could have transformed the world, but the child of God had intervened. The Architect felt an odd sensation. It was an emotion common to those beings that he and his aspects had manipulated over the millennia, but it was new to him.

Anger.

Recoiling from the sphere's explosion, the Overseer watched the child tumble through the air to land on the floor. Verchiel's attack had surprised the Overseer and caused new concerns for his mission.

"Verchiel! What have you done?" the Overseer screamed in displeasure.

What occurred next was another unforeseen turn of events. The Overseer watched as the Nephilim intruder found his way into the Architects' sanctum, flying to attack Verchiel in anger.

The two were locked in battle, and the Overseer could see the situation getting quickly out of hand. It was time to eliminate the most dangerous threat to his plans.

The child called Enoch was sprawled on the floor amid the shattered remains of the sphere that once held him. He was beginning to stir, but the Architect would not allow him to awaken. This child of God, this instrument of discourse, could very easily ruin everything that he had worked so hard to achieve.

The Overseer selected the longest, sharpest piece of the containment sphere that he could find. This would be the quickest and least dangerous way to dispose of the troublesome youth. Carefully, he advanced upon the still stunned child, and then he felt it, a presence close by. At first, the Overseer saw nothing, but as he perceived other realities that existed around him, he saw the spirits of the dead that crammed the room. One in particular, a female, came toward him, a look of determination upon her face.

"You're not going to harm that boy," she said, using an audio spectrum that only he could hear. She stood before him, her fists clenched in repressed anger.

And the Architect simply turned away.

Unconcerned by threats from the dead.

Lorelei had thought that there were more Architects, as the one lunged toward the child.

She had warned the heavenly creature, but it was obvious that he had made his decision.

As she had made hers.

Lorelei radiated energy from her hands in a single, concentrated burst.

It struck the Architect squarely in the back, sending him sprawling to the floor.

"I warned you," she said, sensing the number of dead assembled behind her diminish.

The Architect had dropped his makeshift weapon as he fell, and now he lay perfectly still. Cautiously, Lorelei approached him, wondering if she might have gone too far.

The Architect grabbed her arm with a spidery hand, startling her. How could he touch her?

"The dead never posed a problem before," the Architect said. "I must reconsider that."

Lorelei tried to pull away, but his hold was too strong. As she struggled, A'Dorial and the others slowly drifted away from her. She screamed for their help, but she saw only fear in their haunted stares.

Lorelei could feel her soul's energy grow weaker, less defined, as the Architect's grip strengthened on her arm. She suddenly became painfully aware that it was only a matter of minutes before her essence would blow away like smoke from an extinguished match.

The Architect rose, stronger, as he selected another slice of glass from the floor. "This will do nicely."

Lorelei struggled to break free, her strength dwindling, as he dragged her along toward the child.

Enoch sat where he had fallen, still appearing dazed and confused.

The Architect loomed above the little boy.

Lorelei turned her fading gaze on the other spirits, holding out her hand, desperate for their assistance. She knew what they feared; their soul energies would be consumed, never to return to the source of all things. But she needed their strength, their energy, to save the child without whom the world would be lost.

The Architect drew back his arm to strike, and the mass of dead acted.

A'Dorial took hold of Lorelei's hand, acting as a conduit for the others. Their energies flowed through him, and Lorelei could feel the power of her own soul return twentyfold, giving her the strength to fight back against her aggressor.

The Architect halted his assault in mid-slash.

He tried to wield his weapon, but now it was Lorelei's turn to hold fast.

Glowing with the energies of the other spirits, she looked deeply into the single, bulging eye beneath the Architect's scarlet hood.

"You're not going to like this one little bit."

CHAPTER THIRTY-THREE

The power of God attacked with relentless fury.

It did not care if its host body was caused irreparable harm by its unbridled assault, or if the very world upon which it stood was damaged beyond repair.

It cared for nothing except the eradication of its enemy, light vanquishing darkness.

It was as simple as that.

Simple, but oh so dangerous.

Aaron knew the destructive potential of the power that resided within him, but the longer he spent with it, the less he cared. With every passing moment, he was becoming less Aaron Corbet, and more the Metatron.

The Metatron drove the Darkstar back, his enormous broadsword of fire striking its foe again and again. But the

Darkstar met each of the attacks with his own mighty blade, forged of impenetrable darkness.

What remained of Aaron could not help but feel a twinge of sadness as he looked upon his mortal enemy, who wore the face of his father. He was tempted to pull back on the savagery of his attack, hoping that Lucifer's goodness would re-emerge. But the rage of the God power would hear nothing of it, overwhelming his sympathies with ease.

This was the enemy, and he would be vanquished.

The Metatron's blows rained down upon the Darkstar, driving him back against the great stone slab that held the mystery of the Ladder. But Satan's wings propelled him upward and at the Metatron. Taking advantage of their close quarters, he summoned a small blade of ebony and thrust it with great force into the Metatron's stomach.

Aaron's cries of pain mingled with those of the power of God. Great gouts of burning blood poured from his wound, coating the Darkstar and the stone slab.

The Metatron's wings beat the air savagely, as he retreated from the temple. Kneeling just outside the door, Aaron gazed down at the hilt of the blade still protruding from his gut. With a trembling hand, he gripped the knife and tried to pull it free.

The handle dissolved in his gauntleted hand, but he could still feel the blade inside him.

He looked back into the temple and saw Satan standing over the stone slab. The Darkstar's body was burning from the Metatron's blood, but he did not seem to care. Instead, he wiped the blood on the stone.

With spectacular results.

The stone began to hum with sudden and unbridled power, and its surface began to glow.

Aaron gasped, rising upon trembling, armored legs.

The Darkstar turned ever so slightly, a twisted grin upon his features, as he gloated over his accomplishment. But his happiness was short-lived, for as the blood of the Metatron cooled, so did the activity from the slab.

Satan turned abruptly, his wings of darkness fanned out behind him.

"I think we need to try that again."

The Darkstar flew through the temple and crashed into the Metatron's armored body. The pair connected with fists flying and wings beating, their struggle carrying them down the temple steps to the floor of the crater, where the Unforgiven and the armies of the Darkstar still battled.

Aaron managed to get his knee firmly against Satan's stomach and thrust him away. He quickly examined his wound and saw that the bleeding had stopped, but he could feel that the blade was slowly poisoning him from within.

But he could not think of such things.

This was Armageddon, the ultimate battle of good versus evil.

The Metatron had to defeat the darkness before it could reach Heaven.

Satan hurtled toward him with a scream unlike anything Aaron had ever heard, as if it were dredged up from some heinous nightmare. The Darkstar's sword was raised over one shoulder, poised to strike.

Aaron could sense that there was something different about this blade, the way it crackled and hummed, and knew that it was calling on the dark energies of those fighting nearby, using them to increase its power.

But there was still good in the world, and if evil could forge such a fearsome weapon, so would good.

Using the power of God, Aaron reached out to all the goodness, love, and innocence that still remained, and formed a massive weapon of divine fire and righteousness.

The Metatron and Satan collided, swords connecting with such force that the resultant explosion sheared away the walls of the crater, exposing even more of the ancient city of Megiddo.

Aaron was thrown a good distance away and rose with great difficulty, the pain in his lower body growing even more intense as it radiated from his belly. He forced himself to rally, hefting the mighty blade for the next assault.

The Darkstar landed in a crouch before him, then sprang up with a roar, lunging at the Metatron. As the black sword sliced through the air, Aaron could have sworn that he heard the cries of souls in torment.

The sword appeared to be growing larger, absorbing more evil from the desert battlefield. Aaron used his mighty wings to jump from the path of the sword, fearing that his own mighty blade was weakening against the seemingly endless evil.

Pain was beginning to hamper his speed, and Aaron knew that it was only a matter of time before his luck would run out. He managed to evade the black blade until he saw an opportunity, swinging his own sword across the Darkstar's midsection.

Satan didn't even pause. The black metal was torn and ragged, but it swiftly repaired itself.

"You'll have to do better than that," Satan said, preparing to cleave the Metatron in half.

Aaron stumbled on the uneven ground. The evil blade descended with a predator's scream, but Aaron twisted his body enough to raise his own sword. He managed to deflect the Darkstar's blow, forcing the ebony blade to bury itself deeply in the bleached desert ground.

With perilous results.

The very earth shuddered, as if repulsed.

Satan withdrew his black blade with a hysterical laugh, as the earthquake's damage unfolded before them.

A sharp, whiplike cracking sound filled the air as the desert sands shifted violently beneath their feet, and a giant chasm, miles long, opened like a yawning mouth in the desert surface.

* * *

Vilma stumbled at the awful tremor, watching in growing horror as the ground opened and the enormous crack appeared, zigzagging across the desert floor like a lightning bolt.

While she was distracted by the sight, a goblin warrior was suddenly in front of her, its thick arm pulled back to deliver the killing blow.

She was about to lift her sword of flame to block the thrust when there came a high-pitched whine, followed by a roaring blast, as the goblin's head evaporated in a cloud of red mist.

Vilma turned, sword in hand, to see Taylor Corbet lowering her weapon.

"One needs to pay attention on the battlefield, Ms. Santiago," the woman, whose clothes were torn and covered with dust and blood, said, then took aim and fired her high-tech weapon at yet another foul beast.

They were surrounded by them: foul creatures of every conceivable size and shape. They were like a tidal wave of pure ugliness and evil, but there was no way that Vilma was going to allow them to swallow her.

"So true, Ms. Corbet," Vilma called out, flying at a group of trolls that were beating one of the Unforgiven with clubs. There were four of them and only one of him. It was unfair.

Vilma hated unfair.

She landed in a run, charging the four trolls. Her sword of fire took the hand of one, and the face of another, before the trolls realized how much trouble they were in. The essence of the Nephilim inside her purred with excitement, like the engine of some really fast sports car. It loved when things were like this, feeding its nature for battle. This was what it existed for.

Another troll lost its head, its large body providing her with a kind of springboard as she leaped up on its back, springing into the air, her wings spread wide like a fan, and delivered killing blows to the remaining beasts.

The Unforgiven soldier silently rose to his feet, retrieved his rifle, and returned to the fight.

"Don't mention it," Vilma said, ready for the next confrontation.

The forces of the Unforgiven were more than overwhelmed, but it did not stop them from continuing to fight. The voice of God still echoed in their minds, rousing them to action.

The sound of a fighter jet caused her to look skyward, the Israeli plane firing its missiles and obliterating a dragon from the sky. It gave her hope to see that some of humanity had answered God's call—warriors and civilians emerging from their places of safety to fight for earth, Heaven, and God.

There were human foot soldiers upon the desert battlefield as well. Vilma did not know what nation they had originally sworn their allegiance to, only that they now fought as one against a common threat.

Vilma took to the air above the carnage, looking for where her skills would most have an effect. An explosion came from above, and she darted down to the desert, shielding herself as jagged pieces of jet fighter rained down, the shrapnel taking out some of the demonic fighters, aiding their cause, despite their loss.

Searching for a sign of what had taken out the fighter, Vilma saw a most unusual sight.

There was a large section of sky that seemed to pulse and expand, fiery explosions blossoming in the air above the battleground.

Drawn to the bizarreness of it all, Vilma clutched her sword of fire and flew up toward the strange disturbance, wanting to assess the situation.

Something had begun to appear, and it was huge, temporarily taking her breath away.

Some sort of craft appeared out of the ether. To her, it resembled an enormous seashell—a seashell the size of a football field—but a seashell nonetheless. The craft's smooth surface was marred by explosions, fiery clouds and black smoke blowing from it.

The enormous ship was losing altitude.

Flapping her wings fiercely, Vilma flew to warn the Unforgiven before—

There was an even louder explosion from the seashell-shaped craft, as debris fell from the ship. From the desert below she saw a flash of yellow and Gabriel locked in battle with multiple armored foes.

"Heads up!" she cried, helping out the dog by slicing the

head from one of his assailants, while he dispatched another by ripping out its throat with his powerful jaws.

The dog looked toward the sky, his body starting to shimmer and spark as he left for cover.

The Unforgiven were all fleeing the scene. She quickly scanned the battleground to be certain that everyone had heeded her warning when she saw Taylor Corbet.

Aaron's mother was fighting for her life against something that resembled an awful combination of scorpion and lion. The horrible beast snatched the woman's rifle from her hands, its pincers snapping the weapon in two. Undeterred, Taylor pulled a handgun from the waist of her pants and continued to fire at the abomination.

The strange craft was falling now. There wasn't a second to waste.

Moving as quickly as possible, Vilma flew toward Taylor, grabbing hold of the woman beneath her arms and hauling her into the air, away from her monstrous attacker.

"What the hell are you doing—," Taylor began, but then fell silent as the burning craft rushed by them on its collision course with the desert.

"Dear God, what is it?" Vilma heard Taylor ask, and remained silent, for she did not have the answer.

The craft decimated everyone still on the ground as it hit. And the resounding boom was just as Vilma imagined the end of the world would sound.

* * *

Something had fallen from the sky.

Satan Darkstar saw the strange craft as it plummeted to the blighted land below, trailing fire and smoke as it crashed upon the battlefield, snuffing out many a loyal soldier beneath its enormous mass.

But their sacrifice would not be in vain, for it was exactly the type of distraction he needed.

The Metatron fought tirelessly, but Satan could sense the armored giant's inner struggle.

The Nephilim boy—the son of the Morningstar—had taken on the power of God, assuming the guise of the Metatron, and it was proving a far more daunting task than he had thought.

The power of God, now a whole entity again, no longer divided and weakened between the three Sisters of Umbra, was a force to be reckoned with, and did not care to be controlled.

The Darkstar would be overjoyed to release it from its shackles and put it to use restoring the earthly passage to Heaven, but in order to do that—

The Metatron was momentarily distracted from the battle at hand as it stared into the billowing cloud of dust and sand rolling across the desert toward them from the crash of the enormous craft.

Satan took full advantage of the opportunity, throwing himself at the Metatron.

They fought, blinded by the dust, sand, and smoke, but the Darkstar knew what he was searching for. It was like a beacon, calling out from within the Metatron's mighty form.

"Succumb to me, boy," Satan said. "Surrender what's inside you and be free of its burdensome turmoil."

He created a knife from the darkness inside him, with a hooked blade designed specifically to peel the armor from a godly being, as easily as one would peel the skin from a piece of fruit.

The Lord of Shadows lashed out. The point of the knife dug deeply into the divine metal of the Metatron's chest plate, just below where the human heart would beat.

Satan could barely contain his excitement, leaning all his weight on the knife to open the armor and bring him that much closer to his prize.

But the Metatron did not see the futility of his actions, using one of its mighty wings to swat the Darkstar away.

Satan rose from where he had fallen and felt the ground beneath his armored heel give, and turned to see that he was standing precariously close to the edge of the crack in the earth that their struggle had caused. The fissure descended for miles, most likely into the fiery core of the planet itself.

And all from one little sword strike, Satan Darkstar thought, amused. *I don't know my own strength.*

The Metatron stood at the ready, but Satan could see that the damage had been done. There was a large, gaping wound in the godly being's chest, leaking divine power out into the air.

Such a waste.

"You'll give it up to me or I will cut it from your chest," the Darkstar growled. "Either way would be sufficient, though the cutting would certainly be more"—he smiled at his adversary—"fun."

The Metatron placed a trembling hand over his chest in an attempt to seal the wound.

But Satan would have no such thing.

Satan attacked again.

He landed upon his foe, covering him like the darkest of shadows, driving him back to the ground. The hooked knife was at the ready, poised to peel away the armor forged of divinity.

The air swirled with the blood of God, and Satan Darkstar could feel its corrosive power upon him. The power ate the darkness, but this did not deter the Lord of Shadows. He needed the power to activate the Ladder. It would be his.

The Metatron thrashed, but could not drive the Darkstar back. He was far too close to victory.

The Metatron encased his hands in the stuff of Heaven, his each and every grappling punch searing the Darkstar's body.

But Satan would do anything to bring about Heaven's fall.

"You could have made this easy," Satan Darkstar said. "But I'm overjoyed that you didn't."

Strength surging, the Lord of Shadows drove the Metatron

backward, one tumbling over the other until the Metatron lay at the edge of the abyss.

Straddling his foe, Satan called upon the dark reserve coiled at the center of the form he now called his own, and felt it respond to his request.

Hell always willing to oblige.

Satan pulled back his arm, all the infernal power that roiled about inside him focused for this one, final act.

Darkness thicker than the black of oblivion swirled about his arm and blade, and Satan Darkstar brought his weapon down on the Metatron.

In a killing blow.

It was time.

Hell churned angrily about Lucifer, ready to explode out into the world.

But Lucifer would not stand for it.

This was his burden. Hell's pain and misery belonged to no one else but him.

It was his responsibility, as it had been his responsibility for these many millennia. He was not about to see it unleashed upon his son, never mind a world already besieged by nightmare.

No, it was time now to take it back.

To wrest control from the Darkstar.

"Are we ready, Milton?" Lucifer Morningstar asked, rising

up from where he sat. The tiny, warm body of the rodent resting in his hand brought the Morningstar great comfort.

And in this comfort he found the strength to do what he must.

Placing the mouse on his shoulder, the Son of the Morning readied himself to take matters into his own hands once more.

As Hell carried on as only Hell could do, Lucifer closed his eyes and saw beyond the pocket of his subconscious where he currently resided and looked out through eyes that had once been his.

Lucifer saw his son, and knew at once that a new and dangerous responsibility had been added on to his already gargantuan burden. Realizing this, he allowed himself the chance to listen to the thoughts of the dark thing that lived within his body, repulsed by the depths of its evil.

Fragments of thought so assailed his every sense that he was almost driven back to the safety of his deep subconscious.

Heaven would fall . . . God driven from the light, into the clutches of darkness . . . a Ladder would be restored, giving a means to breach the pearly gates . . . and this would come from Aaron—the Metatron—who held within him the power of God.

The situation was even more dire than Lucifer could have imagined. His essence surged forward, shattering the black, crystalline barriers that held him at bay.

Regaining mastery over his own form.

* * *

Aaron fought to move, but his energy was practically nonexistent; his multiple injuries taking their toll. All he could do was watch the blade fall and pray for the strength to survive the assault.

As the knife approached his chest plate, it stopped. The strangest of expressions passed over the face of his enemy.

It was a look that could only be described as surprise.

Knowing that this might be his only chance, Aaron reacted, focusing every remaining ounce of strength that he had in reserve into one hand igniting a short sword in a rush of divine fire.

The look on Satan's face was almost comical, wide eyes darting about as he struggled to bring the dagger down, but appeared incapable.

Aaron leaped up from where he lay, bringing the cracking sword around, plunging the blade into the Darkstar's side.

There came the most horrible of screams, Satan's ebony wings pounding the air furiously as he attempted to make his escape. Aaron jumped for his injured foe's leg to keep him on the ground, but Satan evaded his grasp. Aaron fell to his knees and watched as the Darkstar's huge, flapping wings carried him off to safety.

A shot echoed across the desert, and Satan Darkstar fell from the sky in an explosion of black feathers.

Aaron whirled around to see his mother, cradling a

smoking weapon in her arms as she came closer. Vilma walked beside her, covered in a thick coating of dust, but never looking more beautiful. Gabriel trotted faithfully beside her, shaking the desert dirt from his coat. Levi and the Unforgiven soldiers, having survived the fall of the mammoth object that had crashed down from the sky, walked behind them.

They waved to him, and Gabriel barked raucously, but reunions would need to wait. There were still matters of evil to be contended with. Satan had not been vanquished.

Aaron flew to where the Darkstar lay.

Satan lay on his stomach, perfectly still. One of his wings was smoldering where it had been shot.

Aaron knelt beside his foe.

The power of God, though weakened, still raged within him, and it demanded retribution. He tried to calm it down, but it would not listen. It wanted to see its foe vanquished, destroyed, not caring that his father was not responsible for his actions.

Summoning a dagger of fire in case, he reached out to turn the villain over. He was surprised to find Satan's eyes wide and focused.

There was something in his enemy's gaze that touched Aaron's soul.

"Dad?" Aaron whispered.

It was no longer Satan that was with him, but the Morningstar.

"I . . . I'm not sure how much longer . . . I can hold him at bay," Lucifer struggled to say.

He reached out, grabbing hold of Aaron's wrist, pulling the knife of fire toward his chest.

"Do it," the Morningstar commanded.

Aaron was horrified by what his father was asking of him. He fought God's power as it urged him to carry out his father's command.

His father's eyes slid away from his, growing wider as they fixed on something behind him.

Aaron turned to see his mother standing there, still holding her weapon at the ready. Vilma, Gabriel, and some of the Unforgiven soldiers stood by her.

"Taylor," Lucifer whispered.

His mother stood rigid, but then her grip relaxed, the rifle falling to the ground.

"Sam?" she asked, her voice quivering.

Sam? Aaron wondered, but the question was swept aside as his mother ran to the Morningstar, throwing her arms around him in an unbridled display of emotion.

CHAPTER THIRTY-FOUR

Lucifer Morningstar had never believed he would hold her in his arms again.

He'd always considered losing Taylor part of his punishment—his penance for the crimes he'd committed against his Holy Father and Heaven. Never had he imagined—especially in a moment such as this—that he would be reunited with his love.

"You look awful," she said to him as he stood up from where he lay.

"I haven't been myself," he told her, reaching to wipe away some of the tears that streamed down her filthy face.

He could not help himself. He brought his mouth to hers. His kiss was eagerly accepted, and it renewed his strength to battle the ancient force that possessed him.

But for how long?

Lucifer knew that his time was limited.

"The beasts of nightmare will be here momentarily," the Morningstar said, pulling away from Taylor and turning his attention to his son.

From a distance, Lucifer saw the legions of monsters who still survived making their way across the desert, as if they were drawn to the lingering malevolence of their master.

Aaron knelt upon the ground, and Lucifer could see that he was struggling with the power that now possessed him.

"What did you do?" Lucifer asked him.

"What I could," Aaron answered, lifting his pain-racked gaze. "I tried to assume the mantle of the Metatron, but I don't think the power of God likes me."

"That extreme power was not meant for you," he said. "It's fighting you . . . eating you alive from within."

"There wasn't any other way," Aaron said. "I had to try and stop the Darkstar."

With a mention of the Lord of Shadow's moniker, Lucifer felt the creature trapped inside him resume its fight. He gasped, using the strength of his love for Taylor and Aaron to keep the monster restrained.

"What can we do?" Taylor asked, coming to stand beside him.

Lucifer smiled, aroused by her selflessness. "You can do what you've obviously been doing since I broke your heart," he told her.

He could see that she was about to protest but stopped her with a glance. "I never believed that I would ever get the chance to say how sorry I am," Lucifer told her. "Leaving you was one of the hardest things I have ever done."

She placed the most tender of kisses upon his lips, and Lucifer thought that if he were to die right then, he would be satisfied.

But there were things that still needed to be done, monster forces to be lessened.

A sword of fire ignited in Vilma's hand as she looked out over the desert. Gabriel had positioned himself at her side, wisps of divine fire leaping from the ends of his hackled coat.

"It won't be long now," she said, turning to look back to them.

Aaron managed to create a sword, despite his weakened condition.

Taylor picked up her weapon from where she'd dropped it.

"Once more into the breach," she said, flicking a switch, causing it to hum loudly as it charged.

Lucifer was amazed by their bravery, proud that he had known them and fought alongside them.

But it was his time.

And his time alone.

The Morningstar strode past them, allowing his wings to emerge. The left wing was still a bit tender, but it had pretty much healed. It would suffice enough to carry him aloft.

"Where are you going?" Taylor asked.

Lucifer didn't want to turn around, knowing how hard it would be to look away, but her voice compelled him.

"There is a task I need to perform," he said.

"We'll back you up," Vilma said. Her wings appeared, and she held her blazing weapon eagerly by her side.

"No," he said with a shake of his head. "Not this time."

"What are you going to do?" Aaron asked.

Lucifer looked to his son and felt nothing but pride.

"What needs to be done," he said. Lucifer pointed to the approaching beasts. "Their numbers must be whittled down," he said. "And I believe I have a way."

His eyes moved past them to the giant crack in the desert. A pulsing orange glow emanated up from the fissure, followed by a thick, noxious cloud.

"Most are simple beasts," Lucifer said, again turning away from them, "and are easily swayed to obey."

"Sam," Taylor tentatively called.

He hesitated, turning back one last time.

"I love you," she told him.

"And I you," he answered. Lucifer took to the sky, feeling stronger at that moment then he had in eons.

Strong enough to hold back the Devil, and the legions of Hell itself.

"I have to go with him," Taylor said.

Vilma reached out to grab her arm, stopping her.

"We need you with us," she said, shifting her eyes to Aaron, who looked worse than he had mere moments ago. "Aaron needs you too."

Taylor gazed after Lucifer's dwindling shape as new tears rolled down her cheeks.

"Okay," she said, hefting her weapon and regaining control over her emotions. "What now?"

Vilma placed an arm around Aaron to keep him from falling. She saw the strain on his face and knew that God's power was killing him.

And that was killing her.

"We have to protect that," he said, slowly turning to point out the stone structure that had been revealed from deep beneath the desert sands. "If my father doesn't make it . . . if the Darkstar regains control . . . we need to keep him from that."

"Beth-El," Levi whispered in reverence, his shaded gaze locked upon the temple. The fallen angel dropped to his knees on the sand. "We stand before the House of God."

The other Unforgiven followed their leader, heads bowed in a deep-residing respect.

Vilma noticed tiny gouts of flame appearing on Aaron's golden armor, flames that seemed to be eating away the divine metal, and she looked at him with concern on her face.

"I'll be all right," he said, forcing a smile.

Gabriel whined pitifully.

"I think this power," Aaron touched his chest with a large, armored hand. "I think that this power is the key to that." He again pointed toward the temple.

"And it's killing you," Gabriel barked.

Aaron didn't argue with the dog; he just pulled himself taller, reaching out a trembling hand to lay it upon the faithful dog's blocky head.

Vilma wanted to throw her arms around him and hold him tight, but she knew that it wasn't the time for such emotional displays.

She needed to be strong for him, for all of them really.

They all seemed to sense it at once, a strange tickling sensation that caused the hair on the back of her neck to prickle. Vilma spun toward the disturbance, a welcome distraction from the sadness that threatened to overwhelm her.

The Unforgiven reacted too, their guns aimed at the strange being that seemed to have stepped out of the air.

Gabriel began to cautiously move toward the strange figure who stood before them, his body seemingly made of metal.

"Gabriel, no," Vilma said, but the dog did not listen.

The Labrador tilted his head back, sniffing the air about the strange metal man. "Dusty?"

The man turned his gray eyes to the dog, his mouth twitching in confirmation.

Vilma lowered her sword, taking in the young man's features.

"Dusty, is that you?" Her mind raced with questions, but

they were quickly forgotten as their friend's stomach began to pulsate and bubble, somehow changing to liquid.

Once more Vilma raised her sword, and the Unforgiven aimed their weapons.

Something coated in a liquid metal fell from Dusty's core. It was small, childlike, and the figure writhed on the ground before finally climbing to its feet.

The metal fluid flowed off the child, returning to Dusty.

They were stunned. The little boy spat liquid metal on the ground, brushing away residue from his bare arms.

"Well, that was disgusting," he said in a voice far more mature than that of a four-year-old.

Gabriel approached the child, giving him a careful sniff.

"Oh dear," the child said, rearing back. "Good doggy." He was obviously afraid. "That's it, be off." He shooed the dog away with his hands.

"Who . . . ?" Vilma began, stunned by this latest bit of insanity. "Where . . . ?"

The child carefully walked around Gabriel, not wanting to get too close, and approached the Metatron.

"I'm Enoch," the child said. He then looked past Aaron, to the Beth-El temple in the distance.

Vilma gasped as Aaron dropped weakly to his knees before the child.

Enoch stood eye to eye with him then.

"I think I can help," the child said, leaning in close, looking deep into Aaron's eyes. "The power that's killing you belongs to me."

Lucifer kept the abominable legions at bay, flying above their heads in a grandiose display.

He circled their diminished number, though there were still quite a few that had managed to survive. Lucifer could see the fear in their eyes as they watched him. None of the beasts wanted to offend their Dark Master in any way.

The ancient evil shrieked and wailed inside him.

"Scream all you like, loathsome thing," Lucifer said. "You are my prisoner now."

This just made the evil fight all the harder, but Lucifer endured, using the love that he'd experienced at seeing Taylor Corbet again as his source of inspiration.

But would it be enough?

It was as if the evil could sense his doubt, slithering its shadowy form about his brain.

"I can feel your reserves weakening, Son of the Morning," the evil cooed. "It is only a matter of time before I usurp control once more, and your body belongs to me."

Lucifer tried to ignore the taunting voice.

"You doubt me?" asked the evil.

Lucifer suddenly experienced the most blinding pain. He dropped from the air like a stone. Landing in a heap, he lay still, hoping the effects would pass.

"What a sight you must be to them," the evil commented. "Their great and powerful leader falling from the sky."

Lucifer picked himself up from the ground, as the monsters circled him.

The fear in his legion's eyes had been replaced by something else.

Caution, perhaps, as they sensed weakness.

The voice of the evil grew stronger, louder, and no matter how hard Lucifer tried, he could not block it out.

"They can smell your fear," the evil purred. "You're not the threat you were when I was in control."

Lucifer spread his wings of black feathers, and the mob leaped back. Slowly, though, they began to converge on him once more.

Something amongst the rabble became brave. A thick tentacle lashed out, whiplike, wrapping around Lucifer's ankle as he tried to ascend, dragging him back to the earth. Landing amongst them, Lucifer conjured a sword of fire and, brandishing it before him, drove the monstrous masses back.

There was suddenly a painful spasm in his hand, and the sword dropped from Lucifer's grasp. It disappeared in a flash before it could even touch the ground.

"Damn you," Lucifer hissed, creating another blade, but the monsters had already started to surge.

"You're far too weak for this," the evil taunted. "All that

time locked away within the recesses of your mind has dulled your strength."

The monsters were atop him now, each desperate for a piece of him. He could feel their claws, tentacles, and teeth frantically attempting to tear him to bits.

So much for loyalty, Lucifer thought, so the evil would hear.

"Loyalty comes from the fear of death," the evil explained. "And you're too pathetic right now to be much of a threat to anyone, but any moment now, when your resolve weakens, I'll show them what death is all about—

And then it will be Heaven's turn."

Satan's words were so fearsome and vile that Lucifer made a most fateful decision.

"Let's get this over with, shall we?" the evil spoke. "Succumb to me, admit your defeat, and I'll allow you to exist as one of my distant memories."

The monsters ripped off pieces of Lucifer's armor, and tore at the flesh beneath. There were so many of them. . . .

"You're right," Lucifer said. "I've let this go on for far too long."

He could feel Satan's joy inside his head. It felt like millions of maggots hatching within a piece of rotting meat and squirming to the surface.

"I fear you and your potential far more."

Lucifer sensed the ancient evil's confusion, which was exactly what he needed. In his mind, he saw the restraints that locked his penance away, a heavy wooden door with chains draped across it.

And standing before that door was the tiniest of sentries with the soul of the most ferocious of lions.

"Hello, Milton," Lucifer said to the mouse. "I'm afraid we're going to need to let it out."

His little friend obediently scampered away from the door as the chains began to disintegrate, large metal links falling to the floor of Lucifer's subconscious.

"What are you doing?" the evil demanded, attempting to inflict all manner of psychic pain upon him, but it was nothing in comparison to the pain Lucifer felt at what he was about to do.

"I'm taking care of you for good," Lucifer explained, waiting before the door, which now trembled and shook, the wood cracking loudly as it was savagely pushed upon from the other side.

"You wouldn't," the evil proclaimed.

"I would," Lucifer replied.

The psychic manifestation of the door exploded outward, and the sinister emotions and sensations that had taken on a life of their own over the ages rushed into Lucifer's being, filling him with the awfulness of their power.

The strength of Hell was now his. Lucifer surged up from the great mound of beasts that tried to claim him, the force his body emitted tossing them miles, reducing their bones to paste.

The monster legions feared him again and fled his wrath, but he would not let them go far.

Lucifer took to the air once more, the power of Hell radiating from his body. He let the dreadfulness flow from his being like some awful pheromone.

The monsters stopped running and gazed up at him. Like bees attracted to the scent of pollen, the nightmares were drawn to the desolation he exuded.

Satan came to the fearful resolution that its own power was dwarfed by the magnitude of what Lucifer had unleashed.

As much as Lucifer loathed it, this was his curse and he was its master, and it filled him with a terrible strength.

Lucifer could feel it already working upon him, Hell eager to spread out to the waiting world. If this dreadful power was to be unleashed, it must be set loose where it could do the least amount of harm.

And the world of man was not such a place.

Satan cowered at Hell's fury, now in Lucifer's control. The ancient evil attempted to retreat, deep into the Morningstar's subconscious, but Lucifer would not allow it.

"You'll stay right here with me," the Son of the Morning said. "Where I can keep an eye on you."

The Darkstar struggled, but even Satan was no match against Hell's might.

Flapping his wings, the Morningstar hovered, waiting for the swarm of monstrosities to catch up to him. He focused his attention on the blighted land, fixating upon the large, jagged scar that Aaron's struggle with the Darkstar had left in the earth.

Would it be deep enough?

The dark miasma leaking from Lucifer's being drew the nightmare throng ever closer. They could taste it on the wind, and were drunk with its promise of misery and sadness.

And all the while Lucifer remembered what he had done to earn such a burden, experiencing it all again as if existing in the moment.

This horrible thing was his, and his alone, but he was its master.

To think this was a power that the Darkstar had hoped to control. The notion was so ridiculous it made the Son of the Morning sadly smile.

Spreading his arms, Lucifer welcomed the swarm of beasts.

"Come to me," he proclaimed. "I am your lord and master."

Legions of nightmare extended as far as the eye could see, and Lucifer hoped that his control over them would reach that far.

"I do this for you," Lucifer whispered upon the gentle desert wind, hoping for his words to be carried to his lover's ear, but knowing that they never would.

As monsters basked in the hellish poison Lucifer exuded, he then addressed his followers.

"This world," he proclaimed. "It is not a place for the likes of you."

The monsters chattered, screamed, screeched, and howled in their agreement, held under his spell.

"Here!" Lucifer announced. He pointed to the open gash in the crust of the earth. "Here is a place better suited to your like!"

The throng responded, their bodies flowing toward the fissure and tumbling into the abyss.

"That's it!" Lucifer cried. "Down into the hole we go."

He flapped his wings, launching himself skyward, and then angled his body down, creating a sword of fire in his hand as he plunged into the chasm.

"A Hell of our own making awaits us!"

Wave after wave of monsters followed.

Following their lord and master down into darkness.

Slowly, Lorelei pulled her corporeal self back together.

In hindsight, releasing the soul energies of thousands probably wasn't the best of ideas, but at that point, she really couldn't think of any better solution.

There were still spirits around her, but their number had lessened dramatically. She hoped that their sacrifice had not been made in vain.

Her vision cleared as she looked at the Architects' headquarters, brought down by the power of the recently dead. It was far larger than she could ever have imagined, a seashell-shaped aircraft carrier broken and buried in the sand.

It was all about saving the child, and she'd tried to convey that to the spirits that had lingered about her: that without him, they were likely lost. It was good that they trusted her, giving her their confidence, as well as their soul energies.

Looking at the extent of damage to the mighty craft, she was surprised at the level of power that had been released. Drifting closer, she began to worry that perhaps the child had not survived the crash, but remembered something that she had seen, appearing in the air behind the little boy, just as she had released the soul energies to stop the Architect.

Lorelei smiled with the memory. Don't ask her how she knew, but she believed the child was fine, and that Dusty somehow had something to do with it.

She had been drifting closer and closer to the craft, when she noticed the extent of the bodies that littered the ground. There were monstrous bodies everywhere, as well as those strange, metal-winged beings that she'd seen at the shopping center when she'd found Jeremy.

It looked as though the Architects' craft had dropped upon some kind of battleground.

Her beliefs were confirmed with a shriek of violence as horrible figures emerged from the clouds of black smoke still billowing from the body of the craft, wielding blood-caked swords and knives, attacking an even smaller group of the metal-winged angelic beings, who looked as though they had seen better days.

She was considering helping them somehow, when there came a tremendous explosion from the seashell-shaped craft. An entire section of pearl-white wall blew open with a fiery gout, the blast so great that it actually scattered the monsters that had been on the attack.

Lorelei, along with the metal-winged angels, stood transfixed before the huge craft, as two shapes locked in furious battle exploded out along with the fire and smoke.

It took a moment to figure out, but at closer inspection she saw that it was Jeremy . . . Jeremy and Verchiel, still joined in battle as they had been before the Architects' home had been knocked from the sky.

Weapons of divine fire hissed and sparked as they struck one another while the two angels continued their struggle, lost in the midst of a battle frenzy. From the looks of their surroundings, she realized that maybe their battle prowess could be better served inflicting damage upon the enemy, rather than each other, and floated across the desert toward them to try and come up with a way to break them up.

Verchiel smashed the fiery pommel of his sword into Jeremy's face, bloodying his nose and knocking him back. She could see by the horrible looks in their eyes that they were functioning now on a barely human level. It was all about the battle now, and destroying one's enemy.

The swarm of goblins came out of nowhere, attacking the angels en masse with their blood-caked weaponry.

Jeremy and Verchiel barely gave them a second thought, until one of the wretched beasts thrust his spear into Verchiel's side.

Lorelei figured that this was certainly a way to get their attention.

Verchiel stopped the progress of his sword in mid-arc, suddenly looking to his left at the ugly beast that bared its ragged teeth at him and pushed on the point of the spear.

Verchiel looked quickly back to Jeremy, and some sort of message seemed to pass between them, something to the effect of, *Let us kill these things first, and then we can get back to killing each other*.

She thought that she'd hit the nail on the head, because the two then attacked the goblins with the same level of fury that they'd had toward each other.

The bald, metal-winged angels had joined the fray as well, as even more monster soldiers appeared on the battlefield, despite the presence of the huge seashell lying in their midst.

She kept her eyes on Jeremy and Verchiel; the two actually appeared to be playing nice at the moment, decimating a squadron of goblin warriors. They were fighting close to the body of the Architects' base when there was another explosion, a blast so great that it shredded the monsters that were close by and sent the two warrior angels tumbling through the air like leaves.

Lorelei knew at once that this was trouble, and went through the motions of sucking in a gasp of air, even though she no longer breathed, as the Architect emerged from his downed craft. Energies that she knew to have a divine origin crackled about his hands as his hooded form stepped out upon the sand.

Sensing immediate danger, Lorelei cried out to Verchiel and Jeremy, and they seemed to hear, even though she knew that this was impossible, as they rose up from the ground, weapons poised to strike as they leaped at their newly appeared foe.

The Architect barely gave them a second glance, swatting one aside, and then the other. They lay very still upon the ground.

Lorelei watched in growing horror as the Architect marched away from the wreckage of his home onto the battlefield with what appeared to be a specific purpose.

Even though a ghost, a churning of great fear roiled in her spectral belly, for she believed she knew where the villain was going.

And for who.

Gabriel looked at Aaron and felt his heart near to breaking.

"Will he be all right?" the dog asked.

The child touched Aaron's face with a small, dirty hand, continuing to look deeply into his eyes.

"I'm not sure," Enoch answered. "That damage might have been done."

"Why is it hurting him?" Gabriel wanted to know.

The child looked at him, a tinge of annoyance evident in his petulant stare.

"You ask an awful lot of questions for a dog," the child said. "I haven't encountered many dogs in my brief existence, but do all your kind act this way? Can't imagine why anybody would want to own one."

"I'm different," Gabriel explained. "Aaron made me different."

"Hooray for us," Enoch mocked with a roll of his eyes.

Gabriel was tempted to give the child a warning nip, to show who was boss, but decided against it. Aaron was his only concern now.

"The power of God doesn't belong in him," the child then said, staring at Aaron's face from multiple angles.

Aaron just knelt there, as if in a trance, swaying ever so slightly as bursts of flame exploded off his armor, making jagged holes and exposing burned and bubbled flesh beneath.

"It's too strong . . . too unwieldy. It's destroying the host body."

"Aaron," Gabriel corrected. "It's destroying Aaron."

"That's what I said," the child answered the dog, annoyed. "The host body Aaron."

Gabriel sensed someone's approach and watched as the transformed Dusty came to join them.

"What happened to him again?" Gabriel asked the child.

Enoch sighed, exasperated with the continuous parade of

questions. "Do you think I'm privy to everything, dog?" he asked. "He's been changed . . . transformed, if you will, into an instrument of God, and it's a good thing, too, for I would have likely been killed when the Architects' base went down, if it wasn't for him."

The child turned his face toward Dusty.

"He knew right where to find me."

Aaron moaned, and he fell heavily to his side, the fire growing larger, hotter, as the armor of the Metatron continued to break down.

"We haven't much time," Enoch said, one of his small hands hovering over the growing divine flames.

"What are you going to do?" Gabriel asked nervously.

"I'm going to attempt to take back what is rightfully mine," he said.

"And Aaron?"

Enoch did not answer him as he rubbed his hands vigorously together, and then laid them upon his boy.

CHAPTER THIRTY-FIVE

Enoch placed his small, delicate hands upon the young man.

In a searing flash that made him cry out, the child found what he sought, wrapped tightly around the man's soul, and was afraid. For after being so violently extracted from its original host, and the countless years it had spent in servitude to a darker power, this power of God had become quite feral.

Enoch called to it, but it did not recognize him. Instead, it surged toward him with a roar, and the child was repelled, falling backward to the sand.

"What's happened?" Aaron's woman, Vilma, asked.

The child could see the fear in her eyes, as well as in those of the dog, Gabriel, and Dusty, as Aaron writhed on the ground, moaning while the force destroyed his body from within.

"Nothing that I didn't expect," Enoch answered shortly,

getting to his feet. "The power has been left too long on its own. It's unfocused, untamed."

"Can you . . . ," Vilma started, but did not finish as the sounds of weapon fire exploded in the air.

Monsters were slowly advancing upon them, the Unforgiven trying to hold them back.

"I can try," the child said, again laying his hands upon Aaron's smoldering, armored form. "But I must not be disturbed. Keep them away," he ordered, gesturing with his head toward the battle.

Without waiting for a reply, Enoch allowed himself to be pulled back into Aaron's psyche, again searching for the power of God that hid there.

"Hello?" he called out over the thrumming of Aaron's heart. It sounded labored, strained, and the child wondered how much more Aaron's body could take.

The force of supreme divinity suddenly emerged to confront this intruder in what had become its den. Enoch was terrified, as he had been so very long ago when the Lord God Almighty had originally joined his frail human form with the glory of His awesomeness.

The God power appeared as many fearsome things as it attempted to drive the child away: a ferocious lion, a shrieking hawk, a hissing cobra. In the blink of an eye, it had morphed into all things that walked, crawled, slithered, and flew upon the planet, showing him the extent of its power.

And even though he was afraid, Enoch extended his hands, calling it to him.

That just enraged the God force all the more. It drew back, away from the interloper, warning him not to come any closer. Then it struck, lunging with blinding speed at the child.

Enoch prepared to meet his fate, but the power of God stopped mere inches from his face.

He stared for a moment at the force, which simply hovered before him. "Do you know me now?" he asked.

The force, integral to the creation of all things, just floated there, considering him.

"You and I," Enoch continued. "We were together once. We were one and the same."

The power drew away.

"And we could be again." He extended his hand once more to the fearsome force, presenting it with all that he had to offer. "Accept me, and I will accept you."

The God power appeared to grow larger with his words.

"Accept me and I will make you whole again."

The power came at him as a wall of pure force, permeating his every aspect.

Knowing him intimately.

Above the whine of the Unforgiven's recharging rifles, Vilma heard the most ear-piercing sound.

Turning from the battle at hand, she saw the child called

Enoch falling away from Aaron's armored body, trails of white fire extending from his small hands. It was as if he were pulling the power from Aaron's body.

And as he did that, the child screamed.

Gabriel barked frantically, lunging forward to help the boy, who was engulfed in white flames, his cries even more shrill and filled with pain.

But the white fire did not care for the dog's interference. A tendril of flame whipped out from the burning body to drive the Labrador back.

Enoch's scream had become like white noise, and all Vilma could do was stare as the fire grew larger and brighter, until the child could no longer be seen. It was as if a miniature sun roiled and burned before them.

Then there was a flash so bright that it threw Vilma to the ground, even temporarily stopping the monsters' attack.

Everything went deathly quiet, and Vilma rapidly blinked her eyes, gradually bringing her vision back.

A striking figure, clad in armor that looked as if it was created from the stuff of stars, stood at least twenty feet high. Its face was hidden by a featureless helmet, but its eyes burned with a supreme intelligence.

The Metatron was reborn.

And then her eyes fell on Aaron, and her heart nearly stopped. He was lying naked on the ground, his body human again, but deathly still. She ran to him, falling to her knees beside him, holding back tears of relief as she realized he was only unconscious. She gathered him into her arms, then gazed up at the godlike entity.

"Will you help us end this?" she asked.

The transformed Dusty went to stand beside the figure, staring at the Metatron as if waiting for its answer as well.

The armored giant said nothing. It looked about at the monster legions that had recovered to once again advance upon them, and then down at Dusty.

Something seemed to pass between the two.

Dusty nodded ever so slightly, as the Metatron turned its broad, armored back on them and walked away.

Vilma couldn't believe her eyes.

"Wait!" she cried out, cradling Aaron's body. "What are you doing? Aren't you going to help us?"

Dusty trailed after the awesome figure, the two of them heading away from the battle, and toward the unearthed temple.

Toward the House of God.

Their last hope was walking away, leaving them to the nightmares.

Taylor and Levi were doing their best to lead the surviving Unforgiven against the remaining monsters, but would it be enough?

Vilma looked down at Aaron lying still in her arms. She didn't want to leave him, but she had no choice.

"Stay with him," she ordered Gabriel. "Protect him at all cost."

"I won't let them hurt him," Gabriel said, his fur beginning to glow and spark.

"You're a good dog." She patted his head.

"You're not so bad yourself," Gabriel replied.

Vilma smiled, calling upon a sword of fire as her wings emerged, and then she flew off into battle once more.

Jeremy sat up suddenly on the desert floor, causing his head to spin.

His eyes drifted about. "Bloody hell," he slurred, as he realized he was surrounded by monsters, that murderous angel, Verchiel, just beginning to stir beside him.

"Hey," Jeremy said to the awakening angel.

"Are you addressing me, Nephilim?" Verchiel spat.

"Yeah, thought you might like to have a look," he responded, slowly getting to his feet.

The beasts were coming for them with bloodlust in their eyes.

Verchiel stood, opening the palm of his hand to summon a weapon. "I never believed I would say such a thing, but killing these beasts is growing tiresome."

Jeremy could not help but chuckle as he called upon his own weapon. "Well, let's get this over with. We might find something more to your liking later."

His wings stretching out as he prepared to launch himself, Verchiel shrugged. "Perhaps."

There was a sudden scream from behind them, and Jeremy spun to meet the attack. But the monsters that swarmed from the cover of the Architects' downed craft seemed to have no interest in them.

"What the . . . ?" Jeremy exclaimed, and glanced over to Verchiel, whose shock gradually turned to amusement.

These monsters laid siege to the others, and although their band was smaller, the other monsters proved no match for their savagery.

"I don't understand," Jeremy said, lowering his flaming ax and watching as their attackers were driven back.

"What's to understand?" Verchiel asked with a disturbing chuckle.

A goblin, clutching a knife and what appeared to be some other beast's scalp, turned and approached them.

"A spoil of war, my master." The goblin bowed before Verchiel, presenting his bloody gift.

"My master?" Jeremy exclaimed, looking from Verchiel to the monsters that stood among those they had vanquished. They were all bowing their misshapen heads to Verchiel. "They follow you?" he asked incredulously.

Verchiel smiled, accepting the tribute. "They do," he said, holding the scalp close to his face, rubbing the course black hair between his thumb and finger.

"And what, pray tell, do you plan to do with them?" Jeremy asked, looking over the gathering of grotesques.

"Do with them?" Verchiel asked, letting the scalp fall to the ground as he raised his fiery sword. "Isn't it obvious, Nephilim? I intend to lead them into battle."

A wall of primitive monsters tried to stop the Overseer's progress, but he would have none of it, turning any and all who tried to halt his forward momentum to a cloud of bloody mist.

For the Architect believed there was a chance that his vision for this world could still be realized.

Chaos had always been a part of the process. The earth's inhabitants had always fought to survive, or died, making way for those strong enough to take back the world that God believed held so much promise.

The Overseer Architect saw earth's promise too, but his vision was so much grander than what his Holy Creator foresaw. This world could be more than Heaven, and he would do everything in his power to make it so.

The armies of darkness were nothing to him, a minor inconvenience, and the Overseer destroyed them without a second thought.

There was still much to be accomplished before his achievement could be viewed by the Lord of Lords. He had to stop the Ladder from being activated, and if that meant the death of the Metatron yet again, so be it.

Up ahead there was a line of defense, warriors who had risen up to do battle with the escalating evil in the world. These were the kinds of beings that inspired his purpose. They had survived so much destruction already; they could help to transform the world into one that surpassed Heaven itself.

But they were in his way. It disturbed the Overseer greatly to remove beings of such enormous potential, but it was the only way.

Time was of the essence if Heaven and earth were to remain disconnected.

"Who the hell is that?" Vilma asked, slashing down a troll, as her eyes fixed on a large, hooded shape that moved with incredible speed across the battlefield, decimating anything that got in its way.

The Unforgiven took notice as well. Vilma saw Levi freeze, concern on his face. It was if suddenly all the monsters attacking them were forgotten.

"Direct all fire!" Levi commanded, and the Unforgiven aimed their weapons at the juggernaut advancing on them.

The fallen angels' high-tech weaponry did nothing to slow the figure, and Vilma realized that it was now up to her. The weapons of the Unforgiven might not be able to deter this new threat, but the power of a Nephilim might.

Wings spread wide, she leaped into the air with a sword of fire, ready to strike. She dropped down into the path of the hooded figure, swinging her blade at where she imagined its legs would be. But the creature captured the burning sword with a spidery hand.

As she tried to pull the blade back from its clutches, she stared, stunned, as the sword fizzled and disappeared. The figure grabbed her by the shoulders and pulled her close. Vilma felt a charge like thousands of volts of electricity passing through her body, totally immobilizing her as the being's single large eye studied her from inside the hood.

"Nephilim," a voice boomed inside her head, and she cried out in pain. "You were to be one of my Inheritors."

The figure released one of her shoulders, bringing a spindly finger up to her face, brushing her forehead.

Vilma cried out again as her mind was invaded by a deluge of terrifying imagery.

And with that imagery came a revelation.

She knew she was in the presence of the Architect, and that he and his kind had toiled for millennia to make this world so much more than what God had intended. From terror, darkness, and despair, a new world would emerge, a phoenix from the ashes of the old.

She saw how the Architects had taken Nephilim from all over the planet and hidden them away, until it was time to repopulate the world. She saw how the Nephilim were to breed, to produce the optimal offspring.

Mated pairs.

The Overseer released Vilma, and she fell limply to the ground, the Architects' plan now seared to her brain.

Vilma was supposed to be part of this grand scheme, but the image of the mate chosen for her by the Architect was not Aaron Corbet.

It was Jeremy Fox.

She lay there, stunned and nearly paralyzed, when she heard a strange sound carried upon the wind.

It started off softly, but then grew steadily louder.

It was the sound of flapping wings.

Many. Flapping. Wings.

Above her, the sky filled with a legion of winged warriors.

Hope exploded inside her as the Architect beheld the vision too.

Nephilim.

The Metatron climbed the enormous steps to the House of God with ease, for this place had been built for a being such as he. At the open doors, he paused for a moment, his eyes scanning the area, searching for A'Dorial, although something told him this angel was no more.

He waited for the guise of the Instrument. Once a tool to sever the ties between earth and Heaven, to prevent the disease of evil from spreading, now it would serve another purpose.

The being who had once been called Dusty struggled up the last step to his side.

Then the Metatron and the Instrument strode through the open doors of the House, to the stone slab in the center of the room. Now in the presence of the mechanism that could unlock the Ladder, the Metatron's body grew even larger.

The stone began to hum, a strange tune filled with the infinite wonders of the universe and of God's love for this simple, yet magnificent world.

The Metatron passed one of his large, armored hands over the flat surface and keyhole-like opening. A light as warm and comforting as the first ray of sun after a storm shone up from the aperture.

He turned his towering gaze to the human manifestation of the Instrument. The reflection of Heaven's light glinted off the Metatron's helmet to shine upon the metallic body of the young man once called Dusty.

The Instrument's metal form began to change, any semblance to the human body quickly disappearing.

Over the centuries the Instrument had been many things: a trumpet to call down the End of Days, a sword so sharp it could sever the ties between Heaven and earth.

And now it took on its newest shape and purpose.

A key.

A key to unlock the passage between the world of man and God; a key to unleash this planet's unlimited potential.

It was time.

The Metatron picked up the key and carefully inserted it

into the lock. Even though the machine had been frozen in place for such a very long time, the key turned easily. There came a series of loud clicks as the cylinders fell into place and the mechanism was activated.

The Metatron stepped back, watching as the machine gradually came to life, its low, gentle hum growing along with its power.

It won't be long now, the Metatron thought just as the Ladder to Heaven emerged in a rush of searing light and fire.

The enormous swirling helix rose through the temple's ceiling to punch through the thick, all-encompassing darkness, glowing brighter, and brighter still, as it burned away the heavy clouds that enshrouded the planet.

And all who lived upon the earth then knew that Heaven was watching once more.

CHAPTER THIRTY-SIX

NOW

Is this the end of the world? Vilma's aunt Edna wondered as the searing light filled every inch of her kitchen, erasing every shadow.

The creature that had invaded their home cried pathetically as it died, the brilliant light burning away the evil that had allowed it to exist.

And though the light was so very bright, Edna and her husband could not help but stare into it as they bathed in its reassuring warmth.

This isn't the end at all, Edna thought. *This is just the beginning.*

Heaven was watching once more.

Charlie didn't know how much longer he could last, how much longer any of them could last within the shelter.

Water was growing scarce, as was their food.

Since they'd put Loretta's body outside the door . . . Charlie fought back tears for the love of his life. Since they'd put her lifeless body outside the door, they'd heard things moving and sniffing around.

It had been days since anyone had dared venture out for food.

Charlie opened his eyes to pitch darkness. The generator had run out of gas a little over a week before. They had a few candles, which they used sparingly, when they could no longer bear the absence of light.

This was one of those times.

The old man got to his knees, gently feeling across the concrete floor for the makeshift table, created from an empty MRE box. He found the candle and reached inside his pocket for the gold lighter his wife had given him on their twenty-fifth wedding anniversary. He'd stopped smoking not long after that because of a cancer scare, but he still carried the lighter. One never knew when one might be in need of a little light.

Charlie brought the candle close as he flicked the flame to life. Now he could see the others. They all were fast asleep, and he couldn't blame them. It was the best escape.

He turned his gaze to the dancing flame, taking comfort in the flickering light.

The flame suddenly began to increase in size, and he just

about had a heart attack as he saw Loretta's face there, in the fire. Charlie thought he might be going crazy, but Tyrone, Scott, Doris, and Maggie had all woken up and gathered around him.

Loretta smiled, and then she began to speak.

She told them that they were safe.

That Heaven was watching once more.

Aaron awoke to the warmth of the sun on his face.

He opened his eyes to find his dog staring down at him.

"Hey," he said.

"Hello, Aaron," the dog answered.

Aaron sat up, in the grass of the Lynn Common, and studied Gabriel's face very carefully. "You're not Gabriel, are you?"

"Perceptive as usual," a now unfamiliar voice spoke through his best friend.

"Who . . . ?" Aaron began.

"Walk with me." The dog started to stroll across the freshly mowed lawn.

Aaron got to his feet and jogged a few steps to catch up. "So who are you?" he asked again.

The dog looked at him briefly, before looking away.

"You're not going to tell me?"

"Is it really necessary?" the dog asked.

Aaron shrugged. "I would like to know who's possessing my dog—and who I'm talking to."

"Let's just say I'm someone who's been watching you for a long time, and I owe you quite a bit of thanks."

Aaron stopped as the dog did.

"You've helped to save a world that I love very much."

"You're God," Aaron said slowly, as understanding washed over him.

"If that's what you wish to know me as. I answer to many names."

"Why are you talking to me through my dog?"

"I've always had a special fondness for canines," God said, with a slight tilt of the Labrador's head. "Or didn't you notice what dog spelled backward is?"

"Seriously?" was all Aaron could manage, not really sure what to think about this being who inhabited his dog.

"When you changed Gabriel, you made him the perfect receptacle for my spirit," God explained. "The perfect host for me to use in delivering my message to you."

They climbed the steps to the Common's bandstand, a large domed gazebo with peeling white paint, where local bands and orchestras often played during the summer.

"I want to thank you for what you and your brothers and sisters have done for this world," God said. The dog's snout turned into the breeze.

Aaron shrugged. "You're welcome, I guess."

"You guess?"

"Well, it wasn't like I really had much of a choice. I was

kind of thrown into the deep end of the pool—we all were really. It was either swim or drown."

"But you decided to swim."

"Yeah," Aaron agreed.

"And I thank you for that," God said.

"All right."

"You sound annoyed," God observed.

Aaron shrugged again, looking out through the open bandstand at the lush green of the Lynn Common before him. He hadn't seen it look this nice—ever.

"Why did you let so much horrible stuff happen?" he asked after a moment of silence.

"Cut right to the chase. Good for you."

"You're God. You're supposed to be loving and kind and look out for the good people." Aaron turned back to his dog, holding his gaze with an icy intensity. "But a lot of good people have died."

The dog sighed. "And for that I am sorry. . . ."

"But?" Aaron prompted.

"But there was no other way."

"So all those innocent people, my foster parents, the other Nephilim—Janice, Kirk, William, Russell, and Samantha—and Lorelei, they were all a part of some bigger plan?"

"They were," God said simply.

"So they were all just some sort of collateral damage."

Gabriel's blocky yellow head nodded ever so slowly.

"What kind of loving God are you?" Aaron blurted out angrily.

"A loving God that does not interfere with the lives of His creations."

"Even though angels and devils and all kinds of other crazies were taking shots at us?" Aaron asked incredulously. "Next you'll be telling me that this was all some sort of test."

"I had to be certain that you and your world were ready," God said.

"Ready? Ready for what?"

"Ready for what comes next."

Aaron remained silent, waiting for God to elaborate.

"Humanity has always been my favorite creation," the dog said after a moment, and Aaron could have sworn that he was smiling. "Despite their obvious failures—their arrogance, their indifference toward their fellow man, and their penchant for violence—humanity has the capability to rise above their imperfections."

The dog paused.

"I have seen that capability in you and the other Nephilim, Aaron Corbet. The Nephilim are what humanity strives to be: the perfect combination of human and divine."

"Not too long ago we were considered abominations," Aaron said, thinking of the Powers angels that had hunted his kind to near extinction.

"Evolution takes many surprising shapes," God said.

"Sometimes perfection isn't quite so obvious, and then of course, there's the matter of jealousy."

The dog lay down in a patch of sunlight and closed his eyes, sighing noisily. "It's time for this world to be Paradise," he said softly.

"But isn't that what the Architects were trying to do?" Aaron asked. "To make the world closer to Heaven's image?"

"I didn't object to what the Architects were trying to do, it was how they were going about it." The dog shivered as if cold. "All that darkness. It never should have been allowed to get so out of hand."

"But it did," Aaron stated flatly. "And you let it."

"You're right," God answered. "Because that is how you and your brothers and sisters came into your own."

Aaron felt himself growing angry. "I really don't like where any of this is going," he said. He gripped the wooden handrail of the bandstand, watching as a father and his small son played Frisbee in the distance.

"What's that old saying? To make an omelet, one must first break a few eggs," God said.

"Eggs," Aaron snapped, trying to keep the anger from his voice—he was talking with God, after all. "Is that all we are to you?"

He turned an accusing gaze on the dog as he waited for an answer.

"You people, humanity," the dog said quietly, his eyes still closed in the warmth of the sun. "Most of the time you have me so wrong. I don't want to be an object of absolute reverence, or someone to be feared. I'm your Creator. I love you all and just want you to be good to one another."

"And when we're not?" Aaron asked.

Gabriel's dark, soulful eyes opened, reflecting the light of the sun.

"That's when evil happens," God said. "That's when events spiral out of control, and I look down upon the world, wanting to intervene, knowing that I shouldn't, but . . ."

"But you did," Aaron said thoughtfully. "You sent the child—you sent Enoch."

"The Architects had been a problem for some time, and I'd been carefully planting the seeds to fix it. Enoch was that last seed."

Aaron found himself drawn to the dog, and squatted down before him.

"You say you don't like to get involved, but . . ."

"But sometimes, in order for things to be the way they have to be, I do."

"And are they?" Aaron asked. "Are things the way they need to be?"

The dog lifted his head to look at the sky. Aaron followed his gaze, surprised to see storm clouds in the distance.

"We're getting there," God said. "We're getting there."

* * *

The Nephilim attacked, violence raining down from a sky now filled with an unearthly light that could only be classified as . . .

Divine.

Vilma rose to her feet, ready to help these welcome, yet unexpected additions to their cause. She had no idea who these Nephilim with Melissa and Cameron were, but they fought the Architect with such ferocity that they actually appeared to be doing some damage.

The Architect drove them back with blasts of concentrated force from his outstretched hands, but these new Nephilim were wild and came back at their foe with twice the aggression.

Vilma called upon her wings and a sword of fire, charging forward to join the fray with a rush of confidence, narrowly avoiding the energies that streamed from the Architect's splayed fingers.

She wished that the poor soul behind her had been as lucky.

The unknown Nephilim cried out, before his body turned to dust and was carried away on the dank desert winds.

For a moment they all knew fear, recoiling from the Architect, but their terror was only temporary, burned away by the anger they felt for their foe.

Whoever these Nephilim are, Vilma thought, turning to fly in for what she hoped would be a killing strike, *they are a force to be reckoned with, and I'm honored to be fighting beside them.*

Nephilim exploded to dust around her, but she was moving

too quickly to pull back now. As if reading her mind, Melissa and Cameron moved to either side of the godlike being, attempting to distract him long enough for her to—

She suddenly spread her wings to their fullest, cupping the air around her and slowing her progress, allowing her to hover in the air before her foe as she swung her mighty blade of fire.

The Architect finally noticed her, extending his arm to block her blow. But it was too late. Her sword sliced cleanly through his pale flesh at the wrist. Without a moment's hesitation, she drew back and plunged the crackling blade into the Architect's chest. The sudden explosion of energies slammed Vilma into the desert sand.

Cautiously, she lifted her head. The blast had leveled the battlefield around the temple and knocked the Nephilim from the sky.

The Architect knelt in the sand, scorched black all around him, Vilma's blade sparking and sputtering where it protruded from his chest.

"Oh you wicked, wicked things," he bellowed inside their heads.

Vilma cried out in pain, as did the others.

The Architect rose. His severed hand had grown back, and he used it to withdraw Vilma's sputtering blade from his chest, absorbing its energy.

"If only you knew the glories that I had planned for you."

And as his words echoed inside the minds of the Nephilim,

a double set of enormous, multicolored wings grew from his back, wings covered with ever-widening eyes.

"But that's all over now," the Architect said with absolute revulsion as he extended his pale arms and began to wave them in the air. "It's time that I take it all back, you ungrateful wretches."

Vilma almost got out a warning for everyone to run, when the pain seized her. It was like nothing she had ever experienced before, as if each of her internal workings was being torn out one at a time. She was paralyzed as the divine power that made her Nephilim was pulled from her body—from all the Nephilim—by the angry Architect.

The Unforgiven opened fire, but their weapons proved little more than an annoyance for the angel. The Architect simply raised a hand, setting loose a wave of energy that caused the Unforgiven's weaponry to overload and explode. The air was filled with twisted fireworks and the cries of fallen angels injured by flying shrapnel.

The Architect returned his attention to the Nephilim, their divine power flowing across the desert to swirl about him.

Vilma struggled to remain conscious, while willing Melissa and Cameron to be strong, to somehow find the strength to fight this, for if they were to stop fighting . . .

She dug her fingers into the sand and used all that she had left to rise. As she looked around her, she saw the others were attempting to do the same.

"Inspiring to the end," the voice of the Architect bellowed inside their heads. He pulled his arms to his body, closing his long, spindly fingers into fists, his wings slowly fanning the air.

All of the Nephilim screamed as the Architect attempted to pull the last of their divine fire from their bodies.

This is what death feels like, Vilma thought. *This is the end.*

At first, she believed the vision was a manifestation of her pain, a glowing mote of energy dancing across her line of sight. But then she watched as, with a roar and a guttural growl, that glowing ball of fire struck the Architect, sending him stumbling backward to the blackened sand.

Stunned, Vilma saw the divinely altered Labrador retriever tear into the Architect, ripping away one of his wings with a ferocious snarl.

The Architect's psychic screams exploded in her mind, and she watched in horror as Gabriel was tossed violently away.

The dog slid across the ground, quickly jumping to his feet and shaking off the sand in a shower of divine sparks. Then he got low to the ground, baring his teeth and growling.

The Architect rose up, his wings torn and leaking heavenly energies, and Vilma feared for Gabriel's safety.

At least she did, until she heard the voice.

"Don't even think about hurting my dog," Aaron Corbet warned, as the Architect spun toward this latest challenge to his supremacy.

Just before all Hell broke loose.

* * *

God had sent him back, and none too soon, from what Aaron could see.

He wasn't quite sure who he was dealing with, but he had his suspicions.

"Let me guess," Aaron said, standing there, adorned in armor of his own design. "An Architect?"

"The only," the robed figure announced, attacking Aaron suddenly with snaking tendrils of snapping fire that sprang from the tips of his long fingers.

Instinctively, Aaron reacted. He captured them in one hand, before they could do any damage.

At least that was what he thought he was doing.

Aaron immediately felt his strength begin to wane. Releasing the writhing filaments, he recoiled as they again attempted to entwine him. He summoned a sword of fire and slashed at the tentacles.

"The great Aaron Corbet," the Architect taunted. "So many of my plans for the future were built around your existence."

Gabriel leaped with a ferocious snarl, only to be caught mid-leap by the Architect. The dog struggled in his grasp.

"Fascinating," the Architect said, studying the animal. "I've never seen anything quite like this. . . .

"You did this," he accused Aaron. "You changed this lowly beast into something . . . better."

Aaron tensed, formulating his plan of attack.

"This is was what we—what I—was attempting to do," the Architect said wistfully. "I wanted to make this world better."

Aaron started toward his enemy, but Gabriel cried out.

"No closer or your canine companion dies all the quicker," the Architect warned.

Aaron froze, feeling completely helpless, as he watched Gabriel's struggles grow weaker in the Architect's grasp.

"If you hurt him . . ."

"When," the Architect confirmed. "There is no doubt that I will hurt him, the question is when."

Aaron glared.

"To prolong the life of your animal, will you give me your divinity?" the angelic being asked.

Aaron forced himself to contain his anger, the slow fanning of his wings the only sign of the rage burning within him.

"Will you, as their leader, command them to surrender the spark of Heaven that still exists within their souls?" the Architect asked, gesturing to Vilma and the other Nephilim, some of whom he knew, and some he did not.

Tendrils of energy wrapped around the dog, draining away his divine energies.

"Say yes, Aaron Corbet," the Architect hissed. "And there might still be hope for this world."

The attack came from the most unexpected place.

Taylor Corbet sprang up from the desert sand, clutching

something metal that glinted sharply in the light of the newly emerged sun.

It was one of the Unforgiven's wings.

She swung the feathered blades with all her might, and the tips of the razor-sharp feathers buried themselves deep within the upper body of the godlike being with a satisfying *thunk*.

For the briefest of moments, the world went deathly still.

"Oh, you nasty little germ," the Architect's voice exploded in their minds.

The surprise of the attack had loosened the Architect's grip on Gabriel, and the dog shot from his grasp in an explosion of divine fire and burning embers. At the same time, Aaron lunged forward, cocooning his fists in the fires of Heaven and putting all his strength behind a punch to the Architect's single eye.

"That's for hurting my dog," he said, as the heavily robed figure collapsed to the ground.

The air beside the Architect began to churn, and a very angry Gabriel appeared in a flash of orange fire. The dog bit into the angel's neck and violently shook his prey.

The Architect appeared stunned, but it didn't last.

A sphere of humming energy surrounded the being, repelling Gabriel. The golden fur around the dog's face had burned away, revealing raw and glistening flesh beneath.

"Gabriel!" Aaron cried out.

"No worries," the dog reassured him. "Just a scratch."

The Architect rose, the protective barrier humming around him like a hive of angry bees.

"We are done here," he announced with great finality, and Aaron had to agree.

It was time for this to be over.

Aaron caught movement around him. Vilma and the other Nephilim had gathered by his side; the surviving Unforgiven had risen to their feet.

It was time for the final battle.

This would be their Armageddon.

The Architect Overseer had never believed this would happen.

His vision for this world was crashing down upon him.

He had failed.

And as he was surrounded by the creatures that he had made the cornerstone of his vision for a new Paradise, he felt a twinge of emotion uncommon to his kind.

An emotion that churned and burned with a fire all its own.

The Architect felt betrayed. He felt anger over the ingratitude that was being heaped upon him.

If only the Nephilim could have seen what he had planned for them. He was sure they would have loved him as much as they loved God.

God.

Is that what this is all about? the first of God's angels

thought as he prepared to bring all that he had worked toward to an end. Do I really wish to be loved and worshipped as God?

In a way he did, for he knew that if given the chance, he could show his Creator the error of His ways. And then the Architect would reign over Heaven and earth, and the universe beyond. And God would be wished away, as the Overseer had once been. God would be finished with His tasks, and the Architect would build a new reality.

That was what the Overseer had always envisioned. Instead, he had only anger and sadness.

Emotions strong enough to fuel what he would do next.

The Architect knew that once he was brought before God, he would be eliminated, and that concept filled him with yet another emotion:

Fear.

Fear of ceasing to be, fear of having everything he had worked toward erased by a disapproving, godly hand.

But fear and sadness were quickly consumed by his blazing anger, and the Architect knew what he would do. If the Lord God was going to ignore his efforts, dismiss his achievements as nothing more than mistakes, then he would make it easier for the Creator.

The Architect would wipe the slate clean himself.

He would make the earth a blank canvas again.

The divine power that he had stolen built to critical mass within the Architect's protective sphere.

It will all be over soon, he wanted to tell the creatures that pummeled his shield with their pitiful weapons and what little remained of their own heavenly energies.

The world wiped clean in the blink of an eye.

Aaron could sense that something was wrong. The Architect just stood in the center of his energy sphere. It was as if he'd given up, but what did that mean for a creature like this?

Then the sphere began to expand, its energy eradicating everything it touched.

Aaron called for everyone to get back, but some of the brave Nephilim either did not hear him, or chose to ignore his request, and were dissolved as the expanding sphere touched them.

"The Architect has created some sort of negation field," Levi said.

"And that means what exactly?" Cameron asked, a sword of flame clutched in each hand.

"It means we're screwed," Aaron said. "You can tell me I'm wrong, but I'm thinking that field is going to keep growing and growing until it wipes out everything."

"A simple description, but sufficient," Levi acknowledged.

"So that's it then?" Vilma asked. "We just let the Architect destroy everything? I can't believe we've come this far only to—"

"We've done all we can do," Aaron said flatly.

He could feel their disappointment. They were expecting him to pull some sort of solution from the air as he would a sword of fire, but they were past that now.

It was time to put their faith in someone other than himself.

All of them had done their part, and now . . .

The House of God rumbled as if besieged by a mighty storm. A searing light flashed from the temple, and they threw their hands before their faces so as not to be blinded.

As the light dimmed before what they believed to be their inevitable end, they saw something that filled them with awe.

And hope.

The Metatron loomed at least a hundred feet over the expanding nullification field. He brought his armored hands down to embrace the sphere of annihilation.

The bubble of dangerous energy became like glass, then started to crack.

Aaron stared in silent wonder, as they all did.

A part of him wanted to cheer, to raise his burning sword to the heavens in victory, but there was something extremely sad about what was happening, and all he could do was watch.

The Architect tried to fight as pieces of his protective shield fell away. Tendrils of energy leaped from his outstretched hands to wrap about the golden, armored giant.

But his efforts had little effect.

The Metatron took hold of the Architect in an armored hand.

“I am God,” the Architect wailed, as the Metatron pulled him closer to his golden chest plate.

The metal became like fluid, and the Metatron hugged the struggling Architect tighter.

“Return to Him,” the Metatron’s voice boomed, drowning out the screams of the Architect as he was absorbed into the armored giant.

Returned to the power that had created him.

CHAPTER THIRTY-SEVEN

Lorelei wanted nothing more than to be with her friends. Standing there, watching as victory was snatched from what appeared to be the jaws of defeat, she cried tears of joy.

"What now?" Lorelei asked, turning to A'Dorial, who stood beside her, the remaining spirits of those who had died while the earth was cut off from Heaven gathered around them.

"Something wonderful," the ghost angel replied.

"I meant for me," she said.

"I know." A'Dorial raised a ghostly arm and pointed toward the Metatron, who had retrieved something from inside the temple after defeating the Architect.

The heavenly giant held an enormous key before him. It began to shift and change into the form of a huge sword.

A sword of light.

The Metatron caressed the blade, making its light shine all the brighter.

Even though a ghost, Lorelei raised a protective arm to shield her eyes, but A'Dorial reached out to push it down.

"This is something you should see," he said. "You've earned it."

And when the sword was glowing brighter than the light of a thousand suns, the Metatron raised the blade toward the heavens. The sky above the Megiddo desert began to swirl, whisking away the remaining dark clouds.

It was like the entire planet's revolution had increased tenfold, and Lorelei wondered foolishly, if they didn't hold on to something, would they fly off into space?

"What's happening?" she asked, wonder in her voice.

Without a word, A'Dorial directed her attention to the great stone temple. The glowing spiral extended from its roof into the sky, spinning ever so gently as it twisted up into the sky and beyond.

The Ladder.

Lorelei thought of her father, wondering if he could see what she had helped to accomplish.

"They should be here any minute," A'Dorial said.

"Who?"

"He's told them that it's safe now," the spirit of the angel said, gesturing to the Metatron, who stood statuelike, arm raised, the light from his mighty sword glowing like a beacon.

Something began to appear in the sky above their heads, from one end of the horizon to the other. It gradually filled her entire view.

"Oh my God," Lorelei gasped, as the image became more distinct.

She'd always imagined Heaven as a magickal place, its lights twinkling in the night like priceless jewels. But as the Golden City drew closer, she realized it was more beautiful than she could ever have believed. Countless hosts of angels stood upon the city's parapets, their armor flecked with gold. And one by one they spread their awesome wings, flying down to the world below them.

One such angel appeared in front of her.

"Hello, Lorelei."

There was no mistaking that Southern twang, and Lorelei smiled widely as the angel's form shifted to one that was most familiar to her. Lehash, her father, stood before her in his faded blue jeans and worn cowboy boots. He wore a flannel shirt, and a Stetson on his head, and around his waist was a gun belt, two golden Peacemakers hanging in their leather holsters.

"Dad," she said, flowing into his arms.

She was surprised and so very glad that she could feel him.

"You done good," the angel Lehash said, hugging her back.

She pulled away from him, her eyes drawn to the city

above them. "Is that the Golden City?" she asked, watching what must have been a hundred angels flying about it.

"It is." Lehash adjusted the hat on his head. "You want a closer look?"

Her gaze dropped. "What about them?" Lorelei asked of the spirits that gathered beside her.

"What about 'em?" Lehash asked, as those who had died when the world was cut off from the glory of Heaven dissipated like smoke, flowing up toward the kingdom of Heaven.

"Is that where I'm going?"

"Eventually," the angel said, hooking his arm around his daughter's. "But fer right now, we got some catchin' up to do."

"I love you, Dad," Lorelei said, as they walked arm in arm into the sun.

Jeremy gazed at the enormous, glowing city that filled the sky above him.

He knew what it was, but to admit it out loud would probably drive him mad.

Jeremy, Verchiel, and a strange assortment of warrior monsters that had sworn their allegiance to the angel had been fighting their way across the desert, moving toward what looked to be the scene of some major happening.

Perhaps a defining moment in the battle.

He'd been thinking of Enoch, somehow knowing that the child was part of whatever battle raged in the distance, and that had just made Jeremy want to get there all the quicker.

But then the sky had started to swirl, as if the revolution of the planet had miraculously increased, and it had appeared above them to fill the sky.

Heaven.

Jeremy didn't want to even think of what it meant for their cause. He looked over at Verchiel, and saw that the angel had fallen to his knees in reverence.

"Is it what I think it is?" Jeremy asked, still clutching a battle-ax of fire, just in case. "Is that . . . is it possible?"

Verchiel turned his blood-flecked face to the glow that now blotted out the blue sky, replacing the sun with a light even more brilliant.

"It is possible, Nephilim," Verchiel said, his normally booming voice little more than a quavering whisper.

"We bask in the glory of Heaven."

Verchiel wanted to avert his gaze from the sight of the Golden City, for he believed himself unworthy, but he could not.

He'd never believed he would see its wonder or bask in the radiance of its splendor again, and he took in the vision of it, gorging his senses upon the miraculous sight.

The gentle sound of weeping distracted him from his adoration, and he looked to see the monstrous warriors that had sworn their loyalty to him cower in fear. Many of them cried at what they perceived to be their end.

The goblin, Ergo, had dropped his weapons and curled into a tight ball, trembling and shaking in the light of the Heaven's city.

"Why do you cower?" Verchiel asked the foul creature that had somehow come to earn his respect.

"I have never seen such a sight," the goblin spoke, his voice muffled, for he refused to raise his misshapen head.

"And I believed I never would again," Verchiel told the goblin.

"Does it not scare you?" the goblin asked, peeking out from between splayed fingers.

"Perhaps it once did," Verchiel said, looking back to the enormity of it all. "But now it just fills me with awe."

Verchiel's words must have given the creature courage, for Ergo cautiously looked to the sky above, the other monsters slowly following his lead.

"Its beauty . . . ," the goblin spoke. "It could most assuredly kill us."

"That it could," Verchiel agreed. "That it could."

And then figures, like falling stars, flew down from the columns and corridors of the floating city, emissaries of light coming to greet them.

Verchiel rose to his feet.

And they came.

The angels of Heaven came.

"Bloody hell," he heard the Nephilim boy say behind him as the flock of Heaven approached.

"Hell has nothing to do with this," Verchiel said, as the first of the angels touched down before the enraptured and terrified gaze of a troll, who presented the divine being with his spiked war club as an offer of peace.

The angel brought forth a sword of flame and struck him down.

The troll wailed in pain, his rocky body burning as he collapsed.

"No!" Verchiel cried out, leaping with wings spread to place himself between the sword of fire and the injured troll.

Multiple blades of divine fire connected with a blinding explosion, as they dropped upon Verchiel's.

"What madness is this?" the angelic soldier shouted, enraged by Verchiel's actions. "Remove yourself, creature of Heaven, or suffer this foul thing's fate."

"I will not," Verchiel stated defiantly, protecting the rock troll from harm, as the other beasts in his army came to the injured creature's aid.

Verchiel held a crackling sword of fire by his side, but at the ready, while other angels dropped down from Heaven above, curious as to what was happening.

"He refuses to let me eradicate this dark blight upon God's chosen world," the angel said to his brethren. More weapons of divine fire immediately appeared in each of their hands.

"These creatures, no matter how foul they may appear, served my cause—our cause. They fought with me in battle, and for that they will receive my protection."

The Nephilim boy came to stand beside Verchiel, his burning ax clutched tightly in his hand.

"I think I can get behind that as well," he said, eyes scrutinizing Heaven's emissaries.

Verchiel chanced a quick look at the Nephilim and felt a certain admiration. When this was over, if they survived, he would have to ask his name.

The angels were agitated by their defiance, and Verchiel considered how many of these fine angelic specimens he could take down, before falling to death himself.

Suddenly, there was a murmuring from the back of the angelic gathering, and they parted as a tall, armored figure made his way toward them.

"What seems to be the problem here?" the great angelic warrior Camael asked.

Verchiel dropped to one knee, his head bowed in reverence and respect to the one who had once led the angelic host Powers. "Forgive my insolence," he said, slowly raising his eyes to look upon his former commander. "But I cannot allow these creatures to be harmed."

Camael considered the monsters with a scrutinizing eye. "You would defend these creatures against your own kind?"

"I would," Verchiel told him.

And then the angelic warrior did the most unexpected thing, a wide and beaming smile appearing upon his bearded face.

"You do me proud, Verchiel," Camael said. "It's gratifying to see that you have learned from your past mistakes." He reached down to haul Verchiel up from where he knelt. "You now see the potential for good in all forms of life, no matter their place of origin."

The angelic warriors gathered round Verchiel, and one by one, they each raised their burning swords.

And finally it was Camael's turn.

"Welcome back, my brother," he said, joining the salute.

"You have been gone too long."

Aaron turned his face to the light of Heaven and gave thanks for what had been done this day.

He felt Vilma's arms slide about his waist and squeeze, and he leaned back into her embrace.

"I thought I would never hold you again," Vilma whispered in his ear.

He turned and gently took her face in his hands, the armored gloves that he'd been wearing dissolving in a flash so he could feel the warmth of her skin. "See, that's the difference between you and me. I couldn't bear the thought, so I never even considered it." With his thumb, he wiped away a tear that ran down her cheek. "Guess that makes me a true optimist, or just incredibly unrealistic."

Aaron kissed her then, and as always, it was like the very first time all over again.

"All I know now is there's nothing more real than this," he said, looking deeply into the eyes of the woman he loved, feeling that same depth of emotion returned to him.

"I love you, Aaron Corbet," Vilma said, holding the back of his head as she now kissed him.

"I love you, too, Vilma Santiago."

And no truer words were ever spoken.

Angels of Heaven flew above their heads, leaving trails of glowing fire.

"What does it all mean?" Vilma asked.

Aaron looked about him. The surviving Unforgiven angels were seeing to their wounded, to their dead. He saw his mother, Taylor Corbet, kneeling upon the sand, a wounded angel's head resting in her lap. Gabriel was there as well, the dog using his unique talent to take away the Unforgiven's fear.

His gaze was again drawn to the wondrous sight in the sky above him, and he remembered his conversation with the Lord God.

He had no idea what it all meant, but then he saw the Metatron moving again and figured they were about to find out.

The armored giant extended his massive arms, palms turned upward.

"Hear me, sons and daughters of earth," the Metatron's voice reverberated inside his head, and inside the heads of every man, woman, and child upon the planet, of that Aaron was sure.

"For I am the voice of God."

Aaron stood transfixed before the manifestation of God upon the earth. A great change had come to the world this day. Not only had the forces of darkness been vanquished by the light, but Heaven and the earth were united again.

Bound more closely than ever before.

The earth was now an extension of God's kingdom.

Watched over by the beings who were the embodiment of both Heaven and earth, divine and human.

Nephilim.

And the name went out over the world for all to hear and know—

Nephilim.

They were to be the guardians of a new world—

Nephilim.

Emissaries of God's light, and scourges of shadow—

Nephilim.

It was their world to watch over and protect from harm—

Nephilim.

And they would do anything, and everything, to keep it safe.

EPILOGUE

ONE YEAR AFTER GOD'S MESSAGE TO THE WORLD

Aaron Corbet stood with hands clasped behind his back as the giant, ghostly simulacrum of the earth slowly spun before him above the floor of the control center.

If there were any dangers that required the attention of the Nephilim, a circle of red would have pulsed with the location. At the moment, there was quiet, as if to acknowledge that a year ago this day, God had made a declaration to the world. Darkness would no longer have a place on earth, and the Nephilim were there to ensure that remained so.

So much has changed in a year, Aaron thought, as he looked about the control center where he and his technicians worked tirelessly to carry out Heaven's wishes.

They had come to the installation in droves, men, women, and children, the young and the old, people eager to help achieve God's vision for the world. For many, the world had lived too long in the shadow of darkness, and they welcomed the Nephilim's efforts.

Others, well, some did not care to see one group endowed with so much power, but they were slowly coming around.

What choice did they have?

Aaron liked to think of this control room as a representation of the world. All people, Nephilim, humans, and even members of the monstrous Community working together toward a common goal.

"Sir?"

Aaron turned to the member of the Unforgiven, Cobb, who had chosen to stay on the earth and not be redeemed by Aaron's touch.

The images of that day briefly filled Aaron's mind. With their mission accomplished, the Unforgiven angels had been given the choice of returning to Heaven, purged of their sins and returned to their glory, or staying on earth. Most had chosen to return, but several embraced a new mission.

"Commander Verchiel wishes to speak to you from the Ukrainian hot spot," Cobb said.

Commander Verchiel, Aaron thought, barely feeling the anger that the angel used to generate. Yes, much had changed in the last year.

"Put him through," Aaron said, directing the operator to open the connection on the command center floor.

There was a slight distortion in the air before him, and then a window opened to reveal the former Powers' leader, murderer of countless Nephilim, who now served their cause.

After what seemed like an eternity, Verchiel had found his calling.

He had a clarity now that he'd never had before.

"Go ahead, Verchiel," Aaron's voice spoke in his ear.

Verchiel scowled at the intrusion, tempted to tear the damnable piece of technology from his ear and melt it to slag in his grip, but he was of a calmer spirit now and accepted his former enemy's more—modern—ways. "Yes." Verchiel tapped the audiovisual device plugged uncomfortably in his ear. "It is me."

"Yeah, I know that. You called me."

"Yes," Verchiel agreed. "I did call."

He heard the sniggering laughter of his monster compatriots behind him and turned to glare at them. There were times that he wondered why he had been so merciful, sparing them from becoming ash and bone.

But then again, if he had reacted to his baser instincts and killed them all, he would never have had the honor of commanding such skilled and ferocious warriors. These beasts rivaled those of the original Powers. Despite their lack of decorum, they were a force to be reckoned with, and one that he was proud to lead.

"What have you found, Verchiel?" Aaron asked.

Verchiel and his warriors had been sent to investigate a possible demonic infestation beneath the tiny village of Korolivka in the Brody Raion region of Ukraine. There had been some unusual seismic activity in the area, and sensors back at the command center had suggested a supernatural threat.

"We thought the village abandoned when we first arrived, but we were wrong."

Verchiel walked around the underground chamber where he and his small army were crammed, stepping over the still-burning bodies of those that had been slain, giving Aaron Corbet a view of what had transpired.

"I'm guessing our suspicions were correct?" the Nephilim leader asked in his ear.

"Indeed they were," Verchiel replied. "We located the disturbance in tunnels beneath the village, where we engaged and eliminated the enemy."

"The missing villagers?" Aaron questioned.

Verchiel knelt down amongst the dead, so Aaron could see the face of the enemy. "One and the same," the angel said.

The face of an older man's corpse was twisted, as if the skull beneath his flesh were taking on a new shape. Horns were beginning to push out through the pale flesh of his forehead.

Even though darkness had been burned from the world by the light of Heaven, evil still managed to hide in the shadows, waiting for an opportunity to flourish.

"Deamons," Aaron commented. "That makes the fourth encounter in three weeks."

The Deamons were just one of the newer threats to the world since the Almighty decreed it part of Heaven. It was as if the ancient species, which possessed the flesh of the living, twisting it into a monstrous mockery, had been patiently waiting to emerge.

Waiting for Heaven to be closer.

Verchiel felt a surge of excitement. This was why he had been given a second chance. This was what the Lord God Almighty had really wanted him to do. And this time there would be no distractions.

Aaron's voice was again in his ear. "So if we're dealing with Deamons here, then we likely have a—"

"Nest," Verchiel finished, turning around in the cramped space to reveal a larger area excavated from the cold, dark stone.

The chamber was filled with large, leathery eggs that seemed to glow from within with an eerie, pulsing green light.

A light that said, *I am evil, and I defy you and the God that you serve.*

The sickly glow within the eggs became brighter, the leathery sacks violently trembling as one after the other split open, and things oh so horrible—

Abominations to the world, and to the sight of God, started to emerge. "Right," Verchiel heard Aaron say in his ear. "You know what to do."

Verchiel could not help but smile as a sword of fire came to life in his hand, and his soldiers readied their own weapons.

"I most certainly do," the mighty angel said, a divine purpose in his voice.

Aaron watched the images from the Ukrainian cave with a certain sense of satisfaction, but also with trepidation. He made a mental note to ask Levi if he could upgrade the equipment, allowing them to locate Deamon incursions before helpless innocents were possessed and killed.

He was about to ask one of his officers to set up an appointment with the former Unforgiven leader, when Melissa arrived.

"Is it that time already?" Aaron asked.

The girl smiled. "It most certainly is."

"Give me one minute and—"

Cameron's sudden appearance interrupted Aaron.

"Cameron," he acknowledged with a polite nod.

Melissa stepped closer. "I was specifically ordered to report to duty now so that you could get to your appointment on time."

Cameron smiled. "And your wife specifically ordered me to escort you."

"My wife?" Aaron asked, looking from Melissa to Cameron. "My wife doesn't trust me to get to our meeting when I'm supposed to?"

He felt Cameron's grip on his arm, guiding him toward the stairs that would lead up and out of the control center.

"I guess she doesn't," the young man said, and Aaron noticed a look pass between Melissa and his head of security. A look that hinted of something more than just camaraderie.

He made a mental note to ask his wife if his suspicions were correct.

Vilma looked out the large picture window of the home that she shared with her husband.

After Heaven's declaration, the Nephilim had decided that the site of the last battle, Armageddon, would be their home. The land had been given to them by the Israeli people, the materials they needed to construct their new homes donated by all the nations of the world.

Going as far as to incorporate the ancient city of Megiddo into its design, signifying their and God's vision, Aerie 2 quickly sprang up from the desert, bringing hope to a changing world.

A changing world.

Her eyes were drawn to the soft blue of the morning desert sky, to the new star that hung there, always visible.

Heaven.

Vilma's eyes followed a flock of Nephilim as they soared joyously above Aerie 2. The Inheritors had adjusted quite well to modern times and the roles they now played.

Some of the flock broke off from the others, touching down

upon the great concrete wall that had been erected around the enormous chasm opened during the battle against the Darkstar and his legions.

She watched as the winged warriors created fearsome weapons of fire, at the ready in case any of the monstrous things that now lived deep beneath the earth decided to make an unexpected appearance.

It had been some time since there had been any contact with the denizens below, but they needed to remain vigilant.

This was their responsibility to a changing world.

Vilma stepped away from the window and quickly gathered up her things to leave for her appointment.

A changing world.

No truer words were ever spoken.

Earlier That Morning

"You know it'll break his heart," Gabriel said, sitting stoically in front of the apartment door.

"Aaron is a big boy now. He'll understand," Taylor Corbet said, as she removed her contents from the dresser and shoved them inside the backpack on the bed, zipping it closed.

She had hoped to leave Aerie 2 before anyone noticed that she was gone, but Gabriel had stopped by for a visit, catching her in the midst of packing. The dog stared at her now, his large, deep-brown eyes prodding at her soul.

"Are you going to try and stop me?" she asked him, hefting the backpack over her shoulder and moving around the bed.

"I could," Gabriel answered. "But I won't."

"I thank you for that," Taylor said. She knelt beside him, patting his soft, velvety head.

"How will you get past the sentries?"

"I've made arrangements," she told him. "I won't say any more."

"Are you sure you need to do this?" the dog asked.

Taylor didn't even hesitate. "Absolutely."

Gabriel rose and stepped out of her way.

"Will you say good-bye for me?" Taylor asked as she grasped the doorknob.

"Of course."

"And that I love him very much."

"Yes."

"And that no mother could ever be more proud of her son."

"I will do that," Gabriel promised.

Taylor pulled the door open and stepped out into the hall.

"If he asks you why I left, tell him that if even the slightest chance exists for me to have what I once did, to feel the way I once felt, I had to go for it."

With that, Taylor Corbet left, no doubt in her mind that what she was doing was right.

As quickly as she could, Taylor made her way down to the lower levels of the building to the paths used to carry maintenance supplies. It was there that she met her contact.

Jeremy Fox stood beside the security door that opened into a tunnel leading to the wall and the edge of the chasm.

He had been put in charge of wall security by Aaron and was the first person Taylor had approached when considering what she was about to do. She'd been surprised at how understanding he'd been when he'd heard her story. She'd half expected him to report her immediately to his superiors.

To her son.

But Jeremy had agreed to help her without hesitation. She didn't know for sure, and did not want to pry, but she guessed there was something in her story that the young man could relate to.

Perhaps he understood what it felt like to be denied a chance at true love.

"Are you certain about this?" he asked her now.

"I am," she said, switching her knapsack from one shoulder to the other.

"Just checking," he said, and turned to punch in a code on the side of the door. There was a loud pinging, followed by the sound of heavy locking mechanisms pulling back, and the door slowly opened.

Jeremy stepped away, turning his back on her. "Didn't see a thing."

"Thank you," she said quietly, as she stepped into the dimly lit corridor.

"You be sure to tell Old Scratch that I said hi."

"I'll do that, Jeremy," Taylor said, proceeding down the passage, as the heavy metal door closed behind her with finality.

There was no turning back now.

Aaron gazed down at his wife, who looked back at him with trepidation.

"We're going to be fine," he told her in his bravest voice.

He squeezed her hand reassuringly, as they watched the strange device of Levi's invention drop from the ceiling, pressing firmly against Vilma's exposed stomach.

"Hold still," Levi ordered, as he disappeared behind a wall of complex machinery.

Aaron's grip on Vilma's hand intensified as the machine began to hum. "Won't be long now," he told her, bringing her hand to his mouth to kiss it. "Almost done."

He had no idea how long the test would take, but he'd do anything to reassure her.

Vilma hadn't been feeling well, something quite uncommon for her, and they'd decided to consult with Levi about the cause.

The machine had grown temporarily louder, before it was silenced and gradually moved away from Vilma's stomach, then back up into its housing on the ceiling.

"Is that it?" Vilma asked, a look of relief on her beautiful face.

"I think it is," Aaron answered, bending down to kiss her sweat-dampened brow.

They waited for what seemed like an eternity before Levi stepped out from behind the cover of machinery.

"Well?" Aaron prodded.

He could feel the Unforgiven's intense stare through the dark goggles that Levi wore.

"Is the baby all right?" Vilma asked, a hint of panic in her voice.

"Baby?" Levi questioned, and Aaron immediately knew that something was wrong. He could feel Vilma stiffen beside him, her hand squeezing his so hard, it was almost painful.

Levi held up an egg-shaped device and depressed a button on its side. Immediately a three-dimensional image appeared, slowly turning before them.

"Not baby," Levi said. "Babies—twins."

Aaron and Vilma could only stare, dumbfounded. It was clear from the holographic image that they were looking at two babies, crowded together inside a womb.

Vilma's womb.

"Those are our babies," Vilma whispered in awe, and started to cry.

"Aren't they sort of big?" Aaron asked, noticing how fully formed they looked for only being a little over a month old. He could already see tiny, feathered wings growing from beneath the shoulder blades.

"The normal gestation period for a human child is nine months," Levi stated, turning his goggle-covered stare to them. "These are not human children. These are Nephilim children."

"So what does that mean?" Vilma asked nervously.

"These children will grow at a far more rapid pace. They should be ready for birth within . . ." Levi returned his gaze to the image of the slowly spinning fetuses. "The next ninety days, give or take."

"Oh my God," Vilma said, fear in her eyes. . . .

Fear that quickly turned to absolute joy, as she threw her arms around Aaron's neck.

"We're going to be parents," she cried. "We're going to have a little boy and a little girl."

He held her tightly, almost afraid to squeeze her too hard. "And they'll be the most special children in the world," he said, then remembering something that Gabriel had told them so very long ago. "They'll be magnificent."

"Magnificent?" she asked, pulling away to look at him. Her eyes twinkled magically. "Yeah," she nodded, answering her own question. "Yeah, they will be. They will be magnificent."

Aaron smiled, pulling her toward him again, and they kissed long and deeply.

"When should we tell my aunt and uncle?" she asked breathlessly, breaking their kiss.

"Maybe after we tell my mom?" he suggested.

The air close by seemed to momentarily catch fire, but it

did not concern them in the least. They'd grown quite used to Gabriel's habit of appearing in a flash of divine fire.

"We're going to have babies!" Vilma screeched, dropping to the floor to throw her arms around the Labrador's thick neck.

"That's wonderful," the dog answered, but Aaron could sense from his tone that something was wrong.

"What is it, Gabe?" he asked.

Vilma leaned back from the animal.

"There's something that I have to tell you," Gabriel said, his gaze and voice both filled with emotion. "It's about your mother."

Lucifer Morningstar sat upon his throne, deep in the bowels of the earth, and dreamed about redemption.

It was not yet time for him.

After all the atrocities he had been responsible for, he'd always known it would be a long road to forgiveness.

But it was not up to him to decide when he got there.

Shifting in his seat of rock, Lucifer asserted his control, not only over the Hell that had been created in the sprawling subterranean habitat, but also the Hell that existed inside him.

Reaching out with his mind, he could sense the world that he'd created; every nook and cranny filled with darkness, every jagged peak and blasted plain of rock, every lake of fire and all the twisted abominations that were capable of living in a place such as this.

This was their home now—their prison.

And he was their jailor.

The ancient evil that he now kept imprisoned inside him stirred, again making an attempt to reassert its dominance. It took all that the Morningstar had to keep it in check, and he prayed for the continued strength to be able to maintain this level of control.

To maintain his hold over both the physical prison that he'd created, and the mental one as well.

There was movement upon the rocks below, and he turned his gaze to a small, red-skinned creature.

This one was named Scox, and he had served the dark entity when it had held possession of his body.

"What is it, imp?" Lucifer Morningstar asked, annoyance dripping from his words.

"I've come to serve you," the red-skinned demon said, wringing his hands.

"I have no need of your service." Lucifer dismissed the creature with a wave of his hand. "Go away."

But Scox did not leave.

"I can help you, master," the creature insisted. "This place. It is so big, but I see things that you do not see." He placed his hands over his eyes, making circular spectacles with his fingers, and looked around.

Lucifer just wanted to be left alone to his misery and his penance.

Maybe this is part of it, he mused. *A wry trick by the Lord God to see how I deal with the most annoying creatures.*

"I see all that I need to see, Scox," Lucifer said, standing up and spreading his black-feathered wings. He dropped down before the scarlet imp.

"Trolls erecting a statue in honor of some long-forgotten troll god in the hopes that the ancient deity might grant their wish and set them free of this loathsome place," Lucifer said as he strode closer to Scox.

"Goblin assassins using their special skills to make weapons to challenge the supremacy of their current lord and master. That would be me," Lucifer said, placing an armored hand to his chest plate.

Scox backed away as the Morningstar continued to advance.

"A pack of demon hounds, hunting at the base of the fissure, about to feast upon a poor creature unlucky enough to—"

Lucifer stopped.

"Yes?" Scox asked, the hint of a smile forming upon his bloodred face. "What do you see? Something out of the ordinary, perhaps?"

Lucifer opened his senses, taking in more of the hellish place than he cared to, but he needed to see this. . . .

The hounds stalked something that did not belong, something that did not stink of the pit, but instead seemed to glow with a brilliant inner light.

A characteristic that this Hell did not have.

A soul.

"I saw her too," Scox said, gleefully clapping his hands. "I saw her as she climbed down from the surface."

Lucifer spread his wings wide to push off against the air, sending him rocketing skyward, the cackling laugh of the red-skinned imp receding below him. He could sense where he needed to be, hoping that he was fleet enough to reach her before it was too late.

Is it possible? he wondered, as his mighty wings pounded the air, propelling him upward. A part of him didn't dare believe it was true, but he had to know for sure. Perhaps it was a trick of one of the foul beasts that he held captive.

And pity upon any who dared rouse his anger in such a way.

The evil entity inside him laughed, waiting to take strength from Lucifer's misery.

The Morningstar flew around the towering black peaks and above the rivers of fire, closer to the base of the chasm wall. His eyes scanned the surface, his vision temporarily obscured by clouds of foul-smelling gas that erupted up from the cavern floor.

And it was within the fog of this viscous stink that he saw movement, and descended.

Lucifer did not hesitate in his attack. With a cry of war, he swung his blade of fire, striking down the lion-sized beasts that had trapped their prey in a dark cavity, too small for their large, muscular bodies to enter.

Enraged by their inability to reach their prey, the demon dogs turned upon him in frustration, oblivious of whom they were attacking.

And what their fate would be for doing so.

The pack came at him as one, snapping jaws and slashing claws, and Lucifer met their assault with equal ferocity. Roars of rage and savagery quickly turned to wails of agony as his sword of fire bit into their taut, muscular flesh, opening them wide to the harsh environment of Hell.

Standing knee deep in the viscera of his foes, Lucifer Morningstar readied for further attack.

Hearing a noise behind him, the Lord of Hell spun, and watched as the monster's prey emerged from the inky blackness of the tiny cave.

Though his eyes told him it was true, he could not believe them, and found himself stepping back and away.

It has to be a trick, the evil thing trapped inside him proclaimed.

Could the dark entity be right?

"Sam?"

And he knew.

It wasn't a trick of this hellish place, or of the powers that he fought so hard to keep locked away inside him.

It was something more.

She came at him, running into his embrace, and he put his arms around her, feeling her warmth even through his thick armor.

And Lucifer Morningstar knew.

His Creator believed that he was truly sorry for his crimes, and that he would continue to make penance until he was fully forgiven.

Lucifer kissed Taylor Corbet and felt his inner strength grow, the darkness that had threatened to overtake him stamped down so deeply that he could barely feel its presence.

Love was the way that his God acknowledged one such as he, guilty of all crimes, but worthy of some compassion.

A show of sympathy.

Sympathy for the Devil.

About the Author

Thomas E. Sniegoski is the author of more than two dozen novels for adults, teens, and children. His books for teens include *Legacy*, *Sleeper Code*, *Sleeper Agenda*, and *Force Majeure*, as well as the series The Brimstone Network.

As a comic book writer, Sniegoski's work includes *Stupid, Stupid Rat-Tails*, a prequel miniseries to the international hit *Bone*. Sniegoski collaborated with *Bone* creator Jeff Smith on the project, making him the only writer Smith has ever asked to work on those characters.

Sniegoski was born and raised in Massachusetts, where he still lives with his wife, LeeAnne, and their French bulldog, Kirby. Visit him on the Web at www.sniegoski.com.

Beneath every beauty, evil stirs. . . .

Darkness Becomes Her

by Kelly Keaton

Under the cafeteria table, my right knee bounced like a jackhammer possessed. Adrenaline snaked through my limbs, urging me to bolt, to hightail it out of Rocquemore House and never look back.

Deep breaths.

If I didn't get my act together and calm down, I'd start hyperventilating and embarrass the shit out of myself. Not a good thing, especially when I was sitting in an insane asylum with rooms to spare.

"Are you sure you want to do this, Miss Selkirk?"

"It's Ari. And, yes, Dr. Giroux." I gave the man seated across from me an encouraging nod. "I didn't come all this way to give up now. I want to know." What I wanted was to get this over with and do something, *anything*, with my hands, but instead I laid them flat on the tabletop. Very still. Very calm.

A reluctant breath blew through the doctor's thin, sun-cracked lips as he fixed me with an *I'm sorry, sweetheart, you asked for it* look. He opened the file in his hand, clearing his throat. "I wasn't working here at the time, but let's see. . . ." He flipped through a few pages. "After your mother gave you up to social services, she spent the remainder of her life here at Rocquemore." His fingers fidgeted with the file. "Self-admitted," he went on. "Was here six months and eighteen days. Committed suicide on the eve of her twenty-first birthday."

An inhale lodged in my throat.

Oh hell. I hadn't expected *that*.

The news left my mind numb. It completely shredded the mental list of questions I'd practiced and prepared for.

Over the years, I'd thought of every possible reason why my mother had given me up. I even explored the idea that she might've passed away sometime during the last thirteen years. But suicide? *Yeah, dumbass, you didn't think of that one.* A long string of curses flew through my mind, and I wanted to bang my forehead against the table—maybe it would help drive home the news.

I'd been given to the state of Louisiana just after my fourth birthday, and six months later, my mother was dead. All those years thinking of her, wondering what she looked like, what she was doing, wondering if she thought of the little girl she left behind, when all this time she was six feet under and not *doing* or *thinking* a goddamn thing.

My chest expanded with a scream I couldn't voice. I stared hard at my hands, my short fingernails like shiny black beetles against the white composite surface of the table. I resisted the urge to curl them under and dig into the laminate, to feel the skin pull away from the nails, to feel something other than the grief squeezing and burning my chest.

"Okay," I said, regrouping. "So, what exactly was wrong with her?" The question was like tar on my tongue and made my face hot. I removed my hands and placed them under the table on my thighs, rubbing my sweaty palms against my jeans.

"Schizophrenia. Delusions—well, *delusion*."

"Just one?"

He opened the file and pretended to scan the page. The guy seemed nervous as hell to tell me, and I couldn't blame him. Who'd want to tell a teenage girl that her mom was so whacked-out that she'd killed herself?

Pink dots bloomed on his cheeks. "Says here"—his throat worked with a hard swallow—"it was snakes . . . claimed snakes were trying to poke through her head, that she could feel them growing and moving under her scalp. On several occasions, she scratched her head bloody. Tried to dig them out with a butter knife stolen from the cafeteria. Nothing the doctors did or gave her could convince her it was all in her mind."

The image coiled around my spine and sent a shiver straight to the back of my neck. I *hated* snakes.

Dr. Giroux closed the file, hurrying to offer whatever comfort he could. "It's important to remember, back then a lot of folks went through post-traumatic stress. . . . You were too young to remember, but—"

"I remember some." How could I forget? Fleeing with hundreds of thousands of people as two Category Four hurricanes, one after another, destroyed New Orleans and the entire southern half of the state. No one was prepared. And no one went back. Even now, thirteen years later, no one in their right mind ventured past The Rim.

Dr. Giroux gave me a sad smile. "Then I don't need to tell you why your mother came here."

"No."

"There were so many cases," he went on sadly, eyes unfocused, and I wondered if he was even talking to me now. "Psychosis, fear of drowning, watching loved ones die. And the snakes, the snakes that were pushed out of the swamps and inland with the floodwaters . . . Your mother probably experienced some horrible real-life event that led to her delusion."

Images of the hurricanes and their aftermath clicked through my mind like a slide projector, images I hardly thought of anymore. I shot to my feet, needing air, needing to get the hell out of this creepy place surrounded by swamps, moss, and gnarly, weeping trees. I wanted to shake my body like a maniac, to throw off the images crawling all over my skin. But instead, I forced myself to remain still, drew in a deep breath, and then tugged the end of my black T-shirt down, clearing my throat. "Thank you, Dr. Giroux, for speaking with me so late. I should probably get going."

I pivoted slowly and made for the door, not knowing where I was going or what I'd do next, only knowing that in order to leave I had to put one foot in front of the other.

"Don't you want her things?" Dr. Giroux asked. My foot paused midstride. "Technically they're yours now." My stomach did a sickening wave as I turned. "I believe there's a box in the storage room. I'll go get it. Please"—he gestured to the bench—"it'll just take a second."

Bench. Sit. *Good idea.* I slumped on the edge of the bench, rested my elbows on my knees, and turned in my toes, staring at the V between my feet until Dr. Giroux hurried back with a faded brown shoe box.

I expected it to be heavier and was surprised, and a little disappointed, by its lightness. "Thanks. Oh, one more thing . . . Was my mother buried around here?"

"No. She was buried in Greece."

I did a double take. "Like small-town-in-America Greece, or . . . ?"

Dr. Giroux smiled, shoved his hands into his pockets, and rocked back on his heels. "Nope. The real thing. Some family came and claimed the body. Like I said, I wasn't working here at the time, but perhaps you could track information through the coroner's office; who signed for her, that sort of thing."

Family.

That word was so alien, so unreal, that I wasn't even sure I'd heard him right. Family. Hope stirred in the center of my chest, light and airy and ready to break into a Disney song complete with adorable bluebirds and singing squirrels.

No. It's too soon for that. One thing at a time.

I glanced down at the box, putting a lid on the hope—I'd been let down too many times to give in to the feeling—wondering what other shocking news I'd uncover tonight.

"Take care, Miss Selkirk."

I paused for a second, watching the doctor head for a group of patients sitting near the bay window, before leaving through the tall double doors. Every step out of the rundown mansion/mental hospital to the car parked out front took me further into the past. My mother's horrible ordeal. My life as a ward of the state. Daughter of an unwed teenage mother who'd killed herself.

Fucking great. Just great.

The soles of my boots crunched across the gravel, echoing over the constant song of crickets and katydids, the occasional splash of water, and the call of bullfrogs. It might be winter to the rest of the country, but January in the deep South was still warm and humid. I gripped the box tighter, trying to see beyond the moss-draped live oaks and cypress trees and into the deepest, darkest shadows of the swampy lake. But a wall of blackness prevented me, a wall that—I blinked—seemed to waver.

But it was just tears rising to the surface.

I could barely breathe. I never expected this . . . *hurt*. I never expected to actually learn what had happened to her. After a quick swipe at the wet corners of my eyes, I set the box on the passenger seat of the car and then drove down the lonely winding road to Covington, Louisiana, and back to something resembling civilization.

Covington hovered on The Rim, the boundary between the land of the forsaken and the rest of the country; a border town with a Holiday Inn Express.

The box stayed on the hotel bed while I kicked off my boots, shrugged out of my old jeans, and jerked the tee over my head. I'd taken a shower that morning, but after my trip to the hospital, I needed to wash off the cloud of depression and the thick film of southern humidity that clung to my skin.

In the bathroom, I turned on the shower and began untying

the thin black ribbon around my neck, making sure not to let my favorite amulet—a platinum crescent moon—slip off the end. The crescent moon has always been my favorite sight in the sky, especially on a clear cold night when it's surrounded by twinkling stars. I love it so much, I had a tiny black crescent tattooed below the corner of my right eye, on the highest rise of my cheekbone—my early high school graduation present to myself. The tattoo reminded me of where I came from, my birthplace. The Crescent City. New Orleans.

But those were old names. Now it was known as New 2, a grand, decaying, lost city that refused to be swept away with the tide. A privately owned city and a beacon, a sanctuary for misfits and things that went bump in the night, or so they said.

Standing in front of the long hotel mirror in my black bra and panties, I leaned closer to my reflection and touched the small black moon, thinking of the mother I'd never really known, the mother who *could've* had the same teal-colored eyes as the ones staring back at me in the mirror, or the same hair. . . .

I sighed, straightened, and reached behind my head to unwind the tight bun at the nape of my neck.

Unnatural. Bizarre. Fucked up.

I'd used all those words and more to describe the thick coil that unwound and fell behind my shoulders, the ends brushing the small of my back. Parted in the middle. All one length. So light in color, it looked silver in the moonlight. My hair. The bane of my existence. Full. Glossy. And so straight it looked like it had taken an army of hairdressers wielding hot irons to get it that way. But it was all natural.

No. Unnatural.

Another tired exhale escaped my lips. I gave up trying a long time ago.

When I'd first realized—back when I was about seven or so—that my hair attracted the *wrong* sort of attention from some of the foster men and boys in my life, I tried everything to get rid of it. Cut it. Dyed it. Shaved it. I'd even lifted hydrochloric acid from the science lab in seventh grade, filled the sink, and then dunked my hair into the solution. It burned my hair into oblivion, but a few days later it was back to the same length, the same color, the same everything. Just like always.

So I hid it the best I could; buns, braids, hats. And I wore enough black, had accumulated enough attitude throughout my teenage years that most guys respected my no's when I said them. And if they didn't, well, I'd learned how to deal with that, too. My current foster parents, Bruce and Casey Sanderson, were both bail bondsmen, which meant they put up the bail money so defendants could avoid jail time until their court appearance. And if the person didn't show for their appointment with the judge, we hunted them down and brought them back to jurisdiction so we weren't stuck footing the bill. Thanks to Bruce and Casey, I could operate six different firearms, drop a two-hundred-pound asshole to the floor in three seconds, and cuff a perp with one hand tied behind my back.

And they called it "family time."

My hazy reflection smiled back at me. The Sandersons were pretty decent, decent enough to let a seventeen-year-old borrow their car and go in search of her past. Casey had been a foster kid too, so she understood my need to know. She knew I had to do this alone. I wished I'd gotten placed with them from the beginning. A snort blew through my nose. Yeah, and if wishes were dollars, I'd be Bill Gates.

Steam filled the bathroom. I knew what I was doing. Avoiding. Classic Ari MO. If I didn't take a shower, I wouldn't get out, put on my pj's, and then open the damn box. "Just get it over with, you big wuss." I stripped off the last of my clothes.

Thirty minutes later, after my fingertips were wrinkled and the air was so saturated with steam it was hard to breathe, I dried off and dressed in my favorite pair of old plaid boxers and a thin cotton tank. Once my wet hair was twisted back into a knot and a pair of fuzzy socks pulled on my forever-cold feet, I sat cross-legged in the middle of the king-size bed.

The box just sat there. In front of me.

My eyes squinted. Goose bumps sprouted on my arms and thighs. My blood pressure rose—I knew it by the way my chest tightened into a painful, anxious knot.

Stop being such a baby!

It was just a dumb box. Just my past.

I settled myself and lifted the lid, pulling the box closer and peering inside to find a few letters and a couple of small jewelry boxes.

Not enough in there to contain an entire life story. No doubt I'd have more questions from this than answers—that's usually how my search went. Already disheartened, I reached inside and grabbed the plain white envelope on top of the pile, flipping it over to see my name scrawled in blue ink.

Aristanae.

My breath left me in an astonished rush. *Holy hell.* My mother had written to me.

It took a moment for it to sink in. I trailed my thumb over the flowing cursive letters with shaky fingers and then opened the envelope and unfolded the single sheet of notebook paper.

My dearest, beautiful Ari,

If you are reading this now, then I know you have found me. I had hoped and prayed that you wouldn't. I am sorry for leaving you, and that sounds so inadequate, I know, but there was no other way. Soon you will understand why, and I'm sorry for that, too. But for now, assuming you were given this box by those at Rocquemore, you must run. Stay away from New Orleans, and away from those who can identify you. How I wish I could save you. My heart aches, knowing you will face what I have faced. I love you so much, Ari. And I am sorry. For everything.

I'm not crazy. Trust me. Please, baby girl, just RUN.

Momma

Spooked, I jumped off the bed and dropped the letter as though it burned. "What the hell?"

Fear made my heart pound like thunder and the fine hairs on my skin lift as though electrified. I went to the window and peeked through the blinds to look one floor down at my car in the back lot. Nothing unusual. I rubbed my hands down my arms and then paced, biting my left pinkie nail.

I stared at the open letter again, with the small cursive script. *I'm not crazy. Trust me. Please, baby girl.*

Baby girl. Baby girl.

I had only a handful of fuzzy memories left, but those words . . . I could almost hear my mother speaking those words. Soft. Loving. A smile in her voice. It was a real memory, I realized, not one of the thousand I'd made up over the years. An ache squeezed my heart, and the dull pain of an oncoming headache began behind my left eye.

All these years . . . It wasn't fair!

A rush of adrenaline pushed against my rib cage and raced down my arm, but instead of screaming and punching the wall like I wanted to, I bit my bottom lip hard and made a tight fist.

No. Forget it.

It was pointless to go down the Life's Not Fair road. Been there before. Lesson learned. That kind of hurt served no purpose.

With a groan, I threw the letter back into the box, shoved the lid on, and then got dressed. Once my things were secured in my backpack, I grabbed the box. My mother hadn't spoken to me in thirteen years and this letter from the grave was telling me to run, to get to safety. Whatever was going on, I felt to the marrow of my bones that something wasn't right. Maybe I was just spooked and paranoid after what I'd learned from Dr. Giroux.

And maybe, I thought, as my suspicious mind kicked into high gear, my mother hadn't committed suicide after all.

ATHENEUM
FICTION

Margaret K. McElderry Books

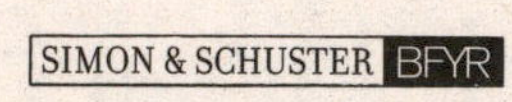
SIMON & SCHUSTER BFYR

SIMON
PULSE